# HISTORICAL

*Your romantic escape to the past.*

**Too Scandalous For The Earl**
Helen Dickson

**How The Duke Met His Match**
Sophia Williams

MILLS & BOON

DID YOU PURCHASE THIS BOOK WITHOUT A COVER?
If you did, you should be aware it is **stolen property** as it was reported
'unsold and destroyed' by a retailer.
Neither the author nor the publisher has received any payment
for this book.

TOO SCANDALOUS FOR THE EARL
© 2023 by Helen Dickson
Philippine Copyright 2023
Australian Copyright 2023
New Zealand Copyright 2023

First Published 2023
First Australian Paperback Edition 2023
ISBN 978 1 867 28670 7

HOW THE DUKE MET HIS MATCH
© 2023 by Jo Lovett-Turner
Philippine Copyright 2023
Australian Copyright 2023
New Zealand Copyright 2023

First Published 2023
First Australian Paperback Edition 2023
ISBN 978 1 867 28670 7

® and ™ (apart from those relating to FSC®) are trademarks of Harlequin Enterprises (Australia) Pty Limited or its corporate affiliates. Trademarks indicated with ® are registered in Australia, New Zealand and in other countries.
Contact admin_legal@Harlequin.ca for details.

Except for use in any review, the reproduction or utilisation of this work in whole or in part in any form by any electronic, mechanical or other means, now known or hereafter invented, including xerography, photocopying and recording, or in any information storage or retrieval system, is forbidden without the permission of the publisher, Harlequin Mills & Boon.

This book is sold subject to the condition that it shall not, by way of trade or otherwise, be lent, resold, hired out or otherwise circulated without the prior consent of the publisher in any form or binding or cover other than that in which it is published and without a similar condition including this condition being imposed on the subsequent purchaser.

All rights reserved including the right of reproduction in whole or in part in any form. This edition is published in arrangement with Harlequin Books S.A..

This is a work of fiction. Names, characters, places, and incidents are either the product of the author's imagination or are used fictitiously, and any resemblance to actual persons, living or dead, business establishments, events, or locales is entirely coincidental.

MIX
Paper | Supporting
responsible forestry
FSC® C001695

Published by
Harlequin Mills & Boon
An imprint of Harlequin Enterprises (Australia) Pty Limited
(ABN 47 001 180 918), a subsidiary of HarperCollins
Publishers Australia Pty Limited
(ABN 36 009 913 517)
Level 19, 201 Elizabeth Street
SYDNEY NSW 2000 AUSTRALIA

Cover art used by arrangement with Harlequin Books S.A.. All rights reserved.

Printed and bound in Australia by McPherson's Printing Group

# Too Scandalous For The Earl
Helen Dickson

MILLS & BOON

**Helen Dickson** was born and still lives in South Yorkshire, UK, with her retired farm-manager husband. Having moved out of the busy farmhouse where she raised their two sons, she now has more time to indulge in her favourite pastimes. She enjoys being outdoors, traveling, reading and listening to music. An incurable romantic, she writes for pleasure. It was a love of history that drove her to writing historical fiction.

Visit the Author Profile page
at millsandboon.com.au for more titles.

## Author Note

*Too Scandalous for the Earl* is the second book in the Cranford Estate Siblings trilogy. The story is set in Devon, which is one of my favourite locations.

Having disgraced herself with a disreputable young man on the eve of her debut, Tilly's sent to Devon by her family until the scandal has blown over. Here she meets Lucas Kingsly, the Earl of Clifton. In the beginning there is conflict between the two, but gradually, against a backdrop of the sea and the beautiful Devon countryside, where smuggling is rife, their conflicts are resolved.

# Chapter One

*1812*

Self-willed, energetic and passionate, with a fierce and undisciplined temper, Tilly had a charm and wit and beauty that more than made up for the deficiencies in her character. She hadn't a bad bone in her body and was just proud and spirited, so determined to have her own way that she had always been prepared to plough straight through any hurdle that stood in her path—but that was before she had made the dubious acquaintance of Richard Coulson.

Summoned to the drawing room by her brother Charles, who had been staying with friends in Sussex for the past month, an inexplicable premonition of dread mounted as she descended the stairs. When Tilly entered the drawing room, Charles was waiting for her.

He was still dressed in his travelling clothes, waiting impatiently by the fireplace, obviously in an angry mood. He had a handsome face—at least he would have been handsome had not a fierce scowl marred his features. The moment she closed the door behind her he embarked on a blistering tirade, denouncing her recent disgraceful behaviour.

'There you are. Aunt Charlotte has filled me in with what you have been getting up to in my absence. Really, Tilly, will you never grow up? You are clever, quick thinking and sharp witted. You are also problematical and a constant headache. You test my patience at every turn. You live for the moment and notice nothing that is not to do with outdoor pursuits and horses. In short, you are hell-bent on self-destruction.'

Tilly sighed. Her brother was adamant when administering discipline. 'I'm sorry, Charles, truly,' she said, only mildly repentant, 'for all the trouble I have caused. I never meant for this to happen. I didn't know.'

'There's a great deal you don't know.'

She nodded. 'It would appear so,' she replied, adopting a meek expression, although anyone who knew Tilly Anderson would know there was nothing meek about her.

'It would seem the task of learning to be the lady our mother intended you to become is seemingly impossible.'

'I am sure I must be a terrible disappointment to you, Charles, but I will try not to let you down in future. I will try harder, I promise.'

'It's too late for that. How could you let it happen? You haven't a grain of sense in you. How could you have been so blind to propriety? Coulson saw you as easy prey. You should have known better than to become entangled with him. You are too young and inexperienced to take on a man of his ilk. He eats young women like you for breakfast. He's played the field and gambled his way through his fortune. He'll beggar his father before he's done. Where did you meet him?'

'In the park when I was out riding.'

'Alone?'

'Well...yes. Aunt Charlotte wasn't very well...'

'And you didn't have the presence of mind to take a maid with you?'

'Aunt Charlotte's maids don't ride—and you know I don't like being confined in a carriage.'

Charles turned away in exasperation. Audacious and bold, Tilly could be a handful without any encouragement. 'Excuses—nothing but excuses, Tilly. Aunt Charlotte does employ two grooms to take care of the horses.'

'And one or the other has accompanied me on occasion.'

'Not often enough. Coulson has ruined your reputation.'

'No, he hasn't. He didn't dishonour me.'

'He might as well have done.'

'He—he did ask me to marry him.'

'And you refused him, thank God. At any other time and with anyone whose character was not mired in decadence I would have insisted you marry him—but Coulson is a rake of the first order. He would lead you a merry dance and you would be downright miserable.'

'I know. I didn't want to marry him. But it's very lonely for me sometimes with just Aunt Charlotte for company.'

'That's no excuse for what you've done. Friends have hastened to inform me of the scandal that is beginning to unfold concerning my own sister—a scandal that is entirely of your own making, if it is to be believed. It has already given you a certain notoriety—and I know perfectly well what happens to a young lady who falls short of society's expectations.

'I am incensed. Not in my wildest dreams did I imagine you would form a liaison with a man whose exploits are the talk of London. And where he is concerned, how dare he have the temerity, the effrontery to interfere with the half-sister of William, the Marquess of Elvington?'

William's father had died when William was just eight years old, and one year later his mother had remarried Sir Edward Anderson. Charles and Tilly were the result of that marriage, and William cared deeply for his half-siblings. Tilly had the grace to lower her eyes and fix them on her hands folded in her lap. No doubt when William heard of this latest escapade he would be as incensed as Charles.

Of course, Charles was quite right. On her rides in the park, she had garnered the favours of several young beaux and Richard Coulson, who stood out from the rest with his raffish good looks and sense of fun, was much sought after. He had approached her when she had managed to shake off her accompanying groom, who despaired of trying to keep up with her since she could ride like the wind with the devil on her tail.

Richard had become enamoured of her and he had soon turned to putty under the assault of her large violet eyes and sweet smiles. It was all a game to Tilly, who had done it out of boredom. His possessive attitude she soon found irritating. He had even had the audacity to kiss her when she had found herself alone with him, which she had thought presumptuous of him, and had shocked her and was not to her liking anyway.

Having captured him completely, the game had turned sour along with what she had seen of society. The idea of a Season and marriage in general—which, after all, was what having a Season was all about—she decided was not for her and had sent the young man packing, blissfully unaware of the consequences of their liaison. Her naivety and inexperience had not prepared her for a young man of Coulson's reputation.

'I could kill Coulson for this,' Charles said. 'The gossip will soon be all over town and you can expect no mercy.' Not to be made a fool of by an ignorant girl, Coulson had let his tongue loose to do its worse and turned the tables on Tilly, laughingly telling his friends that she was a game bird, an amusingly peculiar, pathetic little thing, and, if she was launched, he had no intention of plying his suit.

Charles looked to the door when a maid entered, carrying a letter on a salver.

'A letter has just arrived for you, Mr Anderson,' she said, bobbing a curtsy and leaving the room.

'Thank you, Betty.' Casting an eye over it, he shoved it inside his jacket unopened, turning his attention back to Tilly. Her head was bent, her shock of glossy black curls falling about her face. He sighed, shaking his head wearily.

'You have much to learn about life, Tilly,' he said on a softer note. 'I will take time off from the Company to take you to Cranford. Perhaps William—and Anna—can instil some sense into you, although with your difficult and unyielding nature they will have their work cut out.'

Tilly remembered when she had first seen Cranford Park. It was unlike anything she had imagined. She had been mesmerised by its splendour—imposing without being austere. This was her half-brother William's ancestral home. He had become the Marquess of Elvington on the demise of his grandfather six months earlier. When he had returned from India, he had insisted that his half-siblings made Cranford their home.

Employed by the East India Company in London, Charles resided at the Lancaster town house in Mayfair. Tilly flitted between the houses, recently spending a good deal of her time with Aunt Charlotte in Chelsea village as preparations were being made to launch her into society.

Adored by her family, Tilly had been petted and indulged outrageously by everyone all her life, but all the attention had left her unspoiled. Happy and always smiling, she had a warm and generous heart. Her greatest sorrow had been the loss of her father as a child and then later, on the death of her mother, something vital had gone from her life. She knew nothing of the harsh, cruel world that existed outside her own secure and comfortable existence.

Aunt Charlotte, her father's sister, with her gentle guidance and common sense, had become a kindly presence in her life. Having lost the love of her life in a riding accident, she had never married. She wanted Tilly to have a grand London Season, to associate with fashionable people of note, to attend balls and soirées.

Tilly was always very much aware that the moment she appeared in a room all eyes turned to her and she was soon surrounded by dozens of people, most of them young men, who obviously thought they might have a chance with the Marquess of Elvington's sister when she made her debut. She had a kind of aura about her that made her somehow unique, although she herself was quite unaware of this special quality.

Before her indiscretion with Richard Coulson she was given the distinction of being named as the most beautiful young woman who would grace the next London Season, that she would be the most desirable debutante to join the marriage mart, which was quite an achievement for any girl.

She wished she weren't so attractive because people, especially the young bucks, behaved like complete idiots around her. Aunt Charlotte said that when she was ready, she hoped the man she chose would be right for her—one who would appreciate her free spirit and love her for what she was, not for what he could make her.

But an interesting fact to some was, upon her marriage, the man who married her would become the recipient of a dowry generous enough to elevate his status considerably.

Tilly had met rich men, she had met handsome men, but she had not fallen in love. Disheartened and thoroughly disenchanted with the opposite sex, she scorned them all, much to her Aunt Charlotte's dismay, for she was eager for her to make a good marriage. She was certain that when the scandal had died a death and Tilly made her debut, there would be so many eager young males of good families posturing about that she would have the pick of the bunch.

The sun was sinking behind the gentle rise of the park when the coach carrying Charles and Tilly and Aunt

Charlotte travelled along the stately drive to the house. Despite being the sister-in-law to Charles and Tilly's mother, Aunt Charlotte had never visited Cranford Park. News of their unexpected arrival soon spread through the halls of the great house and it wasn't long before they were ensconced in the drawing room with the tea things arranged on a low table in from of them.

Tilly glanced at William, who stood with Charles across the room. He was as handsome as he had always been, although he possessed a haughty arrogance which some people took for coldness. He was a caring and compassionate man at heart and his love for Anna, his wife, was evident to all. Their first year of marriage had been blessed with a healthy son, Thomas James Lancaster, Lord Lancaster. After proudly presenting him to their visitors, Anna had taken him to the nursery to put him down for his nap.

Aunt Charlotte was an arresting woman. Her hair was no longer the dark brown of her youth and was liberally streaked with grey. She wore it on top her head, which made her appear taller. Besides being quite striking, if not intimidating, despite being short of stature, she conversed with such zest and charm that she could not be ignored. Ever since her sister-in-law's demise when Tilly was fifteen years old, she had stepped in to guide her beloved niece into adulthood.

Unfortunately, nothing had prepared her for the likes of Richard Coulson. With Tilly's reputation about to be shredded before she'd been launched into society, she had agreed with Charles that they should leave for Cranford until the gossip had died and some other unfortunate girl had transgressed for the *ton* to focus their attention on. It was this matter that was being discussed now.

'It was taken for granted that Tilly, a young woman with an impeccable reputation, would have a Season and make a brilliant marriage. It seems foolish to state the obvious,' she said, shaking her head as she spoke, her coiffure wobbling precariously, 'but she cannot do that now. It's out of the question. The *ton* would never stand for it. She would be humiliated and miserable. It cannot happen. At present no one will speak to her, let alone receive her or acknowledge her.'

'You're quite right, Aunt Charlotte,' Charles agreed. 'Of course it can't. Society will tolerate her because she is the half-sister of the Marquess of Elvington, but they will cut her dead whenever the opportunity arises. In short, she will be treated like a pariah.'

'I'm afraid you're right, Charles,' William said gravely. 'For my part I would like to tell the whole of society to go to hell, but that isn't going to do Tilly any good.'

Charles nodded. 'My feelings entirely. With any luck, next year this will all have blown over and she can be presented then.'

William, who had listened to what was being said with a deep regret, shook his head. 'I blame myself for this. Our mother trusted me to keep Tilly safe, not only from rakehells like Coulson, but from any other dangers that may come her way.' His voice was bitter as he added, 'I was so busy at Cranford, sorting out my grandfather's business affairs since my return from India, followed by his passing—and marrying Anna—that I failed to protect her.'

'It was my responsibility too, William,' Charles remarked. 'I have been so damned busy of late that I took my eyes off what matters. But it is important that she has a Season—which was what Mother would have wanted.'

Tilly sat there, listening as all this talk about her went on as if she was absent. 'What about me?' she protested. 'Does it not matter what I want? Who wants a Season anyway? From what I know of them they are a great bore—a gaggle of girls all doing the same thing, seeing all the same people at every event, all of them hoping to make the best catch.

'It doesn't appeal to me in the slightest—all that curtsying and bowing to goodness knows who and making empty conversation with beaus looking for a wife—the wealthier the better. All that time and effort for the sole purpose of procuring a husband. I hate all the restrictions of the social system that enslaves people like me. It all seems so silly,' she said, sitting up straight and raising her nose to a lofty angle.

'Be that as it may, Tilly,' Aunt Charlotte said as she sipped her tea, 'you will have a coming-out ball next Season. As the sister of the Marquess of Elvington you cannot hide yourself away indefinitely. With any luck this unpleasantness will have blown over by then.'

'And if it hasn't? What is to be done with me? I cannot impose myself on William and Anna indefinitely.'

'Do I have to remind you,' William said, 'that this is your home too, Tilly? I told you when I returned from India that Cranford Park is for my entire family.'

'I know—and I am indeed grateful—I do love being here, but I feel…' She faltered, not really knowing what she felt or what she wanted to do.

'You want more...excitement, perhaps?' William said with a twinkle in his eye.

'I suppose I do. But after what happened with Richard Coulson I'm confused as to what I do want to do now. I can't sit twiddling my thumbs until next year when the Season is upon us once more. And my transgressions may not have been forgotten.'

William looked at his sister. Despite this setback with Coulson, with her free and generous spirit and steadfast gaze, he had never been more proud of her, nor loved her more. She had grown more beautiful as she had reached maturity. She might be a handful at times, but with her willingness to please and her exuberance for life, her moods of warmth and generosity redeemed her.

'Perhaps I might make a suggestion,' Charles said. 'I've received a letter from our uncle's lawyer—Uncle Silas who lived in Devon.'

'Oh? What about? He's dead, isn't he?'

'Yes. He died three months ago. Being much older than our father and Aunt Charlotte just a child when he left home to indulge himself in his travels abroad, we didn't see much of him when we were growing up. He rarely got up to London. As you know, he died without issue and it would appear he's left his house—Drayton Manor, and the land that goes with it—to me as next in line. I don't know what to make of it—and I have neither the time nor the inclination to travel down to Devon to inspect it at this time.

'In fact, the Company is considering sending me to India some time next year, I think, which I would like to do. You could go to Devon for me if you like, Tilly. And you, Aunt Charlotte. A change of scene at this time would be good for you. I believe it is close to the sea. A touch of sea air will benefit you no end.'

Tilly stared at him. 'Devon?'

'Why not? I think Uncle Silas left his home in good order, but it will be comforting to know I'm not inheriting a ruin. Although what I will do with it—a house miles away from London—I haven't the faintest idea.'

All three looked at Tilly expectantly, waiting for her to make her decision. She didn't feel grief and shock at her half-uncle's passing. Silas Anderson was a man she had seldom met. She looked at Aunt Charlotte. 'Would you go, Aunt Charlotte? Uncle Silas was your brother, after all.'

Charlotte, who vaguely remembered her older brother and had last seen him on one of his infrequent visits to London, had listened with great interest as he'd talked at length about his extensive travels and his home in Devon. She could not wait to see what he had so avidly described. There was a broad smile of anticipation on her face for the coming trip. 'Yes—of course I would. Charles is right. The sea air might be good for both of us. Don't you agree, Tilly?'

'Oh, yes. It could be just what's needed at this time.'

'I doubt that,' Charles replied with misgivings, but continued in a more affectionate manner. 'When you look at me like that and smile that smile, I begin to understand why our parents and Aunt Charlotte—even you, William—spoiled and pampered you so outrageously. Hopefully there will be nothing in Devon to distract you.'

Tilly looked fondly at her brother and deeply regretted the disappointment he must feel. He was always the soul of discretion. Caught up in the grip of having betrayed her family, of having shamed the proud name she bore and that of William's own, she was aware of the carnage she had wrought by her careless, reckless behaviour with Richard Coulson.

'I meant what I said, Charles, I will do nothing to add to my disgrace.'

'Gossip is mischievous, often cruel and easy to begin, but ruinous and hard to get rid of. It never goes away entirely. People tuck it away, but they don't forget.'

'I know. So, yes, Charles, I rather fancy a visit to the coast.' Her eyes were alight with the spirit of adventure. 'As I recall Uncle Silas never married and when he stopped travelling he became something of recluse. It will be interesting to see where he lived.'

'Married or not, he did very well for himself, enjoying a long period of considerable prosperity with his many investments in Cornish mines and the like. The housekeeper and a caretaker have been kept on in anticipation of my journeying to Devon, so I expect the house will be in good order. I shall make all the arrangements. We can send a message ahead by one of the coaches going that way. Mrs Carstairs will have time to prepare for your arrival.'

The following days passed in a whirl of activity as they prepared for what could be a lengthy stay in Devon. William provided them with a splendid travelling coach drawn by six bay horses, a driver by the name of Dunstan and his son Graham, who acted as groom. Aunt Charlotte's maid, Daphne, was to accompany them. The coach was loaded with boxes above and behind. Goodbyes were said, Tilly promising to write as soon as may be. Anna, holding baby Thomas in her arms, waved, and the coach moved off. Tilly strained from her seat to get the last glimpse of her two brothers. For a moment panic about leaving them threatened to sweep over her, but when Aunt Charlotte squeezed her hand reassuringly, she knew everything would turn out all right.

They reached Devon after an exhausting journey. The early summer days allowed them to keep going. William had sent them off with six of his own carriage horses so the journey did take a little longer to allow the horses to rest, instead of changing horses at coaching inns along the way, but he thought they might be useful when they reached Drayton Manor. Coach travel was not exactly comfortable or relaxing. The roads were frequented by highwaymen and, to alleviate the dangers of being held up, they always stopped for the night at a coaching inn before the light faded.

Tilly had never seen the sea before and she gazed at the vast expanse of water with wonder. Seldom did the English Channel disappear from sight. A warm wind blew off the sea, pushing the clouds inland. Never before had she seen anything like it. She watched in fascination as the waves swelled and rolled in, breaking on the rocky headlands.

They drove through a village which she would later come to know as Biddycombe, where cobbled streets with a jumble of cottages and rooftops cascaded down the hillside to a harbour. Small boats bobbed on the water in the horseshoe-shaped harbour. Two tall-masted ships heading east could be seen on the horizon and triangular-sailed fishing sloops returning with their herring catch were heading for the harbour.

Tilly turned her eyes inland, her attention caught by a large house in the distance. Medieval in its architecture, it was beautiful in its desolation, its stones aged and grey, its mullioned windows facing south. Great chimneys rose proudly to the sky in competition to the backdrop of stately beech and elms.

'I wonder who lives there?' she wondered aloud.

Aunt Charlotte, eager for the coach to reach its destination and a comfortable bed, fought a sneeze and coughed. She had spent the last couple of days dozing in the coach, complaining of a headache. Now she had developed a chill. Tilly and Daphne were concerned about her. Unfortunately, she seemed to be getting worse. Her eyes were bright and feverish.

'I'm sorry you're not feeling well, Aunt Charlotte. As soon as we reach the house you must go straight to bed. I'll ask Mrs Carstairs to send for the doctor.'

Wiping her eyes, Aunt Charlotte looked too poorly to argue. 'I shall not be sorry to go to bed. I do hope the housekeeper has a room ready.'

Dusk had fallen when the heavy travelling coach eventually came to a halt outside the front door of Drayton Manor. The house was set slightly back from the majestic coastal cliffs in a sheltered valley, its origins dating back two centuries. It was certainly not Cranford Park, Tilly thought, with its stately, well-balanced design, but it was charming in its prospect and appearance, with ivy clinging to its grey stone walls.

Dunstan jumped down from the box and rapped on

the door. It was opened by a woman Tilly assumed to be Mrs Carstairs. She was wiping her hands on her apron and wisps of grey hair escaped her white mob cap.

'Welcome to Drayton Manor,' she said. 'We are expecting you.'

'Thank you,' Tilly replied. 'It's a relief to be here at last.'

'Come—come inside. Everything is in readiness for you.'

'This is Aunt Charlotte, Uncle Silas's sister. She isn't feeling well and really must go to bed.'

'Of course,' Mrs Carstairs said, casting a sympathetic eye over Aunt Charlotte as she tried to suppress another sneeze. 'There is a fire in the drawing room and the beds are aired.'

Mrs Carstairs ushered them inside. They were met by the welcoming scent of beeswax, and rosemary and lavender and other scented flower petals in a china bowl in the centre of a round table. With a brief glance, Tilly noted there were pictures of coastal areas and portraits of deceased strangers lining the wall of the curving staircase.

Mrs Carstairs bustled about, showing them into the drawing room and leaving to fetch refreshment. She was a friendly local woman who had been housekeeper at Drayton Manor for a good many years. Tilly sat in a high back chair before the fire while Daphne accompanied Aunt Charlotte to her room.

Gazing about the room with interest, Tilly thought that this would be where Uncle Silas had sat, drinking his brandy, all summer and winter long, listening to the wind sweeping in from the sea as he entertained company.

Mrs Carstairs showed Tilly the room she had selected for her, a pleasant room, aired and polished and the bed dressed with fresh linen. It offered a splendid view of the trimmed and scythed flower-filled garden. It also faced south and, Mrs Carstairs assured her, had an abundant supply of sunlight during the summer months.

'You don't have your own maid?' Mrs Carstairs asked.

'No. Aunt Charlotte and I will share Daphne, but it's not beyond me to take care of myself.'

'Very well, but should it prove too much for her we have maids who are familiar with the work. They come from Biddycombe daily to help with the chores.'

'Thank you, Mrs Carstairs. I'll bear that in mind.'

Later, when Tilly had changed in her room, she went to look in on Aunt Charlotte.

'How is she, Daphne?'

'Sleeping. I think a good night's sleep will put her on the mend.'

'I do hope so. If not, I'll ask Mrs Carstairs to send for a doctor to take a look at her in the morning.'

Downstairs, Tilly ate a solitary dinner. It was a lovely, simple meal and excellently cooked.

Afterwards, with a growing interest about her temporary home, she familiarised herself with the house, impressed by the quality of the furnishings and the library Uncle Silas had built up over the years. Drayton Manor was a house that gave one a feeling of permanence and importance, but Tilly could not see Charles living here, so far away from the bustle and excitement of London and his work at the East India Company.

As she looked out of the library window, in the far distance in the bright moonlight the tall chimneys of the house that had caught Tilly's attention earlier could be seen rising above the trees.

'Who lives in that large house, Mrs Carstairs?' she asked when the housekeeper appeared. 'It looks impressive and rather grand.'

'And so it is,' she said, coming to stand beside her. 'It belongs to the Kingsley family, the Earl of Clifton—Lucas Kingsley. He's the largest landowner in these parts, although he's been absent for the past twelve months. I believe he's kept on a skeleton staff and he employs a bailiff to administer the working of the estate, but apart from that no one knows where he's gone—although they have their suspicions.'

'But the bailiff must know where he is?'

Mr Carstairs shrugged. 'If he does, he isn't saying. I suppose the Earl will turn up one of these days.'

'So the house is empty—no other family living there.'

'Sadly, no.'

'You said everyone had their suspicions. What do they suspect?'

'The Earl has a sister—Cassandra. Everyone calls her Lady Cassie. She ran off—followed the man she was enamoured of to the Peninsula when he went off to fight Bonaparte.'

A romantic at heart, Tilly stared at her, her interest piqued. 'That was a brave thing for her to do, Mrs Carstairs.'

'Reckless, her brother will say. He has a temper. I've no doubt he was furious. Truth to tell, Miss Anderson, I think he's gone after her to bring her back.'

'Goodness me! Do you think he will? Bring her back, I mean.'

She shrugged. 'Only time will tell. If Lady Cassandra doesn't want to come back, she won't.'

'What is she like?'

'Very much like her brother—not just in looks, but in other ways, too. As wild as the countryside and the sea in the sense that is where she has been raised. She's like a bright light among the gentry—too spirited to be tied down. She's inclined towards downright rebellion, a wilful girl, determined to have her own way, becoming truculent when it's denied her.

'There are no conventions that restrict her mind and spirit as they do other young ladies up in London— hence her falling for someone whose spirit is as wild as her own. Lord Clifton often came over to spend time with Mr Anderson, who was a learned man. They would sit together long into the night, talking about things clever people talk about.'

Tilly could well imagine the scene. She looked around the room, at the cabinets full of fine china, beautiful surfaces polished to a shine over the years, the thickly textured carpets and even a harpsichord. Uncle Silas had made this room his own and on occasion invited the Earl of Clifton to share it with him. How she would have loved to have known Uncle Silas better.

The following morning, after looking in on Aunt Charlotte and relieved to hear she was feeling better and wouldn't hear of summoning a doctor, Tilly left the house, wearing a pale yellow dress and a wide-brimmed bonnet of the same colour atop her dark hair, to take a look at the gardens. They were well-kept with beautiful shrubs and flowers in full bloom.

Having looked at the gardens and unable to resist the pull of the sea, she followed a path that took her in the direction of the beach. Wild flowers sprang up everywhere and woodbine and sweet briar grew in tangles along the wayside, but dominating it all was the sea, glinting through the trees, forever beckoning. Breathing deeply of the air and with the taste of salt on her lips, she decided there and then she would be happy to spend the rest of her life within its sight.

She paused on the edge of a low cliff. Before her was a luminous expanse of jewel-bright sea, shading to darker green as it met the rocks jutting out to the water. Several fishing boats bobbed on the water and a sailing ship, its sails billowing as it caught the wind, could be seen further out.

Stepping on to the soft sand, shimmering from the heat, she walked towards the water lapping the shore, pausing to watch the activity on board the large vessel that was anchored some way out. A man climbed over the side into a rowing boat, where another man was manning the oars. A woman followed and when she was settled other items were lowered down to them.

The boat began to approach the shore. Lifting her hand to shield her eyes from the glare of the sun, Tilly watched the boat as it came closer to the shore. Who were these people? Curious, Tilly continued to watch, thinking it strange that the boat hadn't put in at the harbour she had seen the day before.

It took a while for the boat to reach the shore, time enough for a carriage to appear on the smooth wet sand, which told Tilly whoever was in the boat was expected. Ignoring the flutter in her chest, from a respectful distance she watched the tall, lean yet muscular gentleman climb over the side with an agility that bespoke his fitness, his boots landing in the shallow water. Wearing a dark green frock coat and a pair of black leather boots, his black breeches were snug, hugging his thighs.

He then lifted the woman out, placing her down out of reach of the lapping water. A well-rounded, buxom young woman, her skirts were full and a blue bonnet covered her brown hair. When she swayed suddenly, placing her hand over her mouth, Tilly assumed she might be ill. She thought the woman to be in her mid-twenties. She stood on the sand while the gentleman returned to the boat.

He moved with the assurance and lazy grace of a cat, lithe and arrogant. She sensed a tightly coiled strength in the lean body. His thick black hair was untied and waved freely about his dark face, giving him a feral, untamed air.

Extracting a couple of large leather bags and a wicker basket from the boat, he passed the bags to the driver of the carriage and the basket to the woman before turning to address the driver. The woman suddenly placed it on the sand and disappeared behind the carriage, where she noisily relieved her stomach of its contents.

The dark-haired gentleman took an impatient glance in the direction of the young woman, an expression of amused contempt on his face, then carried on talking to the driver, as if she was of no account.

Having seen the woman's distress, it would be unacceptable for Tilly to simply turn and leave without offering her assistance. Without considering her actions, out of concern she headed towards them, her attention focused on the young woman. The gentleman and the driver ceased talking as she approached. Going to the back of the carriage, she handed the young woman a handkerchief, placing her hand on her shoulder.

'Can I be of help?' she said softly.

'Florence is not a good sailor,' a voice said sharply. 'She has been indisposed since she boarded the boat at Le Havre. Get in the carriage, Florence. Now your feet are on *terra firma* you should soon start to feel better.'

Tilly stiffened and faced him squarely. His absolute disregard for the young woman's weakened state made her cheeks burn. 'And you, sir, might have the consideration to allow her a moment to compose herself before subjecting her to further discomfort.'

The stranger seemed momentarily stunned by her elegant speech and haughty manner. Then a sudden glow began to grow in his eyes as he stared at the proud young woman, whose disdain for him was only too obvious. She possessed a certain dignity that impressed him.

'I would thank you not to interfere in what is no concern to you, young lady. There is nothing wrong with Florence that dry land will not cure. Now, if you would be so kind as to step aside, we will be on our way. Well?' he said, when she failed to obey. 'Are you deaf as well as dumb?'

Tilly had to keep a close rein on her temper, for she had never before been spoken to so rudely. He had a hard mouth that curved grimly, if rather mockingly, up at one corner. His eyes darkened as she squinted up at him.

'I can speak and I can hear very well without you resorting to discourtesy. How can I help hearing when you don't have enough self-control to lower your voice?' She stood her ground and looked him contemptuously in the eye. 'You must forgive me if my concern to see someone in such distress seems out of place, but my concern is well meant. If you are an honourable man, you will see she is taken care of in a proper and considerate manner,' she said, appealing to his sensibility.

Any argument the stranger would have raised was silenced by her quiet rebuttal and her refusal to be cowed. He raised one dark brow, a gleam of humour in his eyes as he glanced at the driver.

'Devil take it, Brownlow. It would seem I am being accused of dishonourable conduct.' With his elbows akimbo, he looked down at Tilly from his superior height. 'I see you and I perceive Florence's situation differently. Just to set your mind at rest,' he said, his patience beginning to wear thin with this unexpected delay and wanting to be on his way, 'be assured that Florence will be given all due care and consideration at my disposal. Now,' he said, looking at Florence, 'please get into the carriage, Florence.'

'Yes, sir,' the woman whispered meekly, wiping her mouth with a handkerchief. 'I'm so sorry.'

Tilly turned her head to look at the gentleman. A frown of displeasure creased his brow. His voice was perfectly level, but it had a harsh, metallic quality that reminded her of steel. His face was expressionless, yet he nevertheless seemed far more formidable. He exuded an aura of hard ruthlessness that made her blood run cold. He was handsome, darkly so, and there was something undeniably fascinating about his piercing light blue eyes in a face burned brown by a hot sun. Black brows arched sharply above, brows that flared at the corners.

When Florence stumbled and reached for the carriage for support, on hearing an impatient tut from the stranger Tilly glared at him. 'Give her a moment—or perhaps a hand up would be appreciated.' Her voice was so authoritative that the arrogantly confident gentleman was momentarily stunned. Feeling a hand on her arm, she turned to find the young woman looking at her appealingly.

'It's all right—truly. I can manage quite well.'

'There you are, you see.' The stranger's soft tongue masked what was in danger of becoming outright anger. 'Now, for the last time, get into the carriage, Florence.'

The young woman obeyed him in silence, too much in awe of him and his authority to utter a word. She bowed her head, and Tilly was sure she glimpsed the sheen of tears in her large brown eyes. Picking up the basket, the driver handed it to her. She placed it carefully on the seat beside her. Only then did she look at Tilly.

'You are most kind,' she said softly, 'but please don't concern yourself. I do not travel on sea well. It's good to have my feet on dry land that is not moving up and down like a bucking horse. I shall soon feel better.'

'There, what did I tell you?' the man said, turning to Tilly. 'Florence is a robust young woman. Her discomfort will soon pass.'

Tilly glared at him defiantly, suspecting he was accustomed to total obedience, a tyrant who relished his power over others. She'd already decided that she disliked him immensely. 'Then I will detain you no longer.'

He looked at her, those piercing light blue eyes moving over her, taking in everything, betraying nothing. He raised one thick, well-defined eyebrow, watching her for every shade of thought and emotion in her. His lips lifted at one corner in a faint curl. Did those eyes linger on her face, her body? Was there a flicker of interest in their depths?

She stood back as he hoisted himself up into the carriage. He continued to stare at her boldly, a cool smile tugging at the corners of his mouth. Tilly found herself tensing and unconsciously took another step back, wishing she wasn't alone. Why she felt that way, she could not have said, but there was something in the expression in those piercing ice-blue eyes that warned her that he was no more impressed by her than she was with him.

After he instructed Brownlow to drive on, Tilly saw a feral gleam enter his eyes and realised she had made an enemy out of this ill-tempered man. Of course, that irritated her and she put an unusually haughty expression on her lovely face and her attractive nose firmly in the air. Not that she cared one way or the other for his opinion of her. Her sole concern was for Florence and how unfortunate it was for Florence to be ordered about by such a dreadful man.

Without more ado, she turned on her heel and began walking away in the opposite direction. Only then did she hear the whimpering and the cry of an infant. Spinning round, she watched the carriage make its way across the smooth wet sand, realising what had been in the basket.

A baby! It was the cry of a baby.

Tilly continued to walk along the shore, looking down at the waves lapping her boots while she thought of her encounter with the stranger. He was of good breeding, handsome, too. Handsome enough to tempt any woman. That thought confused her and angered her also because she wanted to feel nothing but the satisfaction of knowing Florence would be taken care of.

## Chapter Two

Lucas felt as if he had been punched in the stomach, hardly able to believe that a girl who looked so feminine and lovely in her yellow dress and bonnet could be so single-minded and outspoken. He couldn't think of anyone, male or female, who would have stood up to him the way she had just done, verbally attack him and walk away as regal as any queen. The girl had spirit that challenged him. Her arrogance was tantamount to disrespect, yet in spite of himself he admired her style. Nor was she afraid of him. That was the intriguing part about her.

On hearing the infant cry, he recollected himself, pulling himself together, angered at the path down which he had allowed his thoughts to wander. For him to be so fixated on the first civilised woman he had seen with a pretty face in a long time, he must be losing his mind as well as his wits.

The carriage left the beach and joined the road to Clifton House. It was the crowning glory of the Devon countryside in these parts. His heart tightened with bittersweet pain as they traversed the fields and woods that lined the road. He was relieved when they passed through the ivy-covered towered gateway into a courtyard, the carriage halting before the entrance to the house.

Their arrival brought half a dozen footmen attired in black-and-gold-striped livery rushing out of the house and taking command of the baggage before the carriage was driven to the stables at the rear. Florence took charge of the basket with the now sleeping child.

As the Earl of Clifton, Lucas was used to the ceremony and scurrying of servants. Everything was quickly and efficiently taken care of, with Florence and the child ensconced in the nursery. With swift steps, he climbed the wide staircase, a magnificent work of carved oak that towered for three storeys.

The walls were lined with impressive family portraits and niches housed an extensive collection of porcelain vases and pieces of china. He moved along the wide, richly carpeted landing until he reached his rooms—large and comfortable and decorated and furnished in masculine tastes, with a view of the beautiful gardens.

Not until then did he pour himself a generous measure of brandy and feel himself start to relax, even though his return came with its share of troubles. His heart was not at rest. How could it be, after what he had seen, what he had experienced and endured in Spain? His beautiful sister was dead. No more would she grace these rooms. No more would her infectious laughter be heard. He found it difficult to think of what had happened, of the raw wound that festered deep in his heart.

In some strange way the woman he had met on the

beach reminded him of his sister. She had a healthy and unblemished beauty that radiated a striking personal confidence. She had an alluring face, captivating and expressive, he decided. Her chin was small and round, with an adorable, tiny little cleft in the centre. A rosy flush had stained her cheeks, her glorious wealth and vibrancy of glossy black hair streaming down her back from beneath the confines of her bonnet.

But it was her eyes he remembered most—enormous, liquid bright, the colour of damp violets, incisive and clear and tilted slightly at the corners—the kind of eyes a man wanted to see looking up at him when he was about to make love.

To Lucas, starved of a woman's beauty—of any kind of beauty—for so long, to behold so much loveliness, to find himself confronted by her, to be surrounded by the sweet scent of her, was torture indeed, yet that torture was sweet to endure. It made him feel that he wasn't entirely devoid of life.

After twelve months or thereabouts he had returned home, an event he viewed with little joy when he thought what he had left behind in Spain and an empty future that spread endlessly ahead. His home needed fresh life injected into it: a wife and children—an heir to inherit Clifton. Now he was home it was important that he made marriage a priority.

When Cassie had died in childbirth, a part of him had died, too. With her young husband killed in battle, with her dying breath she had made him promise that he would take care of her son, that he would raise him as his own, to keep him from the grip of his paternal family, his uncle Jack Price, and to ensure that, as heir to Trevean and the Price shipyard close to Plymouth, he would inherit what was rightfully his. Lucas had made that promise, a promise he intended to keep. But he did not look forward to coming up against Jack Price—a tyrant and a man who was not averse to obtaining money from any criminal means.

At this time news from the Peninsula was that Wellington and his troops were becoming victorious in Spain, giving his allies a tremendous victory. Other news was that the Grand Army, led by the French emperor Napoleon Bonaparte, was invading Russia. Across the Atlantic, America had declared war on the British.

All this was far from Tilly's mind the following morning. She left her room with the intention of taking a short walk. Mrs Carstairs had told her that Uncle Silas, who liked to walk on the shore, had had some steps hewn out of the rocks for easy access to the beach. They were only a short distance from the house and she couldn't miss them.

Climbing down them was easy enough. She gazed at the huge expanse of water with something like awe. The water flashed blue and was speckled with light. Standing on the sand in a horseshoe-shaped cove, unable to resist the pull of the sea, with not a soul in sight and in the shelter of the cliffs, Tilly removed her shoes and stockings along with her bonnet.

Leaving them in the shelter of the rocks, she padded the short distance to where the sea lapped the sand. The tide was on the ebb and the surf barely more than the lapping of wavelets against the beach. She watched as the water washed over her feet, the feeling exquisite.

Deciding to walk to the far end of the cove, curious to see what was beyond the headland, and holding her skirts in front of her, she made her way through the shallows. Driftwood and seaweed had been washed ashore and seashells were embedded in the wet sand. The sun was warm on her face and the breeze lifted her hair from her shoulders.

As she reached the far end of the cove, moving through deeper water now, and before she could round the tall granite cliffs to see what was beyond, a horse and rider came galloping through the surf. For a moment Tilly stood and gaped, then, with the force generated by the horse along with a forceful wave, she lost her balance and toppled into the water.

Suddenly the water was over her head as she was dragged under. The water roared in her ears and her clothes weighted her down as she tried to regain her balance. It felt like minutes before her head finally broke the surface, but it was only seconds. Gasping and spluttering, having swallowed a mouthful of seawater, she opened her eyes.

In the act of bringing his horse under control, the rider looked at the apparition that met his eyes. It was enough to stop all thought for the moment. When he saw the bedraggled head of a woman come spluttering to the surface, he flung himself off his horse and hauled her unceremoniously on to the sand. When she wiped the black hair from her face and he saw who it was, for a moment he couldn't believe his eyes.

'Devil take it! I might have known.' Her dishevelment and the fact that she was coughing and gasping for breath alarmed him. 'Here, take my hand.' Taking a handkerchief from his pocket, he proceeded to wipe her wet face.

Furiously, she shoved his hand away. Recognising the man she had met the day before and remembering their unpleasant altercation, she was tempted to crawl back into the sea he had just hauled her out of. 'Kindly leave me be. I may be half drowned, but I am not helpless.'

'I see you are upset—'

'I am not upset, I am furious.'

The stranger scowled down at her. 'Suit yourself. Not content with giving me a dressing down yesterday, now you almost unseat me from my horse. Do you have some kind of death wish or do you go out of your way to annoy me?'

She got to her feet, unaware as she did so that, from the soaking it had received, her gown clung far too revealingly to every curve of her supple young body. Tilly was so incensed she could hardly speak. Soaked through to the skin and her hair hanging heavy and wet about her face, filled with righteous indignation she looked down and surveyed her bedraggled appearance.

'You blundering idiot,' she fumed. 'You should look where you're going. You could have drowned me riding through the water at such speed. You have ruined my gown.'

'And you, Miss, have ruined my boots.' His voice cut through her accusation like a steel blade.

Almost bursting with rage and mortification, Tilly glared at him while taking the weight of her hair and wringing out as much water as she was able. 'I did nothing of the sort—and I don't care a fig for your boots.

The blame lies with you, not me. I feel sorry for your poor horse. What were you trying to do? Drown the poor beast?'

'That *poor beast* happens to like being ridden through water—he thrives on it, in fact, which is more than I can say for you looking as you do, like some bedraggled sea waif.' Throwing himself down, he proceeded to remove his boots, pouring the offending seawater out on to the sand.

Tilly jerked her head up, looking into his harsh-planed face and his mouth set in a hard line, a mouth she doubted ever smiled, but only curled in a mocking grin. Planting her hands in the small of her waist, she glowered down at him, tempted to snatch one of his boots out of his hand and beat him over the head with it. 'Not content with almost drowning me, now you insult me. This is all your fault, you...you loathsome, unfeeling scoundrel. You are certainly no gentleman... you... Oh!'

In frustration, she cut herself off, unable to find the proper words to insult him with, when he suddenly began to shake with helpless laughter, which only succeeded in incurring her wrath further. Staring at him in disbelief, she moved closer to him as he began to shove one of his stockinged feet back into his wet boot. 'I'm completely baffled at what you can find to laugh at.'

'Can you not? It's your use of the word *scoundrel* to describe me, I'm afraid. Given sober consideration, I suppose it might apply, even if it is rather mild compared to other more colourful terms I've heard to describe me before.'

'If I were acquainted with such terms you are accustomed to, which does not surprise me in the least, then be assured that I would use them.'

'You probably would—given the way you look and the sharpness of your tongue. If only you could see yourself as you are now, you would not dare give yourself airs and graces,' he said with unsympathetic amusement.

Quite suddenly, he no longer felt like laughing at her plight as his gaze took in every detail of her. Having donned one of his boots, he sat holding the other and, with one brow cocked, he studied her carefully, from her slender ankles to the top of her head, noting the way the material of her gown continued to cling to her slender body, emphasising the minuscule waist and the firm roundness of her breasts.

'I do believe,' he said, almost absently, 'that beneath all that wetness, there is a lovely young woman fighting to be released.'

His words hit Tilly like a slap in the face. Realising what was going through his mind and not liking one bit the way he was looking at her, fresh anger threatened to choke her. 'You hateful beast. How dare you be so...so forward?' Almost breathless with fury and mortification, something about the way in which he was looking at her, his eyes dwelling significantly on her breasts, made her suddenly aware of her appearance. 'Have you no shame?'

Lifting his shoulders in a shrug and shaking his head in that infuriating way of his, he said, 'None, I'm afraid. And now I think you have made your point. If indeed I was at fault in tossing you into the sea, then I apologise most humbly.' Ignoring her gasp of surprise, he continued ironically, 'So, you see, your eloquence has moved me enough to touch even my villainous heart.'

'Since my present predicament appears to give you cause for amusement, if you will excuse me, I will be on my way.'

Aware of her wet clothes clinging to her body and the gritty feel of sand against her face and in her hair, wanting to be as far away from this insufferable man as it was possible to be, with a toss of her head Tilly turned and marched across the sand to where she had left her belongings.

Lucas watched her go as if he had taken root. Troubled by his responsibilities since returning from Spain and with a nagging headache brought on by a sleepless night, he'd decided that a long ride would chase it away. After riding across fields and meadows, he'd come to the beach where he gave his horse his head.

He no longer felt his earlier urge to burst into laughter at the young woman's sorry plight. Shoving his foot into his remaining boot, forgetting for the time being that they were now ruined, then getting to his feet, he walked to where his horse stood patiently waiting. Unable to wipe the young woman from his thoughts, he thought of how she had looked—yes, she had been well and truly soaked through, but it did not detract from her temper or her loveliness. In fact, in some strange way, it had enhanced it.

Her breasts were high and firm, tapering to small peaks beneath the fabric of her dress, and her eyes, a wonderful shade of violet, had been huge in her pale face. Her haughty manner had marked her as a strong character whereas there was a certain softness about her, an elusive gentleness.

Clearly, she was a woman of ever-changing moods and subtle contradictions. While her physical beauty first arrested the attention, it was this spectrum, this bewildering, indefinable quality, that held him captive. A strange, sweet melting feeling softened his innermost core without warning, the place in him he usually kept as hard as steel.

Guilt engulfed him. He really should have been more sympathetic. The poor girl had been doused in seawater and no doubt had a long walk home. Feeling like a complete idiot and with the need to make amends, he mounted his horse and galloped across the sands in the direction she had taken, but she was nowhere to be seen.

He was curious as to her identity. He was acquainted with most of the people in and around Biddycombe, but she was a stranger. Although, he thought, having been absent for months on end, how would he know? On a sigh and feeling the discomfort of his wet boots, he headed for home.

As soon as Tilly arrived back at the house, aware of what a sight she must look and making the excuse that she had been knocked off her feet by a large wave, one of the maids who came to help Mrs Carstairs in the house brought hot water and a tub to her room so she could bathe. Nothing would induce her to tell the truth, that an insufferable man had almost drowned her and then insulted her most shockingly. If she was fortunate, she would not see him again.

When she was restored to looking decent, she went

to see Aunt Charlotte, who was seated in a chair by the window, a book on her lap. Glancing up when Tilly appeared in the doorway, she smiled.

'My dear Tilly, do come in and tell me what you have been doing. I hope you're not too bored. You're not used to so much solitude.'

'No, perhaps not, but I like being here very well. How are you feeling?'

'Oh, a little better. I'll soon be up and about. But this is such a restful house—so quiet.'

'So it is,' Tilly replied softly. 'It's certainly a change from the hustle and bustle of London. I'm tempted to asked Charles to keep the house so that I can live here for ever.'

Aunt Charlotte gave her an indulgent smile. 'You say that now, Tilly, but after a couple of months of complete solitude, you might change your mind. Have you been to the beach yet?'

'Yes—I—I was there earlier.'

'And?'

'I like it very well,' she said, having no intention of disclosing her encounter with the arrogant stranger who had knocked her into the sea. 'It's just like I expected. When you are better, we will go together. We can collect seashells.'

'I'm looking forward to seeing it with you. It will be a pleasant way to pass the summer until we have to return to London.'

Tilly laughed, perching on the window seat. 'It most certainly will. Why, you, too, might get to like it so well that you won't want to leave.'

'And miss your debut? Oh, I don't think so.'

'I know you won't miss the chance of playing matchmaker, Aunt Charlotte.'

'Of course not, and you're hardly likely to find a title down here. Not only that, if Charles does go to India, then he will want to see you before he leaves.'

'Yes,' Tilly said absently, listening to a blackbird singing its heart out on the branch of a cherry tree close to the house and thinking how delightful it was. 'Although he doesn't expect to leave for months yet. I'm hoping we'll be here for Christmas. I will miss him dreadfully when he leaves. I would like to see India. Anna loved it, you know—although she was fortunate when her brother made her William's ward when she returned to England.'

'Yes, Tilly,' her aunt said. 'She certainly was. They are so happy together with young Thomas.'

They looked towards the door when Daphne entered, carrying a tray with tea and cakes.

'You will stay and take tea with me, Tilly? See, Daphne has brought two cups.'

'I'd love to,' Tilly said, looking out of the window while Daphne poured the tea, her thoughts turning to her unfortunate encounter with the stranger on the beach, as curious to his identity as he was to know hers.

Two days later, mid-afternoon, while her aunt was resting and Mrs Carstairs was visiting a neighbour, feeling hemmed in and restless at having to remain indoors on such a lovely day, Tilly left her room with the intention of taking a book to read out in the garden. On her way down the stairs she stopped, sensing there was someone in the house.

A man's heavy tread sounded purposefully through the hall, growing nearer from the direction of the kitchen. A tall man appeared, filling the hall with his presence, and then he spoke in the calm, assured voice of a gentleman.

'Ah—so the house is inhabited after all.'

Tilly stared at him. It was that insufferable man she had hoped never to see again.

'Oh—it's you,' she said, continuing down the stairs. 'Do you normally walk into other people's homes uninvited? Sneaking through the house like a thief. You certainly have strange ideas of the way to pay a call on your neighbours.'

One corner of his mouth lifted in a mocking smile. 'Not usually, but this is a house in which I was always welcome.'

There was no mistaking his air of familiarity. He stopped several yards from her, feet apart. She suspected he had no patience for the niceties of life. He had neatened himself up a little and pulled his windblown black hair back and fastened it with a ribbon at the nape, but he still wore the same threadbare coat he had worn on the two occasions they had met. All this was only surface deep and beneath it all the wildness was there.

Alone with him, alarmingly, nerve-rackingly alone, Tilly stood looking at him by the light slanting through the two windows. With his wide shoulders and lean waist, there was no concealing that here was a man alive and virile in every fibre of his being, arrogantly mocking and recklessly attractive. He had far and beyond the most handsome face she had seen in her life.

Tilly found it was impossible to tear her eyes away.

He looked like an aristocratic pirate, arrogant, cold and remote, a man other men would be instinctively wary of and women fascinated by. His eyes in his perfectly chiselled face regarded her with calm intentness, unsmiling but not unfriendly. She looked him contemptuously in the eye before dropping her gaze to his boots.

'I see you have a new pair of boots.'

'I have several—but the boots you ruined were my favourites.'

'You ruined them all by yourself. I know you found the whole incident of almost drowning me highly entertaining, but I did not. Who are you? Why are you here? If it is to see my uncle Silas, then I'm afraid he is no longer with us.'

'So I've been told. So, you are Silas's niece. My commiserations. He was a fine man. A good neighbour. We dined together and visited each other on many occasions.' Despite their differences in age and neither admitting to a certain loneliness in their lives, they had been good friends.

Tilly had nothing to say to this, not having known her uncle well enough to make comment.

The stranger inclined his head slightly. 'I'm Lucas Kingsley, the Earl of Clifton, at your service.'

Tilly stared at him. So, she thought, this was the man who lived in the big house that had raised her curiosity. She was momentarily thrown on hearing this, but her resentment was not diminished. 'I see. And you only recently arrived home. Well, you may be Lord of the manor and own most of the land in these parts, but you do not own Drayton Manor. Do you hear me?'

'How am I to help hearing you when you have no

self-control to lower your voice? I don't know where you come from, but you'll make no friends in these parts if you go about with a face like a thundercloud and a tongue that can flay a man to within an inch of his life.'

'Friends? Ha! I am a stranger to these parts and if my neighbours are all like you, then I can do without them,' she retorted while asking herself what she was doing. She had forgotten her dignity and was shocked at herself and her lack of composure and self-control.

'And you, Miss Whoever-you-are, have a lot to learn. This is a man's world down here and, like it or not, get used to it.'

'I would not take you for a gentleman who indulged in afternoon calls, Lord Clifton.'

'There is always a first time. I apologise for my conduct yesterday. It was unfortunate, and I did try to find you afterwards—when I finally put my wet boots back on, I might add—but you had disappeared.'

'Why on earth would you do that? Come after me, I mean. I think we had said all we had to say to each other.'

'Nevertheless, I wanted to make sure you were all right—to offer you the loan of my horse to see you home—for you were in a sorry state as I recall.'

'Yes, I was. But as you see, Drayton Manor is close to the sea so I did not have very far to walk.'

'And you suffered no ill effects from your tumble into the sea?'

'No. None. Now, suppose you tell me what you are doing letting yourself in without a by your leave. Say what you have to say and leave the way that you entered.'

'Exactly,' he agreed lightly. 'My bailiff told me of Silas's demise. I came to call on Mrs Carstairs.'

'She's visiting a neighbour. She should be back shortly.'

'I brought Silas a keg of French brandy. He was rather partial to the fine stuff. He will have little use of it now. I have left it in the kitchen. Mrs Carstairs will know what to do with it.'

'Feel free to bring Mrs Carstairs a whole distillery, but do not enter this house again unless you are invited.' She thought she saw a look of surprise in his eyes, but it was soon gone.

'Worry not. I will not impose myself on you unless I am invited. We appear to have got off to a bad start,' he said coldly. 'The impression I have of you is that you would not spend your time in useless activities. I think you will get my meaning. With no husband—you do not wear a wedding ring, I see—and therefore no children, you think nothing of interfering wherever you think fit.'

'I believe you refer to my concern for the young lady when I saw her indisposed and rushed to her aid— which is what any decent human being would do. We have met on just two occasions, Lord Clifton, so I fail to see how you have had the time to form any opinion of me at all.'

She felt a moment of unease. It might have been the way his eyes were looking at her, touching her everywhere, an inexplicable, lazy smile sweeping over his lean face as he surveyed her from head to foot, that suddenly made her feel as if she had walked into a seduction scene, which momentarily threw her off balance.

'I recognise a lady who is charitable to others when I see one.'

'Really? I am surprised.'

'Oh, indeed I do. My mother was given to charitable works—quite the saint, in fact.'

'Oh, I am no saint, Lord Clifton. In fact, I am quite the opposite and certainly no lady—which is what my brothers are always telling me. I have an awkward habit of doing things I am not supposed to do and arguing when I should know better. There are times when I don't behave or express myself as a lady is supposed to and if my attitude causes offence, then that is for them to deal with, not me.

'I can be frightfully blunt,' she uttered, looking up into his dark face, which was relaxed into a noble, masculine beauty that drew her gaze like a magnet and brought self-reproach for her weakness.

'So can I,' he replied, his eyes the eyes of a hunter, instantly clear in the moonlight. 'You have inherited Drayton Manor?'

'No. My brother Charles.'

'He is here?'

'No. He remained in London. I am here with my aunt—Uncle Silas's younger sister, who is indisposed at present.'

'And your name?'

'Tilly, short for Matilda, but everyone calls me Tilly—Tilly Anderson.'

Lord Clifton's blue-eyed gaze, alert and watchful, was disconcerting.

'How is the young lady—Florence? Better, I hope?'

'Florence is recovered to perfect health, Miss Anderson. Thank you for asking. The way you leapt to her aid was, of course, laudable.'

'I was concerned.'

'That was obvious.'

'You were not sympathetic to her condition.'

'It is not in my nature. Many people suffer from sea sickness and recover quickly.'

'And you told me not to interfere when I tried to help her.'

'After an absence of many months I was impatient to get to my home.'

'And to be rid of my interference.'

'Yes, since you ask. Florence is a servant and knows her place.'

'She is still a human being and is entitled to be treated with consideration and respect.' Tilly was always one to speak her mind and was too angry to be intimidated by this illustrious neighbour. 'I should tell you that I have a streak to my nature that fiercely rebels against being ordered what to do. I think Florence should do the same.'

'Not if she values her position. I have a formidable temper myself,' he told her with icy calm. 'It may surprise you to learn that when we parted yesterday, I was prepared to give you the benefit of the doubt.'

'And now?'

'That still applies. You virtually accused me of being dishonourable, which was damning in itself. You summed up your opinion of me quickly,' he stated. 'No doubt you have listened to gossip from the locals, but whatever you have heard, forget it. You don't know me.'

Tilly could not look away from him—in fact, unconsciously her feet took her closer to where he stood, her eyes holding his. Angry colour suffused her cheeks. She stood close, her face tilted slightly to look up into his, her unbound black hair spilling down her back, her skirts brushing his black boots.

'You are wrong. I have not been here long enough to listen to gossip—and I wouldn't anyway. I prefer to make up my own mind. I may have met you only twice before, but I have made a very accurate assessment of your character.'

'Do you normally form an opinion of a person after so short an acquaintance?' he asked.

'In your case it was not difficult,' she replied. 'I found you overbearing and dictatorial and with little concern for the feelings of others.'

Lord Clifton arched his brows, mild cynicism and a stirring of respect in the icy depths of his eyes. 'That bad?'

'Worse. You are heartless and I cannot abide your superior male attitude—your insufferable arrogance and conceit.'

He looked at her with condescending amusement. 'And you, Miss Anderson, with a tongue on you that would put a viper to shame, can hardly be called a paragon of perfection.'

'My brothers would agree with you. Especially Charles. We are at war more often than not.'

'And are we at war?'

Tilly eyed him warily. 'I suppose it does seem like that.'

Lord Clifton's face was set in an almost smiling challenge. 'Don't be so certain.'

'Lord Clifton,' she retorted sharply, dark eyes locking with light blue ones, 'if you plan another battle, you can leave right this minute.'

'Nothing so dramatic—merely a mild skirmish. If nothing else, you are forward and recklessly bold.'

'I always believe in being direct and I enjoy walking on the wild side occasionally.'

'And I thought all young ladies sat at their needlepoint and painted pretty pictures.'

'I'm sure you may find it shocking and unfeminine that I do neither, but that's the way I am.'

'I do, but in your case, I will overlook your unfeminine interests. The informality of my call was not meant as an offence. Indeed, I had no idea who you were. I didn't even have the courtesy to ask your name or to thank you for your concern.'

'Because you are arrogant and conceited,' she reminded him.

'You do not take after your uncle.'

'And what is that supposed to mean?'

'You are nothing like him. He was the kind of man who saw the good in everyone and welcomed them into his home. No, you are nothing like him.'

He looked at her with as much dislike as she felt for him and this only increased her anger. 'Do you mean I don't show respect? Oh, dear. How annoying you must find that. I am no sycophant, Lord Clifton, who bows and scrapes to gentlemen and their titles. Those people have to earn my respect. I have met you on two occasions and I believe I have assessed your character correctly.'

When they had met on the beach, she had been angry with him, but that was yesterday. Today he had learned his good friend Silas Anderson was dead and he had come to Drayton Manor with condolences and to commiserate with Mrs Carstairs. Seeping into her consciousness, this thought was telling her that he could not be all bad and that he deserved the benefit of the doubt.

She had no idea how long she was to remain in Devon and, until the time came for her to leave, she could not go around making enemies of everyone, especially not the Earl of Clifton, her uncle's good friend and the most important land owner in these parts. Her manner had been anything but friendly. She must try to practise a little courtesy while he was in her brother's house. But that did not mean to say she had to like him.

'I would like to give you the keg of brandy as a peace offering.'

'I don't drink brandy—my brothers allow me just the one glass of wine, or champagne if I'm lucky.'

'I am not your brothers—and if you don't drink it then you can offer me a glass when I come to call.'

'And do you intend calling, Lord Clifton?'

'If you will allow it?'

'We are neighbours. I would hate to disappoint Mrs Carstairs. She…appears fond of you.'

'Then, in common agreement, we will portray ourselves as being both gracious and mannerly when we are in the presence of Mrs Carstairs.' Surprising her, he abruptly turned on his heel and walked in the direction of the kitchen. 'I will leave you now by the door I came in by. The next time we meet I can only hope you are in a better temper.'

Tilly followed him quickly. Pulling the door open that led into a backyard, he stopped and looked at her.

'You are here for how long?'

'I haven't decided—not that it's any of your business. All I ask is that I am left to live in peace for the duration of my stay.'

'Peace? In Biddycombe?' He laughed and there it was again—that mocking smile. 'You think it's as easy as that?'

She thought he must have read something in her face that made him change his mind about what he was going to say to her.

'When you are ready to listen, I will tell you—or someone else will,' he said flatly. 'A word of advice before I leave. See that your doors and windows are locked and bolted in future—especially at night. You might have the kind of visitors who would not be as amenable or as tolerant as I am.'

They were distracted when Mrs Carstairs entered the yard. When she saw Lord Clifton, her face broke into a welcoming smile. 'Why, Lord Clifton! Good gracious me! I heard you were back. The whole village is abuzz with the news. Welcome home. It's high time, too.'

'I was sorry to hear about Silas. He will be missed.'

'He will that. It's a blessing he didn't suffer. Caught a chill, he did, walking on the beach without his coat. He went out like a light. Can I get you some refreshment?'

'No, thank you. I'll be on my way. I just called to offer my commiserations and to leave a keg of brandy I intended giving Silas.' He looked at Tilly as Mrs Carstairs bustled into the kitchen. 'Good day, Miss Anderson. Thank you for your hospitality.'

Half turning, he hesitated. After some deliberation, when he next spoke his voice was low and serious. 'There is something I would like to ask of you. I'm sorry if it might put you on the spot, but my own need is urgent, which forces me to be blunt. The other day when we met on the beach, to avoid notice, it was my intention to get in the carriage and drive off, not to linger. Unfortunately, Florence put paid to that and I wasn't expecting to encounter a young lady intent on playing the Good Samaritan.'

Tilly looked at him in confusion. 'So, why did that matter?'

'As we were leaving you heard an infant crying.'

'Yes, I did. That was when I realised the contents of the basket was a baby.'

'It is important to me that on no account should anyone know there is a child living at Clifton House—at least, not for the present.'

'Oh, I see. Then...I will tell no one.'

'I would be grateful—not your aunt and certainly not Mrs Carstairs. She is a dear lady, but there are times when she lets her tongue run away with her.'

'I understand. Of course I will keep your confidence. I am not one to gossip. It is your affair, not mine. But you have servants at Clifton House. Can they be trusted to keep your confidence also?'

Frowning, he shook his head. 'As to that, I will have to depend on their loyalty to my family—although there are one or two who are inclined to gossip.'

Tilly followed him out of the yard to where he'd left his mount tethered to a gatepost. Swinging himself up into the saddle, he looked down at her.

'Good day, Miss Anderson. Enjoy your time at Drayton Manor.'

When he unexpectedly smiled broadly, Tilly noticed how white and strong his teeth were and how the tiny lines at the sides of his sharp eyes creased up attractively. He really was so handsome, so well made, so perfect to look at. She wondered at the effect he would have on the ladies who made up London's society.

For a moment she was confused and found herself striving for normality. It was difficult to organise her thoughts when those amazingly light blue eyes were focused on her so intently. Before the rogue thoughts could progress further, she lowered her eyes, quickly shaking off the strangeness of the moment that had caught her unawares. What was she thinking of? This man was practically unknown to her, yet just for a moment she had felt drawn to this handsome, desirable, insufferably arrogant stranger.

But she could not deny that he had a strange and strong effect on her—he invaded her consciousness and took over her mind. She found it hard to explain because it was something she had never experienced before. The way he had of looking at her was a new and very powerful and profound thing.

That something was happening against her will she knew. Men like Lord Clifton found it easy to manipulate a woman's heart and, after her debacle with Richard Coulson, who was a green youth compared to Lord Clifton, she could not allow him to do that.

Tilly stood and watched him ride away, noting his relaxed air and the splendid way he sat on his horse. He was hatless and his loosely tied black hair gave him a jaunty, nonchalant look. Whether or not he had been touched by the reeking decay and stench that hung over the battlefields in Spain, Lord Clifton had not been three days back in England and already he was firmly taking charge of his inheritance at Clifton House. Even with the journey from Spain still present in his mind, he was taking his affairs in hand and seeking her confidence to keep the presence of the child secret.

It was an attitude of which she approved, she thought, almost convincing herself that her admiration had nothing to do with his darkly handsome face, the midnight-blue depths of his eyes and the curl of his lips.

As she stood watching his retreating figure, she pondered the fascination she felt for Lord Clifton. She had met many handsome men in London, yet she'd felt no connection between them, no meeting of the eyes or quickening of her breath that she felt when her eyes were captured by the dark stare of the lord of Clifton House.

What was it about him that had the power to hold her so entranced, to arouse her rampant curiosity? It had to be something other than the classical perfection of his features, for Lord Clifton was an extraordinarily handsome man. She had never experienced with any gentleman that quickening of the blood she felt when his eyes captured hers. And who was the child whose presence at Clifton House he wanted kept secret? Was he the father and, if so, who was the mother and where was she?

## Chapter Three

Lucas had been surprised to find the young woman he had encountered on the beach two days ago in residence at Drayton Manor. When his gaze had come to rest on her, on her violet eyes in which darker flecks blazed—a sure sign that their owner was under some urgent compulsion—he had looked at her with silent fascination.

He was easily moved by the beauty of a woman and the calm coldness with which Miss Anderson had looked at him intrigued him. He had tried to ignore her scent of jasmine and all her delectable attributes that stood just within his easy reach as she had lambasted his character. She was enchanting, part-spitfire, part-angel, and with an independent temperament.

Despite her acid tongue he was drawn to the freshness and vitality with which she carried herself. She was exceptionally beautiful, so beautiful that it was impossible not to stare at her. Her eyes were wide-set and accentuated by black brows. The patrician nose, the heart-shaped face, the fine texture of her skin, the haughty set of the queenly head crowned with a glorious shining black mane—all bespoke good breeding.

There was about her a warm sensuality, something instantly suggestive to him of pleasurable fulfilment. It was something she could not help, something that was an inherent part of her, but of which she was acutely aware. She was obviously intelligent with a poised manner that would charm all present at social events, but beneath her grace and poise she was also full of suppressed energy that lurked just below the surface.

Thoughts such as these brought to mind his need to find a wife, a woman who would be more amenable and biddable than Miss Anderson, who was far too headstrong and opinionated and reminded him far too much of his wild and tenacious sister. Miss Anderson was the type of woman most unsuitable to be his wife. But he was puzzled by her. A young woman with her debut to look forward to? It didn't make sense. What was the real reason her family had decided to bury her in the heart of Devon, in a house once inhabited by an old man?

As so often of late his thoughts turned to his infant nephew. He was a troubled man as he rode back to Clifton House. Jack Price posed a problem. While ever the boy was beneath his roof there was every chance that Price would find out and put two and two together and realise he was his brother's child.

Reaching the house, he made his way to the nursery, which was on the same landing as his own rooms. Pausing for an indecisive moment outside, he pushed open the door. Diaphanous white curtains were drawn across the windows to shut out most of the bright sunshine while the child slept. One of the windows had been opened and the curtain gently stirred in the slight breeze.

Pictures of animals and flowers hung on the walls, shelves crammed with books and baskets of toys were everywhere—toys that had once belonged to himself and Cassie—some more battered than others, but still able to give pleasure to a child. There was a clockwork dog and a doll's house in one corner and a child-size table and chairs. Set at right angles to the hearth were two comfortable easy chairs.

He could hear Florence moving about in the adjoining room. It was to the crib in which the child slept that Lucas directed his gaze. The child was lying on his back, his dark hair on either side of his face, his chubby palms open. He had kicked away the covers so his baby legs were bare. Not wishing to alert Florence to his presence and careful not to wake the child, he edged closer to the crib and looked down.

He was totally unprepared for the feelings and the emotions that almost overwhelmed him. As memories of the child's birth assailed him, remembering how he had taken him from Cassie's arms, promising he would take care of him and guard him from Jack Price with his life, he gulped in the air, trying to drag it into his tortured lungs as he remembered watching Cassie take her final breath.

He couldn't fail her. No matter what, he would honour his promise. She had told him that before he died, Edmund had expressed a wish that, if the child was a boy, he was to be named Tobias. Cassie had agreed, saying it was a lovely name. So Tobias it was.

The servants had been sworn to secrecy. Anyone

who uttered a word about the child's existence would be dismissed immediately. He gazed at Tobias. The fan of his dark lashes shadowed his plump, rosy cheeks. His lips were soft and pink and slightly parted. His head was covered with a mass of glossy brown curls. He accepted that he was his responsibility and his heart was stirred with a sense of pride in his infant beauty. His eyes were blue, the same blue as Cassie's.

Cassie. Remembrance of her twisted his heart. Cassie, glowing and strong, with the power to amuse and infuriate him and with a will of burnished steel as she had stood up to him when he had ordered her to stay away from Edmund Price. Defiant and brave and with blazing eyes, she had ignored him.

When he had caught up with her in Spain, finding her at her lover's bedside where he lay dying from wounds sustained in battle, and seeing she was big with child, he had arranged for them to be married immediately. When she had gone into labour, he could see that she was in pain and tortured with grief for Edmund's loss. Then she had subjected him to the most massive dose of guilt and emotional blackmail to ensure that he would take care of the child should she not make it.

Gently, he stroked Tobias's cheek with his finger. The infant stretched his tiny body and yawned. And then his eyelids fluttered and opened a little in sleep before closing once more, not yet ready to wake, but the man responsible for the disturbance in his nephew smiled to himself, a satisfying smile that warmed his heart.

Aunt Charlotte's recovery proved to be slow. She still refused to allow a doctor to visit, insisting her constitution was strong and she would soon be fully recovered. She was content to spend her time in her room with her embroidery or in the garden with a blanket over her knees, reading one of the many books that filled the shelves in the library.

With each new day that dawned, Tilly loved being at Drayton Manor more and more. During those first days as she was warmly greeted by neighbours as she wandered happily through the countryside and along the coast, she was unable to push the Earl of Clifton, whose house was never far from her sights, from her mind.

One day ran into the next so that she almost lost track of time. Never had she known such freedom, of being able to do as she wished, to live entirely for the present. How pleasant it was. Being out of doors so much, her face took on a golden shade and she had taken to braiding her hair so that it snaked down her back from beneath her bonnet. What did she care what she looked like? There was no one to see her.

Tilly couldn't have said what the sound was that woke her in the early hours. The wind had risen and was buffeting the house, but she thought it must be more than that. She closed her eyes once more as sleep threatened to engulf her, yet her ears continued to strain for the sound that had woken her. But there was nothing, nothing that could account for it.

However, she was restless and got up to look out of the diamond-paned windows. It was a dark, moonless night, but she could just make out the shape of the trees and the outbuildings housing the ivy-clad stables just beyond. Then she heard a sound that alerted all her senses. It was the sound of horse's hooves on the drive leading to the stables. That was the moment she thought she saw a light close to the stable doors. Surely it couldn't be Dunstan or Graham at this ungodly hour, unless there was something amiss with one of the horses.

Not wishing to disturb Mrs Carstairs, she decided to investigate herself. Shrugging herself into a dark blue robe over her nightdress, she left her bedroom and made her way through the dark house, letting herself out by a side door close to the kitchen. She started when a dog fox barked from somewhere beyond the house, shuddered, then pulled herself together, following a path lined on one side by the eerie trunks of ash and beech and guarding like sentries. She made her way silently to the stables.

She couldn't have said what alerted her to danger and caused her to shrink into the secluded, solid darkness of the trees. As her eyes became accustomed to the gloom, she saw the occasional flicker of light and weird shapes and shadows around the stables. There were sounds of movement, of horses shifting restlessly in their stalls. What on earth was going on? she wondered.

Although never of a nervous disposition, beneath the eerie canopy of the trees Tilly felt the chilling hand of fear clutch at her. Her heart began to race. Could someone be trying to steal the horses? About to step out and confront whoever it was, it was then that a powerful pair of hands grabbed her from behind. In an instant, she was pulled back against a hard chest and a hand was placed over her mouth, the fingers that gripped her lower face like a band of steel, stifling any sound she might have made. Then she was held quite still, held so firmly that she was unable to move.

'Hold still. There is danger.'

Hot breath touched her cheek as the warning was uttered softly in her ear. Her body was pressed hard to whoever it was that held her, their faces close together. She moved her head angrily to shake him off and heard a half-stifled noise that might have been a laugh. She could hear the sound of his breathing as the sounds she had heard coming from the stables earlier increased in intensity.

She heard the closing of doors and, in the limited light above her captor's fingers, her eyes grew wide as shapes began to materialise in front of her. She heard the hammering of her heartbeat in her ears as dark-clad figures, some ten or a dozen of them, passed by, some on horseback, each with their heads bent as they hurried on with a deadly-seeming purpose. Did she imagine it, or was that a flash of a scarlet coat she saw in the gloom?

'Be still,' the voice close to her ear repeated in a husky voice. 'Don't utter a sound.'

Unable to struggle, unable to move, Tilly did as he bade, too alarmed and afraid to do anything else. Holding her breath, she stood and watched the figures move quickly by and become swallowed up by the night. Only then did she feel the powerful grip release her and the fingers free her mouth. But he still held her close.

'You can breathe easy now. They have gone.'

Tilly was still tense, still anxious that those men would come back. Taking her shoulders, her assailant turned her to face him. She already knew his identity. Lord Clifton's unseen hands touched the nape of her neck and stroked the length of her hair. His close proximity was disconcerting. Her traitorous body tingled and grew warm. In the leather jerkin he wore, he smelled of the forest, of man and horse, but not unpleasantly so.

'Do you make a habit of prowling the countryside at night, Lord Clifton?'

'A man on foot who knows the land like I do and knows where he's going can hardly be seen—especially at night.'

Tilly looked at him haughtily, mostly to cover her self-consciousness at her state of dishabille. 'And tonight you were drawn to Drayton Manor. May I ask why?'

'For the same reason you were disturbed and came to investigate.'

Aware that his arm still encircled her and the hard set of his muscles flexed against her shoulder as they stood still in the dark shadows of the trees, she felt a shifting deep inside her. It was as if the very essence of him and herself, the very rhythm of his heart, was beating in unison with her own.

For all its intensity, the encounter lasted only a moment. His presence here at this time of night filled her with confusion, yet she was aware of an enormous relief, warmth and pleasure sweeping through her. Placing his finger beneath her chin, he tilted her pale face up to his.

'Are you all right?'

'Yes,' she replied quietly. 'Those men... Who were they? And I want the truth. Were they poachers? But... if so, what were they doing at the stables? Please don't tell me they intended to steal the horses. And why didn't Dunstan or Graham hear them and come to investigate?'

'They weren't poachers, Miss Anderson—nothing so tame.'

Tilly stared at him, trying to make out his features. 'I heard the horses and came to see what was happening.'

'You should have stayed in your room and kept the curtains closed. Those men were smugglers.'

Tilly gasped. 'Smugglers? But...what were they doing here?'

'You have horses?'

'Yes, six, the carriage horses.'

'Then I feel I must warn you that there may be nights when they are needed. I should have made you aware of the smugglers' activities when I called.'

'But...I don't understand. Why would they want our horses?'

'When a large cargo comes in, the smugglers may need extra horses to help carry it away before dawn.'

'You mean they may steal them?' Tilly was astounded by the audacity that such a thing could happen.

'Not steal—merely borrow them.'

Tilly looked at him coldly as the meaning of his words began to sink in. 'Are you telling me the smugglers take them and use them?'

'Exactly. They are always returned, to be used another night. It's a foolish person who tries to keep the smugglers out when their horses might be needed. See your curtains are drawn in future and your lips are sealed and you will find a gift on your doorstep the next morning.'

'And if I don't want a gift?'

'You'll get one anyway for the loan of your horses. The smugglers always pay for people's silence. It suits everyone very well.'

'I see. Well...thank you for telling me, although I'm beginning to wonder what I've let myself in for,' she said, concerned for William's fine carriage horses. 'But I don't understand why Dunstan wasn't wakened by all the activity. He loves those horses and would do anything to protect them if they were in danger. Unless...' She gasped. 'Oh, dear! I do so hope he hasn't come to any harm.'

'Don't worry. Your groom and his son are quite safe. I came to warn them. I was informed of the run—that the contraband would be bigger than usual. I thought your groom should be made aware of what might happen.'

'So that is what you are doing here. Thank you. I do appreciate your consideration.'

'Remember what I have told you. It would be prudent to keep out of the way of the stables at night. The smuggling fraternity is tightly knit and they keep to their own rules.'

'It's still a criminal offence. They make a living by not paying the King his revenue.'

'True. And there are many who say the King is rich enough.'

'Even you?'

He smiled slightly. 'I keep my thoughts to myself. It's easier that way. The smugglers are the law along the coast and they are well organised. Many of the Revenue men are terrified of them.'

'But how do so many horses pass along the road carrying contraband unnoticed?'

'They can and they do.'

'Have they taken the horses or made use of them and brought them back?'

'Relax. They've finished with them for tonight.'

'Thank goodness.'

The moon suddenly appeared from behind the clouds, spreading its light on them. Tilly was aware of him standing close, watching her so intently that he might have been trying to commit every detail of her features to memory.

Dropping his eyes to her waist and taking the ends of the belt which had come loose on her robe, exposing the stark whiteness of her nightdress beneath, he proceeded to tie it, drawing her robe together. Fires ignited inside Tilly at the intimacy of the act, fires that flared to a startling intensity when she found herself standing so close to him that she could almost hear the beating of his heart.

He gave her a long slow look, a twist of humour around his mouth. His direct masculine assurance disconcerted her. She was vividly conscious of his proximity to her. She felt a rush of blood sing through her veins. Instantly, she felt resentful towards him. He had made too much of an impact on her and she was afraid that if he looked at her much longer, he would read her thoughts.

'Come, I'll walk back with you to the house now the danger is past.'

He led the way on to the gravel path. His touch sent a flood of warmth through Tilly's body to settle in a hot flush on her cheeks. She was thankful it was dark and he couldn't see. With a great effort of will, neither of them speaking, she walked slightly ahead of him to the door through which she had exited the house earlier. Before she reached it, she stepped on some stony ground, twisting her ankle beneath her and stumbling in the process, falling painfully to the ground.

In alarm, Lord Clifton knelt beside her. Raising her head, her body feeling bruised and sore, she looked up at him looming over her.

'Here,' he said, reaching out a hand. 'Let me help you to your feet. Are you hurt?'

'I've twisted my ankle.'

'See if you can stand and I'll help you to the house.'

Placing his hands beneath her arms, he helped her to her feet. Putting a little weight on her injured foot, she cried out with the pain that shot through it. It was beginning to throb terribly.

'Here, lean on me.'

'No,' Tilly said quickly as he reached out his hand once more. 'It is only a sprain. I don't need help.'

Lord Clifton scowled at her, noticing the stubborn thrust to her chin which told him she would rather die than accept his help, but in the sudden light from the moon, he could see her eyes were swimming with the silently repressed tears that the pain from her injured ankle was causing her. It was evident that she would not make it to the house unaided. His eyes narrowed.

'I doubt that. Come—don't be difficult,' he said impatiently.

Before Tilly could stop him or protest, he had placed one arm firmly about her waist and the other beneath her knees, swinging her effortlessly up into his arms. Normally, she would have kicked and fought at being handled in such a way, but she was too stunned to say anything at finding herself pressed so close to him. She could feel his warmth and the strength in his hard lean body, which made her feel uncomfortable—and something else as well, something she did not care to analyse just then.

Pushing the door open with his foot, he carried her through the kitchen to the study that doubled up as the library, placing her in a chair by the hearth, where the dying embers of the fire still glowed. Lighting a lamp, he dropped on one knee and removed her slipper, flexing her ankle with the professional expertise of a doctor.

Tilly could feel the firmness of his fingers on her bare flesh as he twisted her foot to one side. She gripped the arms of the chair, almost crying out with the pain this caused her, but bit her lip in her determination not to let him know how much it hurt. At last, he put her foot gently on the carpet and looked up at her directly.

'There doesn't appear to be anything broken—just a slight sprain.'

'Why—*thank you*, Doctor,' she said with emphasis.

Ignoring her sarcastic tone, Lord Clifton curled his lips in a wry smile. 'I'm not a doctor, but I grew up on the hunting field where more people took a tumble than I care to mention. I soon learned how to deal with injured limbs and the like—although I have to say that none of the people I tried to help had such a charming ankle.' He looked to the door when Mrs Carstairs, wrapped in her dressing gown, appeared, carrying a candle.

'Goodness me!' she gasped on seeing Lord Clifton kneeling on the carpet in front of Miss Anderson dressed in her night attire. 'I thought I heard a noise. What on earth has happened—and how do you come to be here, Lord Clifton?' When he cocked an eyebrow at her, she sighed, shaking her head knowingly. 'Don't tell me. It's one of those nights, is it?'

'Yes, Mrs Carstairs. Unfortunately, Miss Anderson was unaware of the strange events that occur on certain nights and went to investigate.'

'Oh, dear. I should have told you,' she said, looking at Tilly with alarm. 'Did they see you? Did they hurt you?'

'They didn't see her—I got to her in time. Don't worry about it. She knows now and will keep to her room in future. On the way back to the house she stumbled in the dark and sprained her ankle. Some cold water and a bandage would not go amiss.'

'Of course. What am I thinking of? I'll get them at once.'

She was soon back. After soaking the bandage in the cold water, Lord Clifton proceeded to wrap Tilly's ankle. When he was done, he stood up and, with his hands on his hips, looked down at her.

'You'll have to rest it for a few days, but it should soon start to feel better.'

'Thank you. I'm sure it will,' Tilly replied, impatient for him to be gone so she could hobble up to bed—but Mrs Carstairs had other ideas.

'You will take a glass of brandy before you leave, Lord Clifton?' Mrs Carstairs asked, always kindly and seeming to have no notion of the impropriety of

Lord Clifton being with Tilly at that late hour, with her dressed only in her night attire.

To Tilly's annoyance, he readily accepted, seating himself in the chair across from her and stretching his long-booted legs out in front of him, looking very much at home. Mrs Carstairs went to the mahogany sideboard and poured a drink from one of several crystal decanters that sat there and handed it to him.

He sniffed and rolled it on his tongue appreciatively. He was silent for a time while he drank. Tilly couldn't believe it when Mrs Carstairs disappeared back to the kitchen, taking the bowl of water with her to be disposed of.

'Do you live in London, Miss Anderson?' Lord Clifton asked, swirling the amber liquid round the bowl of the glass.

'Yes, I do—at least, when I'm not staying with my eldest brother and his wife in Berkshire.'

'Tell me, what brings you to Devon?'

'My brother Charles is employed by the East India Company. He very much wants to work for the Company in India and he plans to leave shortly. He had no time to travel to Devon to see his inheritance.'

'So he sent you instead.'

'Yes, and my aunt.'

'He has no intention of coming to live in Drayton Manor?'

'Not for the foreseeable future, I'm afraid. It's too far away. He may even decide to sell it—which I think would be a shame. It's a lovely house.'

'Your older brother is the Marquess of Elvington, I

believe.' When she gave him a questioning glance he said, 'Silas told me something of your family.'

'I see. William is our half-brother. He spent several years in India with the East India Company until he decided to go it alone.'

Lord Clifton looked at her hard, then he nodded slowly, as if digesting this information. 'I am impressed. I had no idea when I pulled a lovely young lady out of the sea that she was the sister of the Marquess of Elvington.'

'Why? Does it matter? Does that mean you suddenly see me differently?'

'Yes,' he said quietly. 'I have to say it does.'

'Have you met my brother?'

'I know of him, but we have never met. And you are, what, Miss Anderson—eighteen, nineteen?'

'Since you ask, I am nineteen.'

'And ripe for the Season.'

'Next year,' she provided, conscious of his shadowed eyes upon her in quiet appraisal. 'At least, that is, if my aunt and brothers have their way.'

'And you? What do you want?'

'If you must know, the whole idea of the Season terrifies me,' she said, lowering her eyes. 'I have no interest in being paraded in front of society merely to acquire a suitable husband. Besides, I cannot see the point of going to all that bother and expense when I am in no hurry to marry. I'm quite happy as I am.'

Lord Clifton heard the intensity of her statement. It was said with deep conviction and more than a little pain, which stirred his curiosity. 'Perhaps when you return to London, you will have come to see everything in a different light.'

'No, I won't,' she told him with a quiet firmness. 'I meant what I said.'

He gave her a wry look. 'I know how society works, that there are standards to be upheld. As the sister of the Marquess of Elvington, when you fail to make an appearance when the Season starts people will want to know why. You will leave yourself wide open to a great deal of gossip and speculation.'

'I have little interest in what people think.' Tilly wondered how he would react if she were to disclose that she was already the object of gossip and speculation. If Charles allowed her to remain in Devon, then she would be too far away to worry about what people said about her.

As if reluctant to pursue the issue since it clearly troubled her, Lord Clifton stood and sauntered about the room. He looked at everything that had become familiar to him during his visits to his old friend Silas: ancient leather tomes filling the shelves, charts pertaining to the sea on tables and a jumble of magazines on a chair.

'I always thought this to be a pleasant room. I've spent many an hour discussing worldly matters with Silas.' He picked up a much-thumbed leather-bound volume from several on the desk. 'Armies of the world,' he uttered softly. 'The strategies of war always fascinated him. He should have been actively involved. He would have made an excellent leader of men with his common sense and no-nonsense attitude. His knowledge of matters military was as vast as Napoleon's and Wellington's combined.'

Placing it back on the table, he sat back down in the chair, making himself comfortable once more, seeming in no hurry to leave. He looked at the young woman seated opposite. With the orange glow from the lamp, she wasn't to know that her face was like a cameo, something so young and innocent that reminded Lord Clifton of a small bird.

Feeling compelled and at liberty to look his fill, crossing his long legs and resting his elbows on the arms of the chair, steepling his fingers in front of him, he found everything about her pleasing. She must have sensed his perusal because she suddenly raised her eyes, a flash of colour staining her cheeks as he met her gaze with a querying uplifted brow.

'I would be obliged if you would please stop looking at me in that way. Your critical eye pares and dissects me as if I was an insect on a slab.'

'Does it?' he murmured absently, continuing to look at her, at the soft fullness of her mouth and glorious violet eyes.

Her flush deepened. 'I have imperfections enough without you looking for more. Please stop it,' she demanded quietly, 'otherwise I will be forced to ask you to leave—which you should do anyway. The hour is late and your being here with me alone, attired as I am, is not proper.'

Her words brought a slow, teasing smile to his lips and his strongly marked brows were slightly raised, his eyes suddenly glowing with humour. 'And that bothers you, does it? It would be the height of rudeness if you were to do that. After all, am I not a guest? And I have tended your ankle…'

'Which was extremely kind of you, but it does not make me beholden to you,' Tilly retorted tightly.

'Nevertheless, I cannot help looking at you when you are sitting directly in my sights.'

Hot faced and perplexed, Tilly almost retorted that she was not a rabbit in the sights of his gun, but she halted herself in time. She had never known a man to be so provoking. She was suddenly shy of him. There was something in his eyes that made her feel it was impossible to look at him. There was also something in his voice that brought so many new and conflicting themes in her heart and mind that she did not know how to speak to him.

The effect was a combination of fright and excitement and she must put an end to it. She was in danger of becoming hypnotised by that silken voice and those mesmerising light blue eyes. The fact that he knew it, that he was deliberately using his charm to dismantle her determination not to weaken before him, she found annoying. She must learn to control her feelings and emotions where he was concerned. After her debacle with Richard Coulson, she was not looking for any sort of romantic entanglement.

'Will you not find Devon a trifle dull after the excitements of London?' he asked.

'I don't think so. I intend to adjust to the slow pace of country life. I intend to occupy my time getting to know the area—and I love being by the sea. It's the first time I've seen it.'

Lord Clifton smiled. 'Anyone who comes here to settle has much to learn about the place and its people.'

'Whether or not I settle here remains to be seen. It all

depends on what Charles decides to do with the house. I might try to persuade him not to sell it. I would like to know more about Biddycombe. What can you tell me?'

'Only that it's not perhaps what you expect. During the days the locals, the fishermen and country squires go about their mundane work, but when darkness falls it becomes another matter entirely.'

'Why? Is that when the ghosts come out to play?'

His lips curved in a smile. 'Nothing so exciting, Miss Anderson, although some might think so.'

'Well, if not ghosts, then what?'

'Smugglers, Miss Anderson. Smugglers. You have just seen them in action, have you not?'

'Yes, I have—and I have to say it does not sit easy with me. Tell me more about them.'

'Smuggling goes on the length of the entire south coast, from Kent in the east to Cornwall in the west. It's a way of life. For families with many mouths to feed times are hard and smuggling is a way of trying to make ends meet. It's criminal, yes, but it goes on. The coast round Biddycombe is favourable to the smuggling fraternity—reckless, desperate men. Brandy, tobacco, tea—exotic fabrics for the ladies—they break the law by not paying customs duty on them.'

'And do they get rich out of these activities?'

'They can do nicely out of one night's work. Some make fortunes, using any means—even murder. It's foolish to cross them. The smugglers are a law unto themselves along the coast—there's none that can stand against them. The life of anyone who informs on them isn't worth a penny piece. Those who are involved do so at a high cost, for the penalty will be found at the end of a rope.'

'Goodness, it sounds quite dreadful. It would appear I have a lot to learn about coastal affairs.'

'You can't be expected to know the ways of seafaring people. The entire county takes what can be got past the customs men. From the highest to the lowest most people have a hand in it. All it takes is a dark night and to know when the Revenue cutters are about—and even if they are, some go in fear and avoid the smugglers. Most of the community accept what goes on as a way of life and not as a crime.'

'And what of you, Lord Clifton? Do you take what can be got from the smugglers—or perhaps you have a hand in it yourself?'

'I'm not averse to taking the odd keg of brandy for turning a blind eye to their activities, but I am not involved. It would be more than my position is worth. As the Earl of Clifton, it is my duty to uphold the law, not break it.'

'I can understand that—although, where smugglers are concerned, I'm beginning to favour the ghosts.'

Lord Clifton fell silent, considering her carefully, twirling the glass in his fingers.

'How is Florence—and the child? Well, I hope.'

He nodded, suddenly serious. 'There is someone who would do the child harm. I cannot, will not, allow that. If he discovers the child's existence, he will stop at nothing to get his hands on it—one way or another.'

'The child is not yours?'

He shook his head. 'He is my sister's child. She died in Spain—giving it life.'

Tilly's heart contracted with sympathy. There was a deep sadness in his eyes. 'I am so sorry to hear that. You must miss her terribly.'

'Yes, yes, I do. We were close.'

'And how is he—the child?'

'Tobias. Despite the turbulence of his beginning he thrives, thank God. Finding Florence was fortunate for me—for her, less so. Her own child had died several days before, her husband before that. The war in the Peninsula has made many widows. Florence agreed to nurse my sister's child in return that I pay her passage back to England.'

'That must have been difficult for her.'

'It was—but she desperately needed the money. She has also agreed to remain with the child until he no longer needs her. By which time I may have a wife to concern herself with such things.'

Tilly stared at him, surprise registering in her eyes. 'A wife? You are to marry?'

'Eventually, yes—a woman who is eminently suitable to be mistress of Clifton.'

'And of excellent character, I expect—to preside over your house with grace and poise and has been trained to manage the demanding responsibilities of such a large house.' She laughed softly when he looked at her sharply. 'I know all about the way things are done. Aunt Charlotte is forever pointing them out to me for when I make my debut—should I decide to fall in with her wishes. A young lady has to acquire all manner of accomplishments before she makes her curtsy.'

'Of course. As the sister of a marquess, you will know how marriages work among the aristocracy.'

'You, too—and have decided it is time you married and produced an heir. You have a lady in mind?'

'Not yet.'

'It is evident to me that you are thinking with your head and not your heart, Lord Clifton. You are considering marriage to an as yet unknown woman with the same kind of dispassion and practised precision I imagine you employ when dealing with your business transactions.'

He shrugged. 'I am no more sentimental about marriage than anyone else. It's a contract like any other. Marriage to the woman I marry will be...favourable.'

'I think *excruciatingly boring* would be a more appropriate term to use. Do you not feel that where something as important as marriage is concerned, then it is essential that the two people concerned love each other?'

Shaking his head, he met her direct gaze. 'In my opinion that is sentimental nonsense. I cast a blight on love a long time ago, Miss Anderson. So, until the time when I take a wife, I have Tobias to take care of. He is my prime concern at this time.'

'Of course he is. May I ask who it is that is a danger to the child—a name, at least, so I will know who to be wary of?'

He thought for a moment, considering her request, then, deciding he could trust her, he said, 'Jack Price. He lives further along the coast. He's a man whose exploits are talked of all along the south coast. He's earned himself an admirable reputation in his field of free trading. He's a leader. He has agents in his pay—in Devon and beyond.'

'So, others take the risks and he reaps the rewards.'

He nodded. 'Price has the routes and markets for the smuggled goods all worked out. He is a man used to getting his own way and not averse to soiling his hands to get it. He is without common decency, without compassion, his emotions stirred solely by his greed for wealth. He also enjoys the earthly pleasures of life. He's good at impressing people who don't know that beneath his fancy clothes and affectations he is in possession of a ruthlessness and cruelty which will stop at nothing to possess or destroy what he cannot have. But there are those who are law-abiding and will not turn a blind eye to his activities for ever.'

'Then he would do well to remember that he is not beyond the reach of the law.'

'He is the younger brother of the man my sister was married to. Since his brother's death in Spain, he has inherited the property—which is considerable. By rights it is the infant's inheritance, but as yet Price is in ignorance of his existence. Until I can get legal advice on the matter it is imperative that it is kept secret. I have to keep him safe. There is bad blood between our families. That is all you need to know.'

'Then I shall know to avoid him.'

'You will respect my confidence?'

Tilly nodded. 'Yes, yes, I will.'

He fell silent. Tilly waited for him to go on.

'When I encountered you on the beach on my arrival back in England,' he said at length, 'you were the first civilised young woman I'd seen in a long time, Miss Anderson. It was a long way back to Devon.'

'Was it very bad in the Peninsula? We hear things—

about battles fought and won, or lost—but no one knows for certain what it is like.'

'It is bad. It was not what I hoped to find among the forces of the British and French armies and the utter carnage of the battle.' He got to his feet, looking down at her. 'Do you ride by any chance?'

'Yes—I love riding. Mrs Carstairs has told me I can hire a horse from the farrier in Biddycombe. I intend sending Dunstan to find something suitable for me to ride.'

'Thank you for the brandy. You are right. The hour is late. Will you manage to get to bed or would you like me to assist you?'

'Certainly not,' Tilly replied, prepared to climb the stairs on her hands and knees rather than ask his help. 'Mrs Carstairs will give me a hand and I am capable of hopping.'

'In which case I will leave you.'

'Thank you,' Tilly said stiffly. 'I'm glad you had the foresight to come and warn us about the smugglers coming to take the horses. I will speak to Dunstan in the morning and make sure they are unharmed.'

Lord Clifton nodded, crossing to the door. 'They won't be harmed. Now you are aware of what goes on after dark, you'll be prepared. Remember to turn a blind eye in the future.'

And then he was gone, melting into the shadows of the hall. Tilly waited and after a moment she heard a horse galloping away from the house.

With the help of Mrs Carstairs, Tilly returned to her bed.

'You know Lord Clifton quite well, don't you, Mrs Carstairs?' she asked, curious to know more about him.

'As well as most in these parts. Why do you ask?'

'His sister. Did you know that she died in Spain—along with her young man?'

She nodded. 'Lord Clifton told me himself. Terrible tragedy it was—such a lovely young lady—and coming so soon after the vessel carrying his parents went down in the Channel during a storm. They were going to Jersey to visit friends. What a dreadful time that was. It was a miracle their bodies were recovered and brought back to Clifton House. The whole of Biddycombe and the surrounding towns and villages were in mourning. In the space of two years Lord Clifton lost his entire family.'

'That is tragic indeed, Mrs Carstairs. He has never married and he must be, what, twenty-eight or nine?'

'Twenty-nine, he is. Of course he should have married—when he was just a young man—but it all went wrong.'

'Oh? What happened?' Tilly asked, her curiosity piqued.

'Ran off with somebody else, she did—when her parents took her to London. Miranda, her name was. Some rich American gentleman, apparently. Broke Lord Clifton's heart, she did. Never looked at a woman in that way since. I doubt he'll ever get over it.' On a sigh, she turned to the door. 'He's had nothing but bad luck in the past. It's time something good happened to him.'

Left to her thoughts, Tilly was deeply saddened and ashamed of the way she had behaved towards Lord Clifton. His suffering must be great indeed. There was something about him that seemed to bring out the worst in her and made her act more outrageous than she thought was wise. Why couldn't she learn to control her tongue? Knowing what she now did, her conscience smote her. She had been quite horrid towards him. Should they meet again, she would try to be more amiable towards him.

And who was the woman he'd wanted to marry—the woman who had broken his heart? Having been let down so badly in the past, little wonder he spoke with such cold indifference about love.

Shrouded in darkness, as he rode, Lucas thought of what Miss Anderson had told him about having no wish to have a Season and her seeming reluctance to marry. He applauded her honesty, but suspected there was more than what she had divulged she was concerned about. There had been an unmistakable pain and desperation behind her words that had reached out and touched him in half-forgotten, obscure places. He had been made to feel uneasy by it, leaving him puzzled and with a curiosity to know more.

## Chapter Four

Tilly slept badly that night. Her imagination was running rife. The night was dark and she tried to settle, but found her conversation with Lord Clifton played on her mind. She listened for sounds that would tell her the smugglers were active, but they were gone now. She was distressed at the thought of William's beautiful carriage horses being used to carry heavy contraband to goodness knew where for someone else's gain.

The following morning, the sun was already high when Tilly rose. Placing her injured foot gingerly on the floor, she was relieved to find it not as painful as she thought. Hobbling to the window, she looked out. Everything was still, with no sign of the disturbance in the early hours.

Later, managing to hobble to the stables, she found Dunstan putting fresh straw and hay into the stalls. He was a big man, a middle-aged widower, but tough and stubbornly dedicated to his work. He loved working with horses and had been more than happy to come down to Devon with his son Graham, who she could hear moving about up in the loft.

'I know what happened during the night, Dunstan. Lord Clifton told me. How are the horses this morning?

'They seem to be all right. No harm done. I gave them a rub down earlier.'

'I have been told that this may happen on a regular basis.'

'So I understand. Bit queer if you ask me.'

'I agree, but we have no choice apparently. Make sure you look the other way in future and that you come to no harm. It is the way of things down here. Lock the stable doors to keep the smugglers out and they will think nothing to burning them down.'

Sitting astride his black gelding, its shining mane gently lifting as he rode, Lucas surveyed Clifton's precious acres for the first time since arriving home from Spain. The house was surrounded by woodlands of ancient oak, elms and beech, interspaced with sunny glades where streams meandered gently along on their journey to the sea. Berries and brambles clambered over the walls surrounding verdant fields and rabbits and deer darted for cover as he approached.

Riding out of the trees, he brought the horse to a halt atop a low hill and gazed at the gently rolling vista all around him. Each view kindled a memory—of his mother walking in the gardens at Clifton and the surrounding lanes, shielded from the sun by a gaily decorated parasol, of his father galloping hell-for-leather in the hunt, Cassie doing her ferocious utmost to keep up with him. He realised how empty the house was without Cassie and his heart wrenched when he remembered how she had filled the rooms with laughter. He couldn't bear the silence. And what was to become of Tobias? He couldn't keep him hidden for ever.

Clifton had always been the one place where he had felt in complete control of his life. It had always given him a feeling of fulfilment, of well-being, but no more. The house had never seemed so empty or so still. The servants had looked at him with anticipation on his return from Spain. On learning of that bright golden girl's death, they said little, but shared the silence on remembering. Never had he felt so alone, so bereft of family. It was as if all Clifton's life blood had been drained out of it with their loss.

And before that there had been Miranda, passionate and with a golden beauty, the daughter of Baron Enys and his wife who lived in a grand house in Truro. At twenty-one he had been unable to resist her. She had sent fire through his youthful veins, the woman whom he had so deeply loved, and at whose hands his pride had suffered so badly.

They met whenever he could travel into Cornwall and she would often come to Clifton House with her parents. Twining her slender arms about his neck and using all her wiles to captivate him, she'd made him her pliant, willing slave. She was a bright and beautiful beacon in his life. An honest man, who would later deplore the fact that he had such a large streak of naivety in his make-up, Lucas found it hard to grasp the guile behind the soft smiles or fond words, especially when they came from the mouth of this exotic creature.

He had believed Miranda loved him, but how purring

and persuasive and soothing the voice of hers could be. He could not have guessed for a moment what weight of treachery it concealed. On a visit to London with her parents she'd met a very wealthy American, who—her parents had told him when they had come to explain the conduct of their daughter—had swept her off her feet, married her and whisked her off to America. To his knowledge she never did return to Truro.

Lucas had been deeply hurt by what she had done. For the first time in his adult life his eyes had been blinded by a rush of scalding tears. When at last the tears had gone, what had come to take their place was rage at his own weakness. Never, he had vowed, would he allow a woman to do to him what Miranda had done.

As he lingered on that hill, still and silent with his thoughts, his eyes were shadowed by memories that haunted him, memories that banked the fires of his anger, anger at the unfairness of it all, of his life, of having his entire family taken from him in the space of two years. Both his parents had been lost to the sea during a storm, followed so soon by Cassie leaving for Spain and the tragedy of her death. Cassie's child brought so brutally into the world had awakened a response of warmth and love in him and he felt a need to protect the child.

The added worry at this time was that Tobias was his heir until he had offspring of his own. How Jack Price would react when he learned of the boy's existence, his own brother's child, remained to be seen. But it concerned him greatly. Should he himself meet with some unfortunate accident, he had no doubt that Jack

Price would lose no time in trying to control the actions and decisions on how the Clifton estate would be run.

Should he not provide Clifton with an heir of his own, he had to prepare for every eventuality. At some point he would travel to Oxford to see his lawyers. To prevent Jack Price taking charge of the estate, he intended setting up a board of trustees to run the things until Tobias was of age.

He still loved every blade of grass, every tree, every hollow and hill of Clifton, in all its seasons, but it was no longer the same. He was struggling with his feelings of fear that everything else he held dear would be wrenched from him. Now there was something missing, something vital, something of immense value he had always taken for granted. Would he ever know peace?

Seeing the tall chimneys of his home above the trees brought a lump of emotion to his throat. Clifton House, with its air of solidity and permanence, had been in the Kingsley family since the Commonwealth and he vowed on the memory of those he held most dear, though lost to him, that he would create for his descendants the greatness of its heritage. The Kingsley name was a loved and revered one, one he was proud to belong to.

He must marry and produce heirs in order to go forward. But first he must find himself a wife. Since his unfortunate experience with Miranda, he no longer believed in love matches. It would be a marriage of convenience. He sighed dejectedly. There wasn't enough fire in the world to thaw him out and make him feel the way he had for Miranda in those heady, golden days of his youth when he had fallen in love, and even if there were, he could not let it happen again. Behaving like a lovesick calf was not his style.

Unable to sleep and impatient to be out of doors, Tilly left the house before anyone was awake and made her way to the steps that would take her to the shore below. Halfway down she found herself a perfect vantage spot between the rocks. Settling herself between them, she took in her surroundings.

How beautiful it was, a magical, enchanted place, especially as early as this, with the dawn breaking and the sun just peeking over the horizon, a perfect example of the beauty of nature itself. How gentle the sea was, with hardly a wave to break its smooth surface. It was a place where one could disappear into the realms of fantasy and imagine herself to be a fairy princess, to float on the surface of the water and close her eyes and wait for her prince to come.

And then there he was, entering her fevered imagination. Sitting there languidly, she watched him ride on to the beach and dismount, tethering his horse to a rock. Sitting on the sand, the man removed his boots and threw off his upper garments, before striding across the sand towards the sea.

Losing all power of motion and scarcely capable of thought, she could not take her eyes off his naked chest, covered with a smattering of dark hair. He was like a Greek Adonis. There were the muscles rippling beneath the smooth, golden skin, the width of his shoulders narrowing down to the hips. For a moment she wondered if she'd conjured up some spirit by accident.

From her vantage point she watched him walk into

the sea until it was up to his chest. He dived underwater like a fish and came up some moments later to shake back his black hair before beginning to cleave his way from the shore, as if some unnamed nightmare could be banished only with an early-morning dunking in the sea. Tilly tried not to dwell on what it was that he felt the need to wash away, what he needed to exorcise, but it did not seem to have worked because the dark, troubled shadow in his eyes when next they met would still be there.

She continued to watch him, her knees drawn up to her chin. She was mesmerised by him, in some kind of trance as a dreamlike feeling of unreality had taken hold of her. He swam out to sea so far that he almost disappeared from view. Afraid that he might be caught in a strong current or an undertow, anxiously, she waited for him to reappear.

And then there he was, his head bobbing just above the waves as his arms stretched out before him, strong and sure. Closer to the shore, he stopped swimming and turned on to his back, floating lazily, letting the swell of the water rock him while he stared up at the sky. When he reached a place where he could put his feet down, he stood, shaking wet hair from his face.

Completely unaware that he was being observed, he walked across the sand to his waiting horse. Dressing quickly, he leaped on to its back and rode away. Tilly remained where she was, unable to believe that what she had just witnessed had really happened and was not a figment of her imagination. She remained there another few minutes before she got to her feet and returned to the house.

\* \* \*

Tilly was surprised when a groom from Clifton House appeared with a horse gifted to her by Lord Clifton for the time she was in Devon. She was deeply touched by his generosity. It was a lovely horse, a spirited grey mare called Gracie, which suited her well. With no visitors paying calls, or when not sitting with Aunt Charlotte, Tilly enjoyed riding Gracie, accompanied by Graham on one of the carriage horses following at a sedate pace in her wake.

It was a fine and sunny day when Tilly accompanied Mrs Carstairs into Biddycombe. She had asked Aunt Charlotte to accompany them, but she had declined, preferring to sit in the garden and read. It was market day and Mrs Carstairs wanted one or two things. Tilly had not been as far as the village. Dunstan hitched two of the horses to a carriage that had belonged to Uncle Silas and off they went. Tilly's ankle was feeling much better, so walking about the village shouldn't be too taxing for her.

Biddycombe was a picturesque coastal village, with a huddle of thatched and slate-roofed cottages and bay-windowed shops. Being market day, the traders had set up their brightly coloured stalls in the market square. People were milling about along with horses and wagons carrying all manner of goods. The pungent smell of fish came from the work sheds where, Mrs Carstairs explained, the wives and daughters of the fishermen gutted, salted and packed the fish.

The quayside was an animated scene, alive in a chaos of sight and smell and the laughter of children. Lobster pots were stacked high and sailors sat about mending nets and talking among themselves, seagulls circling overhead. It was a scene that would have changed little over the centuries.

Accompanying Mrs Carstairs round the market stalls, she became the focus of everyone's scrutiny because they had heard that a Miss Anderson had taken up residence at Drayton Manor. Had it been a larger seaport, with strangers coming and going all the time, her presence would not have been noted, but Biddycombe was a small fishing village where strangers were conspicuous.

When Mrs Carstairs had acquired what she had come for, Tilly left her basket in the carriage watched over by Dunstan and decided to have lunch before returning to the manor. Mrs Carstairs assured Tilly that the local tavern was a respectable place to eat and the food was good. It was close to the market square and had a wooden sign above it bearing the name the Lobster Pot.

It did appear to be a pleasant enough place, catering to tradesmen, farmers, travellers and local people alike. Being market day, the inn was busy. Despite the warmth of the day, a fire burned brightly in the hearth, the flames reflected in the gleaming tankards on the wooden bar, where men quaffed tankards of ale and conversed and laughed in good-natured ribaldry, enjoying themselves immensely.

'It's always like this on market days,' Mrs Carstairs explained. 'We'll find a quiet corner to eat.'

Serving girls threaded their way through the crowded room. They were assailed with the fragrant odour of tobacco, along with the appetising smell of roasting meats and spices, increasing Tilly's pangs of hunger. They sat at one of the oak tables, where they were served with a good wholesome meal.

As they were ready to leave, someone entered and Tilly's eyes were drawn to the door. It was filled with the figure of a tall man. Sweeping off his hat to reveal sandy locks of hair secured at his nape, he had to duck his head as he came into the room. He was followed by several other men, but it was the man in front that riveted Tilly's attention.

She had risen from her seat and when his eyes picked her out for his attention he paused, oblivious to the awkward silence that had fallen on the usually noisy room. Tilly eyed the man who stood boldly before her, eyeing her with a look not to her liking. He was a large man, firm of muscle, a sensual attractiveness in his coarse features, which carried a countenance that was merciless. It instilled fear. He sauntered towards her as she was about to follow Mrs Carstairs out of the inn.

'Well, and who have we here? Never seen you before so you must be new to these parts.' Looking from Tilly to Mrs Carstairs, he put two and two together. 'So, staying at Drayton Manor, are you? Now old Silas has gone to keep his maker company. I heard someone had moved in. I should come round and welcome you proper like—if you'd care to extend an invitation.'

'I would not,' Tilly said coolly. 'I am not receiving visitors.'

'Excuse us, Mr Price. We are just leaving,' Mrs Carstairs said, edging further to the door.

Tilly eyed the man with distaste. So, this was Jack

Price, the man Lord Clifton had told her about—a smuggler and disreputable sort. She recalled Lord Clifton telling her that he liked to cut a dash. As if to prove it he was flamboyantly dressed in scarlet velvet braided with gold and an embroidered waistcoat beneath, a froth of lace at his throat and wrists—clothing more fitting for a soirée in London than riding the waves in a smuggler's sloop in Devon. Two pistols were thrust into a black sash about his waist and the hilt of a knife was visible above his black riding boots. The man was obnoxious and there was an ugly glint in his eye. Little wonder people feared him.

'Why the hurry?' He looked at Tilly. 'You'll stay and have a dram with Jack Price?'

'I don't think so,' Tilly said in her clear-cut voice, which told Jack Price and his loyal vassals standing around—accomplished thieves every one—that she was a lady. Lord Clifton had told her Jack Price was dangerous, a man to avoid. 'Mrs Carstairs is right. We are leaving.' She didn't bother to hide her distaste, much to Jack Price's amusement. He liked a woman with fight in her.

Tilly turned to leave the inn, aware that all eyes were on her. Turning her back on Jack Price, dismissing him with no more attention than she would give an annoying fly, she was about to walk away when a heavy hand landed on her shoulder, the bejewelled fingers digging into her flesh.

'Not so fast,' Jack Price said, his voice close to her ear. 'Uppity, aren't you? There's no need to be unfriendly, is there now?'

'Tell her where you live, Jack,' someone shouted. 'She might like to pay you a visit some time.'

He leaned closer to Tilly. 'If I thought she might find her way to my lair to help me wile away the daylight hours, I would tell her, but since she isn't too friendly and might take it into that pretty head to turn me in, she's better off not knowing.'

He spun her round and Tilly found herself looking up into his coarse features. 'Kindly let go of my shoulder.' She spoke in a commanding voice, trying not to show her fear or that she was in the least intimidated by him.

'I beg your pardon, my lady,' he said sarcastically, bowing his head in mock respect. 'I meant no offence. But when a man sees something as sweet as you, pretty and smelling of roses, how can he resist such a tempting morsel? This is an unexpected surprise to find someone as lovely as you in Biddycombe. You can't blame me for trying to be friendly now, can you?'

'Then find someone else to be friendly with, Mr Price.'

'You're a proud one,' he said with a quick, dangerous sneer, but he schooled it to a taut smile. 'Elude me if you will, but now we've met I intend to spend some of my time getting to know you. We might find we have things in common, things we can share. Biddycombe is a small place—with not many hiding places that Jack Price doesn't know about.'

'I have no intention of hiding from anyone, Mr Price. You may be accustomed to easy conquests, but I find the thought of sharing anything at all with you utterly distasteful.'

Jack Price's eyes narrowed. The mockery had gone and his voice was purposeful. 'Maybe so—but you won't always feel that way—and you have a stable of fine horses by the way,' he said quietly, close to her ear. 'I look forward to making use of them again—very soon as it happens.'

Tilly glared at him, unable to think of anything to say that would not jeopardise matters for her and Aunt Charlotte while at Drayton Manor.

'You will learn to be nice to me,' he went on, 'not now, not tomorrow, but you will, and you will no longer speak to me with such haughty disfavour.'

She stared at him, emotionless and defiant. 'Threaten me all you like—it means nothing to me. Just leave me be.' Hoping to make her escape, turning away, once again she felt the heavy hand fall on her shoulder.

'What's the hurry? Don't you like Jack Price?' His gaze lingered on her lips.

'Don't think you're going to have any luck there, Jack,' someone called, the words followed by the sound of raucous laughter.

Jack Price laughed, a horrible, brittle sound that bounced off the walls of the tavern. 'You think not? Me and this little lady are just getting to know each other.'

Tilly tried to step away from him, but he held her shoulder in an iron grip. Her flesh crawled at his nearness. His eyes slid over her, making her flinch. Instinct told her that he was a man who would find resistance and cold indifference far more intriguing than mere submission. She lifted her chin with a show of bravado. There was arrogance in the tilt of his head and a single-minded determination in the set of his firm jaw that was not to her liking. She had an uncomfortable feeling that her angry words, far from discouraging him, had acted as bait to this obnoxious man.

'Release me at once,' she demanded, enunciating each word clearly, her voice quivering with anger. In spite of herself, even surrounded by a room full of people, she flinched.

'Not yet.' He was enjoying her discomfort. 'Forgive me if am so enamoured of you that I want to keep you with me a while longer. I reckon I'll find my way to the Manor one of these days—to pay my respects.'

'Please get out of my way. We are in a hurry.'

'Please, is it? I like politeness in a woman.'

Tilly realised no one would come to her aid. The men whose services Price enlisted were afraid of him. According to Lord Clifton, smuggling was his forte and upon it he profited. His men feared him, some would die for him—any death was preferable to the fury that would rain down on them should they fail him.

Mrs Carstairs stood near the door, observing what was happening with fear in her eyes. Everyone else, cowed by this man, observed what was happening with fear. None had the nerve to speak up. Aware of his rampant maleness, Tilly felt an instinctive awareness of the danger she was in. This man was not the kind of London fop she was used to. What he wanted he took.

Encouraged when she didn't pull away and unaware of the moment when all eyes turned to the door, he pulled her close, his grin widening. Not until someone let out a curse did he look above the head of his captive towards the door. The smile of triumph on having this young woman almost at his mercy froze on his face.

Tilly's head spun round. Lord Clifton stood there. His tall, broad-shouldered figure blocked out the light and seemed to fill the whole room. With his hand resting on the pistol at his hip, he was looking directly at Jack Price.

Tilly's gaze never left Lord Clifton's eyes, which were narrowed and savagely furious as he looked at his adversary in murderous silence, his lips curling with disgust as he absorbed the scene. Such a transformation had come over his features that she recoiled before the change. All that had been controlled and good-humoured when he had visited Drayton Manor had given way to hot fury and positive revulsion.

'Release her, Price.' He spoke calmly, but with deadly intent.

The atmosphere inside the inn was heavy with tension. The arrogance had gone from Jack Price's eyes, replaced with a murderous glint. His expression tightened as he stared at the tall figure in the doorway watching him closely. Tall, handsome and carelessly dressed in a snug-fitting leather jerkin, his shirt neck loose, his hair untidy, his high leather boots accentuating the long lines of his body, she might have taken him for a local tradesman, if the voice and stance had not been so firm, so sure. It was impossible not to respond to this man as his masculine magnetism was dominant in the room.

'I said, release the lady, Price,' Lord Clifton demanded, walking further into the room.

When Jack Price's eyes rested on the cold, steely features, he released his iron grip on Tilly's shoulder and stared at him, momentarily stunned speechless, as if he were looking at the Devil himself. 'So, Kingsley, you're back in one piece. You survived your time in Spain.'

Lord Clifton's lips curled in derision. 'I am the sort who clings to life, Price.'

'So...you went after that whorin' sister of yours.'

Lord Clifton would not be drawn in by Price's vile slur.

'Find her, did you—and that renegade brother of mine? Bring her back, did you?'

'I buried her,' Lord Clifton provided, 'alongside her husband, your brother—in Spain.'

If Price was surprised, shocked or aggrieved by this in any way, he didn't show it. He merely stepped towards the bar, a sneer on his lips as he said callously, 'Then be thankful for small mercies. Edmund made his own bed when he took up with your sister and took himself off to Spain to fight the Frenchies. There's no remorse on my part.'

He glanced towards Tilly, who had made her way closer to Lord Clifton. 'I was just getting friendly with Drayton's newest resident—until you showed up.'

'You're a scurrilous villain, Price. I don't want to know what you intended—I can guess. I do not think it's an association she desires. If you make any forward move to touch her again, I'll blow your head off. And if you don't think I have it in me to kill you, you are mistaken.'

Price met his opponent's gaze and, reading the simmering anger in his eyes, knew he was dealing with a dangerous man. Price's eyes glittered with malice. A dangerous tension emanated between the two of them. 'I do, Kingsley. I have no illusions where you are concerned.'

Tilly watched and listened to the two men with bated breath. Jack Price's anger was barely held in check as he parried words with Lord Clifton—none too successfully, which riled the smuggler. There was an uneasy muttering among the men who stood around.

Lord Clifton continued to glare at him. Price was a criminal, a scoundrel, with blood on his hands. A powerful force within the smuggling fraternity, he intimidated, seduced, deceived others into obeying his will and thought nothing of resorting to violence. The idea of him touching the delicate flesh of Miss Anderson, having possession of all that beauty, woke the sleeping demon inside him. 'Move away from her,' he demanded.

Indecision written clearly across his features, Jack Price gazed at Tilly. Her hands were clenched by her sides, her head thrown back as she glared at him with defiance and pride, her hair in a plait as thick as a man's wrist snaking down her spine. She was lovely and Jack Price felt lust stirring within him, but then he looked at Lucas Kingsley, his greatest enemy.

As if deciding that nothing was to be gained from furthering hostilities just then, he backed away. He seemed to hesitate for a moment. Something in Lord Clifton's words and the way he was looking at him must have awakened a curiosity inside him to know more about his brother's death.

'They were married, you say—Edmund and your sister?'

'On your brother's deathbed. I found a priest. It was what they both wanted.'

Price looked at him sharply, eyes narrowed. 'Why the hell would Edmund do that if he was dying? And your sister—dead, you say. How did that come about?'

'Let's just say the toils of war and a broken heart.'

Price's lips curled and his nostrils flared. 'There's

more to this—things you aren't telling me, Kingsley. If I find you have been lying to me, keeping things back, you'll regret it.'

'You're nothing but a black-hearted villain, Price. Threaten me all you like—the law will catch up with you eventually.'

Neither man was aware of those who stood around. They only saw each other. The hatred they felt was a tangible thing as they looked at each other over the distance that separated them.

'If you do have the audacity to touch me again, Jack Price, I will kill you myself,' Tilly retorted scathingly.

In spite of herself, despite her brave words and even with Lord Clifton's intervention, Tilly flinched when Price's lascivious gaze slid over her slim form—the pressure he had applied to her shoulder she still felt. Her revulsion was plain to see, but not one bit of his cocksure attitude faded.

'Don't be too sure of that,' he said nastily. 'The next time we meet you won't have His Lordship on hand to give you protection.'

'If I were you,' Lord Clifton drawled dangerously, 'I would not make promises that you haven't a hope in hell of keeping.'

'Is that so?'

'At the end of the day you will have me to reckon with.' Lord Clifton looked at Tilly. 'You have finished your meal?'

'Yes. We were just leaving.'

'Then allow me to escort you to your carriage.'

## Chapter Five

They drew notice as they emerged from the tavern. Lord Clifton was a well-known figure in the community and everyone was happy to see him back at Clifton House, although they felt a great sadness on hearing that Lady Cassandra wouldn't be coming back.

Lord Clifton took Tilly's arm. 'Come, let's get away from here—away from Price. Do you have to get back to Drayton Manor right away or will you walk with me, if your ankle will permit?'

'I'm with Mrs Carstairs—but I don't think you will mind if I have a word with Lord Clifton, will you, Mrs Carstairs?' Tilly said to the housekeeper standing beside her.

'No, in fact I've seen a friend of mine I would very much like to speak to.'

'Then I'll see you back at the carriage shortly.'

Tilly realised her mistake immediately. They would be seen walking off together and, in such a close-knit community as Biddycombe where nothing ever happened, she suspected they were in danger of becoming the subject of a good deal of senseless gossip and conjecture. But it was too late to do anything about it now.

'How is your ankle? Easier, I hope.'

'It is much improved,' Tilly said in answer to his enquiry. 'I am able to walk very well.'

'I'm glad to hear it.'

'I want to thank you for your generous loan of Gracie. I certainly wasn't expecting it. She's a lovely horse. We get on well.'

'I knew you would. Gracie belonged to my sister, Cassie.'

'Oh…then…then perhaps I shouldn't—'

'Of course you must. She has to be exercised. The grooms have enough to do as it is.'

'Well…thank you. I'll take good care of her.'

He looked down at her. 'I knew you would, otherwise I would not have trusted her to you. And you needn't worry about her being taken and used by the smugglers. Dunstan knows to move her elsewhere on the nights when the other horses might be needed.'

'That's a relief. She's not as sturdy as the carriage horses. I'd hate to think of her carrying a great weight.'

They began to walk away from the market and down to the quay. Taking a turn, they strolled along the beach, which was sheltered by a steep cliff. Few people were about so it offered them some privacy.

'So,' Tilly said when they found a quiet place to sit on some boulders on the edge of the beach, 'that was Jack Price.'

'That's right.' There was concern in his eyes when he looked at her. 'I'm sorry you were subjected to that.'

'Why? It wasn't your fault.'

'Did he hurt you?'

'No,' she replied, taking comfort from him, his presence and manner helping to dispel any lingering effects of her encounter with Jack Price.

'Please tell me you are glad I turned up to rescue you from our obnoxious neighbour.'

'Relieved, I think. Your arrival was timely. I was beginning to wonder how I was going to extricate myself from his unwelcome advances without resorting to violence,' she joked.

He cocked an eyebrow in mock horror. 'Violence? I would never believe it of you.'

'Nevertheless, I'm glad you arrived when you did.'

'I had people to see in Biddycombe. I've been shut away in my study for the past week with my bailiff, concentrating on estate matters—of which there are many that need taking care of. Most are routine, easily delegated to those who work on the estate.'

It was warm. They could hear the sounds from the market and the gentle sloughing of the sea as it caressed the shore. Tilly gazed at the channel, wrapping her arms round her drawn-up knees and breathing deeply of the salty air.

'It's so beautiful here.' She turned her head and looked at him. 'I imagine you have grown up with the sea, that it's as familiar to you as the woods and the fields that surround you.'

'It is. I have to confess that whenever I go away, further inland, I miss the sight and sound of it. I'm always glad to get back to it.'

'Do you travel much—to London or other faraway places?'

'I've done my share. London is not high on the list of places I like to visit. I have extended family, cousins, in London. Some of them often come down to Devon to take advantage of my hospitality—more often than not to escape some scandal or other or if they wish to escape the high life for a while. They enjoy nothing better than to come down here for the fishing and hunting and any other country pursuit they like to indulge in.'

'Have you always been at loggerheads with the Price family?'

He nodded. 'Always. It started when Elizabeth, my grandmother, rejected Jack Price's grandfather when he wanted to marry her. She was a widow by then—still a very beautiful woman. My grandfather died after ten years of marriage. They had three children—my father was the eldest. By all accounts, Jack Price's grandfather was a violent man—not unlike his grandson. When my grandmother became a widow, old man Price wanted her for himself. She did not reciprocate his feelings— quite the opposite.'

'I cannot blame her if the grandfather was anything like Jack Price. What did she do?'

'Unable to accept rejection, he abducted her and violated her. Unable to live with what had been done to her, she threw herself off a cliff. Her body was found on the rocks below. It was a great blow to my father— he was eight years old at the time—but he soon learned to hate the Prices. So you see, the vendetta that started with my grandmother is still there.

'There is a portrait of Elizabeth at Clifton House and, every time I gaze upon it, I thank the Lord she had the courage to escape him, that she preferred death to living with what he had done to her. The enmity is still there.'

'Yet your sister married one of them.' Tilly glanced at him. Although she could not blame him for his hatred of the Price family, she could not help but wonder what Jack Price would do when he discovered the existence of the child and that Lord Clifton had kept it from him.

He nodded. 'She did. Cassie didn't care about such things. She loved Edmund Price and that was that, even though I tried to dissuade her—even though he was nothing like his brother and grandfather. Because of who he was, I couldn't sanction the match.

'Edmund was the elder of the two brothers. He was not by nature or inclination a smuggler. The family own a boatyard further along the coast. Jack Price has never shown any interest in the business—unlike Edmund, whose whole life revolved around the yard. Edmund didn't see eye to eye with his brother. His nefarious activities were the cause of many a battle between them. He chose a military career to get away from him. But no good could come from him marrying Cassie.'

'Perhaps the child, a product of both families, will bring reconciliation.'

Lord Clifton threw her a dark look. 'That will never happen. Our families have been enemies for too long, the elders passing their loathing on to the next generation.'

'Is it not foolish to keep up these old feuds?'

'The Prices have kept up the feuds as firmly as any of us. If I were to let Tobias go to them, he would be raised to be like the rest of the Prices—of whom there are several scattered up and down the coast—who think they are some kind of divine beings put there to rule over everyone else.'

'I dare say that is what the Prices think about the Kingsleys.'

Lord Clifton frowned, looking at her. 'You've met Jack Price. Do you really think he would want to bury the hatchet?'

'No, perhaps not,' she agreed, 'unless it's in your head. I don't think he is a man to reason with.'

'Quite.'

'Tell me about your sister. What was she like?'

'Cassie was a wilful girl, determined to have her own way in all things. She would try my patience on a daily basis. Our parents coped with her as best they could, but in the end, they found it was easier to let her have her way, to do as she pleased, within reason, than face the awesome force of her hot temper.

'The death of our parents affected her very badly. She was inconsolable and when she met Edmund Price there was no reasoning with her. When I finally tracked her down in Spain, she was still in love with him, still defended him.'

'Then he must have loved him very deeply.' It was evident to Tilly that his sister had mattered to him, and to lose her so soon after their parents must have been devastating for him. Her gaze focused on his bent head. She felt the sudden urge to shove back the heavy lock of his hair that had fallen forward to better see his features.

With a strength of will, he lifted his head and stared unseeingly before him. She looked into his proud face. His eyes were dark with suffering. Did he ever give in to the struggle of emotions that must tear him apart?

'She did,' Lord Clifton said at length. 'To the very end.'

'And she was his wife.'

He nodded. 'Yes, she was.'

When he spoke of the loss of his sister, he looked up. Tilly was trapped by the intensity of those thickly lashed light blue eyes. There was such suffering in their depths, such anguish that she wanted to reach out to him, to offer him comfort. Yet, despite his evident pain, there was also something else warring with the anguish—the hatred he felt for Jack Price.

'Before I left for Spain, I encountered Jack Price. I damned his black soul to hell. It was because of him that his brother went to Spain to fight—that my sister followed him and is now dead. He stood arrogantly before me and laughed at my concern, showing no emotion.'

He got up and leaned against the rocks, looking down at her. He was smiling slightly. It was more reflective, even with a trace of wistfulness in it. Her questions had recalled memories to him.

'Is Jack Price's father still alive?'

'Ned Price. Yes, but he suffers ill health.'

'And Jack is his only remaining son?'

'Now Edmund has gone, yes—Jack revels in the power he has over others.'

'You say the family own a boatyard. Who works it?'

'Ned Price, when he's able, and they employ an overseer. When Jack deems to show up, he works the men for a pittance. My bailiff informs me his father is thinking of selling the yard. If so, then I intend to buy it.'

'Do you know anything about building boats? Is it a profitable business?'

He shook his head. 'I know nothing about the business. I know Edmund turned over enough work to secure its future. The craftsmen are still there. Edmund and his father shared a love of boat building. Ned taught Edmund all he knew. He was disappointed by Jack's lack of interest and turned a blind eye to his smuggling. If the yard does come up for sale, then I will buy it and not disclose ownership to Jack Price or his father until I decide how to handle it. They would never accept it, but I have to do this for Tobias's future.'

'And if he doesn't want to build boats?'

'Then he can do with it what he will. He can sell it or pass it on to any offspring he might have.'

'You have it all worked out, don't you?' Tilly said in a quiet voice.

'I have to do this for Cassie.'

'Why are you telling me this? I am a virtual stranger to you.'

'My instinct tells me you are trustworthy, Miss Anderson—and I always follow my instinct.'

'Thank you.'

He smiled at her. 'You're welcome.' Falling silent, he stared out to sea. 'So much has happened to me over the past two years that I have lost track of what is important,' he said quietly, as if speaking his thoughts aloud. 'Several months ago, I wouldn't have thought that I would be dashing across to Spain to find my sister—and yet here I am, Cassie dead and with the responsibility of a child whose life is dependent on me.'

'And you still insist his existence is kept from Jack Price.'

'To keep Tobias safe, it has to be.'

'What I don't understand is that if he is a free trader, why has he not been arrested before now?'

'To be suspected of smuggling is one thing, but to be caught doing it is another matter entirely. He also has some of the Revenue men in his pocket. They fear him, along with everyone else hereabouts. He doesn't always dirty his hands with the smuggling. He controls activities from Trevean—his home. He has his spies scattered about—knows where the patrols are going to be, both on land and at sea.

'Over the years he's forged his own kind of power. He thumbs his nose at the powers that be—the only way to settle disputes is with fists. Few men are foolish enough to cross him. When my parents were crossing to Guernsey to visit friends, their boat went down. It was reported that it was as a result of a storm and not at the hands of smugglers, which was what I suspected— the vessel my parents were on was perfectly sound and there was no storm that day.

'Afterwards I listened to words spoken furtively here and there and began to envision what had happened, unable to tear the ugly pictures from my mind. I knew Price was on a run at that time. Whether he was involved I never did find out—but I am almost certain he had something to do with it.'

'And if he was? What would you do?'

'He would not escape justice. I would see to that.'

'And you are such an important figure in the community you would be able to bring that about.'

'Yes, yes, I would.' He looked at her for a long moment and Tilly fancied there was a strange expression on his face she had not seen before. 'Because you have met Jack Price, because he knows you are alone at Drayton Manor, be wary.'

'Why? Do you think I may be in some kind of danger?'

'One never knows with Price what he will do. If, at any time, you should find yourself in danger, will you promise to come to me? I will help you. I promise you.'

Tilly paused to look at him. He was sincere, that she knew. She nodded. 'Thank you—although I imagine he has more to do than trouble me.'

He was smiling, a smile Tilly found almost endearing. He did seem to have a way about him and she could not fault any woman for falling under his spell, for she found to her amazement that her heart was not as distantly detached as she might have imagined it to be. Even his deep mellow voice seemed like a warm caress over her senses.

Shoving himself away from the rock, he held out his hand. She took it and he drew her to her feet. 'I would like to show you Clifton House.'

'You would? Mrs Carstairs tells me it is quite magnificent.'

'So it is—but then, I am biased.'

'I would love to see it.'

'And what about its owner? Are you not tempted to know me better?'

'It is true. I hardly know you.'

'We could soon remedy that. I think you would find it interesting to discover more.'

'I am sure you are right, Lord Clifton,' she replied, trying to still the rapid beating of her heart.

'I am having a few friends to dinner next week—the first time I've entertained anyone since returning home. So, will you honour me by joining us? You and your aunt, of course. She is recovered, I hope.'

'Yes, quite recovered—although she gets more tired than usual.' Tilly smiled. 'She puts it down to the sea air. I am sure I can speak for her when I accept your invitation.'

'It will give you the opportunity to meet the local parson, Reverend Leighton, and his wife, and Mr and Mrs Ainsley. Mr Ainsley is a magistrate.'

Tilly glanced up at him to find he was looking at her strangely, as if he was preoccupied. She was bewildered by his mood and, caught up in a rush of irrational confusion, she looked away from him—she felt mesmerised, uncertainty flooding over her.

He touched a lock of hair that had escaped the confines of her braid and rested on her neck and she felt the brush of his fingers on her flesh. When they lingered, her heart beat erratically, a thrill of anticipation spreading through her. Brief though the touch was, his fingers left their imprint upon her flesh.

Every nerve in her body piqued at the feel of his touch, which was like a brand of fire against her skin, and a searing excitement shot through her. She felt overpowered by his nearness. Her whole body throbbed with an awareness of him, but she would not give any hint of her weakness. She was conscious of the power of his masculinity, so great was the pull.

His face creased with concentration as he studied her upturned face. Slowly, his finger gently traced the line of her jaw. It was strong and soothing, his touch impersonal, as if he were examining an object, yet it was gentle and Tilly did not feel like an object—far from it. She felt cosseted. There was something agreeable in his touch, almost sensuous. Her whole body felt as if it were unwinding, growing weak with the pleasure of what the tip of his finger was doing to her.

Vividly conscious of the strange things happening to her, she abruptly turned her thoughts away from this new and dangerous direction and averted her head, before he could realise just how much he affected her.

'You are a lovely young woman, Miss Anderson. I don't imagine I am the first man to say that to you.'

'No, as a matter of fact, you aren't. My brothers can be complimentary when the mood takes them, which isn't very often. They only flatter me to improve my humour.'

'I am tempted to taste what your lips offer.'

'I am certain they offer nothing that is different to what you have experienced before, Lord Clifton,' she said, feeling the heat and vibrancy of him reaching out to her. For her own safety, and her own sanity, she knew she had to try to stay one step ahead of him. 'So, if it's seduction you have in mind, then please forget it.'

His lips curled in a crooked smile. 'Here on an empty beach, hidden from prying eyes, with the sun shining and the sea as blue as can be, with a beautiful woman—what man in his right mind would not have seduction on his mind?'

'Then please don't. If you tried, I'd resist you with all my strength—only I'm afraid I don't know how my strength would hold out with you.'

He tilted his head at her. 'Afraid?' he said. 'Are you afraid of me, Miss Anderson?'

'Yes,' she whispered. 'I'm afraid of both of us.'

With the sun warm on her face, a tautness began in her breast, a delicious ache that was like a languorous, honeyed warmth.

As he sensed the change in her, Lord Clifton drew her towards him. Curling his long masculine fingers round her chin, he tilted her face up to his. Her eyes were large, her lips soft and quivering. It seemed a lifetime passed as they gazed at each other. In that lifetime each lived through a range of deep, tender emotions new to them both, exquisite emotions that neither of them could put into words.

'Are you still afraid, Miss Anderson?'

'No,' she murmured. 'I'm not afraid.'

'And will you resist me if I kiss you?'

'No.' The word issued forth from her lips. It was uttered softly, barely audible, her breath warm on his flesh.

As though in slow motion, unable to resist the temptation her mouth offered, slowly Lord Clifton's own moved inexorably closer. His gaze was gentle and compelling, when, in a sweet, mesmeric sensation, his mouth found hers. Tilly melted into him. The kiss was lingeringly slow.

Raising his head, Lord Clifton gazed down at her in wonder. Her magnificent eyes were naked and defenceless. 'My God, Miss Anderson,' he whispered, his voice hoarse, 'what a delightful surprise you are turning out to be.'

The pressure of his body, those feral eyes glittering with power and primeval hunger, washed away any measure of comfort Tilly might have left. A strange, alien feeling fluttered within her breast and she was halted for a brief passage of time when she found her lips entrapped by his once more and, though they were soft and tender, they burned with a fire that scorched her.

Closing her eyes, she yielded to it, melting against him, finding herself at the mercy of her emotions as he savoured each intoxicating pleasure, glorying in her purity.

When they finally drew apart, Tilly could not believe how easily she had succumbed to his kiss. She turned her head away, wanting to conceal how deeply she was affected by what had just happened between them. 'I—I think we should be getting back.'

Raising her hand to his lips, he pressed them to the soft centre of her palm. 'Yes. We should stop now before things go too far. I'll escort you to your carriage before Mrs Carstairs comes looking for you—and since I am impatient to see you again, I will call the day after tomorrow. I would like to show you more of the area. Do you approve?'

Tilly was about to refuse, but the words died on her lips when she looked at the lazy, relaxed man with the slightly smiling mouth and eyes like soft blue velvet. Suddenly a ride in the countryside or wherever he chose to take her seemed immensely appealing. 'Why— I—yes, that would do very well. I shall look forward to it.'

'Excellent. We'll lunch at a tavern I know some miles from Biddycombe. It provides the best food in the area.'

Lucas took her hand to help her over the boulders that littered the beach. He was unable to believe this innocent temptress had surrendered in his arms and returned his passion with such intoxicating sweetness. The times they had been together, the tension and explosive emotions that her presence elicited had been disturbing. Like a siren in Greek mythology whose singing was believed to lure sailors to destruction on the rocks, her vulnerability had finally broken all bounds of his restraint.

He walked beside her to where Dunstan waited with the carriage. Mrs Carstairs was already seated inside. He stared at his companion's profile, tracing with his eyes the beautiful classical lines of her face, the softness of her shapely mouth and the brush of lustrous dark eyelashes shadowing her cheeks. A strand of her hair nestled in a dark spiral in the hollow of her neck. She really was quite extraordinarily lovely.

He sensed an untamed freedom of spirit hovering just below the surface, yet, haughty in bearing, she was undoubtedly a true lady and represented everything that appealed to him, everything that was most desirable in a woman.

He had seen the way Jack Price had looked at her and the remembrance of such familiarity sent a sudden surge of cold fury through him. Seeing Price with his hands on her when he had entered the inn had caused something to snap inside him, shattering his emotions almost beyond all rational control. The intoxicating beauty before Jack Price would arouse lust in any man and, dressed in a pale yellow day dress, she looked so damned lovely.

The smugglers came again. Tilly heard them in the early hours. She had promised Lord Clifton she would turn a blind eye and she had meant it, but her curiosity got the better of her. Going to the window, she half opened the curtains. The sky was moonless, but she was able to make out the eerie figures of men and horses. They were leaving the stables, which were in darkness. The front rider was a big man wearing a cocked hat, his frock coat spread over his horse's flanks. Instinct told her it was of a scarlet hue, that the rider was none other than Jack Price.

As if sensing her watching, he lifted his head and directed his gaze to her window. She didn't move or attempt to hide herself. She sensed he was laughing at her. When he removed his hat and waved it with a flourish in her direction, she knew he was.

It was a lovely morning for their ride, carrying the promise of a lovely summer's day in the faint sea breeze. Looking extremely fetching in a ruby-red riding dress, with a matching hat cocked at an impudent angle atop bunches of delectable ringlets that bounced delightfully when she moved her head, Tilly went to the stables. Lord Clifton rode into the yard. Bringing his horse to a halt, he dismounted, the heat of his gaze travelling the full length of her in a slow, appreciative perusal, before making a leisurely inspection of her upturned face.

'You're looking very fine this morning, Miss Anderson,' he said as Dunstan appeared leading Gracie.

'Why, thank you, sir. I'm looking forward to the ride.'

Placing his hands on her waist, he lifted her with gentle strength into the saddle. Wide-eyed, she met his gaze and saw his brows lift, a quizzical expression in his eyes. He watched as she hooked her knee around the pommel and placed her foot in the stirrup before settling her skirts, then he hoisted himself on to his mount.

'I've never seen you ride. Do you ride well?'

'As well as most,' she replied, taking the reins as Gracie moved restlessly. She controlled the horse effortlessly. 'You can judge for yourself.' She turned and looked behind her to where Graham was already mounted. 'Are you ready, Graham?'

'I am, Miss Anderson.'

Lord Clifton looked from Graham to Tilly, a scowl on his face. 'Graham is to come with us?'

'But of course. It wouldn't be proper for me to ride out with you alone now, would it? When I told Aunt Charlotte I was to go riding with you, she insisted Graham accompanied me.'

'Of course, and your aunt is quite right. Now, shall we get going?'

Tilly urged Gracie forward. Lord Clifton on his mount moved off from the stable yard and along one of the paths that led off into the woods. There was no room for them to ride abreast, so they didn't speak as they went through the deep shade, a kaleidoscope of shapes and colour. Sometimes they had to duck under low branches.

It was beautiful in this shadowed world, with the smell of damp earth and the coolness of the trees. Eventually they came out of the woods where the vegetation grew thick and rampant and they were able to ride side by side across the rolling countryside. Graham kept at a discreet distance. Fresh, cool breezes were fragranced with an invigorating scent of the sea.

Casting a sidelong glance at her companion, Tilly admired the way his body flowed easily with the big gelding's stride, both horse and master strong, a picture of combined, harnessed power. For a man of such imposing herculean stature, he had an elegant way of moving in his casual clothes.

He wore a tan coat, his long legs encased in biscuit-coloured trousers and highly polished dark brown riding boots. His hair was dishevelled from the ride, the black curls brushing the edge of his collar. The sun illuminated his bold, lean profile and that aquiline nose that gave him a look of such stark, brooding intensity.

Lord Clifton was no less admiring of her, gracefully perched side-saddle. When she soared over a wide ditch, he grinned approvingly. Tilly was light and lovely on horseback, managing her horse with expert skill. She urged it into a gallop, her skirts flying out behind her. She let the horse have its head as she charged full pelt laughingly along the rutted track. The speed and the air brought colour to her cheeks and made her feel more alive than she had in days.

After riding for several miles, Graham doing his level best to keep up with them on the heavier carriage horse, Lord Clifton drew up on the clifftop overlooking the sea and dismounted, then walked over to lift Tilly down from her horse. Graham pulled his horse to a halt some way away from them and sat on the soft grass with his knees drawn up, looking out at the sea.

'My compliments, Miss Anderson. I know few men who ride as well as you,' Lord Clifton told her. 'I am certain that the huntress Diana could not rival you.'

'That is a compliment indeed.' The genuine warmth and admiration in his voice and in his eyes flooded Tilly's heart with joy.

'Gracie is clearly to your liking.'

'She most certainly is.'

'The ride has done you good,' Lord Clifton said, noting the blooming colour in her cheeks and sparkling eyes.

'I always enjoy riding. I try to ride most days, but never venture very far from Biddycombe.'

'It's good for you to explore, to learn to see your surroundings through your own eyes. I am biased about the charms of Devon, but I've no doubt you shall fall in love with it, too, and want to come back.'

'That's up to Charles. I shall have to wait and see what he intends doing with the house,' she told him, perching on a large rock and smiling up at him. 'But I do like Devon—at least what I have seen of it—and the people seem to be friendly enough. You are fortunate having been raised by the sea. I can't imagine anyone would want to leave it for the city.'

'It does make one feel like that, although one gets used to it.'

'Do you swim in the sea?'

He nodded, walking towards the edge of the cliff and gazing over the water to where a large brigantine was heading east. 'Often.'

Tilly wondered what he would say if he knew she had watched him that day from the cliff as he cleaved his way through the water. She hugged the memory to her, considering it prudent not to reveal her voyeuristic moment.

'I don't sleep well and I come to the beach early in the morning,' he went on. 'It's the best time of day— the stillness, everything fresh and at peace. Sometimes

I come before daybreak when the sky is still dark and the stars so low you imagine you could reach out and touch them. There's something mystical about that time of day.

'I like to watch the dawn. It's as though, with the faint light on the horizon, the whole universe is holding its breath—waiting. I can sit among the rocks and listen to the scurrying of the land crabs and a multitude of other creatures that make up the sounds of the night. And then there's the sound of the surf.'

Tilly listened to his voice, which was soft and wistful. *Yes*, she thought, *he really does love this place.* 'I envy you your sense of belonging. I haven't lived anywhere long enough to feel that way—not even when my mother was alive—and then when I went to live with Aunt Charlotte. And as much as William wants me to make Cranford my home, as beautiful as it is, I have no sense of belonging. But you have Clifton House and a fine estate in this glorious part of the country. Knowing of the loss of your family, it must have been a difficult time for you of late.'

'Yes, it has, but I have no choice but to carry on.'

Tilly seemed to have touched on a tender spot of his vulnerability. 'You are strong. It is not impossible. I am sure you have the will to survive.'

They sat in silence for a while, content to sit and admire the view and watch the sweeping, squawking gulls circle the rocks. Tilly watched as her companion lifted his hand and, as he absently rubbed the muscles at the back of his neck, her treacherous mind suddenly imagined how skilfully those long fingers might caress her body and the exquisite pleasure he would make her feel.

Her heart suddenly swelled—with what? Admiration? Affection? Love? No, not that. She did not know him well enough to feel that. Recollecting herself, she shook away such thoughts angrily. She was being an utter fool romanticising Lord Clifton, simply because he was an attractive man, sleek and fierce as a bird of prey, with his raven-black hair. He had been incredibly skilled at raising her desire when the only time he had touched her was on the night when the smugglers had come and as they had shared the kiss on the beach, because she was helplessly attracted to him.

Standing up, she took a few steps to stand by his side. He was preoccupied with his thoughts, his gaze fixed on the distant horizon. Looking up at him, she wondered what he was thinking. Was it the loss of his family, or was it because he was pining for the woman who had stolen his heart?

'What are you thinking?' she asked softly.

As if he hadn't heard her, he continued to look straight ahead. When her voice finally penetrated his thoughts, he looked down at her and then fixed his gaze on the distant horizon once more.

Something hard flared in his eyes for a moment, but then he shrugged resignedly. 'I was thinking of nothing in particular—nothing that would interest you.'

'You could try me. I'm a good listener.'

'I was thinking of Spain—but you were not there. You would not understand.'

'That's nonsensical. Perhaps if you were to speak of it, the pain would ease. I am persuaded that you must talk about it. Why have you closed your mind to it?'

'Out of necessity.'

Something about the way he looked stirred Tilly's sympathy and she felt her heart wrench agonisingly. 'I would like to think you could talk to me,' she said quietly. He turned his head and looked at her. Her eyes were full of concern. 'How else can I understand? Is it your sister you are thinking about—or about the war?'

'Both. After all, I would not have been there had it not been for Cassie.' His eyes had grown as distant as the horizon, as if he had withdrawn into himself, into that painful time still so recent.

'Where did you find her?'

'I eventually tracked her down to a town called Ciudad Rodrigo, not far from the Portuguese border, where the French garrison was besieged by Wellington's Anglo-Portuguese army. It was January and it was very cold. Cassie was with more soldiers' wives and those who follow the army. She was heavily pregnant. I begged her to return with me to England, but she wouldn't hear of it. I was shocked by the conditions she was having to endure—it was not for the faint-hearted.'

'And you saw Edmund Price.'

'Yes. He was concerned about Cassie and he didn't want her there any more than I did, but there was nothing he could do. She was dead set on remaining. Aware of Cassie's condition, I made sure they were wed. When the town walls were breached by the British artillery, the British and Portuguese armies went on the rampage. There were hundreds of casualties—many killed. Edmund eventually died of the wounds he sustained in battle. Just hours after he was buried Cassie was delivered of her child and followed Edmund into the earth.'

'That must have been dreadful for you,' Tilly whispered.

'It was the worst. Before I left for Spain, I was sure that the men who'd gone to fight, so valiant in the field, with military discipline instilled into them, would deal with whatever was thrown at them. But what I witnessed at Ciudad Rodrigo—the mindless slaughter and deplorable lapse in human nature—shocked and horrified me to the core of my being. My saving grace was finding Florence to take care of Tobias. We travelled overland for many weeks, dodging French soldiers and desperate men. Eventually, we reached northern France and took ship for England.'

When he fell silent, Tilly moved closer to him, feeling his pain. 'I'm sorry, truly. There is nothing I can say to ease what you went through. But in time, in another life, that terrible time in Spain will ease.' *But it will not be forgotten*, she thought. What he had seen would continue to haunt him for evermore.

'What can I say except that I hope you are right.' He looked at her and held her eyes captive. 'You were right. You are a good listener and I apologise if what I have told you has caused you distress.' Suddenly, he smiled—it was as if the sun had suddenly broken through a dark cloud. 'Come, let's be on our way. I promised you lunch. The Bell Inn is not far from here. The ride has given me an appetite.'

## Chapter Six

They spurred their horses on, riding some considerable distance following the coast before arriving at the Bell Inn on the edge of a large village. It was a respectable establishment, frequented by ship's masters, owners and brokers of merchant vessels based in nearby Plymouth. Carriages were drawn up outside. Inside, it was plain from the bustling clientele that business was good.

The landlord was a genial sort with a sunburnt face and a thick black beard and looked more like a sea captain than an innkeeper. On recognising Lord Clifton, honoured that one of the most important gentlemen in the district should visit his hostelry, he ushered them to a quiet alcove that offered a degree of privacy. Graham hung back, preferring to eat outside at one of the tables.

'Might I suggest that you aid the digestion of your food with fine wine and brandy brought in from France?'

'It surprises me that such luxuries are available, when Britain and France have been at war for so many years,' Tilly remarked, making herself comfortable across from Lord Clifton.

'A war fought by soldiers on behalf of politicians,' the landlord replied.

'And we in Devon—and Cornwall—have never allowed such considerations to stand in the way of trade, have we, Landlord?' Lord Clifton remarked with a knowing wink.

'By God, never! It benefits us all.'

The landlord left them alone to order one of the serving girls to take their order. Tilly glanced around the inn, observing the looks cast their way.

'You are a popular man, Lord Clifton. You are attracting attention.'

'Not just me. Who could not but notice you? And I must say that you look extremely fetching in your riding dress.'

She laughed. 'Why, thank you.' She took a sip of the lemonade a maid had set before her. 'Tell me, how is Tobias?'

'Thriving. He's a fine boy.'

'And Florence?'

'She is well—glad to be settled for the time being. She's had a difficult time.'

'Will she stay with Tobias permanently, or does she have family of her own?'

'She has a sister in Dawlish. She mourns her husband—and her child.'

'That's understandable. Her suffering must have been great indeed. It must have been a godsend to her when you befriended her.'

'I needed her very badly at the time. She's devoted to Tobias, but she's a sensible, educated young woman and realises the time will come when she will no longer be needed. But that will be discussed at a later date. For now, I'm glad to have her.'

'And Jack Price is still unaware of his existence?'

'As to that, I cannot be sure. People talk. Most of the servants at Clifton House have family connected to the smuggling fraternity one way or another. It's just a matter of time before Jack Price learns of his existence.'

Their meal came and they ate in companionable silence. Tilly enjoyed watching a variety of people come and go, greeting each other and going on their way or staying to enjoy a meal. And then it was over and they were heading home, riding through the woods once more.

'Who do the woods belong to?' Tilly asked casually when the track opened up and they were able to ride side by side.

'I own them.'

'I see. And do you mind people using them?'

He laughed. 'Not at all. I am not mean-spirited. The woods are too vast to patrol. Besides, people need to pass through them to go from here to there. All I ask is that they are sensible and do not damage the trees or light fires.'

She looked at him. His eyes were brilliant—full of laughter. 'And poaching?'

'Ah, now that is a different matter entirely. I employ gamekeepers to keep an eye out for poachers—although I'm not averse to anyone taking the odd rabbit or two. Those pesky animals do a lot of damage to crops when they come through.'

'And they provide a good meal for a family.'

'Exactly.'

Suddenly, they emerged into the open and ahead of

them was Clifton House. Seeing it from a different viewpoint, Tilly caught her breath.

'Oh, it's quite magnificent.'

'I totally agree. I shall enjoy entertaining you and your aunt when you come to dine. It is quite impressive—but then I am biased.'

'And so you should be. I look forward to seeing it.'

They rode on, eventually arriving at Drayton Manor.

'Won't you come in and meet my aunt?' Tilly offered.

'I will look forward to meeting her when you come to Clifton House. I have business in Biddycombe shortly. I must get back.'

'Of course.' Tilly was sorry the ride was over. 'Thank you for today. I've enjoyed it so much.'

'You're welcome. We must do it again soon.'

Tilly watched him ride away. Something was happening to her. She was too much aware of him—and he of her. Physically. He gave her a feeling of disquiet, yet at the same time he stimulated and excited her. Was their banter and meetings leading up to something, and, if so, what? Would he have kissed her if he hadn't intended to take their relationship forward?

He had been let down in the past—had he not told her that he did not believe in love and that when he married it would be one of convenience? It was early days and Tilly had no experience of men like Lucas Kingsley. Where was their relationship leading? Clearly his former lover had broken his heart. Could she, Tilly, be the one to put it back together again?'

They rode together again, but this time he took her up on to the high moor. It was a place where misleading mists often took travellers by surprise, mists in which one could get hopelessly lost, even those who believed they knew the moor. On the hem of the mist the moor was like some petrified and silent world. It was rich with legend, of highwaymen and smugglers and ghosts. The ground was strewn with rocks and for miles around it was littered with ruined druid temples and ancient stone circles. When darkness came it infused itself into the rock rising like sharp blades into the sky. Tilly felt drawn to the moor, finding beauty in its bleak and desolate landscape.

Having left Tilly after their ride, thinking how ravishing and invigorated she always looked, her cheeks adorably pink and her eyes sparkling, alone at Clifton House Lucas had much to think about. Finding a wife was very much on his mind. Perhaps he wouldn't have too far to look. Did he not have the ideal woman, with all the proper requisites to grace the halls of Clifton House?

Having overcome her initial hostility towards him, he felt that she enjoyed his company the more they were together—and he had the whole of the summer to win her over. Most of the women he was acquainted with were available to him at the crook of his finger, some of the most beautiful women in Devon and beyond, but none of them especially stood out and appealed to him—only one, who had particularly warm violet eyes and a wealth of gleaming black hair.

He had no doubt the chase could prove both difficult and exciting. He sensed her wariness. This young woman with her beauty and spirit affected him and she was not immune to him, as the kiss they had shared on the beach confirmed. Whenever they met, he felt a current of emotion between them, like the charged air on the sea before a storm strikes with all its devastating violence. He didn't have the slightest doubt of his own ability to lure her into his arms.

He was aware that she was young and that her brothers might insist that she make her debut, but he was prepared to wait. Before she had to return to London, he would court her with such ardour that she would return to Devon as soon as her brother left for India.

The next time Tilly rode out Lord Clifton was not with her. Having ridden through a shadowy world of muted sounds, where damp and decay rose from the undergrowth and assailed her nostrils, and squirrels skittered in the upper branches of the trees, without the sun a bitter chill had fallen on this twilight world.

Relieved when she came out into the open, Tilly looked about her, having ridden further than she'd intended. Accompanied by Graham, she had been tempted to ride once more to the high moor, with its craggy peaks and purple heather, but instead she had followed the coast to the west, seeing the occasional tall chimneys of the engine houses of tin and copper mines. Slowing her horse to a walk, she rode in the direction of the sea just ahead of her. She could make out the phosphorescence of the breaking waves below.

A large stone house was perched on a promontory high above the sea where it was under siege by the storms that blew in from the Channel, buffeting its walls during the winter months. Its surrounding battlemented wall gave it the look of a castle rather than a house. Never had Tilly seen a more desolate or gloomy place.

Hearing the sound of sawing and hammering, she looked down a steep hill to an inlet, seeing a large boatyard. Labourers' cottages lined the hillside set further back from the inlet. The not-unpleasant smell of sawdust and tar assailed her nostrils. There was a good deal of activity as labouring men went about their work, carpenters sawing planks and caulking the hull of a large vessel. A dry dock held a large vessel having barnacles scraped from its hull, another was being painted and cradles held the keels of fishing smacks. A prepared launch way ran down to the sea.

Could this be the Prices' boatyard? she wondered. She turned to wait for Graham. Then she heard the barking of dogs. They sounded fierce and angry. And then there they were, two great big black hounds, bounding towards her. Gracie half reared and shied away. The dogs stopped and looked straight at her. Then they began to bark again. It intensified.

Her heart almost ceased to beat when a tall figure suddenly stepped out of the trees in front of her horse. It was Jack Price. His eyes were gleaming coldly. There was a sneer on his mouth, and it was a cruel mouth, twisting in perpetual contempt for those who were beneath him. He was looking at her with impudent admiration, letting his gaze travel from her eyes to her mouth and then, after lingering on its soft fullness, moving down to the gentle swell of her breasts beneath the bodice of her sapphire-blue riding habit.

'Well, well, if it isn't Miss Anderson! They do say as how, if one is patient enough, one will get what one wants in the end. I had no idea you would come calling to Trevean quite so soon. I am flattered.'

All the colour drained out of Tilly's face. At this point her pride played the better part of furthering her association with Jack Price. 'Don't be. I had no idea you lived this way. If I had, I would have taken a different route. Call off your dogs.'

Surprisingly, he did. They ceased their barking and retreated to sit beside their owner, but their eyes remained on Tilly. She glanced at a worried-looking Graham, who had halted his horse close by. 'It's all right, Graham. Mr Price and I are already acquainted.' She patted Gracie and murmured soothing words. She shivered, still disturbed by the dogs. 'She does not like your dogs,' she said to Jack Price.

'Not many people do. They do what I tell them.'

'I imagine they do. Kindly step out of my way,' she said coldly.

He smiled thinly, unconcerned by her hostile demeanour. 'What? You are wanting to leave so soon? You offend me, Miss Anderson. You don't know me well enough to show me such hostility.'

'I know *what* you are, Mr Price.' In the depths of his cold eyes something stirred and she felt a strong desire to ride away. There was an air of menace about him that entered her heart like a sliver of ice.

'Do you now? And you newly come to Devon. How much do you know, Miss Anderson? I should hate you to be under a misconception and will put you right if you are.'

'I know that you are a smuggler, that even the cleverest smuggler will make a mistake eventually and then he will be arrested or dead.'

His brows rose imperturbably. 'Is that so? I—and more than half the population in Devon and Cornwall—do not see free trading as a crime. Those involved in various ways either buy, sell, or drink—respectable ministers of the church, doctors, lawyers and, yes, even magistrates and Excise men. They all look the other way for a drop of French brandy or a bolt of silk or lace for their ladies.'

He moved closer to her horse, holding its bridle and touching her leg in a familiar way. 'What of you, Miss Anderson? Tell me what would please you—silk? Satin? The softest velvet, perhaps, to wear next to your soft skin?'

He was taunting her and she stiffened with anger. She met his eyes, so bold, gazing at her, taking in every detail of her face. 'I want nothing from you, Mr Price.'

'No? Not even in return for the loan of your horses? They're fine horses, by the way—worth much more than a keg of brandy.'

'I don't drink brandy—and I would prefer it if you didn't make use of the horses.'

'Too late, Miss Anderson. There are nights when they are needed and brave is the man—or woman—who refuses to help the traders.'

'You are quite mad.'

'No, not mad. It takes a very sane person to plan the things I do.'

'As you say. Now please let go of my horse and I will be on my way.'

'Your horse?' He stroked its mane, leaving his hand

to rest there. 'You must have become friendly with Kingsley for him to let you ride his sister's horse.'

'What he chooses to do is nothing to do with you.'

'No, it isn't, but to see you riding Lady Cassandra's horse is bound to raise a few eyebrows.'

'Lord Clifton's sister is dead, Mr Price, as you well know. The horse needs to be ridden.'

'There are grooms aplenty at Clifton House to take care of that. Although—when I saw the two of you walk off together in Biddycombe—to the beach... Very cosy the two of you looked.'

'It is none of your business.'

He laughed, a deep, low sound. 'Maybe not, although, with an infant to take care of, His Lordship must have his hands full.'

Tilly felt her heart flip over. 'Infant?'

His lips stretched in an odious smile. 'Oh, yes, an infant. With a house full of servants, more than one is willing to inform Jack Price what goes on in that fine house.'

Tilly looked at him with intense dislike burning in the depths of her eyes. 'You have a black heart, Jack Price. It will be your own wickedness and greed that will bring about your destruction.'

'You could be right.'

Immediately, she pulled her horse away from him. 'Good day, Mr Price.'

'Good day, Miss Anderson.' He half turned and then looked back at her, capturing her gaze. 'The infant? Who is he? Who does he belong to?'

Tilly stared at him. He had spoken softly, slowly, a hidden purpose in the depths of his evil eyes. She tossed her head. 'How on earth would I know that? Lord Clifton's affairs are his own.' On that note, she rode away from him.

'Are you all right, Miss Anderson?' Graham asked, looking at her with concern. 'I saw the man step out in front of you and recognised him as the man who sometimes takes the horses in the night.'

'I'm all right, Graham. Let's go home. I don't like this place.'

'Nor me, Miss,' Graham mumbled. 'I don't like him either.'

The night Tilly went to Clifton House would always stand out in her memory. It was early evening, the heat of the day having left the land, but it was pleasant and warm, the air heavily perfumed with wild honeysuckle. Aunt Charlotte was excited to be visiting and was looking forward to being introduced to the Earl of Clifton at last.

Tilly was strangely excited, more about seeing Lord Clifton than anything else. Wanting to look her best, she had taken care over her toilette and had chosen to wear a high-waisted, square-necked gown with puffed sleeves in powder blue. It was a lovely contrast to her ebony hair, which she wore loose, held back with a broad ribbon to match her dress.

Driving the carriage drawn by four of the bay carriage horses, Dunstan negotiated the narrow lanes with care. It rocked gently from side to side, the harness jangling. The sunlight was warm and a faint breeze blew in from the sea towards the high moor. They passed through parkland with enormous oaks, beneath which a small herd of deer grazed serenely, looking up with a singular lack of interest as the carriage passed by.

They entered through the high gilded gates of Clifton House, which was magnificent, with its tall chimneys and mullioned windows. Two cylindrical towers flanked either side. There was something medieval about it. Tilly felt that she was passing into another age, a time long past. The stately gardens and carefully maintained parkland were surrounded by woodlands of ancient trees and in the distance the English Channel.

A butler admitted them to the house, where two liveried, bewigged footmen waited to take any outer garments. Handing one of them her bonnet and the light shawl she wore round her shoulders, Tilly looked about her. She recalled the time William had taken her to Cranford and how awestruck she had been as she had tried to take in all the grandeur and that was how she felt at that moment, for Clifton House was just as grand but in a different way.

'So, you have arrived.'

The voice came from above and Tilly turned and looked up the wide staircase. Lord Clifton was coming down. When she saw him, with a strange sensation of fatality she was aware of the stir the sight of him caused in her heart as he continued to advance. Everything about her disappeared into a haze. Her attention was focused entirely on him. Had she wanted to look away she could not have done. She was not even conscious that her aunt was watching her.

Never had Tilly seen such a fine figure of masculine elegance and as handsome as a god with those perfectly chiselled features. In contrast to the times when she had seen him, Lord Clifton looked so poised, so proud and debonair. His movements, his habitual air of languid indolence, hung about him like a cloak. The perfect fit of his claret coat and the tapering trousers accentuated the long lines of his body, his white neckcloth pristine against his sun-bronzed features.

With his hair brushed back, he looked every inch the well-heeled titled nobleman—and a great deal more dangerous than the average country gentleman. It was impossible not to respond to this man as his masculine magnetism dominated the scene.

When Tilly met his eyes, at that moment she became convinced that there were no eyes in all the world that were brighter than those which now smiled at her. Mentally casting off the spell he unwittingly cast, she scolded herself for acting as addled as a dazzled schoolgirl. Closer now, a half-smile curved his lips. He looked down at her.

'Welcome to Clifton House.' He shifted his gaze to her aunt standing beside her. 'And you must be Miss Charlotte Anderson, Silas's younger sister. Commiserations on your loss. Silas was a fine man—one of the best. I am delighted to meet you at last. I have encountered your niece on one or two occasions—a most interesting young lady. I thought it was time you both visited Clifton House.'

'And what a lovely house it is,' Aunt Charlotte said.

They were unable to say more for at that moment the butler admitted a gentleman and his wife. Lord Clifton went to greet them, bringing them to where Tilly stood with her aunt.

'I would like to introduce you to Reverend Leighton and his wife. They are old and valued friends of the Kingsleys. And this is Miss Charlotte Anderson and her niece Miss Tilly Anderson. They are in residence at Drayton Manor at present. Silas was Miss Charlotte Anderson's brother, Miss Anderson Silas's niece.'

'May I say we are truly delighted to meet you both and welcome you to Devon,' Reverend Leighton said as he raised Tilly's hand to his lips. 'I am delighted to see Lord Clifton has lost no time in inviting you to Clifton House.'

'Lord Clifton is a very persuasive man, Reverend,' Tilly replied without looking at their host, but she suspected there was a mocking gleam in his eyes.

'I understand we are to be neighbours, that you have taken up residence in Drayton Manor,' Reverend Leighton said. 'Such a lovely old house. Silas was a good friend of ours and we were sorry when he passed on. He was a great asset to the community and will be sadly missed in these parts.'

'Reverend Leighton spent the early years of his ministry in London and moved to Biddycombe fifteen years ago when the appointment became available,' Lord Clifton explained.

'And I bless the day I did. I enjoy ministering to the parishioners who belong to the fishing community, the farmers and the miners. I look forward to seeing you at church one of these Sundays, Miss Anderson. I think you will enjoy my sermons.'

'You will,' Lord Clifton said, laughing. 'Reverend Leighton delivers them with tremendous enthusiasm in case any of his parishioners are indiscreet enough to be caught nodding off.'

Their conversation was interrupted when Lord Clifton's other guests arrived—Mr and Mrs Ainsley. Mr Ainsley was a stout, jovial man, with a warm smile and the relaxed congeniality and confidence that came with the privileged position he held as the local magistrate. His wife was a handsome woman, with an easy, open manner.

They took a moment for introductions and for them to get to know each other before Lord Clifton led them towards the drawing room where drinks were to be served.

Tilly's attention was caught by a gilt-edged portrait tucked away in the corner of the hall. She stopped to look at it. The subject was a lady of perhaps twenty-five or more, wearing a gown in a style no longer fashionable. Mesmerised, she stared at the fair features. The lady was wearing a wig so she was unable to note the colour of her hair. Her features were delicate, giving her an air of fragility, but the artist had captured a steely determination in her blue eyes. Tilly knew instinctively that this was Elizabeth, Lord Clifton's grandmother, the lady who had preferred death to living with the violation inflicted on her by Jack Price's grandfather.

Lord Clifton turned as he was about to enter the drawing room to see what had captured her attention. He came to stand beside her.

'Is this your grandmother?' Tilly asked, her gaze on the painting.

'Yes. That is Elizabeth.'

'She was beautiful.'

He nodded. 'She was also very brave.'

\* \* \*

When dinner was announced they progressed into the dining room of Jacobean design, with chestnut panelling and a great impressive fireplace showing the arms of the Kingsley family. It was a large and high room, with an elaborate plaster frieze depicting a forest with the court of Diana and attendant assortment of animals along with scenes of country life and hunting. Tilly loved it and began to relax, pleased to see Aunt Charlotte was enjoying herself.

They dined in generous style, the conversation light and lively as they talked of local matters and people known to them all. But Tilly had the disconcerting impression that Lord Clifton's other guests were weighing her up with every move she made and every word she uttered, though she was sure they meant to be kind.

'You must learn to swim, Miss Anderson,' Mrs Ainsley said, wiping her mouth with her napkin, 'living so close to the sea. Silas loved the sea. He was a regular swimmer—every night and morning, I believe. He had some steps hewn out of the cliff to save walking half a mile along the cliff path.'

'Yes, I have found them. It's an advantage being able to get to the beach quickly. Do you swim, Mrs Ainsley?'

'Goodness me, no. I never go near the sea—can't stand the way the sand gets into everything. Most unpleasant it is.'

'Miss Anderson expressed to me only the other day when we...er...met quite by chance on the beach her desire to learn to swim. Is that not so, Miss Anderson?' Lord Clifton said, his penetrating eyes watching her intently, a mischievous twinkle in his eyes. 'I think she would take to it like a duck to water.'

'Yes, Lord Clifton, I do remember,' Tilly said, looking at him directly, remembering all too clearly how he had dragged her on to the sand after the wave swept her off her feet. 'But I have had a change of heart since then. I prefer my feet on dry land and will be in no hurry to take to the water.'

Over the glowing expanse of white tablecloth and gleaming plates and cutlery, Aunt Charlotte was regarding her with suspicion. Tilly had told her she had met Lord Clifton when he had called at the house to see Mrs Carstairs and again in Biddycombe, which was where he had invited them to dine at Clifton House. She had failed to inform her they had met before that on the beach.

The meal was a relaxed affair, the food delicious. Seated at the head of the table, Lucas found his eyes drawn to Tilly Anderson like a magnet, where she sat on his right and next to Reverend Leighton. When she had entered the house, the vision she had presented in her blue gown had snatched his breath.

She was beautiful and bewitching and he was drawn to her in a way he wouldn't have thought possible when he'd arrived from Spain. She lit the room simply by being present. Looking for unease or nervousness on her face, he found nothing but calm and the soft glow of light in her velvet-dark eyes.

She had been fully tutored in the conventions of society and was clearly experienced in social repartee. She was lively, amiable, a laughing, beautiful young woman in possession of a natural wit and intelligence. The more he saw of her, the more his need to know more about her grew—and the more he wanted her to be his wife.

'What has been happening in my absence?' Mr Ainsley asked. 'No doubt the smuggling fraternity are as busy as ever.'

'They are.' Mrs Ainsley leaned towards Miss Anderson and her aunt. 'Have you seen anything untoward at Drayton Manor? You know—smugglers, that sort of thing?'

'Aunt Charlotte was not well when we arrived and has been confined to her room,' Miss Tilly Anderson said. 'But there was one occasion when I was awakened in the early hours by strange sounds and, peering from behind my bedroom curtains, I have seen horses being moved.'

A twinkle entered her eyes when she flashed a look at Lucas, reminding him of that night when the smugglers had come to Drayton Manor to return the horses, and he smiled in collaboration.

'And what did you do?' Mrs Leighton asked eagerly.

'What could I do? Not that I would wish to do anything. One thing I have learned since coming to Devon is that the gentlemen are not openly discussed. The men involved in the illicit trade have a reputation for brutality and it would be most unwise to apprehend them.'

'Not without foundation,' Mr Ainsley said. 'They have no respect for anyone—be it man or woman— who gets in their way. They are quite unscrupulous.'

'Then I will take the greatest of care not to get in their way,' Tilly replied.

'Very sensible, my dear,' Mrs Ainsley said. 'The matter of smuggling must be treated with levity. Half a dozen free traders were captured along with their cargo a sennight past off Liskeard and imprisoned. They are awaiting trial. The new Revenue Officer, Lieutenant Foster, is like a man possessed in his desire to eradicate smuggling in this area. He has achieved more than his predecessors—although Jack Price is still at large. He's grown rich on the trade.'

'Then why don't you arrest him?' Miss Charlotte Anderson asked, having finished eating the fish course and sipping her wine.

'Because there has to be tangible proof and because he's clever, Miss Anderson. He's also feared among the smuggling fraternity. No one dares to speak against him. Too many men are in his debt. He manages to escape the Revenue men every time and the Dragoons. The Revenue men are vigilant in these waters, but it grieves me to say they are not all honest. Some of them are in Price's pay.

'Price is greedy, but as careful and as slippery as an eel. He has the distribution routes well planned and has markets for the smuggled goods. He knows all the inlets and coves where a vessel might hide. He also acts as agent and banker with the merchants across the Channel, where the goods to be smuggled to England are purchased.'

'Price is the uncontested victor over his counterparts, but the lucrative trade will turn against him,' Lucas said. 'His days are numbered.'

'Maybe so. I hear old Ned Price is thinking of selling the boatyard. Now Edmund has gone he's reluctant to hang on to it. Jack hasn't raised any objections about selling it.'

'He never did show an interest in ship building,' Lucas said quietly, 'unless the yard was building boats to service his own smuggling needs. I'm not surprised he's thinking of selling. The Price family own enough property up and down the coast to live in comfort. The boatyard will be a prosperous business for somebody—and Edmund kept the workers' cottages in good repair. He would have been saddened to see it sold off.'

With the signal that dinner was at an end, they convened to the drawing room, where coffee was served and something stronger for the gentlemen.

While Reverend Leighton and Mr Ainsley indulged in a game of cards with brandy on the side, the ladies were content to sit and gossip and drink their coffee. Tilly, who was feeling restless, was happy to oblige when Mrs Leighton asked if she played the pianoforte. She was reasonably proficient and played a few easy pieces she had learned by heart. When she had finished, she was applauded and complimented.

'You play well, Miss Anderson,' Lord Clifton said. 'You are a young lady of many talents.'

'My mother made me practise religiously every day. She was of the opinion that every young lady should be able to play the pianoforte—and to sing—but I have not been blessed with a voice I would inflict on others.'

Feeling the need of some fresh air, Tilly slipped out through the French doors on to the terrace, walking down a flight of shallow steps. The terraced gardens were filled with flowers and sweet-smelling shrubs and an enormous fountain shot plumes of water into the air. The sun was sinking, casting long shadows on the smooth lawn.

On a sigh, she breathed in the sweet fragrance of the garden. The night was so quiet. She had come to Devon to escape a scandal, hoping for a few weeks' respite before returning in the hope it would have died a death and she could resume her life as it had been before she had encountered Richard Coulson. Instead, she had inadvertently become embroiled in something quite new to her.

She was tempted to return to London and leave it all behind, but a pair of warm blue eyes held her. She felt bemused. She sensed there were many different facets to Lord Clifton. He was dangerous to her sensibilities and yet she still found him attractive. She was never a rational person—her misdemeanour with Richard Coulson gave evidence to that—but this time she should have the good sense to heed the warning and walk away.

What she could not understand, and what worried her, was this strange, magnetic pull she felt towards her illustrious neighbour emotionally. There were times when he spoke to her in that deep, compelling voice of his, or looked at her with those penetrating eyes, that she almost felt as if he were quietly reaching out to her and inexorably drawing her closer and closer to him. Her mind was telling her to dismiss his sensuality and the attraction she felt for him, but her heart was saying something else entirely.

A footfall sounded behind her. A pulse fluttered in her throat when she turned her head and saw Lord Clifton.

'Oh,' she said softly. 'I thought I was alone.'

'I beg your pardon, Miss Anderson. I didn't mean to startle you. I saw you leave and thought you might like some company. Reverend Leighton is happily drinking his brandy and his wife and your aunt are deep in conversation.'

'So you thought you would come and find me.'

'Something like that. To talk with a lovely young woman on a moonlit night in a beautiful garden is a pleasure beyond compare. I hope you don't mind.'

Feeling her heartbeat quicken alarmingly, Tilly was amazed by the effect his sudden presence was having on her, but she was resolved not to let it show. 'Not at all. It's your house, Lord Clifton, your garden. You are allowed to go where you please.'

'I am—but I will return to the house if you would prefer to be alone.'

'No—please stay. There is something I would like to talk to you about—two things, actually.'

'Oh? I am all ears.'

'It's about the smugglers.' Immediately his expression became serious.

'Have they visited Drayton Manor again?'

'Yes—once. I did as you told me to do, but I couldn't resist having just a peek. They were leaving the manor and I'm certain one of them was Jack Price.'

'I expect you're right, but as long as he doesn't approach the house you shouldn't be in any danger. They have drop-off points inland to use when necessary.'

'Where?'

'Anywhere that is suitable.'

'Is it likely they would use the stables at the manor?'

'I think it's highly likely. Since Silas died the outbuildings will provide the perfect hiding place.'

'But...what if they were using it before Uncle Silas died? Would he have known?'

'I imagine he did, but as I told you before, it's a foolish man who doesn't turn a blind eye to the workings of the smugglers. They often pay people to keep quiet—especially if there's a big run. Usually it's small fishing boats, their owners out to make a little money, but for those who have got rich out of the business—Jack Price coming to mind—they have bigger, faster craft that will outrun the Revenue men. When they come ashore with the cargo, that's where the horses come in, a great number of horses, to carry a large cargo away from the coast before dawn.'

Having come to a wall separating one part of the garden from another at a lower level, he paused, leaning against it and holding her gaze with his own. 'There is something else. You said there were two things you wanted to talk to me about.'

'Yes. When I was out riding the other day, I rode further than I intended. I ended up at Trevean—which I now know is where Jack Price lives.'

Immediately, his expression hardened. 'It is. Did he see you?'

'I'm afraid so.'

'Please don't tell me you were alone.'

'No. Graham was with me. We exchanged few words, but what he did divulge was that he knows about Tobias—that you have a child here at Clifton House. He asked me what I knew about it. I told him I knew nothing about a child.'

'Someone must have talked. I expected it to happen at some time.'

'What will you do?'

He shrugged. 'What can I do? I will have to be extra-vigilant.' He moved closer to where she stood so still. 'Now, if I am to stay, what would you like to talk about? Excluding smugglers and children.'

Standing beside him and looking at the garden below, she said, 'About anything. What do you suggest?'

The answer was slow in coming. 'Anything? Then why don't you begin by telling me something about yourself?'

Tilly laughed softly. 'About me? But I'm not in the least interesting.'

'I disagree. Everyone has something interesting to tell about themselves, Miss Anderson—even you. All my sins have been revealed to you.'

'What? All of them?' she teased.

'Maybe not all.' Reaching out, he gently fingered one of her glossy curls admiringly. 'You have beautiful hair, Miss Anderson—the most beautiful hair I have seen on a woman.'

'And you have known many to measure me by,' she remarked.

'Some,' he said, not bothering to deny it. 'I freely admit that I didn't live the life of a saint before I went to Spain.'

'And now you have returned? Will you revert to your old ways?'

He smiled and shook his head. 'I don't think so. A lot has happened to me in the past year.' His eyes captured Tilly's, a lazy, seductive smile passing across his handsome face, curling his lips, and against her will she felt herself being drawn towards him, knowing the sensible thing to do would be to step back, but she was too inexperienced and affected by him to do that. Belated warning bells screamed through her head and her eyes became fixed on his finely sculptured mouth as he came closer still and she knew he was going to kiss her.

## Chapter Seven

Tilly was trapped and she knew it. She was mesmerised by him, like a moth to a flame, and she felt her heart suddenly start pounding in a quite unpredictable manner. He was looking into her eyes, holding her spellbound, weaving some magic web around her from which there was no escape.

She favoured him with a melting smile, which made Lord Clifton's blood run warm in his veins and the heat of it move to his belly. 'I want to kiss you, Miss Anderson—if you don't mind, that is.'

'Yes—I mean, no…'

Taking her hand, he drew her close, his mouth almost brushing her lips. 'It doesn't matter,' he said huskily.

The darkening of his eyes, the naked passion she saw in their depths, seemed to work a strange spell on Tilly, but it was his tone and not his words that conquered her, and, without knowing what she was doing, she found herself moving closer still.

His arms came around her and her entire body began to tremble with desire and fear. There was nothing she could do to still the quiver of anticipation as he lowered his head and covered her mouth with his own. The contact was like an exquisite explosion inside her.

The shock of his lips on hers was one of wild, indescribable sweetness and sensuality as he claimed a kiss of violent tenderness, evoking feelings she had never felt before. Richard Coulson had kissed her once, but it had been nothing like this. This was a man several years older, experienced, worldly, who could have any woman he wanted at his feet.

Imprisoned by his protective embrace and seduced by his mouth and strong, caressing hands, which slid down the curve of her spine to the swell of her buttocks and back to her arms, her neck, burning wherever they touched, Tilly clung to him. Her body responded eagerly, melting with the primitive sensations that went soaring through her, her lips beginning to move against his with increasing abandon as she felt his hunger, unwittingly increasing it.

The sweetness of the kiss, of yielding to it, made her confused with longing. When he finally withdrew his mouth from hers an eternity later, Tilly reluctantly surfaced from the glorious Eden where he had sent her, her face suffused with languor and passion, her eyes luminous. His powerful masculinity had been an assault on her senses. She had been unable to resist him. She swallowed a smile. Aunt Charlotte would have an apoplectic fit if she should see her kissing their host.

Lord Clifton touched her cheek with his finger, looking down at her upturned face, and in that instant they both acknowledged that a flame had ignited between them. 'I do believe you have cast a spell on me, for I do not seem to have the strength or the inclination to resist you. I have been too long alone, too long on the move, too long looking for Cassie, my life often fraught with danger. Little did I know that as soon as I reached Devon, I would encounter someone like you.'

Tilly laughed softly. 'I think we will both remember our first encounter. I had only been in Devon twenty-four hours myself when you landed on the beach and played havoc with my temper.'

'So,' he said, leaning against the wall and folding his arms across his chest. He was a tactician by nature and a frontal assault wasn't always to be relied upon. There were often more effective ways, but he wanted to know all there was to know about her. 'What of you? I am curious as to the real reason that brought you to Devon. You are a beautiful young woman. I would have thought you would have the whole of London at your feet.'

'Not quite,' she said carefully as she gathered her thoughts, deciding to stick as close to the truth as possible while disclosing nothing about her unpleasant affair with Richard Coulson. Having grown closer to Lord Clifton over the past weeks, she sensed that their relationship might progress. And now that he had kissed her once more, she was beginning to think he was of a mind to take things further—perhaps even to offer marriage.

If she told him about Richard, there was a danger that it would fundamentally change the newly developed accord between them. Perhaps it was selfish of her, but she hoped he would never find out.

'My coming out is next Season—if I agree to fall in with everyone's wishes, that is. When Charles got the letter informing him that Uncle Silas had left him his property in Devon, but was unable to come himself, Aunt Charlotte and I couldn't resist coming to take a look.'

'And now you have seen it, do you think you could you live here—in Devon?'

He seemed to be watching her carefully, waiting for her response to his question. Half turning, she let her gaze drift towards the sea in the distance. 'Yes, I think I could,' she said softly. Turning her head, she looked at him. He, too, had turned and was looking at the sea.

She looked at his proud profile etched against the sky, strands of his dark hair stirring slightly in the breeze. His strong hands were by his side, his feet planted firmly on familiar ground. Here was a man in his own element—a man she believed she could love. Suddenly, she could not bear the thought of taking up her life in London—or the thought that she might lose him.

'I think we should return to the house,' she said. 'We will have been missed and Aunt Charlotte will more than likely scold me for being out here alone with you.'

'In which case I agree. We should return—but I will invite you back to Clifton House very soon.'

'You are a very gracious host.'

'I can be charming when I am doing what I like to do.'

'I suppose we all can.'

'I want to know all about you, Miss Anderson. Are you happy in London—with your family and the hustle and bustle of town?'

'I'm as happy as most people,' she replied as they made their way slowly back to the house. 'Although happiness is rarely a permanent state. One would be fortunate to achieve that.'

'And are you happy now—at this moment?' he asked, glancing sideways at her.

She hesitated before answering. 'Yes—I am. I am interested in this change to my environment—being close to the sea and the solitude. It is all so new to me.'

He walked on, seeming to contemplate her reply in thoughtful silence. Tilly found a certain pleasure in watching him. She felt very strongly about him. He was the sort of person she disliked most. It was more amusing and interesting to have deep feelings about people and she was one to have such feelings. She disliked or she loved—and she did both most intensely, which often made life most exhausting. One thing she was certain about was that she was looking forward to the days ahead spent in this man's company and getting to know him better.

The evening over, Lord Clifton handed them up into the carriage and closed the door. They drove past the oaks and deer that had so delighted Tilly earlier. In the gathering dusk a lowering copper-and-gold-toned sun cast elongated shadows across the land.

Settling against the upholstery, she let her eyes drift to the sea in the distance. It was still light enough for her to see where it met the sky on the horizon. She was unable to still the confusion of thoughts in her head. Her mind was preoccupied with that moment of intimacy in the garden, when Lord Clifton had kissed her.

Closing her eyes, she allowed the memory of the kiss to invade her mind—the kiss, vibrant and alive, soft, insistent and sensual. When he'd bent his head and placed his lips on hers, she'd wanted it to go on and on and to kiss him back with soul-destroying passion, to feel his hands on her bare flesh—and more.

Dear, sweet Lord! How could she have felt like that? That one kiss and the strange feelings and emotions it had brought had changed her. A peculiar inner excitement touched her cheeks with a flush of soft pink, and a special sparkle was in her eyes at the memory. Aunt Charlotte was seated across from her and her sharp eyes picked up on it.

'You are enjoying your time in Devon, Tilly?' she asked. 'You look pensive—has something happened? I noted you were gone a while—as was Lord Clifton.'

'We took a walk in the garden. Where Devon is concerned, I could live all my life here. I love everything about it—the scent of the woods and the sea. It's so clean and fresh—so very different from London.'

'And much kinder to one's health than the dirt and grime and the smog of the city, although Cranford is a lovely place to live. You could spend more time there if you wished. I am sure Anna would love to have you stay for longer periods.'

'Yes—I know she would. But I do so love it here—so much so that I would not mind if we were never to return to London.'

'Which we will have to do when Charles leaves for India.'

'I expect we will, but I don't see why I should live there. I'm going to ask Charles to let me come back—to live in the house indefinitely. Let's face it, Aunt Charlotte, when he goes to India he could be away for years—and he has no desire to live in Devon anyway. I don't see why he would object.'

'Are you serious about this, Tilly?'

'Very. It's what I want. All I have to do is persuade Charles. And if I do, Aunt Charlotte, if you have a mind to, you can come and live with me. I know you like it down here.'

'I do—very much. I believe you could find real happiness here—and then, of course,' she said, with a knowing smile, 'there is Lord Clifton. Such a charming man.'

'Yes—he is,' Tilly replied, averting her eyes.

'I have noted your sudden interest in His Lordship. You told me you met on two occasions and yet he mentioned meeting you on the beach.'

'Yes, briefly—and again when he came to the house to visit Mrs Carstairs. I did tell you.' Tilly hadn't told her about the night when the smugglers had come for the horses. She couldn't see the point in worrying her aunt unnecessarily. But when it had entered the conversation at the dinner table, her aunt had picked up on it.

'Did you really see the smugglers come during the night?'

'Yes, Aunt Charlotte—briefly. Apparently, when they have a lot of contraband to move, they borrow people's horses, returning them before sunrise.'

'Goodness me! That is shocking.'

'I agree, but there is nothing one can do about it.'

'You will have to be careful, Tilly.'

'Don't worry about me, Aunt Charlotte. I can take care of myself.'

'And if Lord Clifton decides to pursue you? He is a handsome man—and you are an attractive young woman.'

'I'm sure Lord Clifton has enough to deal with just

now. He is grieving for his sister, don't forget, and he lost both his parents just before that. I doubt he has a mind to pursue anyone at present.'

Tilly did not see Lord Clifton for several days. Aunt Charlotte was keen to see something of the surrounding countryside and they spent their days exploring and walking on the beach. They even managed a trip into Plymouth to do some shopping and went in to Biddycombe often. Mr and Mrs Ainsley came to tea, as did Reverend Leighton and his wife. The Reverend was pleased to see them among the congregation on a Sunday.

Two weeks passed in this manner and then one day a letter came from Charles informing them that he was to leave for India with the Company sooner than he had expected and he would like them to return to London before he went. A cloud descended on Tilly, less over the mention of Charles leaving than because she would miss seeing Lord Clifton. She would live in hope that Charles would agree to allow her to return to Drayton Manor indefinitely.

The sharpness of her disappointment that he might not took her by surprise. God alone knew what she had been hoping for. Perhaps that the close relationship that had developed between her and Lord Clifton would oblige him to ask her to stay. He could not know how much he had come to matter to her and his absence from her life would be a source of grief.

There was no use denying it or fighting her attraction for him. Nor could she regret it. How could she regret knowing this man, even if it was for such a short time?

Until then her heart and body had been dormant, waiting for the spark that would make it explode into life.

If Lord Clifton had not ignited it, she would have spent her whole existence not knowing what it felt like to have a fire inside her soul, would never have known that such a wild, sweet passion could exist. Better by far to experience that passion for such a short time than never to have known it at all, even if it brought such pain and heartache, or to die not knowing such joy was possible.

It was unfortunate that now she had had a taste of the intoxicating sweetness of Lord Clifton's kiss, she realised it was completely separate from what she really yearned for—an intimacy of the heart.

Although Tilly didn't know it, Lucas was missing her and, try as he might, being kept busy with important estate matters, he couldn't get to see her. Having been told by Reverend Leighton that having received a letter from her brother, she was to return to London shortly, he was determined to see her.

He had hoped they would have had more time together, to get to know each other better, to eventually ask her to be his wife. She was young and had yet to make her debut and for some reason she was opposed to marriage, which did puzzle him somewhat, but if her willing response to his kiss was an indication of her feelings for him, then he felt she could be persuaded. He could not bear to lose her.

He found it impossible to banish her from his mind. She had a way of getting under his skin and insinuating herself into his mind. No other woman could outshine her. She was physically appealing, with a face and body that drugged his mind, but she was also appealing in other ways, with an intelligent sharpness of mind and a clever wit that he admired, making her pleasant company and interesting to be with.

He was woken when Florence screamed—indeed, it was so loud that it woke the whole house. Immediately, he was out of bed, thrusting his arms into his robe and dashing along the landing to the nursery. Florence, in her night attire, was utterly distraught.

'Oh, My Lord,' she wailed when he appeared. 'Such a terrible thing has happened. Tobias has gone—disappeared. He wasn't there when I went to feed him. Where can he be?' she said, looking wildly around her as though the child might, at the age of five months, have climbed out of his cot and be somewhere in the room. 'I fed him and put him down. He was asleep in no time like the good baby he is.'

Her voice rose to fever pitch, for Florence had experienced the horrors of the battlefields in Spain and witnessed the full horror of nightmares of losing her own child at birth, but surely this was the worst.

Immediately, Lucas took charge of the hysterical Florence, sitting her in a chair.

'Calm down, Florence, and tell me what has happened. Did you hear anything, see anything?'

She shook her head, her eyes filled with fear. By now, servants had gathered on the landing and were peering inside the nursery, curious as to what all the fuss was about. Lucas went out to them.

'The child has gone. I want every one of you to search the house—inside and out. He must be found.'

Florence came forcefully towards him, a fierce look in her eyes. 'She's got him. She's taken him, I just know it.'

Lucas stared at her. 'Who, Florence? Who has got him?'

'That Lizzy who works in the kitchen. Lizzy Tomlinson. She's a sly one, that girl, always creeping about up here on one pretext or another, asking questions—questions about Tobias.' Suddenly, she seemed to crumple and tears flowed from her eyes. 'Oh, where is he—my lamb? Why would she do such a cruel thing as to snatch a baby from his cot—and who will feed him?'

Lucas indicated to one of the maids to come inside and console Florence. Fury burned inside him. He knew exactly who was capable of kidnapping Tobias. Jack Price. It had to be him. Had not Miss Anderson told him that Price knew there was a child at Clifton House? He was surprised he had not taken him before. Returning to his room, he dressed quickly and was soon striding to the stables.

He didn't have to ride far. Lizzy Tomlinson was found outside the gates with the baby in her arms. She was about to pass him to two of Jack Price's men waiting there with a wagon. The child had started to cry, alerting those who were looking for him. The two miscreants absconded without the child and, after being questioned and confirming it was Jack Price who had ordered the child's kidnapping, Lizzy Tomlinson was dismissed from her position at Clifton House.

## Chapter Eight

Jack Price's attempted abduction of Tobias had given Lucas much to think about. He could no longer keep Tobias's existence secret and while ever Jack Price lived, he would pose a constant danger to the child. Something had to be done. After decades of feuding with the Price family, Lucas decided it was time to face up to the old man, Ned Price.

On the day he rode to Trevean, Lucas had no doubt in his mind about Ned Price's feelings toward him or his unexpected visit. He hadn't seen the old man for a good many years. Ned might refuse to see him in retaliation for past grievances, but Lucas refused to dwell on that possibility. Prior to this, he had made quite sure Jack was out of the area.

Fortunately, Ned Price agreed to see him. He was admitted into the large, sprawling building perched on the cliffs above the sea. Without the touch of a woman— Ned Price's wife had died many years ago and he had never remarried—the house was badly in need of renovation and modernisation.

Ned Price was a man of around seventy years and not in the best of health. He used to be a big, upright man, but now he was gaunt and stooped with a sparse covering of white hair.

He greeted Lucas warily in his study, studying him closely with penetrating grey eyes.

'Lord Clifton! Forgive me if I appear surprised,' he said, his voice deep and rasping. 'A lot of tides have rolled on to Devon's shores since any Kingsley graced the halls of Trevean.'

'Yes—and many more will roll in before there is another.'

'It must be an important matter to bring you here.'

'It is—and I am not here to heal the breach. Had I the choice I would not be here at all. I will be brief and to the point and as civil as I can be.'

'I would appreciate that. As you see, my health is not what it was.'

Ned Price lounged back in a high-backed chair, motioning for Lucas to be seated in the one opposite. He did so, eyeing the man across from him.

'I intend to get this ordeal over with as quickly as possible.'

'You know Edmund is dead?' Ned said quietly.

'Yes—I was in Spain at the time.'

The old man nodded. 'He should not have gone. He took after me—not wild and headstrong like Jack. They were always at odds with each other. I taught Edmund all I know about building boats. Jack was a disappointment. The days are gone when I begged him to find an honourable profession.'

'You have no one to blame but Jack and yourself for

what happened. Jack resented the fact that Edmund was the eldest, the heir, that he would inherit your estate and boatyard on your death. Edmund was content to work the boatyard—it was what he was good at.'

Ned glanced resentfully at him. 'I don't need you to tell me that.'

'No. Rumour has it that you are to sell it.'

'So, that's why you've come. And if I am, what's that to do with you? Don't tell me you want to buy it.'

'Yes. And when I tell you what I know you will agree.'

He laughed, a harsh, humourless sound. 'You fool, Kingsley. Jack would never agree. A Kingsley owning the Price boatyard? Never.' He shook his head, looking away. 'I have to sell. Jack is only interested in one thing—you don't need me to spell it out. When he's not up to his illegal activities, he's wenching and gaming over in Plymouth. He profits from the smuggling he's invested in.'

He grimaced. 'It won't last. Jack has a streak which will get him into trouble with the law, which he cannot evade for ever, which is why I've decided to sell the boatyard. Trevean and the yard have always been locked together. It's a hard thing for a man to acknowledge his son has no interest in what keeps the family afloat. But Jack would rather see it go to rack and ruin before letting a Kingsley set foot in it.'

'Jack doesn't have to know.'

Ned Price looked at him closely, eyes narrowed. 'What are you saying?' he demanded. 'That I deceive my son?'

'That is precisely what I'm saying. What I am about to disclose is for your ears alone. Do you understand?'

'I am intrigued. You'd better tell me?'

'Two nights ago, a child was kidnapped from Clifton House, a child who is just five months old. Fortunately, we managed to apprehend the servant who was working for your son. It was Jack who arranged to have the child abducted.'

Ned Price stared at him in confusion. 'Jack? What in God's name are you talking about? What would Jack want with a child?'

'The child is called Tobias. He is Edmund's son. His mother was my sister, Cassie.' His words rendered Ned speechless. 'They wanted to be together. I refused to sanction the match—which I am sure is what you would have done. My sister was determined they would be together, that not even Bonaparte's army would come between them. She followed Edmund to Spain.

'When I discovered what she had done, I went after her. It was no easy matter tracking her down. I saw Edmund before he went into battle. I also saw that Cassie was with child, his child. I arranged for them to be married—shortly before Edmund was killed.'

'And your sister?'

'She died in childbirth. Edmund and Cassie are buried together in Spain.'

'And the boy?'

'He is at Clifton House. I promised Cassie before she died that I would take care of him. Somehow, Jack got wind of it and tried to abduct him. I have no doubt he sees Tobias as a threat to his inheritance. With Edmund's death your estate would have passed to Jack. I will leave you to imagine what Jack would do with a five-month-old child who stands in the way of what he now considers to be his inheritance.'

'So, I have a grandson—Edmund's son.'

'He's a fine boy.'

'But...what has all this to do with you buying the boatyard? If the boy is indeed Edmund's son, then it will pass to him in time. Knowing this, I will not sell.'

'No? Think about it. Yes, it is what Edmund would have wanted, but will Jack allow it? I cannot trust him and you will not be around for ever. Can you imagine that Jack will let such an injustice go unavenged? Jack rules by brutality. He served a year in prison for assaulting a man—in fact, he will probably end his days in gaol. Is that anything to be proud of?

'Leave Jack Trevean if you must. That is your affair. The only way to safeguard the boatyard for Tobias's future is to sell it to me on the understanding that when he comes of age it will be his to do with as he sees fit. If you allow me to buy the yard, it will be Tobias's when he is of an age to work it himself. That I promise you.'

'And Jack?'

'Would not know that I am the buyer—not for a long time.'

'You are asking me to deceive my son?'

'I am asking you to do this for Edmund.'

'And in the meantime? Who will work the yard?'

'There will be no change. You have some skilled workers. It will continue to be worked as you yourself have done.'

Ned Price nodded slowly, thinking it over. 'It is profitable now, but I'll not pretend. The shipbuilding business needs careful scheduling to run efficiently and profitably. You also have competition. The Price boatyard is not the only boatyard on the coast. There are times when customers cannot meet their investments. Terms have to be renegotiated, but often you are left with a half-built vessel. Overheads of a shipyard are immense.'

'I have the income of the Clifton Estate to help support it in times of crisis. I am willing to take the risk for Tobias's sake.'

'There will be legalities involved. The investors will have to be told that the yard has changed hands.'

'I deal with legalities on a daily basis. I will ensure that everything is done legally and above board and with your approval. I have a lawyer who will act as my representative and therefore my name will not appear. It will secure Tobias's future.'

'You have it all worked out.'

'I am up against Jack. It has to be done this way. If you agree, I will have my lawyer draw up the documents. It's a complicated business, but it will work providing Jack doesn't find out I am the owner.'

'How do I know I can trust you?'

Lucas produced a letter from the inside pocket of his coat. 'This should convince you. It is from Edmund. Fearing he would not come through, hoping Cassie would bear a son, he wrote it before he went into battle.'

With trembling fingers, Ned Price opened the letter and read it. At length he raised his head. 'He says he wants your sister to raise the child at Clifton House.'

'Since Cassie is no longer able to do that, the onus is on me to do it for her.'

'May I keep this?'

Lucas ignored the mistiness he saw in those grey eyes. 'Yes, of course.'

'And my grandson? Can I see him?'

'It will be arranged at a time when Jack is not around.'

The old man lowered his head, deep in thought. When he again looked at Lucas, there was a determined look in his eyes, as if he had come to a decision. 'I'm not ignorant of Jack's way of doing things. I have no sway over what he does any more. You are right. Jack is a danger to the child. How will you keep him safe?'

'That is something I have already decided. I intend to send him away for the time being—somewhere Jack will not think of looking.' When Lucas made to walk away, Ned Price's next words halted him.

'One more thing. Your parents—I heard what happened to them. For what it's worth I was sorry to hear of it. A storm, they said.'

Lucas paused in his stride and then he turned and fixed him with a hard gaze. 'There was no storm that day.'

'Then...what happened?'

'I think you should ask your son about that. I have proof his vessel was in the vicinity that day, but no one will talk. If I find he was responsible for the death of my parents... That he should still be walking about is unthinkable.'

A darkness entered Ned Price's eyes. 'If it is true, then I will finish him myself—even though he is my son.'

Lucas nodded and said nothing more.

Lucas arrived at Drayton Manor with the intention of seeing Miss Anderson's Aunt Charlotte, only to be told by the maid that Miss Charlotte Anderson was resting and her niece was in the garden.

'I shall go and fetch her this instant if you will be so good as to wait in the library.'

'No,' he said, as she was about to disappear. 'Thank you, but do not trouble yourself. I shall find her myself.'

He stepped briskly outside and was walking along the paths, drawn towards the sound of something creaking among a group of trees way beyond the house. He moved through the shrubbery, following the winding narrow path until he eventually came to a clearing.

There seemed to be a golden mist about him, heightening the hues of a beautiful copper beech, resplendent in all its summer glory, its branches spread out like a gigantic parasol. Hanging from one of them was a swing and sitting on its board was Miss Anderson, gently swooping to and fro, careful not to let her feet touch the ground, her wonderful mane of raven-black hair flowing behind her.

Momentarily taken aback by the sight of her, Lucas paused, transfixed on seeing her like this. He had forgotten what a wonderful rich colour her hair was and seeing her again made every one of his senses clamour for her. There was that same fierce tug to his senses on being near her as there had been that time he had seen her on the beach when she had fallen into the sea.

She really was a beautiful young woman, with her softly rounded limbs, the way her head moved with a swaying grace and a soft, inviting, lilting expression to her lips. He watched as her skirts and petticoats lifted when she stretched out her legs to gather momentum on the swing, revealing her shapely stockinged calves and fancy blue garters.

With her translucent skin and her violet eyes, which were as wide and solemn as a baby owl's, she had an ethereal quality. His heart took a savage, painful leap at the sight of her. She seemed like someone looking more at home here than she would in the salons of London.

He wanted to go to her, take her in his arms, kiss her and tell her how he felt. Ever since they had met, he had been plagued with so many conflicting emotions where she was concerned, becoming lost in a turmoil of contradiction and insoluble dilemma.

Yet until he had settled the business of buying the Price boatyard and making sure that Tobias was safe—and waiting to see what Miss Anderson's brothers had in store for her in London—he was resolute in his decision not to further their relationship until it was over.

Absorbed in her thoughts, Tilly did not realise Lord Clifton was there until he stepped in front of the swing a short distance away. Shocked out of her reverie, immediately she scraped her feet on the ground and stopped, the intimacy of their time spent in the garden at Clifton House springing instantly to the fore.

Lightning seemed to scorch across the space between them, burning, eliminating everything in its path. Everything was obliterated but that invisible physical force searing through her body, so that she felt her flesh throb in agony as every nerve sprang to a trembling awareness of him—and instinctively, she knew it was the same for him.

An unbidden flare of excitement rose up in the pit of her stomach. She watched him, wishing she could cool the waves of heat that mounted her cheeks. She left the swing and stood utterly still. Like a free spirit she faced him, her head poised at a questioning angle, her hair spread over her shoulders like a shining black cape. Until that moment she had thought she remembered exactly what he looked like, his well-chiselled features stamped indelibly on her mind.

'Lord Clifton—you take me by surprise,' she said, forcing herself to ignore the fluttering in her stomach.

'I didn't mean to do that. So,' he said, stopping in front of her, 'no sooner do you arrive in Devon than you are to return to London.'

'Yes. How do you know that?'

'Reverend Leighton told me. Were you going to leave without telling me?'

She shook her head, brushing back a stray lock of dark hair from her eyes, eyes that were bright and inquiring. 'I would have written. It's come as something of a surprise. I was hoping Charles would not be leaving for India until next year.'

'I came to see your aunt, but I was told she is resting. The maid said this was where I would find you.'

'As you see.'

Lord Clifton's eyes softened and a slow smile curved his lips as his eyes swept slowly over her. 'You looked charming on the swing,' he murmured. 'There was a moment when the tantalising young lady eluded me and I saw how you must have looked as a girl.'

A rush of warmth pervaded Tilly's whole being, reawakening the nerve centre which had been numbed since she had last seen him. Hearing the warm words, being here with him now, she felt a sudden, keener awareness of her feelings for him.

The feeling was so strong that for an instant she had a wild impulse to tell him how she felt, but she recollected herself just in time. The man in front of her had merely complimented her on how she looked on the swing and might not wish to listen to a declaration of her feelings.

'It isn't so long ago that I was just a girl. But something tells me you have not come to talk about the garden—or the swing, which Graham very kindly made for me. You have something on your mind—I can tell.'

He smiled. 'How perceptive you are. You are right. The reason I am here is because I wish to enlist your aid in a matter that is of extreme importance, which you will no doubt consider a gross imposition. It concerns Tobias—and Jack Price.'

Lord Clifton's handsome, aggressive face became hard in that particular way Tilly had seen before when he had mentioned Jack Price. His eyes were filled with a mixture of rage, apprehension and dread—dread that Price would succeed in harming Tobias.

'Price has shown his hand. I thought he would,' he said bitterly. 'How dare he make a child the instrument of his vengeance?'

'I am sorry to hear that. But I cannot see what that has to do with me or my aunt. Why are you here, Lord Clifton? Although if you would prefer to wait and speak to Aunt Charlotte then you may do so.'

'No, you would have to know anyway. You are to leave for London. Would you take Tobias and Florence with you? While ever he is here, he is in danger.'

Tilly stared at him. He was watching her uncertainly.

She could feel the tension in him. This really was important to him. 'You...want us to take Tobias with us?'

'Believe me, Miss Anderson, I do not ask this lightly. I did not want to come here...to burden you with this. I have no right, but I am desperate.'

'Why? Has something happened?'

'You might say that. Two nights ago, Florence woke to find Tobias had been taken from his crib. One of the servants whose family is answerable to Jack Price took him. Fortunately, she had only taken him minutes before and we managed to apprehend her as she was leaving the grounds.'

'But that is terrible. Was he harmed in any way?'

'No—just hungry. Apparently, the maid was to have passed him on to one of Price's cohorts waiting in the lane outside the gates.'

'I see. Then if you have him back and he is unharmed, I fail to see how we can be of help. London is a long way to travel with a small child.'

'So was Spain, Miss Anderson,' he said pointedly.

'Yes,' she said quietly. She didn't have to be told what an arduous journey, fraught with many dangers, that must have been for both him and Florence with a young baby. 'I—I am sure it was.'

Noting her hesitation, his lips set in a grim line. 'If you have an aversion to my request, then I will bother you no longer.'

Tilly stared at him as if he had struck her. Lord Clifton saw the pupils of her eyes dilate until the violet had almost disappeared, and all the blood drained from her face until even her lips were pale.

'If you think that, then you do not know me. You

have never been more wrong. No matter what my circumstances are, if I were the meanest, poorest creature on God's earth, I would put the welfare, the safety, of any child before myself.'

His jaw tightened, his eyes burning furiously down into hers, while feeling a surge of relief and thankfulness that she had spoken as she had. 'In all conscience it would appear I have no alternative but to ask your help if I am to keep Tobias safe. His very life is at stake if he remains in Devon. Price will not give up. While ever Tobias is alive, he is a threat to Price.'

'Are the servants aware that Tobias is your sister's son?'

'It's difficult to keep something like that secret. Florence keeps very much to herself in the nursery, but servants talk—so, yes, I believe they will know by now.'

'What will you tell them when Florence and Tobias leave Clifton House?'

'Florence will let it be known she is visiting her sick sister in Dawlish. Since Tobias is dependent on her then it is only natural that he goes with her.'

'And the girl who tried to abduct him?'

'Has been dismissed.'

Tilly hesitated. How could she possibly travel all the way to London with a baby—and how on earth would she explain that to Charles and William? Then came the realisation that there was no guarantee that Charles would allow her to return to Devon.

Even though Lord Clifton had made her no promises, agreeing to take Tobias and Florence to London had given her a link to him. Everything paled beside this. She did not want the strands which tied them together to unravel just yet—if at all.

'Very well,' she conceded. 'You are right. Tobias must be kept safe at all costs. I would never forgive myself if anything were to happen to him because we refused to take him to London. I will help you—*we* will help you—I am sure Aunt Charlotte will agree with me. Tobias has to come first.'

Lord Clifton's expression softened. 'Thank you. I can't tell you how grateful I am. When do you expect to leave for London?'

'Two days. Naturally we are going to have to speak to Aunt Charlotte before anything can be arranged for definite about Tobias, but I cannot see a problem, although I imagine she will have a few choice words to say to me when she finds out I have known about your nephew all along. We will go inside and see if she is available. So you see, Lord Clifton, I may have been painted many things, but I am not uncaring.'

His gaze lingered on her face. 'I do not recall saying you were,' he murmured.

Hearing the tenderness in his tone, Tilly felt her stomach lurch and she turned her head to hide her confusion. 'No, perhaps not.'

On a more tender note that made Tilly's heart flutter and brought her head up, he said, 'There is nothing ordinary about you, is there, Miss Anderson?'

'I hope not. I should hate to be predictable. No doubt you disapprove.'

'Most certainly not. I applaud the wildness and individuality I first saw in you.'

'As I recall it was my bad temper that you noticed the day when we met on the beach.'

Lord Clifton laughed quietly as he fell in to step beside her as they walked back to the house. 'That is something I will always remember about you.'

'Will you take Gracie back with you? Thank you for letting me ride her.'

'She will be at Clifton House, if you manage to persuade your brother to let you return.'

'Yes, thank you. I hope he will.'

'The smugglers are going to miss the use of your horses.'

'That's too bad. I was never comfortable with that. I can only hope that when the time comes for us to leave, they have not made use of them during the night, otherwise we will not get very far before they have to rest.'

'We must work out what is to be done. I intend leaving for London myself shortly. I have some business to take care of, but I have yet to finalise my plans. By that time, I hope to have bought the boatyard, or at least set proceedings into motion. Will you be making for London or Berkshire? I must give you the address of my cousin and his wife. They won't mind taking care of Tobias and Florence until I can get there.'

'If Aunt Charlotte agrees to Tobias coming with us, then we will be going to her house in Chelsea village before I go on to Cranford. If, for some reason, your cousin is not at home or there is a problem, then we will take him to Cranford. William and Anna have a son who is of a similar age to Tobias. Anna is involved in many charitable works, including opening a school for less advantaged children, so I'm sure they wouldn't mind us staying there.'

Having reached the house, they went inside to find Aunt Charlotte had come down from her rest and was in the parlour.

'Ah, Lord Clifton,' she said, smiling broadly at the sight of their visitor. 'How nice to see you again. I'm sorry I was not able to receive you—I do like my little nap in the afternoons, more so since coming to Devon, which I put down to the sea air—but I see my niece has been taking care of you.'

'Aunt Charlotte, Lord Clifton has something to ask of you—something you need to consider very carefully. He is faced with a problem and he believes we can help.'

'Oh?' she said, looking from one to the other. 'I am intrigued. Please, Lord Clifton, take a seat and tell me how I can help you.'

Lord Clifton did as she bade, seating himself opposite and crossing his long legs as he proceeded to tell her his reason for coming to Drayton Manor. He went on to tell her a good deal of what had transpired since he had arrived back in England—all about Jack Price and his illicit activities, the attempted abduction and the threat he posed to Tobias. She listened avidly, her eyes fixed on him in fascination, sometimes with shock, but mainly with great concern.

'Dear me,' she said when he fell silent. 'What a tragedy. That poor motherless child. I can't believe anyone would want to hurt him.'

'What do you think, Aunt Charlotte? Will you agree to take the child with us? If Lord Clifton truly believes that he is in danger at this present time, then we cannot refuse to help in any way we can if he is to be kept safe. He has asked that we take him to his cousin in London. Lord Clifton is to travel to London himself shortly. Maybe by then it will be safe for Tobias to return to Devon with him.'

Aunt Charlotte nodded. 'I see. If it will help you, then we will take him with us. There is room enough in the coach for all of us.'

'Thank you. I am most grateful.'

'I will leave you to make the arrangements, Lord Clifton.'

'Should Lord Clifton's relatives not be at home, I thought Tobias and Florence could go to Cranford, Aunt Charlotte. I'm sure William and Anna won't mind—Tobias will be company for their Thomas.'

'You seem to have it all thought out.'

'Not really. It just seems to be the most sensible thing to do.'

'Very well,' her aunt said. 'I can only hope the journey will not be too taxing with a baby in the coach.'

'I don't think there will be a problem about my cousin not being at home. It is normal practice for them to go to their estate in Oxford closer to Christmas. I will write telling them to expect you. In the meantime, I would appreciate it if you did not mention this to anyone—especially Mrs Carstairs. No one must know Tobias is to go with you to London. I will arrange the time and place where we can meet. It must be kept from Dunstan and Graham until you are away from here.'

'Do not worry, Lord Clifton,' Charlotte said when Lord Clifton got up to leave. 'You can rest assured that our lips are sealed.'

Tilly walked with Lord Clifton to the door, when she paused and looked at him. 'We will take Tobias to London and keep him there until the time when it is safe for him to return to Devon.'

'I know you will.'

He wanted to say more, Tilly could tell, but he remained silent. She wanted to say more, too, words that would make it easier for them both, but the words remained clogged in her throat.

'I will let you know the details,' he said. 'Until then we will go about our daily lives with no hint of what we intend.'

'Very well. If we don't hear from you, we will know you have changed your mind about the whole thing and we will leave for London.'

'I won't change my mind. This is the only thing I can think of to keep Tobias safe for the present.'

## Chapter Nine

When Ned Price arrived at Clifton House and was introduced to his grandson, Lucas saw the raw emotion in the man's face. Losing Edmund had affected him deeply, but knowing he had left him his son went a long way to lessening the pain.

Afterwards the two men sat over a brandy to discuss Tobias's future and the sale of the boatyard.

''Tis ironic, wouldn't you say, Lord Clifton, the two of us discussing a business proposition? After all, I and many of my forebears were enemies of your family.'

'The irony of it has crossed my mind,' Lucas said smoothly.

'Aye, well, it's done with. I've paid many times for past mistakes and it's a wonder I'm not long since dead. The young lad is what matters now—and he's a fine lad. I trust you to do what is right by him.'

Lucas was silent for a long moment. 'You have my word.'

Ned nodded slowly; his eyes narrowed on the man opposite him. 'I will come and see him again. It's an odd thing, but you are the only person I feel that I can trust.

I knew your grandmother and father and you, Lord Clifton, all as opponents. Sometimes a man comes to respect an enemy more than a friend. There have been few men I would turn my back on, but you I would do so without a qualm.'

Draining his glass, he stood up and without another word left the house to where his carriage waited in the drive. Lucas watched him go. Ned Price's admission had surprised and touched him as few other things had done.

Everything was arranged, the luggage strapped to the coach and Mrs Carstairs was waving them off. She would carry on running the house in her usual efficient way until further notice.

An anxious Tilly sat back with a deep sigh, knowing she would not be at ease until they had left Devon behind.

The coach had passed Biddycombe when they met up with Lord Clifton. He was in a closed carriage with Florence and Tobias. Immediately, he got out and held the door open for Florence. Taking Tobias in his arms, he waited until Florence was seated beside Daphne before passing the child to her. Dunstan and Graham secured their baggage behind the coach.

Tilly climbed out, sensing Lord Clifton's pain on this parting from his nephew. The remorse that gripped her was powerful and sudden.

'I can understand how difficult this is for you,' she said quietly.

'Yes, it is. The last thing I wanted was to send him away.'

He spoke softly and she looked at him. The sheer male beauty of him took her breath. Morning sunlight speared his hair to shining jet. She wondered what he would say if she were to reveal what was in her heart. He didn't know the extent of her feelings, feelings she had for him, deep and abiding feelings, feelings that would last a lifetime. She didn't really know him, either. Beneath the surface he was deep and complex, a man of moods, a man of principle, who cared deeply about his commitments and about those he had lost.

'You have Aunt Charlotte's address in London and Cranford in Berkshire. Should your cousin not be at home, that is where we will take him. You have written to your cousin telling him to expect us?'

'I have.'

'Have you encountered any further trouble from Jack Price?'

'No, none. I pray it remains that way until you are well on your way to London.'

'Yes, we won't delay lest we are seen. Tobias will be well looked after; you can depend on that.'

'I know. It saddens my heart to part with him, but it is for the best.'

'Yes.' She turned from him and as she was about to get into the coach she turned back. She saw his eyes fixed upon her with an expression of such sadness in them that it wrenched her heart.

'Farewell, Lord Clifton.'

And so they began their return journey to London. Florence was a friendly young woman who was excited to be going to London. Tobias was a lovely baby.

His hair was dark brown with tawny lights in it. When he was awake, he gazed at them wonderingly, his little hands curling round anything within his reach.

He was clearly a contented baby and that was something to be relieved about. It would make the journey so much easier. Florence was clearly fond of him. When she dozed Daphne was more than happy to take the child on her knee and entertain him.

'I've never been to London,' Florence said on leaving Devon. 'In fact, until I followed Edgar, my husband, to Spain, I'd never been further than Dawlish, which is where my sister lives. I've all sorts of ideas about it. I've read about it and heard people talk of it and it sounds daunting and exciting at the same time.'

'So it is,' Tilly told her. 'It's a big city, with lots to see and everybody bustling about. It has its lovely, fashionable parts with big houses and parks to see and enjoy, but there is also the other side where poverty abounds. Should Lord Clifton's cousin be out of town we will go on to my brother's house in Berkshire. It's called Cranford and is not unlike Clifton House.'

'I was so grateful to Lord Clifton when he asked me to take care of Tobias. When I lost my husband and then when my baby died, I didn't know what to do. Nothing seemed to matter any more. The conditions were so awful out there.'

'I am so sorry for your loss, Florence. What an awful time you've had. What happened to you happened to Lord Clifton's sister also.'

'I know. We knew each other—being in the same boat, so to speak, with both of us losing our husbands. Except that poor lady lost her life, leaving her baby without a mother—poor little mite. Lord Clifton's arrival was a godsend, I can tell you—although, at the time, his sister gave him what for for following her. I'm right glad he did, otherwise there's no telling where her bairn would have ended up—or me, for that matter.

'He applied himself to the matter at hand and did what had to be done about getting back to England. With so many people displaced because of the war, some dangerous individuals who would think nothing of shooting you for a coin or a horse, we could not allow fear to take hold. Meeting him made me realise that even though I had lost so much, I still had a lot to live for.'

Only then did Tilly begin to realise what a terrible experience it must have been for Florence. Her heart went out to her. She was also aware of a new side to Lord Clifton she had not seen before, of the way he had taken care of Tobias and Florence with a doggedness and determination born of pain and hopelessness that had pushed him to get back home. An immense pity welled up from the bottom of her heart towards this man and Florence, whose sufferings she was beginning to understand.

'I'm so very sorry for what happened to you, Florence, and I'm glad things turned out for the best.'

'So am I. At least I have a roof over my head—although what I'll do when His little Lordship has no further need of me, I shudder to think.'

'Plenty of time for that later,' Tilly said. 'Perhaps Lord Clifton will keep you on as Tobias's nanny?'

Florence's face broke into a wide smile. 'I don't mind telling you I would welcome that.'

\* \* \*

After five long, tedious days of travel they finally arrived in London. Heading for Mayfair where Lord Clifton's cousins, Lord and Lady Marchant, lived, they traversed the streets that were congested and noisy with traffic of every description. London was a city made up of theatres, churches, palaces and lovely parks, the skyline dominated by the twin towers of Westminster Abbey.

The river was a busy waterway, with barges and wherries and boats of every description scurrying up and down like busy beetles. The darker side of the city, where squalor abounded, was made up of gin houses and brothels, where thieves and prostitutes, clerks and thieves rubbed shoulders with members of the nobility looking for less refined entertainment. It was a city of the destitute, of piles of rotting rubbish, but it was also a city of vibrancy and splendour that was the unique essence of London.

Not until they reached the more salubrious area of Mayfair did the roadways become quieter. On finding the house of Lord Marchant, they were informed by his butler that Lady Marchant was not in the best of health so Lord Marchant had taken her to their estate in the country. With that, they had no option other than to go to Charlotte's house in Chelsea village. When Charlotte had received Charles's letter in Devon, asking them to return to London forthwith, she had written to her housekeeper instructing her to have rooms prepared for their arrival.

The house was a large three-storey red brick Queen Anne house with Dutch gables. It was a large comfortable residence close to the river. To the rear was a coach house and stables and a well-planted substantial garden. Once inside, with Tobias nestled against her shoulder wrapped in a shawl and sound asleep, Florence followed the housekeeper and Daphne up the stairs where a room was prepared.

As soon as Charles arrived and called her name, Tilly flew into his arms. After giving her a welcoming hug, then holding her at arm's length, he laughed on seeing her sunburnt face.

'Well, just look at you. Devon clearly suited you.'

'It did, Charles, and I simply love Drayton Manor, as did Aunt Charlotte. It's a lovely old house. You should see it. It's perfect.'

'I don't doubt that. But it's a long way from London.'

'I do so hope you won't sell it. It's close to the sea and the most delightful villages,' she enthused. 'In fact, Charles, I would very much like to live there—if you permit it and keep the house.'

Charles stared at her as if she had taken leave of her senses. 'Live there—permanently? I think you're suffering from too much sun, Tilly. Your place is here—with your family.'

'We'll talk about it later—Aunt Charlotte also loves it down there. We could live there together, but come and see her,' she said, taking his hand and pulling him into the drawing room to greet Aunt Charlotte.

Tilly was proud of her brother. Tall and slim, with deep blue eyes and terribly good-looking, he appeared every inch the successful businessman, which he indubitably was, which the smile he cast on his two favourite people seemed to say.

Aunt Charlotte's face was wreathed in delight as she watched her nephew stride into the room. 'Charles! I can't tell you how good it is to see you at last.'

The following ten minutes were taken up with excited chatter—mostly from Tilly as she told her brother all she had learned about Devon. He was quite happy to listen until the distinct cry of a baby was heard coming from the upper regions of the house.

For a moment silence reigned, then, looking up as if he expected the perpetrator of the cry to materialise through the ceiling, he said, 'Would either of you care to explain why there is a screaming baby in the house?'

Aunt Charlotte looked at Tilly perched on the edge of the sofa. The moment when she would have to inform Charles about their tiny guest could not be put off any longer.

'His name is Tobias, Charles. He is five months old and the nephew of Lucas Kingsley, the Earl of Clifton. Lord Clifton was deeply concerned about the child's safety and asked if we could bring him with us to London.'

Charles stared at her in disbelief. 'Are you completely mad?'

'Not at all. We have our reasons for bringing him here. If you will sit down and listen, I will tell you.'

Which she did as well as she could, while her brother stared at her wide-eyed, trying to take in what she was telling him.

'I cannot believe you have done this,' Charles said flatly when she had finished. 'It was a blasted foolish thing to do. I don't know what possessed you to agree to it.'

'The child was in danger, Charles...'

'From his own uncle? What manner of man would threaten his own nephew—a baby, for heaven's sake?'

'A man as wicked as Jack Price.'

Charles drew himself up out of the chair in frustration, combing his fingers through his hair. 'You have gone too far, Tilly. I sent you to Devon in the hope that you would see the error of your ways over that sordid affair with Richard Coulson—the scandal is still raging, by the way—and you come back with fantastical tales of smugglers and kidnappings.'

'Just the one kidnapping,' Tilly interjected.

'Don't be flippant. It doesn't matter how many. Here we are with a baby to take care of—the nephew of a man none of us has ever heard of.'

'He knows William—at least he has heard of him.'

'Of course he has. William is the Marquess of Elvington, for heaven's sake. Everyone in England and beyond has heard of him.'

'Please, Charles, don't be cross. I know when you sent me to Devon you were only trying to protect me, but I can't bear to think of it. I realise now that I was wrong and stupid and I'm sorry for all the trouble I've caused, but please be reasonable about this. Lord Clifton needed our help at a difficult time. We could not refuse to help him.'

'In fairness to Lord Clifton, Charles,' Aunt Charlotte said quietly, 'he belongs to an important and highly revered family in Devon, whose ancestry is as proud and impressive as that of the Lancasters, with a noble pile to equal that of Cranford. Lord Clifton has suffered greatly recently—losing both his parents at sea followed closely by his beloved sister in Spain. Tobias is the only member of his immediate family he has left.

'The man is desperately trying to get some normality back into his life, but he is bedevilled by the child's paternal uncle—a violent individual who threatens the child's existence. Lord Clifton is to come to London himself shortly. Until then I ask you to bear with the situation.'

'How old is Lord Clifton, Aunt Charlotte?'

'Oh, I wouldn't know—perhaps twenty-eight or nine.'

Charles looked at his sister. 'And you have become friendly with Lord Clifton, Tilly? How friendly?'

Tilly flushed a delicate shade of raspberry. 'A...a little. He...invited us to dine one evening, along with other guests.'

Charles scowled. Always protective of his sister, he had a proprietorial air as he regarded her and was not prepared to see another philanderer such as Richard Coulson take advantage of her. 'Aunt Charlotte will know better than I what mischief you have been up to in Devon, Tilly.' When the flush deepened on her cheeks, he added, 'I think you have developed a special interest in this gentleman.'

'We...saw each other on occasion. Lord Clifton and Uncle Silas were good friends.'

'Lord Clifton is also a handsome devil,' Aunt Charlotte said with a low chuckle, 'and has the charm to match. Any young woman would be flattered by his attention—and those not so old,' she muttered to herself.

Charles considered what she had said for a moment, then gave a philosophical sigh. 'Very well. Where the child is concerned, I can hardly turn him out on to the streets, can I? But I will have a few choice words to say to this gentleman when I meet him—if he turns up before I have to leave for India. Lord knows what William is going to say to all this. He will not be best pleased.'

'Thank you, Charles,' Tilly said, throwing her arms about his neck. 'I knew you would understand when I explained it all—and I'm sure William will be just as understanding as you are. We intend having a couple of days here before travelling to Cranford. Will you come with us?'

'Not immediately,' Charles replied, beginning to relax and looking at his sister fondly. 'But I will if I have the time—which shouldn't be a problem since the voyage to India has been delayed. I would like to spend a little time with you before I have to leave.' He caught her in a warm embrace. 'I'm so glad you came back. I'm so used to having you around. I missed your funny face. What am I going to do without you in India?'

In the brilliant sunshine of a lovely July day, Tilly gazed out of the coach window at Cranford's splendid façade. She had only been away a few weeks, but she had missed the warmth of the family to be found within.

They were welcomed warmly by William and Anna. There was a great deal of fuss as they settled in and explanations to be made regarding Tobias. William was concerned while Anna took it all in her stride and Tobias was soon ensconced in the nursery with Thomas.

Tilly soon fell into a daily routine of pleasurable country pursuits and assisting Anna with her many charitable works.

After an invigorating ride out with Anna, the two sat on the terrace overlooking the garden, a tea tray in front of them. Tilly took great pleasure in her friendship with her sister-in-law. Tilly had made many friends when she had been at the academy, but since she had left, Anna was the closest friend she had. She found she could talk to her sister-in-law freely and she was sure she felt the same about her. Although Anna was three years older, they shared the same pleasures in life.

'I'm so glad you're back, Tilly,' Anna said, pouring the tea and handing a cup to Tilly before helping herself to a dainty piece of cake. 'We've missed you—especially William. He does so enjoy your company.'

'William has you, Anna. Never have I seen a married couple who are so absurdly happy. You make a splendid case for the married state.'

Anna laughed, flicking cake crumbs off her lap. 'It is truly a happy state to be in, Tilly, and the fact that we fought so hard to achieve it only makes me appreciate it more. I feel a love so strong for William and Thomas that it scares me. I hope one day you will feel it for yourself.'

'Yes—perhaps one day,' Tilly said, envying Anna her happiness.

'Tobias is a lovely child, Tilly—and Florence is so good with him. It's such a tragedy what happened to his parents—although his uncle obviously cares for him.'

'Yes, he does. Lord Clifton and Lady Cassie were very close.'

'And this Lord Clifton?' Anna said with a curious light in her eyes. 'Do you find him handsome, Tilly?'

'I think some would consider him so,' she answered with an artificially bright smile.

'That wasn't what I asked you. Do *you* find him handsome?'

'Yes—yes, I do.' She sighed, taking a sip of her tea as she watched one of the peacocks strut across the lawn beneath the terrace, trailing its exotic feathers behind him. 'We were getting on so well—and then I had to leave.'

'Did you tell him about what happened—with Richard Coulson?'

'No. I—I didn't want to spoil things.'

'I see. Well, if he cares for you, it shouldn't matter.'

'Perhaps not, but I couldn't tell him.'

Anna studied her calmly. 'I think you care for Lord Clifton more than you are letting on, Tilly. Tell me about him.'

Once Tilly had begun her confidence, she seemed unable to stop. She told Anna about their volatile first encounters and how, as they had got to know each other better, she had begun to see a different side to him and a new accord had grown between them.

'Charles was right when he told me that nothing good comes of a woman who falls short of society's expectations. I broke the rules and I really don't know how I'm going to move on from it, least of all tell Lord Clifton.'

'You didn't break all the rules.'

'No—maybe not all of them. Although everyone believes I did. In a fit of spite, because I refused his proposal of marriage, Richard Coulson let everyone believe the worst of me.'

'When Lord Clifton comes to London for Tobias, if

he has a mind to take things further in your relationship, Tilly, will you tell him?'

'I don't know. I honestly don't think I can.'

'Better coming from you than someone else. There is still gossip.'

Tilly looked at her beseechingly. 'I don't think I can manage to do that, Anna,' she said at last.

'He will be arriving shortly to take Tobias away. William received a letter from him explaining the reason why he begged your help in the unfortunate matter. But, what of you, Tilly? What is it *you* want?'

Tilly fixed her gaze on the peacock once more. 'I knew you would ask me that and the answer is, I don't know.'

'Can you not wait and see what happens? See what the day brings when he comes for Tobias? You really like him, don't you, Tilly?'

She nodded. Her parting from Lord Clifton had been like a pain in her heart, a pain mingled with an odd sort of longing. She dared not call it love. In another woman she would think it foolish, yet this feeling had such a hold on her heart.

'I think if I am not careful, he will break my heart. There was a woman in his life some time ago. I don't know what happened, but when it ended, he never got over it, apparently.'

'He has spoken to you about this woman?'

'Not much—and it is not my place to ask him. But… how can I live with a man who mourns the woman he still loves?' A man who, she thought, because of that one tragic experience, now considered marriage to any other woman a convenience—without love.

'When he comes for Tobias he will return to Devon. I've asked Charles to keep Drayton Manor on, to let me live there—me and Aunt Charlotte, who loves Devon. I would still see Lord Clifton.'

'And what did Charles say?'

'He will consider it.' Placing her cup and saucer on the tray in front of them, she looked at Anna and smiled. 'Now enough of Lord Clifton. Tell me what you have planned in the way of entertainment now I'm back.'

Lucas arrived at Cranford Park three weeks after Tilly. He had set off at first light so he could return to London with Tobias and Florence before dark. He was impatient to see Tilly. He had missed her more than he'd thought possible. He couldn't explain it, nor could he understand it, but marriage to Tilly just seemed right, as if it was meant to be. It was not as if he hadn't been looking for a bride anyway, and Tilly was eminently suitable—well-born and well-connected.

Smiling inwardly, he thought he'd hardly behaved like a perfect gentleman, taking advantage of her by kissing her, which would have insinuated in her mind that he wanted to take their relationship further, and, if not, risking her reputation should it become known. Marrying Tilly Anderson was simply the right and honourable thing to do and he had the feeling that she would not need much persuading to accept.

Seeing Cranford in all its splendid magnificence, he could not fail to be impressed. It was fascinating because of its overall effect, not just due to the splendour or beauty of the architecture and the rich golden-yellow stone of which it was built, but because it was enormous, ancient, powerful and beautiful. With dramatic grace, it stood against a backdrop of sweeping lawns and a terraced courtyard.

A smiling Lord Elvington received him as though it were the most natural thing to receive unknown visitors. On arriving in London and going to his club in St James's, he had made discreet inquiries concerning the Marquess of Elvington. His name was not unknown to him, but they had never met.

Everything he was told was favourable. The same was said about his half-brother, Charles Anderson—although it would appear that their sister had got herself into a bit of a tangle some weeks back. Considering it was in her best interests for her to disappear for a while, she had been sent away to spend some time in the country.

Lucas hated gossip and avoided it whenever he could. No doubt it was over something and nothing and Miss Anderson would enlighten him when next they met.

'I have to thank you for the kindness you showed my sister and her aunt in Devon,' Lord Elvington said, handing him a brandy as they sat opposite each other in his study.

'We were neighbours—indeed, Silas and I were friends for a good many years. He was a fine man, a clever man, and he is sadly missed in the community. I am indebted to you for taking care of my nephew. I assumed my cousin Lord Marchant would be at home to care for him. It was indeed kind of Miss Charlotte Anderson to take him in. I explained the unfortunate circumstances of why it was necessary to remove him from Clifton House in my letter—and I am sure your sister and her aunt have filled you in on the matter.'

'Of course. We are happy to help in any way we can. I trust the situation is resolved and it is safe for Tobias to return to Devon?'

'Unfortunately not, but I will take him back with me. I have several matters to take care of in London so I will be there for a while longer.'

'Aunt Charlotte did not accompany Tilly to Cranford. After journeying up from Devon she was tired of travelling and preferred to remain in town. Charles is here...somewhere. You'll meet him later. You are welcome to stay with us overnight and travel back in the morning if you prefer.'

'That's very kind of you. Thank you. That would suit me—although I have to see my lawyers in Oxford. It would help me greatly if Tobias could reside here a few more days until I return. I could travel on to Oxford from here in the morning.'

'That won't be a problem. Make yourself at home. The servants will see to your every need while you are a guest under my roof. I'm afraid my wife has become besotted by Tobias and will be reluctant to see him go. She is in the nursery at present. Come, let us go up. I will introduce you—and I am sure you are impatient to see your nephew.'

'And, Miss Anderson, your sister? Is she at home?' Lucas asked, trying not to sound too eager to speak to her, to feast his eyes on her again, to hear her soft, musical voice and to know the exquisite sensation of being close to her.

Lord Elvington gave him a long, considered look and

then he smiled. 'I believe she is out riding somewhere—spends most of her time on horseback. Perhaps you would like to take a stroll to the stables? She should be back shortly.'

Glad of the opportunity to stretch his legs, Lucas found his way to the two-storeyed stable block and coach houses to the rear of the house, built round a central yard with a huge fountain spouting water up into the sky in the centre. He paused, taking in the activities of the grooms and stable boys, all busy with their tasks.

Turning his attention to the deer park beyond, his eyes lit on the person he was looking for. He had been driven by a ridiculous eagerness to see her. His loins tightened as he recalled the way she had yielded her lips to him in the garden at Clifton House. The sweet desire she had felt for him had been there. She had wanted him, and he had wanted her more than he had ever wanted anything in his life.

Atop a spirited mount, she was cantering across the grass towards the stables, riding expertly in the side-saddle, urging the raw-boned gelding, a glossy chestnut horse, on. She presented a slender figure and it seemed incomprehensible that she could control the great beast, so much stronger and more powerful than Gracie. The groom in the Lancaster livery rode some distance behind, hard pressed to keep up. Her hair beneath her riding hat was loose and rippled gracefully behind her and the long skirts of her riding habit billowed against her horse's flank.

Since parting from her in Devon, it had been a time of great bemusement for Lucas. The longer they were apart and the more she was in his thoughts, the deeper he fell under her spell. Watching her deftly controlling her mount as it frolicked and pranced beneath her, he was reminded of the days they had ridden together, and his heart swelled with tenderness.

He observed her from some distance away, but she was unaware of his presence as she rode into the yard and dismounted, her cheeks as rosy as a delicious apple. Her riding habit was a shade of apple green and simple in its cut, but not even her plain clothing could hide Tilly Anderson's beauty. Her shining hair framed a face of striking, flawless beauty and glowing with health he remembered so well.

His mind drifted back to the times they had been together. How exquisite she had been when she had emerged from the sea that day, with her dress all wet and clinging to her perfect body, her face as pink as a rose in the warm sunlight glinting off the sea, the sight of her making him light-headed, reeling with her sensuality. What a firebrand she was.

## Chapter Ten

Tilly had risen early, the sun shining out of a speedwell-blue sky. The torrential rain which had saturated everything the day before had stopped shortly after she had gone to bed. She entered the stable yard—the sight of the horses' heads peering out over the half-stable doors and their soft whickering never failed to excite and cheer her.

She breathed deeply, inhaling the familiar smell of the tack room, of warm leather and saddle soap. She acknowledged the polite, respectful good mornings cast her way by the grooms with a smile and asked for William's horse to be saddled. The groom set about it without question. Miss Anderson was a competent horsewoman and His Lordship allowed her to ride his horse whenever she had a mind.

She had taken her time to enjoy her ride, so it was some time later when she rode into the stable yard. Feeling relaxed and invigorated, she dismounted and handed the horse to a groom. Suddenly, she saw Lord Clifton coming towards her, lean and immaculate. Her heart gave a leap of surprise, consternation and excitement.

He stopped in front of her, wearing a look of unconcealed appreciation on his handsome face, his glorious blue eyes locked on hers, which, unbeknown to her, shone with a heart-stopping brilliance. During the time she had been without him, she had done nothing but think of him—now they were face to face, all she could do was stare at him, feeling painfully self-conscious.

There was a silence about them. They stood quite still in those first few moments, savouring each other, their eyes seeking the truth, which was what they had felt for one another when they had kissed was still there.

'Lord Clifton. You take me by surprise.'

'Do you think we could drop the Lord Clifton and you call me Lucas?'

'If that is what you want.'

'You look well.'

The tone in which it was said brought a warm glow to her cheeks and her voice trembled a little when she spoke. 'I am. You have met my brothers?'

'I have met Lord Elvington and his charming wife. I'm here to take Tobias back to London. I'm staying in my cousin's house for a couple of weeks or so—I have several matters of business to take care of. How has Tobias been? No trouble, I hope?'

'No, he's such a good baby. We...will miss him when you take him away. How were things in Devon when you left? Have you managed to do anything about buying the boatyard?'

He nodded. 'Ned Price agreed to the sale. It's going through.'

'Did he get a chance to see Tobias before we left for London?'

'He did. He tried hard not to show it, but it was an emotional moment for him. He was closer to Edmund than Jack. His death hit him harder than he cares to admit. The fact that he has a grandson has given him a new lease of life. There will have to be some adjustments made to his will and he doesn't intend losing any time in doing so. How he will deal with Jack is his business. The fact that he said not a word about Tobias has angered him.

'Had I not called on him to offer to buy the boatyard he would have been none the wiser that he had a grandson. What Jack intended to do with Tobias if the kidnap had been successful, I shudder to think. Which brings me to the reason why I had to come to London.'

'Oh? Please,' she said as they left the stables, unsure that she wanted to be privy to his private affairs, 'don't feel that you have to tell me. It is your affair.'

'I would like to tell you. I'm probably jumping the gun, so to speak, but I have to be practical and consider the future logically. It is important that I prepare for every eventuality should anything happen to me.'

Tilly's eyes flew to his in alarm. 'Why? Are you in danger?'

Having no illusions about Jack Price and what he could expect—a bullet or a knife in the back—he nodded. 'I may be—from Jack Price. Until I produce offspring of my own, Tobias is my heir. When Jack Price works it out—which he will—then he will move heaven and earth to get his hands on the Clifton estate through Tobias. He is devious and ruthless and will stop at nothing, even murder.'

'Surely you exaggerate. Jack Price would not go that

far.' As soon as the words had left her mouth, on recalling her own encounters with the smuggler, she acknowledged Lucas had good reason to fear what he would do. She could see and almost feel the tension in his body. He was not a man to lie or exaggerate. It made her suddenly fear for him. 'What precautions will you take to deter him?'

'In case the worst should happen, then I intend to set up a board of trustees to administer the estate until Tobias is of age. I will have to travel to Oxford to see my lawyers.'

'I can understand that. It is a wise move. What about the boatyard? Does Jack Price know you are buying it?'

'He's raised no objections to the sale, although it would be a different matter should he discover I am the one buying it before the sale goes through.'

'Then I hope that everything is finalised before he finds out. Are you travelling back to London today, or has William invited you to spend the night at Cranford?'

'He has, and I was happy to accept. He has been most generous. His wife is more than happy for Tobias to remain here while I travel on to Oxford to meet with my lawyers tomorrow. I shouldn't be gone more than a couple of days. I will be for ever in Lord Elvington's debt for the care he and his family have taken with Tobias.'

'Have you seen him—Tobias?'

'I certainly have. He has grown since I last saw him.' His face became set in serious lines. 'Florence looks better than she has for a while. She has become indispensable to me. Out of our misfortune came the luckiest moment of my life when I met her,' he said quietly, his expression grave, which left Tilly in no doubt as to the strong bond that had developed out of extreme hardship between Lord Clifton and Tobias's nursemaid.

'I imagine it was—and I am sure Florence feels the same. What will you do when Tobias no longer needs her?'

'Keep her on—if that is what she wants. There will always be a place for her at Clifton House—and if I am so blessed, there will be other children to care for in time.' He paused, pronouncing his next words carefully. 'My coming to Cranford to see Tobias is only half the reason.'

'Oh? Then pray tell me what else brings you all this way.'

'To see you—although I thought you might have returned to London to enjoy the short Season and whatever other pleasures are to be had. Are you not sad to have left Devon?'

'Yes, yes, I am, although I am happy now to be at Cranford.'

'I can understand that. When I was in Spain, I, too, knew how it felt to be far away from home.' As he took in a deep, appreciative breath, his gaze did a wide sweep of the house and beautifully landscaped gardens. 'I have to say Cranford Park is quite splendid. I imagine you will be reluctant to leave here for the city—although,' he said, turning to look at her, 'you may be impatient to partake of the frivolities there after your time in Devon.'

She met his gaze, a frown creasing her brow. 'Why on earth would you think that? I thought you understood that I much prefer the country.'

'And it has nothing to do with you getting yourself

into some kind of tangle and your brothers thinking it wise for you to have a spell away from town?'

Alarm shot through Tilly. She stood rigid, fighting against the fear and nausea. He must have heard the gossip. She felt the pain of memory—those awful days following her reckless behaviour with Richard Coulson and the horrible scandal about to burst hanging over her.

'Now you are frowning,' he said. 'You are remembering something unpleasant, I think.'

'Disastrous, more like.'

'As bad as that?'

Taking a deep breath, she stood and faced him. Since he had raised the issue she had hoped to avoid, she realised she could do so no longer. 'Yes, I'm afraid it was. If you know anything at all about London society, you will know there is no surer way for a girl to ruin herself than to take up with a profligate nobleman. No self-respecting gentleman would want to marry her after that.'

He frowned, a growing suspicion in his eyes. 'And that is what happened to you?'

She nodded. 'Yes. Something like that. Charles handled the matter as discreetly as he could—and then decided it would be prudent for me to disappear for a while, which is why I found myself in Devon.' Throwing caution to the winds, she found herself telling him about Richard Coulson, how she had misjudged him and how he had meant to ruin her reputation for rejecting him.

'And he was believed?'

'He's popular, so yes. Everyone believed him because it gave the gossipmongers something to talk about—

and they love to gossip—especially when every word is true.'

Lucas's eyes narrowed below a frown. 'True, you say?'

'Why—yes. I cannot deny my friendship with Richard and every damning word that dripped from his mouth was believed. Besides, he is a man and they'll ignore his part in the nasty affair because he's charming and very rich.'

'Why did you reject him? With your reputation in question, did your brothers not insist that you marry him?'

'No—I had no wish to marry him. I will not be pushed into some misalliance. Marriage was not on my agenda at that time—although,' she said, laughing lightly, 'he did offer me a diamond engagement ring as big as a dinner plate if I accepted him.'

'Was he in love with you?'

'Goodness me, no. He was something of a narcissist—completely in love with himself.'

'And you have returned to London in the hope that your ruination is only temporary?'

'Yes, exactly. London did not smile kindly on me and I left in somewhat of a hurry. Apparently, the scandal hasn't gone away and if I were to appear in society I am sure I would be treated with contempt and condemnation. At all costs I will try very hard to hold on to my dignity. It's true that I am no lady and I hold my place in society through the generosity of my half-brother. At present, my place in society is too insecure for me to risk making any more mistakes.'

Lucas looked down at her. 'Tell me something. Did you enjoy my kiss—when we kissed in the garden at Clifton House?'

She stared at him in bewilderment, thinking it a strange thing for him to ask. He stood there, a perturbed look in his eyes, his mouth in a tight line, and a frown cut a furrow in his brow. What was wrong? Why had he suddenly changed? 'Yes, of course I did. I—I've never felt that way before.'

'Then the young man you say compromised you cannot have been a proficient lover if he neglected to give you pleasure. As for myself, I don't like being played for a fool.'

'I wouldn't do that.'

His frown grew deeper, his mouth grew tighter, and the expression in his eyes was a mixture of reproach and accusation. 'I didn't know you well enough and yet you kissed me—twice, as I recall. Why did you do that?'

'Because I wanted to. In the light of what you've just told me, I'm beginning to think that it was a mistake.'

A deep flush spread over Tilly's cheeks. To her dismay she realised he thought she had done this before, that she and Richard Coulson had been lovers in every sense. But she hadn't. She'd been the recipient of nothing more than a few chaste kisses. She might be prone to scandal, but she wasn't wanton. His expression was unforgiving. There was a silence.

Tilly averted her eyes, never having felt so wretched. She forced herself to look at him, having no trouble reading his expression, and her heart sank. She had been hoping he would look more kindly upon such an admission than its concealment. He was disgusted, yet she could not regret telling him the truth.

Now he knew what she had done, she could not blame him for his reaction, nor had she expected it to hurt quite so much. But she would not be cowed. Stepping away from him, she averted her eyes. If Lord Clifton had decided to judge her and think the worst, then so be it.

'Yes—I agree with you. Goodness me! I didn't expect you to make the ritualistic proposal that follows a kiss.' She glanced at him sharply. 'Please tell me you weren't going to do that.' He remained silent, watching her intently. She laughed mirthlessly. 'You were, weren't you? Well, if it will make you feel any better, I will tell you now that I don't want to marry you—and if you had offered for me I would have respectfully refused.'

His lips twisted in a mirthless smile as he looked down into her deceptively innocent eyes. 'Then it's as well for both our sakes that I didn't make you an offer.'

'Absolutely,' she uttered flippantly, his utter lack of caring causing her heart to squeeze in the most inexplicable way. She longed to say that of course she wanted him to make an offer, but the words wouldn't form. She simply stood looking at him, the familiar ache in her heart. She wanted to reach out to him, but her body stayed still, unbending.

'I am also fresh out of diamonds,' Lucas told her coldly. 'How can I possibly put my life in order and restore some kind of peace to my house if I have to defend my wife's reputation? You have beauty, wit and spirit and you are exciting to be with—I actually *like* being with you, but if your recent scandalous behaviour is anything to go by you will make an abominable wife.'

Her chin lifted in self-defence. 'And you, My Lord, would make an abominable husband. I really don't want to marry you—or anyone else for that matter. I'm not in the market for a husband,' she said, trying to sound as indifferent as he.

'Then you shouldn't have allowed yourself to be compromised. You certainly have a propensity for scandal and a disdain for the rules of society.'

'Oh, dear me,' Tilly uttered mockingly. 'That is bad indeed. I was raised to understand that society makes the rules and if one wants to live among society then life must be lived according to them. I failed at the first hurdle. If you must know, I made an utter fool of myself and I am ashamed because of the hurt it brought to my family. But it's too late now to change that.

'So, you see, you really must look elsewhere for someone to wed. I cannot for the life of me see that you and I have anything in common. You say you like my spirit and find me exciting to be with, but after your severe and unfair condemnation of my character I fail to understand how you can possibly feel that way.'

'Then I ask your pardon. But when you made me aware of your reason for going down to Devon, I had to wonder at your ethics.'

'Then don't,' she cried firmly, uncaring that she was unable to defuse his wrath. 'What I do is none of your business. Yes, I was a silly, naive fool and I make no excuses for becoming involved with Richard Coulson. You have clearly misinterpreted what I said, but that is beside the point now.'

'If I have done so, then perhaps you would care to explain.' He was trying to hold on to his anger.

'No, I do not. You do not have the right to judge or condemn me. Not that it will matter since you will be leaving for Devon shortly so I doubt we will meet again—even if I do decide to return to Drayton Manor in the future. I realise that you must despise me for what I might or might not have done, but that is for you to deal with, not me.'

'I do not despise you, quite the opposite, but what you did no respectable woman would have dreamed of doing—which is a category from which you chose to eliminate yourself when you took up relations with the likes of this...this Richard Coulson,' he said derisively.

Tilly stood before him, straight and erect, as if carved from stone. Her cheeks burned from the casual cruelty of the remark. 'That is condemnation indeed.'

His eyes narrowed, but otherwise he ignored her comment. 'There are times when you remind me of Cassie—when you are angry.'

His tone was sombre while something sad and bleak tugged at her heart, despite his animosity towards her of a moment before. She had forgotten for the moment that his own past was not bereft of tragedy. He was still mourning his sister's death and the woman he had loved in the past still had a hold on him.

Stiffening her spine, she steeled herself and hardened her heart against any sympathetic urges she felt. She didn't want to feel that way lest it weakened her resolve to preserve all her resources for herself. Stepping away from him, she squared her shoulders and lifted her chin.

'And for that very reason I would refuse to be your wife. I am my own person. I think and feel and do what I like. I will not be any man's wife because I bear some resemblance to his sister. You can go to the devil, Lucas Kingsley—and take Richard Coulson with you. When I look in the mirror, I want to see a strong woman, not a victim. My reputation might be in tatters now, but that is my problem. It is certainly not your place to lecture me or to sit in judgement.'

He looked at her, his face sculpted against the brightness of the sun. It was without expression. He seemed remote, untouchable. 'I think you have said quite enough.'

'It is clear to me that because of the scandal I have created, my presence offends you. Since you are to stay the night, to show courtesy to my family we will behave as if nothing untoward has happened between us. You have made it plain that you don't approve of me, but there is no need to turn this into a spectacle.'

As they walked towards the house, the atmosphere between them was charged with a subtle tension. When Tilly had seen him waiting for her at the stables, she had wanted nothing more than for him to take hold of her, to crush her in his arms, to feel his lips on hers once more, but he had done none of that.

A strange, icy calm came over her. Taking a look at the hard planes of his face, the subtle aggression in the line of his jaw, and the clear intent that stared at her from the depths of his deep blue eyes, she felt a slight trembling sensation skitter over her skin. Ignoring it, she looked straight ahead and continued to walk on.

There was a pain in her heart she couldn't identify. All the days leading up to seeing him again she had looked forward to, but now...? Nothing. She had felt excited in a way she had never felt before as something was beginning to grow inside her, something bright and beautiful that filled her heart like a gentle piece of music, soft and sweet that would grow and burst into a crescendo of... What? She tried to identify the elusive feeling inside her, but she couldn't.

She wondered why the thought of losing the man who did not care for her should affect her heart in such a pitiless manner. It was an enigma too complex for her to analyse. And yet it should be simple. She cared deeply for him. He did not care for her. But that was for her head to work out, not her heart, which could only feel the hurt, the pain, the emptiness. And yet the heart still mourned, still grieved.

Reaching the house and seeing Charles in the entrance to the hall, she waved. He came to meet them, shaking Lord Clifton's hand warmly on Tilly's introduction. When they began to indulge in polite conversation, she managed to make her getaway.

For the rest of the day and through dinner Tilly was reeling between confusion and dread—and more than a little anger because Lucas had been so ready to judge her. Where she was concerned, his eyes were always guarded. They were polite with one another, pleasant even, both of them doing their best to begin the process of making something of being together under William's roof.

Whatever illusions Tilly might have had where Lucas was concerned were gone. When she anticipated his visit to Cranford, there had been a soaring of her spirit and excitement had heated her blood. Now she swallowed against an overwhelming sense of loss. The pain of her emotion was sharp. She tamped it down and reminded herself that if his reaction to her fall from grace was what she could expect if she conceded to Aunt

Charlotte's wish and made her debut, then what was the point of it all? She was ruined by her own stupidity.

Maybe she was judging Lucas too harshly. If she told him the whole truth—that her virtue had not been violated—maybe he would no longer feel the disgust she had seen in his eyes when he looked at her. At least then, with time to mull things over, there was the possibility that his attitude would become soft with understanding.

Lucas had much to think about when he left Cranford for Oxford. Tilly's confession, followed by the sense of betrayal he felt, was as powerful as anything he'd ever experienced before. When she had told him about the scandal she had created in London, it had taken a moment for the full significance of her words to sink in. His mind had registered disbelief. It started to shout denial, even while something inside him slowly cracked and began to crumble.

Was she just some shallow little rich girl looking for excitement? No well-bred young lady, who would normally have been seen exclusively among the company of the social elite, would have risked her reputation by indulging in such wanton behaviour that would damage any chance she might have of making a decent marriage. He had to admire her courage, he thought with much bitterness, if not her standards. At least she had been honest.

He'd believed Tilly was different to other women. Discovering that she was not so pure was like being kicked in the gut. It puzzled him that it should make him angry that she could give herself so easily and his anger was exacerbated both by a kind of rage that she should demean herself and by an inexplicable disappointment. He'd been so enamoured by the wonder of her, by her wilfulness and the spirit of her, by her freshness, that he'd been blind to her real nature.

What she had told him touched the part of a man's life that was sacrosanct—his woman—even though she'd never declared herself as such. There could be no kind of relationship, no future for them together with the scandal she had created lying between them like some eternal obstacle. Her weak moral standards left her wanting in his eyes. Everything he'd felt for her, all his expectations of forming some kind of future for them together, left him abruptly. All that remained was a cold, sick rage.

And yet nothing could be softer than those eyes, or softer than that skin, those lips, nothing purer than that face or more exquisite than that form, but that was just a small part of her. He had been hurt by a previous lover, beautiful, treacherous Miranda, who had shown the kind of betrayal her kind were capable of once their love had paled and someone else came along. The experience had left him wary of all women. He had vowed never to fall into the same trap twice.

Lucas's meeting with his lawyers to set up a board of trustees for Tobias should something untoward happen to him was dealt with to his satisfaction. He spent an extra night in Oxford to put other matters affecting his life into perspective. Gradually, his anger towards Tilly diminished and there followed a time of soul searching. There had been so many adversities in his life. Fate had been cruel to him, it had mocked him, but it would not triumph. Fate could be overcome.

He could not escape the fact that Tilly was branded deep inside him and he could not hold out against his need. She had a way of getting under his skin and insinuating herself into his mind and his heart that troubled him. Where she was concerned, he felt the same aching loss he had felt when Miranda left him, followed by the loss of his parents and then again when Cassie had died.

He had reacted to what she had told him very badly and assumed the worst. Now, as though to punish him for his condemnation of her, it was all turned about. Something about what she had said nagged at his mind—that he had misinterpreted what she had told him. How? What had she meant by that? It puzzled him. Had he indeed misconstrued her words?

Guilty or innocent, it no longer mattered. He would not abandon her. If she would have him, he would marry her in spite of everything. After the upheaval of his feelings and emotions he realised at last that he wanted her in his life, that he did not want to lose her.

Would she forgive him? he wondered—that defiant, wilful woman with a spirit and a will to match his own. She was clever, she was lovely and as slick as oil, and yet, for all that, she was as vulnerable as a child. She could not have known what she was doing when she had taken up with Coulson.

Memories of his sister came to mind, of how she had fled to Spain to be with her lover and how he had gone after her to bring her back before she came to harm in a war-torn land. He had failed to do that and the memory of his failure haunted him still.

High-spirited Tilly reminded him of Cassie. With this scandal hanging over her, her future looked bleak. He could not let that happen to her. He would not abandon her. He would go to her and fall to his knees if need be and beg her forgiveness.

The hour was late when Lucas arrived at Cranford. The ladies had retired, but William and Charles were seated before the fire in the library enjoying a late-night glass of William's excellent brandy. They insisted Lucas join them. He had never known the companionship of brothers and he envied them their closeness.

The three of them talked companionably about their various business interests and Charles's imminent departure for India, and they showed a particular interest in the smuggling operations in Devon and Tobias's future. Having discussed these topics at length, they turned their attention to what was uppermost in all their minds—Tilly. Charles was hoping she'd return to London with him.

William propped his feet on the low table between them, loosening his cravat. 'She's reluctant, Charles. Accept it. She really doesn't want to go and I'm quite happy for her to remain here. Your aunt will be disappointed, I expect, but there's no point in forcing her into the maelstrom of society until she's ready.'

'Perhaps she's afraid of meeting the young man who damaged her reputation,' Lucas remarked casually, swirling his brandy round the bowl of his glass.

Surprised, Charles stiffened as if he were trying to withstand a physical blow. 'She told you about Coulson—the scandal that ensued?'

'Yes, she did.'

'Then...you must have become...close, for her to do that. It's not something she likes to hear mentioned, let alone discussed. Coulson is a rake of the first order, for God's sake. Tilly did not lose her virtue—if that's what she told you—but when she rejected him, he spread malicious gossip about her wantonness and laughed about it with his friends. He was believed.

'When I found out I wanted to strike out at him for what he had done to my lovely, vulnerable sister. From the moment she was born I have never stopped thanking God for the gift of her, for the beauty of her, the joy of her. And now Richard Coulson has brought her to this. I am not a violent man by nature, Lord Clifton, but when it comes to something as serious as this—when a damned reprobate has intentionally damaged Tilly's reputation, then I can be as outraged as the next man. I could kill him for this.'

William looked at his brother with concern. 'Don't upset yourself, Charles—and for God's sake don't suggest she goes with you to India. I've worked for the Company in India, don't forget. You'll have enough to take care of without a wilful sister hanging on to your coat tails.'

'Where is this Coulson to be found?' Lucas asked.

Charles shook his head. 'As to that I can't say. He disappeared weeks ago. I heard he'd gone for an extended tour of the Continent.'

'He proposed marriage to her?' Lucas asked.

'Yes—although we never knew how serious he was. We couldn't consider it, of course. Coulson is a philanderer—a reprobate. He would have made her life a misery. We couldn't allow that, not for Tilly. She was not yet nineteen and she was to make her debut—have a Season. The whole of London would have been at her feet.

'Coulson—with an inflated opinion of himself—took that from her, making her the victim of malicious tongues. She was young, vulnerable, wilful and when he gave her his attention she was flattered and besotted as any innocent young woman would be by the attentions of such a handsome, well-favoured young man.

'I've always looked out for her, and when it wasn't me, then Aunt Charlotte or William when he came back from India. Collectively, we failed. She fell prey for the first dissolute character that came along. That beautiful girl was put in such an impossible situation by him that we felt compelled to send her away—hence her departure for Devon.'

'Where she met me,' Lucas remarked quietly. 'Why on earth did she lead me to believe her virtue had been taken from her?'

'Lord knows! I've ceased wondering how my sister's mind works. If you offended her when you believed the worst and you want to make amends, you must apologise to her—and hope she'll accept it. But then again, she might very well tell you to go to the devil.'

Lucas grimaced. 'She already has.'

'The gossip is proving hard to get rid of,' William said. 'It's been blown out of all proportion. We hoped that by the time she came back from Devon it would have died and some other unfortunate would have become the topic of malicious tongues. I hate to think of the damage and the heartache this has caused her. Before she met Coulson, she was like any other young lady looking forward to her debut.'

'I will not stand idly by while our sister's name is sneered at and pulled apart,' Charles declared, his lips tight with anger. 'I hate to be going off to India and leaving her like this.'

'Then allow me to offer a solution before you go that far,' Lucas said.

The two brothers looked at him. 'How?' they asked in unison.

'Since my arrival at Cranford I have been a detached observer, but I am not inexperienced in dealing with the female mind—my sister was very much like Tilly. However, your sister has right on her side. The way I see it is simple. Her name has been unfairly besmirched. She no longer has the desire to make her debut into society, yet she cannot hide herself away—that would be a scandal in itself.'

'Then what is it you suggest?' Charles asked.

'That she gives the gossips something to gossip about. Instead of retreating from the battlefield, she takes the initiative...and marries me.' The brothers stared at him in astonishment.

As Lucas watched their reaction to his suggestion, now that he had admitted to himself his desire to marry Tilly, he wanted her with an urgency that was almost irrational. The desire she ignited in him every time they met was eating at him like a fire licking at his insides. He wanted her so badly that he ached with it.

His growing need for her made him feel vulnerable and uneasy, for he knew from past experience how vicious, how treacherous, the female sex could be. Despite this, he could not stop himself from wanting her and his firm hope was that she would want him, too.

'You would do that?' Charles said, looking at him, his piercing eyes alive with anticipation.

'I would. Marrying Tilly was very much on my mind before she left Devon, but there was so much going on in my life—having just returned from Spain, having lost my sister, Tobias to take care of and a damned smuggler out for my blood. I was shaken when she implied she and Coulson had been lovers.'

'And now you know the truth.'

'I do—although I had become so enamoured of your sister that I had decided to set her lapse from grace aside. As her guardians it is the correct thing for me to ask your permission to marry her.'

William nodded slowly, thinking it over. 'At present it would stop the gossip that will surely ruin Tilly if it carries on much longer. There are many kinds of persecution that are not readily apparent, such as the whispered conjectures, the gossip and subtle innuendoes that can destroy a reputation and inflict a lifetime of damage.'

'Which marriage to me will put an end to. I have much to offer her. My name, my title and an estate that has belonged to the Cliftons for generations. I would have it remain so for many more generations.'

'Do you have feelings for Tilly?' Charles asked.

Lucas nodded. 'I have come to have a high regard for her—and, yes, I adore her.'

William gave him a considering look. 'So—you have come to realise what a dear, sweet girl she is.'

Lucas laughed softly. 'I would not describe Tilly as

sweet. It didn't take me long to appreciate that that high-minded woman is the most exasperating female I have known in my entire life—although she only comes a close second to my dear, departed sister. Tilly is also the woman I want for my wife.'

Charles, having taken special note of the way Lord Clifton's gaze had lingered tenderly on his sister momentarily before he had left for Oxford, was not surprised by this. 'And Tilly? How do you think she will react when she knows you want to marry her? Has it not occurred to you that she might very well turn you down?'

'It has, but I am confident she can be persuaded. I care for her—more than I have ever cared for any other woman, which is why I want her to be my wife. I want to marry her as soon as it can be arranged.'

William nodded and looked at his brother. 'What are your thoughts, Charles? Do we give this gentleman permission to wed our wilful, spirited, troublesome yet adorable sister?'

'Gladly—although I must insist you woo her first, to observe all proprieties. We don't want to intimidate her, nor do we want to do anything that might exacerbate the situation with society. Let people see you together before you announce your betrothal. When it's announced, I have no doubt it will be received with tremendous shock.'

'Four weeks,' Lucas stated.

'Four weeks?' Charles gasped. 'But surely that's too soon.'

'Three weeks is the time it will take for the banns to be called.' Lucas smiled, catching Charles's eye. 'You are due to leave for India shortly. Do you think Tilly would not want her brother to be present on her wedding day?'

'Yes, I suppose there is that. I shall have to extend my leaving if it can be arranged.'

'I also have to return to Devon. There are important matters that need my personal attention.'

'It will certainly give society something else to talk about,' William remarked, draining his glass.

'This is quite splendid,' Charles enthused, crossing to the sideboard. 'Now that's out of the way, I think a toast is in order—and we will sit and discuss the kind of wedding we want for Tilly—along with the terms of the betrothal and the dowry.'

Picking up the decanter of brandy, he filled their glasses, already thinking how much easier it would be for him to go to India without the worry of Tilly's predicament hanging over him. 'I pray she looks on you with favour, Lucas, and agrees to be your wife without argument—otherwise we are all going to have dreadful headaches in the morning without anything to show for it.'

The following morning found Tilly up with the lark and riding over Cranford's luscious acres. She loved to ride through the park when the dew was heavy on the grass and the deer were grazing nearby.

As he had done on his arrival at Cranford, Lucas walked to the stables, hoping to meet her on her return. He was not disappointed. Her ride concluded, she was on her way back to the house.

He'd paused, as if distracted, and turned his gaze

to the beautiful panorama that stretched out as far as the eye could see. He was already lost in his thoughts.

As she slowly approached him, Tilly studied him. For a man of such herculean stature, he had an elegant way of moving. Wearing a dark green coat, his long legs were once again encased in biscuit-coloured trousers and highly polished dark brown riding boots.

His hair was dishevelled from the breeze, the black curls brushing the edge of his collar. The sun illuminated his bold, lean profile and that aquiline nose that gave him a look of such stark, brooding intensity. His mouth seemed hard and grim. She watched him raise his hand and, as he absently rubbed the muscles at the back of his neck, her treacherous mind suddenly thought of the exquisite pleasure he would make her feel were his hand to caress her in that way.

On the times they had been together she had made no effort to know the man who lived beneath the surface of the man who dwelt there, who had seen her as a future bride, a woman he could wed before, like a silly girl, she had told him of her association with Richard Coulson, leaving him to believe her virtue was no longer intact. How could she have done that? It had mattered to him. She should have seen that, instead of seeing only how it affected her and had taken offence.

Her heart suddenly swelled—with what? Admiration? Affection? Love? No, not that. She could never love a man who was in love with another woman. Could she? However hard she tried, she couldn't help but want him. But then, hadn't Aunt Charlotte once told her that the heart wasn't always wise when one's body was driven by base desires.

Recollecting herself, she shook away such thoughts. She was being an utter fool romanticising Lucas Kingsley, simply because he was a handsome man, sleek and fierce as a bird of prey and incredibly skilled in arousing her desire—and because she was a spineless idiot who was disgustingly and helplessly attracted to him.

Becoming aware of her approach, he turned and looked at her. Her cheeks were flushed and her eyes glowed from her ride. 'At last,' he said. 'I was beginning to think I would never get you alone. I thought I would have seen you at breakfast.'

'I like to ride early. I heard you were back. You are leaving for London shortly, taking Florence and Tobias with you. It is doubtful we will see each other again.' She was doing her best to hold in the resentment she felt, to be dignified, as a lady of her class would be, but it was very hard and her expression was softening.

'And that pleases you—that you and I will part without resolving our differences?'

'Really, Lucas,' she said, walking round him and proceeding to walk on, 'I cannot for the life of me think what else you and I have to say to one another.'

'I disagree. I merely want to talk with you privately for a few moments. After all that has happened, I thought it especially needful before I leave Cranford.'

'Why on earth would you think that? What is the point?'

Deeply moved by her outburst, Lucas took hold of her arm and turned her to face him. 'Tilly, please stop this. I am sorry if I upset you when you told me about Coulson. I should have been more understanding—but I am not your enemy.'

'No? Then what are you?'

'The man who wants to marry you.'

A silence fell between them that could be sliced with a knife. Tilly stared at him through eyes huge with shock and disbelief. 'Marry me? You *want* to marry me?'

'That is what I said. Is it so strange that I want you to be my wife?'

'Yes, yes, it is when I think of the harsh words we exchanged before you left for Oxford. I told you that I didn't want to marry you or anyone else come to that."

'It was a misunderstanding, Tilly.'

'But—but why do you want to marry me? Isn't that a bit extreme? It's quite ridiculous.'

'I see nothing ridiculous about a man asking a woman to be his wife. I have approached your brothers on the matter and they think it's a splendid idea—providing I court you in the proper manner of course.'

'I would have to go to London?' He nodded. 'I'm trying to avoid being seen, remember,' Tilly retorted cuttingly. 'What will everyone say when we suddenly appear together?'

He grinned. 'They'll see how weak you are, that you find it impossible to resist my manly charms.'

She looked at him coolly. 'Don't flatter yourself—and don't you think you should seek Aunt Charlotte's favour first?'

'I don't think your aunt will raise any objections and will be happy to combine forces if it stills the gossip.'

'You mean I'm not completely ruined?'

'Not if you marry me.'

'I recall you telling me in no uncertain terms that

you didn't want to marry me,' she said with cool dignity, lifting her chin and stiffening her spine.

'That was then. This is now. The way I see it, you have been unfairly maligned.'

'Thank you for your concern,' she remarked with heavily laden sarcasm, 'if it is genuine. You didn't think so before.'

'That was partly down to you leading me to believe the worst. I realise that I have done you a terrible injustice—but I still cannot understand why you did that.'

'No, neither can I,' she said, her mood beginning to soften. 'It was very stupid of me; I know that now. At the time I think I wanted you to think I was sophisticated and more experienced than my nineteen years. It was wrong of me. I suppose my brothers told you the truth.'

'They did, but it didn't make any difference. I had time to think in Oxford and I realised that I want you in my life. I'd already decided that I wanted to marry you before I reached Cranford.'

Gazing at the cool, dispassionate man standing before her, looking so powerful, aloof and completely self-assured, Tilly managed a nervous little laugh. 'It would seem that you and my brothers have it all arranged. Pity you didn't think to ask me first. Is it pity or guilt that has prompted you to ask me?'

He shook his head, knowing she would suspect that—and as proud as she was, her pride would make her oppose him. 'Neither. I care enough about you to be hurt by the dreadful way you have been treated by society. You do not deserve that.'

'No, I don't—but please do not feel under any obligation to marry me.'

'I don't. It just so happens that I want to marry you. That aside, I am offering you a lifeline, to enable you to hold up your head in society and not have to listen to the slights and slurs, the whispers and jeers. I ask you to put aside any objections you might have of marrying me and see marriage to me as a way forward, otherwise...'

'Otherwise?'

'You will be terribly unhappy—as I will be.'

'And you expect me to be grateful for your generosity? You speak of marrying me as if you're discussing a business arrangement—without any feeling or emotion, without even the pretence of...'

'Of what, Tilly? Of love?' His eyes suddenly became warm as his hands went to her shoulders and he drew her near, his voice low and seductive. 'I find myself attracted to you. When we are apart I think of you all the time. It just so happens that I want you, Tilly—you cannot condemn me for that—and I know you want me. We have wanted each other every time we have been together. You are beautiful, innocent and courageous, passionate and stubborn—and I hope you will forgive my wrongdoings and get to like me.'

Feeling perilously close to tears, Tilly dropped her gaze, unable to absorb the amazing revelation that he was actually attracted to her. 'I can understand your reaction when I told you about Richard Coulson, but I acted in all innocence, unmindful of propriety and plain good sense.

'I liked Coulson when we first met,' she whispered. 'After a while I couldn't stand the sight of him and couldn't wait to be rid of him. It would seem that I have poor judgement in the matter of men. Maybe I should change my mind about considering marriage to you or anyone other man for that matter.'

'Tilly,' he said softly, 'you have no choice if you want to come out of this with your reputation intact. Come, let me look at you,' he cajoled gently. When she complied by raising her head, his brows gathered in perplexity. The tears glistening in the long, silken lashes were hard to ignore. Laying a hand alongside her cheek, he gently wiped away a droplet with his thumb. 'What has happened is not so bad that you should feel a need to cry.'

Embarrassed because she couldn't contain her emotions, Tilly responded with a shake of her head, wiping away the remainder of her tears with the back of her hand in frustration. 'I never cry. It's a silly weakness I could do without.'

'Why? If you are unhappy, it's the most natural thing in the world to cry.'

'I'm not unhappy,' she argued. 'Quite the opposite.'

'That's a relief to hear. Marry me and we'll be ecstatically happy together. I would like us to reach an understanding before I leave Cranford today. As the Earl of Clifton, I have much to offer you, Tilly. I want to give you my name and everything a woman could want. Our wedding will be the likes of which London has not seen in an age and afterwards a grand ball to which everyone who is anybody will want an invite. Before you know it, you will have every distinguished family in London leaving cards and you can thumb your nose at the lot of them and come to Devon with me.'

## Chapter Eleven

'You make it sound so easy,' Tilly murmured. He had told her he wanted to give her everything, everything a woman could want—everything but love. She was unable to fathom that cynical remark, because he took her hand and drew her into the shrubbery, away from the sight of prying eyes, his firmly chiselled lips beginning a slow, deliberate descent towards her.

'I'll give you riches beyond anything you've ever dreamed of,' he murmured, his free hand cupping the back of her head and tilting her face up to his for his kiss. 'In return, all you have to give me is yourself.'

Strangely, Tilly thought he was selling himself too cheaply, asking so little of her when he was prepared to give her so much. His eyes peering down at her were like flames of fire, scorching her. She was astounded at her body's reaction on being held so close to him and she tilted her head to make her lips more accommodating to kiss.

Then he was kissing her face, her cheeks, caressing her lips with his own. His lips moved on hers, the fierceness changing to softness, to the velvet touch of intoxication. An eternity later he pulled his mouth from hers and looked down into her eyes, which were warm and velvety soft.

'Oh, dear,' Tilly murmured, her senses all over the place. 'That was a mistake.'

His lips quirked in a faint smile. 'Then let's make another one.'

As he spoke, he drew her further into the gloom of the shrubbery. His tall figure dark against the shadows, he pulled her to him once more.

Tilly was astounded at her body's reaction to this man. A touch, a kiss, a look and he could rouse her and something rose and shouted for the joy of it. Her heart was pounding in her breast and she could feel his beating against hers to the same rapid rhythm.

She pressed herself close to him, not with fury but with delight, with something she had felt before when he had kissed her, which she knew was the female in her responding to the male in him. It was madness. She made a sound in her throat and she threw back her head in the exultation of the moment.

'You *do* want me, don't you, Tilly?' Lucas said triumphantly, softly, her breath sweet and warm against his mouth as she still clung to him. 'Say it. Your heart beats far too quickly for you to claim uninterest, my love.'

'Yes,' she whispered, 'I do want you, Lucas.' She was dazed, her eyes unfocused with that soft loveliness that comes when a woman is deep in the pleasures of love, her senses completely overruled by this magic that had sprung up between them. Cupping her chin, he began to kiss her face, her eyelids, her cheeks. Her lips trembled as he claimed them fiercely with his own.

'My God,' he whispered hoarsely, his blue eyes even deeper in the gloom as he looked at her upturned face. 'You are the most beautiful, wilful woman I have ever met, traits I admire in any woman. But you are also so lovely and desirable. Do you enjoy being kissed?'

Regardless of all the raw emotions quivering through her, Tilly gave him a wobbly smile. 'Yes, but I'm not used to being kissed twice in one day.'

'You must expect to be kissed more than that if you consent to being my wife. For the present, I will try to control my urges.' He gave her the ghost of a smile. 'But it will be no easy matter.' For a moment neither of them spoke, then he said, 'I promise you I will not take advantage of you. For now, you are quite safe from me.'

May God help her, she did not wish to be safe from him. As he turned his head away, she wanted to beg him to kiss her like he had a moment before, to ignore all his good intentions, but he was already drawing her out of the gloom.

Emerging into the open once more, they continued to walk on in silence.

Tilly went through a great deal of deliberation and heart searching, deciding that, with cool calculation, marriage to Lucas might not be so terrible after all. She could hardly believe how deep her feelings were running and the joy coursing through her body melted the core of her heart. The feeling was so strong there was no room for anything ese. Ever since their first meeting they had moved towards this end and now there was no doubt in her heart.

Lucas represented security and a release from the gnawing fear and uncertainty of being shoved into an alliance with a stranger. But it was all so sudden. Was she about to give in too quickly? Could it be? Could it work? It was, as yet, only a whisper inside her, but it was growing, becoming more insistent. She allowed the whisper to extend to the hope that Lucas might one day feel for her what he had felt—might still feel—for that other woman he had once fallen in love with.

On reaching the house, Tilly stopped walking and turned to him. 'You said you wanted the matter settled before you have to go to London.'

'That is what I want. May I have your answer? Will you marry me, Tilly?'

She kissed him then. That was her answer. 'I hope I can make you happy, Lucas. I think I can.'

Lucas raised her hand to his lips and kissed the soft white skin of her wrist. 'I have no doubts about that. What do you think? Are we compatible?'

'Yes. Yes, I believe we are. You have twisted my emotions from the very first.'

An incredibly tender smile flitted across his lips. 'I adore you, Tilly. It's as simple as that.'

'I see,' Tilly exclaimed, unable to believe the evidence of her eyes. But there it was for her to see, the powerful emotions that moved him. She could hear it in the vibrant tones of his voice. Hardly daring to believe what her heart told her, a frisson of delight shot through her, her own feelings revealed by the bright flush on her cheeks. His arms closed around her; his lips brushed hers.

When they parted, he glanced towards the double doors of the great house and, seeing the three figures standing there, he laughed. 'I see we have a reception committee. Are you ready to face your family and tell them what we have decided?'

'Yes. Let's do it.'

'I am surprised,' William remarked as he watched Lord Clifton walk towards them with Tilly on his arm. 'Who would have thought our sister would make such a grand match? Even if it did come about in an unorthodox fashion. What do you think of the Earl of Clifton, Charles?'

'I am impressed by him. He is well-born, titled—an old and venerated title. He is rich and honourable, and if what we have just witnessed is to be believed, Tilly is enamoured of him. I believe he will treat her well.'

William nodded. 'Then with all that to recommend him, I have no objections to a marriage between them. With the scandal still running, it would solve the problem of what to do about a Season for Tilly.'

'That's all very well,' Anna said, having listened with interest to the conversation between the brothers, 'but does Tilly love him?'

Charles looked at her. 'Yes, Anna, I believe she does.'

'Then she must marry him.'

William cast his wife a loving look. 'To my darling wife, Charles, love is the mainspring of any marriage. Without love she is convinced a marriage cannot survive.'

Charles smiled. 'Then it would be prudent to take note of those pearls of wisdom, dear Brother. As for myself, I will never know—not for the foreseeable future anyway. When I finally set sail for India, I would like nothing better than to see my dear sister happily married and tucked away—out of mischief—in Devon, before I go.'

'And Drayton Manor?' William asked. 'Have you decided what you are going to do with it?'

'Not yet. At some point I will go and take a look at it myself. I know Aunt Charlotte grew rather fond of the house when she was there and has fallen completely in love with Devon. I believe she will be quite happy to return and to continue living there for the present.'

'And with Tilly living nearby,' Anna said, 'she will have her darling niece for her neighbour.'

Everyone was delighted at the way things had turned out. It was suggested that since Cranford had its own chapel the ceremony could be performed there. But Lucas intended for it to be a large affair and, since the guests were mainly centred in London, it was decided that they would be married at St George's Church in Hanover Square with the wedding breakfast and ball to follow at the Lancaster town house. No expense was to be spared.

With business matters to attend to in town, Lucas had left Cranford, accompanied by Florence and Tobias. Tilly and Charles had followed a day later to inform Aunt Charlotte of the latest developments.

Tilly found that she had very little time in which to think during those heady days in London. Every minute seemed crammed with activities. It was a happy time. Tilly's feelings were too newly acknowledged to be the firm bond that would develop over time. She and Lucas trod an uncertain path, learning about each other, and there were still some dark areas that lurked in the shadows—Tobias's future being one of them and how to keep him and Lucas safe from Jack Price. The other dark cloud that bedevilled Tilly was Lucas's past love. Did he still harbour feelings for her? It was something that must be confronted eventually, but for the time being, she was too happy not to let that or anything else spoil her world.

Aunt Charlotte had been surprised and highly delighted when she was told that Lucas and Tilly were to be married and in no time at all, although she would have liked a little longer to prepare for it.

'There really is so much to do,' she said when they all sat around drinking tea on the terrace of her lovely house in Chelsea village. 'If it is to be the grand affair you intend, then a guest list has to be drawn up before the wedding invitations can be sent out and there are the menu and the flowers to be taken care of—not to mention Tilly's bridal gown. Really, Lord Clifton, it is obvious you have never been married, otherwise you would know it is virtually impossible to arrange a wedding on a scale that befits the sister of the Marquess of Elvington in four weeks. And do not forget that we have bridesmaids to find and dresses to be made.'

'I don't see why that should be a problem,' Tilly said. 'There are children in abundance among your close friends to choose from who might like a trip up the aisle.'

'Yes, of course, although I still think more time is needed,' her aunt argued.

'Really, Aunt Charlotte,' Tilly said, laughing softly. 'You are one of the most competent and capable women I know. I have every confidence that you will cope splendidly. I will help, too, don't forget—and William's secretary. He will assist us in the preparations and knows how to go about getting things done.'

'Very well,' Aunt Charlotte conceded, knowing everyone's mind was made up about an early wedding and there was no point arguing, but she insisted on the requisite rituals of courtship with equanimity until the wedding and chaperoned Tilly wherever she went.

'There is bound to be a great deal of speculation as to why Tilly has skipped her coming out,' she remarked, 'but you, Lord Clifton, are exactly the kind of bridegroom that all young ladies enter the marriage market for—which is precisely what it is—to catch a titled and wealthy husband. When they see that Tilly has managed to achieve what many young ladies have failed to do, they and their ambitious parents will turn green with envy.'

'But I have no desire to go anywhere before the wedding, Aunt Charlotte. I'm simply not ready to face everyone just yet.'

'Yes, you are,' Lucas countered. 'You have to do it some time. I have every faith in you.'

'I can't do it,' she said, throwing up her arms in despair. 'I simply cannot.'

'Yes, you can.' He spoke in a tone that brooked no argument.

'And it doesn't concern you that I shall be flayed alive by malicious tongues?'

Unbelievably, he laughed outright at that. 'Not a bit. From the conversation I've had with your brothers concerning your behaviour before you ran away and sought sanctuary in Devon, then you deserve it,' he joked, knowing as he said it that she would rear up in indignation. He wasn't disappointed.

His remark made her cheeks flame. 'I did not run away,' she retorted adamantly.

'No?' he said, chuckling softly. 'It sounded very much like it to me.'

It was the sort of thing she would have expected him to say as an act of revenge. 'And I have no doubt that you will enjoy every minute of my suffering.'

Crossing his long legs in front of him, he captured her gaze. 'I may be many things, Tilly, but I am neither cruel nor sadistic. If we are to be married, you have to face society at some point. Since you have a scandal hanging over your head, I suggest the sooner we are seen together the better.

'For your first public appearance since returning to London I've reserved a box at the theatre. We can all go so you will be well chaperoned. There is every chance the scandal will be forgotten when the performance is over.'

Tilly paled at the mention of the scandal. 'I can't. I have no desire whatever to enter society. I can't face anyone just yet.'

'You can and you will,' he said in his determination to convince her of the feasibility and the necessity of the plan. To soften his words, he took her hand and raised it to his lips. 'Take my word for it, you will be a sensation.'

'How can you possibly know that? You are being very stubborn, Lucas, expecting me to do this with no consideration for my feelings.'

Her words were unjust, but Lucas cast them aside

and, when he spoke, the tenderness in his voice was teasing and persuasive. 'I have every consideration for both you and your feelings. It is you who are being stubborn, my love, and if I knew you couldn't do this, I wouldn't put you through it. But you are more than capable of looking every one of your adversaries in the eye and telling them to go to the devil—as you did me on one occasion.'

'Yes, I did—and you deserved it.' Having no wish to argue further, for deep down she knew he was right, and unable to endure his close scrutiny any longer, she shot out of the chair and, ramrod straight, stood apart from him. With a superhuman effort, she took control of her rampaging ire. She looked straight into his enigmatic eyes. 'Going to the theatre to be gawped at in a box by all and sundry is not the solution. It's a nightmare.'

Without another word, she stalked into the house.

Suppressing a smile, Anna placed her cup and saucer on the table and rose. 'Oh, dear. She's still highly sensitive about the whole thing. I'll go and try to calm her down.'

Anna managed to work her magic on Tilly, but not entirely. In the warmth of her bedchamber as she prepared for the theatre, the face that looked back at Tilly in the pier-glass was glowing. Colour flushed her cheeks and her deep violet eyes seemed to have become almost luminous. It was not the heat, but rather the suppressed uneasiness and tension within herself that was responsible.

Standing with William and Charles in the hall, in a moment of stunned silence Lucas saw a vision in a drift of lavender lace coming down the stairs. The neckline of her gown was scooped low, offering a tantalising view of smooth creamy flesh above a minuscule waist.

Her glossy black hair was swept back off her forehead and held in place with a diamond clip, then left to fall artlessly about her shoulders and down her back. Beneath arched brows and long curling lashes, her glowing violet eyes were watching him carefully.

Moving forward, he waited for her to descend, holding his hand out for her to take. Her unparalleled beauty proved a strong lodestone from which he could not drag his gaze. 'I am almost speechless,' he murmured, taking her hand and kissing it lightly. 'You are exquisite.'

Trying to fight down her growing trepidation, she gave him a wobbly smile. 'Thank you, Lucas,' she said, staring up at the handsome, dynamic man standing before her. He looked powerful, aloof and self-assured. 'You look quite handsome yourself.'

'We should be going,' Anna said, looking incredibly beautiful in a creation of pale green silk and lace as she stood beside William and Charles. 'We are late.'

'Don't worry. We can be there in no time,' William replied. 'Besides, Lucas wants everyone there when Tilly arrives.'

The theatre was athrong with theatregoers and every pair of eyes seemed to shift to Tilly as she alighted from the coach. No one looking at her would guess how nervous she was. For a moment as Lucas paused to assist Anna out of the carriage, she stood beside Charles outside the theatre, looking at a sea of nameless faces. Then Lucas suddenly appeared by her side and held out his hand. Tilly placed her hand in his and he tucked it possessively in the crook of his arm.

Lucas felt it tremble and, bending over her, murmured, 'You are nervous, aren't you? I can tell.'

'Terrified,' she amended, pinning a smile to her lips. 'Everyone is looking at us.'

'Tilly,' he said severely, but with a dazzling smile for the benefit of onlookers, 'you are the young woman who brazenly confronted an arrogant stranger on the beach and several times thereafter. Compared to that this is child's play.'

Tilly stared at him askance. 'Did I really do that?'

He grinned down at her. 'Yes, you did. So do not dare turn cowardly now.'

Tilly glanced round at the curious faces, some craning their necks better to see her. 'I'll try not to,' she replied, 'but it won't be easy. Don't they know that it's impolite to stare?'

'Probably not. Ignore them,' Lucas quipped, seeming completely impervious to the stir they were creating. But when he looked at the fashionable throng, how these same people had shunned her and whispered about her, he was angry, but managed to appear superbly relaxed.

The attention that Lucas attracted did not go unnoticed either, as, during the interval when one group after another entered their box, in a flurry of curtsies and flirtatious smiles, inviting glances and a fluttering of fans, the ladies almost fell over each other in their foolish desperation to be introduced.

William and Charles watched it all with amused understanding. 'How does it feel, Lucas,' William enquired as the curtain went up for the second act and the last group departed their box, 'to have become, overnight, London's most sought-after bachelor?'

Relieved that Tilly had been left unscathed, Lucas laughed. 'Bachelor maybe, but no longer eligible—and they will all see that when our betrothal is announced tomorrow.'

All those people who had maliciously maligned Tilly, looking at her as she sat serene and secure in her box, had to admit that Tilly Anderson was beautiful. She had no lack of admiring smiles from the gentlemen who watched from the auditorium and other boxes to where she sat with her siblings. Some of the more adult theatregoers knew Lord Clifton from the days when he had come up to London and had been no stranger on the social scene, but the younger generation were curious to know who that rakishly handsome man who remained attentively by Miss Anderson's side through the evening could be.

They found out the following morning, when their betrothal was announced in the *Post*, giving rise to further gossip, no longer malicious but full of complimentary speculation and excitement as to who would be on the guest list for the wedding.

Nothing seemed real for Tilly during the days leading up to the wedding. She moved into the Lancaster town house in Mayfair where she went through several fittings for her wedding gown. Aunt Charlotte was in her element as she busied herself with arranging the flowers and bridesmaids—six in total with a variety of ages. She was determined that everything would go well on the day. The guest list for the ceremony was for a select assortment of close friends and family, the ball to follow a truly grand affair with guests that would fill the Lancaster town house to overflowing.

It was a happy group that rode into Hyde Park late one afternoon to partake of exercise and fresh air. It was where the *beau monde* congregated, to see and to be seen. Ladies attired in the height of fashion, gentlemen on high-stepping horses and carriages bearing the gilded family crests of the *ton*, liveried servants and matched teams of horses glided along in majestic splendour.

William, Charles, Tilly and Anna were to meet Lucas in the park. They had done a circuit of Rotten Row, jostling along with other riders, when Tilly saw her betrothed astride his horse. He was accosted by a group of other riders and fell into conversation with them. She slanted a long, considering look at him as he sat astride his strong, well-muscled mount. Attired in a dark green coat, gleaming brown leather boots and a pair of buckskin riding breeches that fit to perfection, in her opinion he was by far the most attractive man present.

She watched him as he talked and joked with lazy good humour with those around him, looking completely relaxed. On seeing her he excused himself, but unfortunately he was too far away to reach her before Sir John Paterson, one of the sporting gentlemen in their group who had latched on to them, challenged her to a ride. With an angry scowl on his face Lucas watched her gallop off in light-hearted abandon across the green grass, scattering other riders in their path, leaping over a ditch and clearing a low hedge effortlessly.

Her mare held her own until they turned and headed back to the others, slowing their mounts to a sedate walk. Tilly was happy to converse with the young man about the pleasant afternoon, when a sudden awareness swept over her. One moment she was thoroughly occupied learning the identity of others in the park and the next she was oblivious to everything but the inexplicable realisation that Lucas was close at hand.

The perception was quickly confirmed when his cool voice said, 'If you don't mind, Paterson, I would like a word with my betrothed.' His eyes passed over them both, considering each of them, instilling some discomfort in Sir John.

Even though there had not been the slightest hint of impropriety, Sir John stiffened apprehensively. 'I beg your pardon, Clifton, but Miss Anderson expressed an interest in some of the people present.'

'Then I shall be happy to familiarise her with them myself.'

Sir John fell back and, after excusing himself, rode away.

One quick look at Lucas's face convinced Tilly that he was furious with her. Not only were his eyes glinting like shards of ice, but the muscles in his cheeks were tensing to a degree that she had never seen before.

'It's a pity your riding skill is not exceeded by your common sense, Tilly,' he reproached her severely. 'Did you have to ride off alone with Sir John? And did you have to take those jumps? You could have broken your neck.'

'Really, Lucas, there's no need to get all hot and bothered about a few measly ditches and hedges. You've seen me ride harder terrain than this and jump obstacles far worse in Devon. And you should not have spoken to Sir John like that—making him think you are jealous...'

Lucas squinted in the sun's bright glare. 'Damn it, Tilly. I *am* jealous.'

His simple acknowledgement confused Tilly so completely that for a moment she could think of nothing to say. To feel jealousy, one had to care. As usual, his tall, hard body radiated strength and vitality, but his eyes held a dangerous glitter. A winsome smile touched her lips. 'Why, Lucas, you really are quite terrifying when you're angry—and jealous.'

'I'm jealous of any man who claims even a moment of your time when that moment could be spent with me. Was it too much for you to wait and ride with me?'

Tilly gasped, astounded that he should argue about something so trivial. 'Really, Lucas, I was just enjoying myself—and I could see you were engaged in conversation with others. But there is no need to be jealous of Sir John.'

'He's a handsome fellow with many conquests. The very idea of you being pursued by another rankles sorely.'

'It wasn't like that,' she answered softly, truthfully, in an attempt to placate his ire. What he said confused her, for it was in complete variance to his behaviour of late. Unhooking her leg from the pommel, she slipped off her mount with an easy grace. 'Of late we've spent little time together, Lucas, and our wedding is only days away. The others are riding along the Row so let's walk together. There is something I would like to talk to you about.'

Dismounting and leading their horses to where the park was less busy, Lucas took her arm and drew her into the shade of a large beech tree, out of sight of prying eyes.

'I'm sorry if I've made you angry,' she said. 'I didn't mean to.'

'You are right,' he said. 'We've had precious little time to ourselves of late. I'll be relieved when the wedding is over and we can leave for Devon.' Placing a finger lightly under her chin, he tipped her face up to his, his anger of a moment earlier dissolving. 'I'm sorry, too. I didn't mean to speak so harshly. What is it you want to talk to me about?'

Biting her lip, Tilly hesitated. Would what she was about to ask him make him angry? But she had to know about Miranda. How much had he loved her? Had he grieved for her so much that he wanted to die? Would he ever come to terms with their parting? Would he ever be free of her? Until she had the answers to these questions, how could their marriage succeed?

'I—I would like you to tell me about Miranda, Lucas. Before you marry me, I need to know if you are still mourning her loss?'

Pain clouded his eyes. 'Miranda? How do you know about her?'

When Tilly saw the taut line of his jaw and how his expression had hardened slightly, her mouth went dry and her heart began to beat in heavy, terrifying dread as she sensed that he had withdrawn from her. 'Mrs Carstairs told me. I know you are a private person, but if I am to be your wife, if you cannot be open with me, then it bodes ill for the future.'

'You are right. You should know about Miranda—and why I am marrying you. When you told me about Coulson I was repulsed by the very idea of marrying a woman without any regard to the morality of the situation you were in. But I was so consumed with anger that another man had taken what I cherished that I was blind to anything else. Yet much as I wanted to rebel against it, I found myself wanting you.'

Tilly's heart soared and his confession brought a smile to her lips, but the grim expression that suddenly appeared on his face gave her a sense of unease and made her wary. 'I was a fool to let you think Richard Coulson and I had been lovers and I am sorry. I didn't mean for you to suffer. I thank God all was not lost.'

'No, it is not and I will show you,' he murmured, taking her face between his hands.

The sound of his deep, reassuring voice, combined with the feeling of his strong gentle fingers closing around her face and his lips placed tenderly on hers, did much to dissolve Tilly's misgivings. When his lips left hers, her gaze searching his face, she said, 'It would mean a great deal to me, and to our future together, if we could put this behind us, so will you not tell me about Miranda? I don't want to pry into your relationship with her, but it is perfectly natural for a wife to want to know if her husband's old love is still a threat.'

'You do me a grave injustice, Tilly, to imply I would love another woman when you are to be my wife.'

'I'm sorry. I didn't mean to. I know you loved her and that she hurt you when you parted.'

For a long moment his gaze met hers with penetrating intensity. 'Yes, I loved her. I thought she felt the same. I was young and dazzled by her. We were to be married—the wedding was arranged until she went to London and met someone else. She was beautiful—she was also deceitful and treacherous as sin. There had been other men before me—men known to me, who mocked my youth, my ignorance and my innocence.'

Tilly stared at him. 'You are saying that you do not still love her?'

He nodded. 'I came to realise that when I met you. What I felt for her was something more primitive than love. Whatever it was that bound me to her was so powerful that I was in danger of losing my immortal soul. She lived in Truro with her parents, who also had a house in London. It was where Miranda met a rich American gentleman, married him and went to live in America.'

Tilly bowed her head. At last she understood why he had behaved the way he had when she had told him about Richard Coulson, why he would not let his feelings and emotions get the better of him. She could not blame him for not wanting to love any woman. Her heart ached with remorse. For a man as proud as Lucas to have his proposal of marriage flung back in his face, which was what Miranda had done, must have made him furious.

'She hurt you very badly, I can tell.'

'I chided myself relentlessly for having been tempted by her, for having believed she felt as I felt. Remembering, I hated myself with a hatred and contempt that were absolutely bottomless and I swore that the woman I took for my wife would not be like she was. I vowed that my emotions would never again be engaged by a woman. I wanted none of their treachery and deceit.'

'And you thought I was like that. I am not Miranda, Lucas—although I am sorry I gave you reason to believe I was like her.'

'And yet, my love,' he said, 'before I knew the truth, I came to realise that I wanted you so much that it no longer mattered. What I feel for you transcends anything I have felt before. It seems impossible and yet I know it is true, for here I am, totally enamoured with you.'

Tilly looked up at him, his achingly handsome face languid and his blue eyes dark with passion as his fingers gently traced the line of her throat. 'Thank you for telling me about Miranda. We'll be man and wife in just a few days and I can't tell you how relieved I am knowing there will be just me and you, with no other woman in the shadows.'

Walking towards where their horses were grazing on the soft turf, Lucas slipped his arm about her waist and paused, looking down at her. 'There is no one else, Tilly. There never will be. It is important to me that you believe that.'

The intensity of his gaze ploughed through Tilly's composure. The yearning in his eyes smote her. 'I do—now.' Kissing him lightly on the lips, she smiled, looking towards where the riders were parading ahead of them. 'I think I see Anna waving to us. We should go. Just a few more days, Lucas, and we will be man and wife.'

And then suddenly it was the wedding day and as servants and footmen scurried about in a frenzy of preparations and bridesmaids ran excitedly about the house, Tilly was in her room being dressed in a creation of champagne silk gauze. Anna and her maid had spent all morning getting her ready. Her hair was brushed until it shone and then drawn back from her face into a heavy chignon. Round her throat she wore a necklace made of amethyst gemstones with matching earrings to match the colour of her eyes. They were a wedding gift from Lucas. He would have given her diamonds, but ever since she had told him how Richard Coulson had promised her diamonds if she married him, he had developed a strong aversion for that particular gemstone.

When she was ready and it was almost time to leave for the church, Charles, who was to walk her down the aisle, came to see her.

'Well,' he said, his voice hoarse with emotion and pride as his eyes passed over her appraisingly. 'You look…you look beautiful, Tilly—like a princess,' he said reverently. 'How I wish our parents were here to see you today. They would be so proud of you. Are you nervous?'

'Terribly—but I'm also happy.'

'We should be leaving. William said there are crowds of spectators around the church, with congestion on the roads. It's as if the whole of London has turned out to see you wed.'

'Oh, dear, I never imagined I would be so popular—unless it's the handsome man I am to marry who has drawn the crowd, or even my terribly attractive brothers. I never can decide which of you is the most handsome.'

Charles grinned, adjusting his cravat. 'As far as I'm concerned there's no contest. It's me, of course. Besides, everyone turns out to see the bride on her wedding day and to look at what she's wearing. They won't be disappointed.'

## Chapter Twelve

Charles was right. The crowds and vehicles blocked the streets around the church in Hanover Square. The bridesmaids being kept in check by Anna were waiting. The church was bedecked with urns of sweet-scented flowers. The organ music swelled. Drawing a deep breath and taking Charles's arm, Tilly walked slowly down the aisle, bearing a spray of white lilies.

All the radiance in the world was shining from her eyes which were drawn irresistibly to the man who was waiting for her at the front of the church, overwhelming in stature, his ebony hair smoothly brushed and gleaming. His claret-coloured coat, dove-grey trousers hugging his long legs, matching waistcoat and crisp white cravat were simple but impeccably cut. Anna had taken her seat beside Aunt Charlotte, who looked proudly on, dabbing a tear from her eye.

The blue eyes of her husband-to-be held hers, narrowing, assessing, the woman walking towards him snatching his breath away and pride exploding throughout his entire body until he ached with it, for no bride had ever looked so lovely. He stretched out his strong hand and offered it to her. She lifted her own and placed it in his much larger, much warmer one. Lucas felt the trembling of her fingers and saw the anxiety in her large eyes. He gave her hand a little squeeze in an attempt to reassure her.

The music drew to a close. As Tilly spoke her vows, firm and sure, she was aware of little more than his close proximity and his firm hands when they slipped the ring on her finger. At that moment she felt herself possessed and at the same time a rush of happiness that he was the possessor. To this man she had committed her life and at that moment she recognised the emotion that had struck her when he had kissed her at Clifton House. She no longer had any doubts that she was deeply and irresistibly in love and this revelation sealed the bond between them.

They were pronounced man and wife and the next thing Tilly knew was her husband's lips on hers, sealing their union, and they were walking back down the aisle with a drift of bridesmaids behind, smiling broadly to all those who had come to witness their union.

With the aid of grooms outside the church, they were ensconced in the shiny black carriage and managed to get through the snarl up. Along with the rest of the wedding cortège, they were soon at William's house for the wedding breakfast.

Already anticipating the night to come, food was served and wine and liquor flowed. Gifts were received and congratulations given, wedding cake cut. The whole day had an air of unreality about it.

The wedding breakfast over, Tilly went to her room to prepare for the ball.

\* \* \*

When she was ready, with a smile pinned to her face and with Anna by her side, she passed through some of the anterooms to the ballroom. It was exquisitely decorated and festooned with flowers on pedestals.

Some of the fashionable, overdressed gentlemen lounged against pillars, drinking wine and talking and laughing much too loudly as the liquor loosened their inhibitions. Tilly was confidently aware of the gleam of her beautiful wedding dress hinting at the contours of her long shapely legs as she walked. Long gloves encased her arms and her shining dark hair was caught up at the crown in a mass of thick, glossy curls.

She was surrounded by other ladies, beautiful, bejewelled ladies, but when Tilly put her mind to it only she had that perfect self-conscious way of walking. She moved as if every man present was watching her. She walked as if she were irresistible, such was the power of her conviction that she would achieve her goal in what she had set out to do—to retrieve her good name. Even the jewels adorning the throats of the ladies winked at her like bright-eyed conspirators as they caught the prisms of the chandeliers.

Looking ahead, she saw Lucas waiting for her. His midnight-blue evening clothes accentuated his long lean body to perfection, his hair as dark as her own brushed to perfection. The pleasure of seeing him again eclipsed her earlier panic about attending the ball. Lucas Kingsley was as handsome of physique as he was of face. His chiselled features were touched by the light and a gentle ache in her bosom that grew and grew attested to the degree of his attractiveness. His masculine perfection dominated the scene.

A half-smile curved his lips as he watched her come closer. He raised his fine, dark eyebrows. She completely ignored the young women eyeing him with encouraging, flirtatious glances over their fans, tittering and giggling. Where other women might have succumbed to the irresistible pull to see behind the cool façade and start uncovering the man beneath, Tilly merely returned his smile, knowing perfectly well what lay beneath.

Taking her hand, he smiled down at her. 'You look exquisite, my love. Are you ready to take to the floor with me for the first dance? Everyone is impatient to join us on the dance floor, but it would be bad etiquette for them to do so before the bride and groom.'

'Then we'd best not keep them waiting any longer.'

It was quite magical when Lucas led her on to the dance floor and gathered her into his arms for the first waltz. Feeling terribly conspicuous, with all eyes upon them, she hoped she wouldn't trip up and make a fool of herself.

Aware of her nervousness, Lucas murmured, 'Relax.' She almost missed her step, but his arm tightened, holding her steady. 'Focus your eyes on me and you'll be fine.' He steered her into the first graceful steps as the music washed over them.

Gradually, other couples began to step on to the floor. Of their own volition Tilly's feet followed where Lucas led and her mind opened to the sensations of the dance. She was aware of the subtle play of her skirts about her legs and the hardness of her husband's thighs against hers. The closeness of his body lent to her nostrils a scent of his cologne, fleeting, inoffensive, a clean masculine smell. The seductive notes of the music were mirrored in their movements and the sway was a sensual delight. Lucas's hand at her waist was firm, his touch confident as he whisked her smoothly around the ballroom.

The ball became lively as everyone threw themselves into enjoying themselves. Tilly danced with Charles and William and other gentlemen she could not put a name to, for all her thoughts were focused on just the one. Her husband.

They were to spend the first night of their marriage at William's town house. It was almost midnight when they managed to slip away while everyone was still enjoying the festivities. Tilly said goodnight to Aunt Charlotte, who was having a rare old time, the madeira she had consumed having flushed her cheeks a bright pink. Kissing her soundly and wishing her all the luck in the world, Charles and William ushered her on up the stairs, and when she looked back at them, they were still watching her, grinning like a pair of hyenas.

Having removed her wedding finery and the pins from her hair, and wearing a cream silk dressing gown, she dismissed her maid. The room was sumptuously furnished, tastefully decorated in pastel cream and green, with a huge, canopied bed fit for a king.

Tilly sat before the mirrored vanity, brushing her hair until it shone. She tried to ignore her nervousness, not knowing what to expect beyond the basic facts as told her by Aunt Charlotte. Knowing Lucas would be joining her from the connecting room at any minute, her anxiety increased.

When he stepped into the room, dressed in a dark blue silk robe, through the mirror she watched him come close and paused her brushing. Standing behind her, he placed his hands on her shoulders and, lowering his head, pushed aside her hair and placed his lips on her neck before meeting her eyes in the mirror.

'So, here we are at last,' he murmured. 'Happy?'

His warm breath caressed the back of her neck, and then his lips trailed over her sensitive flesh to her ear, while she turned liquid inside. 'Yes—you know I am,' she said, closing her eyes as she enjoyed the feel of his closeness. 'Are you happy, Lucas?'

'Absolutely. I am the luckiest man alive to have you for my wife—and my lady. Countess of Clifton. How does that feel?'

Tilly's heart swelled to hear him say that and her mouth curved in a smile. 'Strange, but I suppose I'll get used to it. It's been a lovely day—although I swear, I only remember the half of it. Did we really get married?'

Laughing softly, he again bent his head to nuzzle her neck with his lips. 'Believe it, my love. It happened—and you looked like an angel in your wedding gown. But I prefer you like this—with your hair loose and wearing nothing but a robe.' Meeting her gaze once more in the mirror, her eyes warm with passion, he gave her a lazy grin and said, 'Shall we go to bed?'

Standing up, she walked into his arms, wrapping her arms around his neck and tilting her head back to look at his handsome face. 'I would like that. But…you…you realise that this is all new to me, don't you, Lucas?'

'Why, what's this? A fit of nerves?'

'A bit.'

'Then don't be. I will be consideration and gentleness personified,' he murmured, slipping the knot on the belt of her robe and sliding it off her shoulders where it settled in a pool at her feet. 'You have the loveliest eyes I have ever seen and I like the way they sparkle when you laugh, and darken when we kiss. I remember an unbelievable softness when I kissed your lips, and a warmth the likes of which set my heart afire.'

A wicked grin highlighted his lips as he glanced at her. 'I also like the way you look in your nightdress—but I would like you better without it.'

Tilly felt the soft caress of his gaze which caused a familiar twist of her heart, an addictive mix of pleasure and discomfort. His warm eyes looked at her in undisguised admiration as his gaze took in her silk nightdress to match her robe. 'You are very eloquent, Lucas, but please don't go on. I would prefer you to show me with your lips.'

'My thoughts exactly.'

Again, his arms went round her and he found her lips, drawing her senses into the heated depths of a kiss, as his hands deftly slipped the straps of her nightdress off her shoulders, revealing the cleft between the round fullness of her breasts. Her cheeks flushed scarlet at his boldness.

Bending his head to pay homage to the soft flesh glowing like creamy pearls in the soft light, he placed his lips in the hollow of her throat where a pulse throbbed. Heat blossomed and spread inside her. But the heat building inside Lucas, fed and steadily stoked, was escalating into urgency. He needed to touch more, to explore without the encumbrance of fabric.

Standing her away from him, he slipped the offending nightdress down over the curves of her hips and thighs, where it joined her robe on the carpet. Her glorious body was a shade of pale gold in the wavering blur of the candles.

Chest tight, eager to seize, to devour, to slake the lust that drove him, every nerve Lucas possessed stilled as slowly, his gaze traced up the curves of her long legs, the gentle swell of her thighs, over her taut stomach and minuscule waist to her breasts, full tipped with rosy peaks.

Tilly's throat dried. His eyes focused upon her figure and the ardour in his dark gaze was like a flame to her senses. Fuelled by a whirlpool of emotions she didn't recognise, much less understand, she fled to the bed, climbed in and pulled the covers over her nakedness.

'When you've finished ogling me, Lucas, kindly remember you're supposed to be a gentleman and take off your clothes, too—unless you intend to make love to me with them on.'

Desire having become a physical torment, he disposed of his robe and joined her in the bed.

'That's better,' she said. 'Now we're the same—and I have to say, Lucas Kingsley, that you're a fine-looking man without your shirt on—although,' she said, remembering another time she had seen him minus his shirt, 'I have a confession to make.'

'You have? Then you had better tell me—although I feel I must tell you that I have an aversion to a divorce,' he teased.

'It's nothing like that…only… Do you promise you won't be cross?'

'Absolutely. It is our wedding night. I'll forgive you anything. I'm curious. What is it?'

'One day—I didn't know you very well, I saw you on the beach. You stripped off to your trousers and went for a swim. You swim very well, by the way. Despite my previous dunking, I would like you to teach me some time.'

'It will be my pleasure. But why on earth didn't you make your presence known? Where were you hiding, ogling me?'

'I wasn't hiding—nor was I ogling. I was sitting among the rocks when you appeared. I liked watching you, which is why I stayed where I was.'

'I see. Well, what can I say, only that I hope you weren't disappointed.'

'No, I wasn't. Quite the opposite, in fact,' she said, snuggling close to him. 'Now, will you please kiss me.'

'It will be my pleasure.'

Gathering her into his arms, as he held her tight against him, his kisses consumed her in the violent storm of his passion. Lowering his head, his mouth moved to circle her breasts, kissing each in turn, before travelling down to her stomach. Operating wholly on instinct since her wits had flown, Tilly craned her neck back and her fingers laced through his thick hair as she abandoned herself to his lips, his hands—intimate and evocative, exploring the secrets of her body like a knowledgeable lover, savouring what he found—and the pleasure that burned through her, expanding, mounting, until her body shuddered with the force of her passion.

When he shifted position to take control, the warmth of his body pressing close against her own, wrapping her arms about him, Tilly opened up to him, her kisses driving him on, inciting his passion until he could no longer control the force that had claimed him. Her hands tensed on his shoulders, but she did not cry out when he entered her. He paused and looked down at her.

'Are you all right, Tilly? Did I hurt you?'

She shook her head slightly, hardly daring to breathe.

'That's good, my love,' he said, his voice low with passion, soothing her so seductively as he began to move.

The discomfort she had felt passed and her body came alive with pleasure, unfolding like the petals of an exotic flower. Never in her imagination had she experienced anything so erotic as this. All her senses became heightened and focused on him and what he was doing until nothing else mattered.

This was how she wanted him, all his iron will stripped from him, his passion for her driving him on. There was no hiding for either of them when they were in the throes of passion, of pleasure, consuming them in undulating waves.

They reached their climax in unison. A blissful aura broke over them. Spent and exhausted, slowly they drifted back to earth, drained and incapable of any movement other than holding each other close. Tilly sighed, the physicality of their lovemaking, her vulnerability and her implicit surrender sweeping over her as her hand caressed Lucas's furred chest.

He eased away from her, and, drifting on a tide of glory, in the aftermath of their passion she curled against him, her body aglow, her limbs weighted with contentment, firm in the belief that her husband was a man of extraordinary prowess. Finding his lips, she kissed him softly, then, lost in the wonder of completeness, naked limbs entwined, with a soft sigh she let exhaustion claim her.

Lucas leaned on his elbow and gazed down at the young woman with a mass of silky hair who was now his wife in every sense of the word. He thought of all the nights to come and his blood stirred hotly at the mere thought. He was engulfed in a swirling mass of emotions, emotions that were new to him, emotions he could not recognise and could not put a name to.

His every instinct reacted to the fact that he had this woman in thrall, that he'd finally breached the walls and captured the elusive creature at its core. He gloried in the fact that she was his, here, without reserve. Gently, he touched her hair, brushing her flesh with his arm, feeling the warm reality of her.

Conscious of the languor that weighted his limbs, of the satiation that was bone deep, he realised that this state had been reached not by mere self-gratification, but by a deep contentment more profound than at any other time in his life. Tilly had succeeded in tapping the source of his well-being where every other woman he had known had failed.

They were soon to leave for Devon. He looked forward to showing her her new home and all the things he had come to cherish as a boy and throughout his life into manhood. Nostalgia swamped him, for it was at a time such as this that he missed his parents and Cassie.

They would have taken to Tilly and welcomed her into the family with open arms.

Tilly sensed the presence of a warm, naked masculine form pressed against her as she floated in a comforting grey mist.

'Good morning,' Lucas murmured huskily. 'I trust you slept well.'

Opening her eyes, she gazed up at him and her lips curved in a smile as she stretched her lithe body. 'I slept very well. In fact, I cannot believe I slept at all after what we did.'

Kissing the tip of her nose, he nuzzled his lips against her cheek. 'Are you ready for breakfast?'

'Absolutely not,' she uttered with mock indignation. 'I have a different kind of appetite now and I am not ready to face the world for, well, another two hours at least. Besides, I must look a complete mess.'

'You, Countess, look quite delectable, but you are also wanton. Despite that, I am willing to oblige you in any way you choose.'

He laughed. She liked it when he laughed. His tousled hair, with an errant wave falling over his brow, was dark against the snowy whiteness of the pillows, and sleep had softened the rugged contours of his handsome face. He was utterly irresistible in his naked state.

Remembering their loving, of how he had lingered over her, guiding her to peak after peak of quivering ecstasy, caressing and kissing her with the skill and expertise of a virtuoso playing a violin, a warm glow engulfed her and she found herself reaching for him again.

Later, she was to look back on this night when Lucas

had lit the spark within her that was like having a fire in her soul. She would never have known such wild, sweeping passion existed were it not for Lucas. Better by far to experience that passion for such a short time, than never to have known it at all, even if it brought such pain and heartache, or to die not knowing such joy, such intoxicating sweetness was possible.

It was a lovely early autumn day when Charles embarked on the East Indiaman, which was to take him to India. They all went to East India dock to wave him off. He had delayed his sailing due to Tilly's wedding. He was excited by the prospect of India and impatient to be on the high seas. Tilly was sad to see him go and cried a little, but her joy in her marriage and the excitement of returning to Devon overshadowed everything else.

They were to travel with Florence and Tobias the day after Charles's departure. William and Anna were to return to Cranford, promising to visit them at Clifton House in the spring. Quite worn out with all the wedding arrangements and looking forward to a quiet time, Aunt Charlotte would travel down to Drayton Manor at a later date.

Their journey to Devon was uneventful. The weather held and, changing horses frequently at the coaching inns, they made good time. Florence had enjoyed her time in London, but was glad to be returning south. Tobias was restless and often fretful at being confined to the coach for long periods. Keeping him entertained was often difficult and, his patience running thin, Lucas would climb up front with the driver and leave them to it.

Both Lucas and Tilly looked forward to the nights they spent at the inns along the way when they could be together. Tilly fell more in love with her husband with each passing day. She would anticipate the nights of love and she would tremble, in part from an inexplicable excitement that his mere touch never failed to evoke in her.

She was delighted to see the sea again and the thought of it being available to her for the rest of her life gave her a warm glow. And then suddenly they were at Clifton House, gracious and almost shining in the clean air. One of the peacocks appropriately appeared on the lawn, strutting along with its head high in his desire for admiration, a peahen following sedately behind.

Lucas had notified the butler when to expect them. Everything had been prepared for their arrival. It was cool inside the lofty hall. Tilly had insisted she didn't want any fuss, but the housekeeper had other ideas on the proper way to welcome the new Countess of Clifton. The servants were lined up in the hall to be introduced to the new mistress, although many of them were already acquainted with her from her previous visit.

Tilly had ridden to pay a visit to Mrs Carstairs and returned, only to find Florence and Tobias were nowhere to be found. Thinking Florence might have taken Tobias into the garden, she scoured the secluded places she might have gone. She was not to be found anywhere. Deeply worried and with a feeling that something was very wrong after speaking to one of the maids who helped Florence in the nursery, she went to find Lucas in his study to alert him to her disappearance.

He looked up when she entered, frowning when he saw the anxiety on her face. 'Tilly? What is it? Is something wrong?'

'It's Florence. She's nowhere to be found. She's taken Tobias.'

Lucas's face hardened and his eyes darkened. Anger flared in them, as sudden and as bright as quicksilver. 'When was she last seen?'

'Mid-morning. One of the maids who helps her in the nursery told me her sister's husband arrived from Dawlish with a message that her sister is very poorly and wanted to see her.'

'And has she gone?'

'Yes—at least she's gone somewhere. I don't like it, Lucas. Something is not right. Wherever she's gone, she's taken Tobias with her.'

'I'll arrange for a search party,' he said, getting up and striding to the door. 'If she was last seen mid-morning—two hours ago—she could be anywhere. Did anyone see her speak to this individual?'

'Apparently not,' Tilly said, following in his wake as she went out into the hall. 'She returned to the nursery for Tobias and no one has seen her since. Where can he have taken her?'

'But why did she not speak to you...or me?' Lucas said, raking his fingers through his hair. 'And why take Tobias? Why do I sense Jack Price is behind this? If he is, I shudder to think what he will do to them.'

At that moment the butler was opening the door to a caller. Two mounted Dragoons waited in the drive. The visitor, a tall man with a gaunt face and piercing grey eyes, introduced himself as the Revenue Officer, Lieutenant Owen Foster. Lucas remembered his name being mentioned when the Reverend Leighton and the magistrate had been for dinner before his trip to London.

'Pardon me for coming unannounced, Lord Clifton, but it is necessary that I speak with you.'

'Why are you here, Lieutenant?'

'You are aware that the smugglers use this part of the coast for their runs, Lord Clifton?'

'Very much so. What of it?'

'I have it on good authority that there is to be a large delivery of contraband tonight. We've been waiting for this for a long time and hope to arrest some key figures. The Coastguard and Excise men and the Dragoons will all be ready.

'The sea is choppy, the winds fair, but not a problem at present—no moon, so the conditions are favourable for the free traders. I thought you should know since it may turn violent when the smugglers realise their plans have been blown wide open. If some of them manage to get away, then they will try to make it north over your land.'

Lucas nodded. 'I don't think I need ask the name of the man you seek.'

'Jack Price.'

'I have a problem of my own at present, Lieutenant. I believe my nephew has been abducted—roughly two hours ago. For reasons I do not wish to go into, I believe it is Jack Price who has taken him. The child is seven months old. His nurse is with him. I have to find Price myself before the child comes to harm.'

'And you think your prediction is correct?'

'Yes, I do.'

'I understand your concern, Lord Clifton, but I am compelled to ask you not to try to find him for the present—in fact, I will go so far as to forbid it. If he has taken your nephew we will find him, but Jack Price is a man who must be apprehended. I have been after him for too long to have my plans jeopardised.'

Lucas stiffened. He didn't like being denied by anyone, but he had to admit that the Lieutenant might have a legitimate point.

For the rest of the day both Lucas and Tilly waited in a state of suspended anguish for darkness to come. Despite Lieutenant Foster's orders to leave what was to happen later to him, Lucas was determined to be there to see Jack Price brought down and to retrieve Tobias and Florence. Tilly insisted on going with him. When Lucas objected, she set her jaw mutinously, her eyes shining with determination.

'I will do nothing of the sort. I'm going with you.'

'No, Tilly. You'll be safer here.' His mouth was set in a grim line. 'For once in your life you will do exactly as you're told. You are far too stubborn for your own good.'

Tilly, not to be deterred, squared her chin and met his gaze head on. 'You say what you like, but I will not stay here. Besides, Florence or Tobias might have need of me.'

Reluctantly Lucas relented. 'Very well. But when I tell you to keep out of sight you do as I say. Is that clear?' Tilly nodded. 'You are being extremely difficult,' Lucas remarked, raising a disgruntled brow at her.

'I would have you know I am never difficult,' Tilly

was quick to insist, 'save, of course, for those times when you aggravate me into being so.'

'It will be hazardous on the beach,' he reminded her. 'I'd never forgive myself if some harm came to you. I couldn't bear to lose you.'

The genuine concern in his voice touched Tilly and warmed her heart. She prayed to God that it was so, that he was all hers and would be so for evermore, but until he told her that he loved her a shadow of doubt would always remain. 'Don't look so gloomy. You need have no fears for me. I will behave and not do anything rash. I promise you.'

Lucas drew her close to him. 'If you do, my love, I will tell you now that I will never forgive you.'

'Worry not, Lucas,' she whispered, momentarily managing to overcome her anxiety for Florence and Tobias and force a little smile to her lips. 'I shall still be here to plague you.'

When darkness shrouded the land, Lucas, with Tilly by his side, took to the saddle and vengeance rode with him. His nephew had been taken by a man who he was convinced was responsible for the death of his parents. No man had ever set forth with a blacker rage filling his heart.

The moon was hidden behind a bank of cloud. Her eyes having become accustomed to the dark, Tilly glanced across at her husband. He was bent low over the horse's neck. She caught the gleam of a pistol butt at his waist. Beneath his French cocked hat, his face was set and intense.

This self-contained man with a single-mindedness

had his thoughts on a purpose. He knew they were facing a grave emergency, that from now on the momentum would build until it reached its inevitable climax, and for him there could only be one conclusion.

Tilly found the inky blackness total and terrifying. Gradually their eyes became accustomed to the gloom. Coming to the edge of the cliff, they dismounted and tethered their horses out of the way. Suddenly, she started when half a dozen figures materialised out of the dark. One of them was Lieutenant Foster, two of them Excise men, and the other three Dragoons. All were armed with pistols and swords.

'Everything seems to be going to plan,' Lieutenant Foster told Lucas in a low voice. 'They are not expecting us. Price placed two lookouts on the cliff-top, but they've been taken care of, having given us the signal they were to use with a little coercion. I let it be known I'd be in Plymouth. It's a night of no moon—perfect for a run. I hope to catch Price red-handed. Hopefully they'll run straight into the trap we've set for them. They cannot escape.' His words carried conviction.

'Where are the rest of the troops?'

'They're placed strategically around the cove. They have orders to hold their fire unless any of the smugglers try to escape and not to invade the beach until I give the signal. Price has his men waiting in the gully that opens on to the beach further along with the pack horses. They cannot see the Dragoons waiting on top of the cliffs. The Revenue cutter with the Coastguard on board is round the headland and will appear when the boat is sighted with the contraband.'

Lucas nodded, his face grim. 'Congratulations, Lieutenant. You appear to have thought of everything.'

'I hope to God I have. I've been after Price too long to allow him to slip through my fingers tonight.'

'But what of Florence and Tobias?' Tilly asked, fearful for the nurse and her charge.

'I've received reliable information that Price has them. He's ashore—probably waiting in one of the caves for the vessel to land. When the contraband has been unloaded, he plans to have the lad and his nurse put on the boat and taken to France. What fate he has worked out for them I shudder to think.

'We must apprehend them before the boat sails off—although there's no chance of it getting away if the Revenue Cutter appears on time. Don't worry, Lady Clifton, we'll get to them in time, but we won't make a move until the contraband has been brought ashore.'

For the next hour they played a waiting game. The wind rose and then the vessel they waited for was sighted, its ghostly shape riding the waves towards the shore. The one-masted cutter which brought the contraband from France carried no light. It bobbed about like a cockleshell on the heaving water, perilously close to the cliffs. On shore and on the surrounding cliffs the Dragoons waited.

There was a flash of light from the shore followed by two more signalling it was safe for the vessel to land. When the contraband had been taken off, the smugglers would load their haul on to the backs of horses and make the long climb up the high moor.

Lucas saw men at the oars struggling in well-drilled

unison against the swell of the sea, using brute strength to keep it from smashing into the rocks. A man stepped over the side and climbed into a rowing boat. They watched him row towards the shore, where he climbed out and dragged the boat over the shingle and some way up the sands.

He rapped out orders to some of the men waiting in the shadows, the wind whipping the words from his lips as the sloop delivered her cargo into small waiting boats. At that moment men and horses pulling carts appeared from the gully, scattering like ants over the sand to load the contraband on to the backs of the horses, and from one of the caves further along the beach a man appeared, shoving a woman in front of him, a woman holding a child in her arms.

'Florence,' Tilly said. 'Lucas, that's Florence—and she has Tobias.'

When she made a move to run down to the cove, Lucas took hold of her arm and drew her back. Knowing how headstrong and wilful she could be, he placed his hands on her shoulders and gripped them hard, forcing her to meet the intensity of his gaze. 'What I said to you earlier applies now more than ever, Tilly. Listen to me and listen well. No matter what happens from now on, you will remain out of sight at all times. Is that understood?'

He saw the spark of defiance gleam from the velvety depths of her eyes and the stubborn tilt to her chin. His mouth tightened, his dark brows coming together, and he spoke with grinding resolution. 'I mean it, Tilly. I want you to find it in your defiant heart to obey me on this, otherwise I shall have one of these soldiers escort you back to the house, where you will remain until I return.'

Tilly opened her mouth to argue with him, but his gaze was so hard and unyielding that she bit back any words she was about to utter. 'But what about Florence and Tobias?'

'When I manage to get down there, I will bring them to you, but until then you keep out of sight.'

She nodded dully. 'I will do as you say. But please take care, Lucas.'

He nodded, thrusting her further back. His pistol at the ready, gripped firmly in his hand, he moved to the edge of the cliff and disappeared down the path.

The contraband was unloaded with well-practised precision. From his stance behind some rocks, Lucas had his eyes firmly fixed on Jack Price standing close to the sea edge. He was holding on to Florence while issuing orders to the men. Suddenly, pandemonium broke out as the Dragoons poured on to the beach, firing warning shots into the air.

Lieutenant Foster shouted to the smugglers to stop or they would be fired upon. They ignored the command and began scattering in every direction, half-crazed with fear. They didn't know in which direction to run. Ahead of them were the soldiers, behind them the sea. Soon swords were brandished and torchlight glinted on the cold steel.

Seeing what was happening, Jack Price shoved Florence, holding on to Tobias, towards an empty rowing boat, ordering her to get in. Florence stumbled, almost dropping a mewling Tobias into the water. When he would have hauled her on to her feet and tossed her into the boat, Lucas came up behind Price, his pistol in his back.

'Let her go, Price,' he ordered. 'Move and you're a dead man.'

Slowly, Price turned and faced his enemy, his eyes gleaming like bright slits. 'By whose hand, Kingsley?' he challenged boldly. 'Yours?'

'Why not? I hold the weapon.'

Price had seen the red-coated Dragoons and splashing through the surf towards him was Lieutenant Foster. 'Foster! I might have known,' Price sneered.

Lieutenant Foster nodded, moving closer. 'Surprised, Price? Did you expect to find me absent from Biddycombe?' He laughed derisively. 'How unfortunate for you that I'm not. You've led us a merry dance up to now. But you're finished, Price.'

Price was visibly furious at this unexpected turn of events, and he felt at a disadvantage—a unique experience for him. His presence was noted and from that moment he knew there was no escape. He might be Devon's most successful smuggler, prepared to use any misbegotten, contemptible method to achieve his aims, but nothing had been more important to him than to rid himself of his brother's child, whose very existence threatened everything he considered was his from the moment he had learned of Edmund's death.

'You are guilty of many things, Price,' Lucas said contemptuously as the Lieutenant helped Florence out of the water, 'but the one that concerns me is the crime of kidnap—and you can only think yourself lucky that your crime has not extended to the murder of an innocent babe,' Lucas said with icy calm, 'otherwise I would kill you myself.'

Seeing what was going on around him, that his men were fleeing the scene and the cutter about to set sail, Price saw the imminent threat of defeat, but he was not prepared to give in now. His hard mouth curled in a savage sneer. 'So, Kingsley, you thought to deceive me when you brought my brother's brat from Spain to steal my inheritance.'

'The child is Edmund's son, the inheritance of Trevean his by right.'

'A child with the blood of our enemy—your sister. Do you think I would let a Kingsley take what is mine?'

'Not for one minute—which is why I bought the boatyard. Yes,' Lucas informed him when fury propelled Price towards him. He stepped back. 'I bought the boatyard for Tobias to make sure when you played your dastardly game, he had something that had belonged to his father. Even your own father wanted it kept out of your hands.'

'Damn him.' Price spat. 'I damn him to hell.'

'As you did my parents when you tried sending them to the bottom of the sea? The truth, Price,' Lucas said, ramming the barrel of his pistol against his chest, his free hand clenched into a fist and his eyes as cold and hard as obsidian blackness. 'I've waited a long time to hear it—and since this is your day of reckoning, you might as well tell me the truth before I decide to put a hole through your black heart.'

'The truth is it you want? Then look no further and I will tell you,' Price hissed, a wild hatred filling his eyes as he thrust his face contorted with rage at his most hated enemy. 'I was on a run—me and my fellow traders. The skipper of the sloop your parents were on saw me and tried to stop me. By the time their vessel caught up with me they'd seen our faces. They knew too much.'

Lucas was deadly quiet. 'So, you and your gang of murderers sent the boat and all those on board to the bottom of the sea. There were no survivors—but bodies were retrieved.'

'Aye, so I heard and a grand send-off you gave those who sired you—better than was deserved for the dastardly Kingsleys.'

Lucas would have gone for him then if Lieutenant Foster and one of the Dragoons hadn't pulled him back.

'Enough,' the Lieutenant ordered. 'The man isn't worth hanging for. He'll get his just deserts in the end.'

From her vantage point on the cliff, Tilly watched everything that was happening. She saw Lucas confront Jack Price and the Lieutenant take charge of Florence and Tobias. Suddenly, there was pandemonium as the escaping smugglers made a dash for the sea, milling around Lucas and the Lieutenant. She watched as Jack Price made a lunge for the rowing boat he had tried to shove Florence into. He threw himself into the boat and began to row out to the cutter for all he was worth, trying to widen the distance between him and the shore. But the men on the cutter had seen what was happening on the beach and were equally desperate to escape.

It began to move away, faster now she was lighter, having shed her cargo. But not far away were the lights and outline of another vessel bearing down on them. Tilly realised this must be the Revenue cutter. The smugglers were caught like rats in a trap, and as a fusillade of shots broke out from all around the cove, the desperate scramble for life went on.

From the shore Lieutenant Foster shouted to Jack Price to stop or he would be fired upon. He ignored the command, rowing faster against the incoming tide. Suddenly, there was a loud report and a sudden flash or orange flame shot across the night sky as the soldiers opened fire on the boat. The cutter began its own desperate battle to escape the Revenue cutter, only a few lengths away.

The soldiers hauled the boat back to the shore and hauled Jack Price out on to the sand. At first, they thought he was dead but, as if sensing their presence, he opened his eyes, sunk deep in their sockets, forcing them to focus on Lucas. They were filled with so much hatred and contempt that Lucas was seared by it. He tried to speak, but before any word could pass his lips his whole body convulsed. When his head rolled to one side and his lids sagged over his eyes, devoid of life, Lucas knew he was dead.

Tilly, who had ventured on to the beach when she saw the soldiers had everything in control, stood beside Florence, who was clutching Tobias to her. She was numb with shock and cold from her stumble into the sea. Lucas came and placed an arm comfortingly around Tilly's shoulder and drew her to him. He was accompanied by Lieutenant Foster, who draped a cloak over Florence's trembling shoulders.

'Why would he want to get rid of the boy?' he asked Lucas, staring down at Jack Price.

'His reason is complicated—it is a long story, Lieutenant, one that will keep until later.' He clasped his wife tight and placed a kiss on the top of her head, feeling her tremble. 'Come, Tilly. You shouldn't be here.'

'I'll get someone to accompany you and the nurse back to the house,' Lieutenant Foster offered. 'I'm sure your husband will be along shortly.'

'Yes, you go, Tilly—you, too, Florence. Is Tobias unharmed?'

Florence nodded, gazing down at the child in her arms. 'He is. He's been a brave little chap. So very brave—just like his father.'

# *Epilogue*

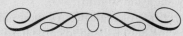

Later, with Florence and Tobias safely tucked up in the nursery, hopefully none the worse for their ordeal at the hands of Jack Price, Tilly waited for her husband to return. When he walked in, wet and dishevelled and slipped his arms around her, she sighed with contentment, breathing in the manly scent of him—of soap, leather and the smell of the sea.

'Is it over?' she asked softly.

She felt him smile before he lowered his head and placed his mouth on her neck, gently nuzzling her warm flesh. 'Yes, my love,' he murmured. 'It is over. Jack Price is dead. His body is being taken to Trevean. His fellow smugglers have been rounded up, and the cargo impounded by His Majesty's Customs.'

'I can't believe he's dead,' Tilly whispered.

'I have to say that it is no more than he deserved. He was a rogue and a blackguard to the end, who manipulated and cheated all those involved in his illegal operations. He lived a villain and died a villain and leaves a legacy of torture and plunder—excessive evils indeed in a country where smuggling is almost a way of life.

He also confessed to the murder of my parents and all those on board the vessel they were on.'

Tilly's heart went out to him. 'I'm so very sorry, Lucas, but you always suspected him of having something to do with their deaths. At least now you know the truth.'

'Yes—and he's paid the ultimate price. Did Florence tell you why she went to him?'

'Apparently one of Jack Price's men paid a visit to her sister, forcing her husband to come here. He told her Jack Price had asked for her—and to take Tobias with her, otherwise her sister's family would be harmed.'

Lucas's arms tightened around her. 'What a terrible ordeal it's been for her. But it's over now and we can all move on—no more of Jack Price's threats.'

'And his father? He has lost both his sons. The enmity between you will have to end, Lucas.'

'The enmity between our families goes back decades. It became more virulent as the years passed, and when Jack came along, but Ned was never my enemy. I cannot forgive his son for what he tried to do to Tobias. God knows what he intended doing when they got to France—probably to be sold into slavery or some such thing.

'Despite his son, I think Ned has suffered in his own way when he lost Edmund. It left him with a well of loneliness and bitterness. I'd like to think we could become friends.'

'Reconciliation and redemption can defy anything that's gone before, Lucas—forgiveness, too, if you let it. One thing I learned when I was growing up is that it's easy to condemn, but harder being compassionate.

It seems to me you have shown compassion for Ned Price, even if the reason is hard for you to understand just now.'

With his arms around her, he smiled softly. 'You have a beautiful head on your shoulders, Tilly—and a wise one. Ned Price has a grandson—we will have to decide where and how he is to be raised, which we will do between us. I will be neighbourly towards him and welcome the hand of friendship if he offers it, but at this moment it is you who fills my thoughts, you I care about, you I adore and love.'

Filled with a feeling that was part-joy and part-reverence, with love passing between them in silent communication, Lucas kissed her softly, tenderly. Raising his head, he sighed heavily. 'I am so fortunate to have found such a wonderful Countess. I love, admire and respect you. During the past few years, I have lost my close family and there were times when I thought I would never come through.

'But then I met you. You have reinvented my life for me and I am never more content than when we are together. I bless the day I landed on that beach and met you. You have brought purpose and meaning to my life and you make me feel human again—to forget the heartache the loss of my parents caused me, followed so soon by Cassie.'

Tilly lifted her thickly lashed eyelids, and the dazzling brilliance of her wonderful violet eyes lovingly caressed her husband's handsome face. His eyes burned with all the love and passion she had once despaired of ever seeing there and, for the first time in her life, she was able to savour the joy of loving and being loved.

Through a blur of tears, she smiled tremulously. 'Thank you for saying that, Lucas. You already had my heart—and now I know I have yours.'

\* \* \* \* \*

# How The Duke Met His Match
Sophia Williams

MILLS & BOON

**Sophia Williams** lives in London with her family. She has loved reading Regency romances for as long as she can remember and is delighted now to be writing them for Harlequin. When she isn't chasing her children around or writing (or pretending to write but actually googling for hero inspiration and pictures of gorgeous Regency dresses), she enjoys reading, tennis and wine.

Visit the Author Profile page at millsandboon.com.au.

## Author Note

I hope you enjoy reading *How the Duke Met His Match* as much as I enjoyed writing it!

We know that women in England had far fewer rights and career options in the Regency era than they do today, but that didn't mean that there weren't a lot of strong, independently minded women who did their best to live their lives the way they wanted to. I wanted to write about one of those women, someone who would do her best to maintain her independence no matter what life and the laws and customs of her time threw at her. And that was Emma!

She was of course more than a match for Alex, the duke—a still-grieving widower with a sometimes-cold exterior covering a heart of gold. But I think that she also met her match in him in that he was perfect for her: open-minded and caring enough to respect women more than a lot of men at that time did, and also of course very good company and devastatingly attractive...

I also enjoyed setting the story mainly in England's beautiful Somerset, a southern county with rolling countryside and many picturesque villages.

Thank you so much for reading!

# DEDICATION

To George

# Chapter One

*London, 1817*

Alexander, Duke of Harwell, froze for a second as Lady Cowbridge, smiling broadly, ushered her daughter towards him. She couldn't have indicated her intent more clearly had she produced a bishop and had their wedding banns read.

This had to be about the tenth such approach made to him in the past hour. Enough was enough. Alex unfroze, inclined his head very slightly in the direction of the two ladies, and turned to march himself straight out of the ballroom's nearest doors.

Before he'd managed to cover the ten feet or so to the end of the room, yet another dowager placed herself in his path. This one was resplendent in a jade-green dress and was holding a bejewelled hand outstretched towards him. She gave the lavender-clad young lady she was accompanying a little push with her other hand, so that she stumbled almost right into Alex.

As he executed a swift sidestep to avoid a collision, Alex caught a glimpse of the younger lady's expression.

Her eyes were downcast, long dark lashes against her cheeks, and her brow was furrowed in a slight frown. By contrast, the older woman was looking straight at him with her wide smile increasing, as though she was about to address him.

Alex muttered, 'Excuse me,' and almost leaped out of the long, glass-panelled doors ahead of him into the garden.

He should have resisted his friends' entreaties to attend this ball. He didn't remember the season being quite as awful as this, though. Had the mothers and guardians of marriageable young ladies been as determined in their pursuit of him—like vultures circling their prey—the last time he was single? He didn't think so. But perhaps the full decade that had passed since then had dulled his memory. Or perhaps his elevation from viscount to duke had increased their determination.

Safely through the French doors, he was hit first by intense heat from the remarkable profusion of lanterns clustered around the door-frame, and then, as he moved a little to his left along a terrace that seemed to run all the way beside the house, by the freshness of the clear February night. And, God, that was good.

He closed his eyes and leaned his head back against the wall of the house, allowing himself a long moment to appreciate the peace, the coolness of the air on his cheeks after the claustrophobic warmth of the ballroom and the faint scent of the autumn leaves from the trees in the mansion's small garden, infinitely more agreeable than the cloying perfume inside.

Amazing to think that he'd actually loved London life ten years ago.

Right now, all he wanted to do was to go home to

Somerset. In fact, maybe he'd bring forward his return to the country. He missed his land, the open space, the opportunity for long walks and hard riding. And his local friends and tenants. And, of course, he missed the boys, his sons. It didn't feel right to be away from them for any extended period since they'd lost their mother. Yes, maybe he'd return home tomorrow. Ask his man of business and his lawyers to attend him there.

His thoughts were interrupted within a couple of minutes by a couple crashing out through the doors and coming to a halt only a few feet from him. Instinctively, he moved further along the terrace into the shadows. He had no desire to stand right next to a lovemaking couple, and he wasn't ready to re-enter the ballroom. So shadows it was.

He hadn't moved far enough. The couple's voices carried very clearly to him across the still night.

'Let go of me,' the woman hissed.

Not a lovemaking couple, apparently.

Alex turned reluctantly to look at them, illuminated by the lanterns, as the woman seemed to struggle in her partner's hold. The man pulled her close to him with one arm and with his other hand gripped her face far more tightly than a lover would. The woman continued to struggle, and then suddenly went quite limp.

Alex took a couple of steps closer. He had no desire to get involved in any lovers' tiff, but what he'd seen so far indicated that this was something more sinister than that. He should check that the woman was all right. If he was sure then that all was well, he would apologise for interrupting them and leave them to it.

He opened his mouth to speak just as the woman, as suddenly as she'd gone limp, dipped her head and bit the man's arm, and simultaneously seemed to kick him on the shin from beneath her dress. The dress was a pale lavender, like the one that the green-clad lady's younger companion had been wearing. Perhaps the same woman.

The man jerked and let go of her, spitting the words, 'You vixen,' as she picked up her skirts and began to run towards the ballroom.

Alex was contemplating landing a punch to the man's face, to teach him a lesson in addition to the kick and the bite, when the man lunged forward and caught the young woman around the waist, pulling her back against him.

'You'll pay for that,' he growled as she tried to resist his pull, her arms flailing.

Alex sighed internally—he'd so much rather just go home and go to bed than get involved with this, but clearly he had no choice—and stepped forward.

'It appears that the lady doesn't wish to be mauled by you,' he said.

'Mind your own business.' The man's voice was slightly familiar, maybe someone Alex had known in town in his younger days.

Alex shook his head. 'Let go of her now,' he said, injecting as much steel into his voice as he could.

He could see the man properly now in the flickering light. Sir Peter Something. Always with a group of men scrabbling at the edge of polite society. He could see the woman's heart-shaped face too. She had clear, light brown skin and deep brown eyes, which were glistening right now. Definitely the young lady who'd been with the woman in green just inside the ballroom.

Sir Peter looked up at him and shrank away, as though scared, but pulled the lady with him. She did something with her leg and Sir Peter gave an unattractively high-pitched little howl and then shook her a little.

'Enough.' Alex took a step towards them and clamped his hand round Sir Peter's—puny—forearm, until he let go of the lady with another little mewl of pain. Truly pathetic. Alex moved between the two of them and held his arm out to the lady.

She looked at Sir Peter, and then at Alex, and then took the proffered arm. 'Thank you, sir.' Her voice was remarkably steady, given the situation.

They began to move together towards the steps, away from Sir Peter, the young lady gripping Alex's arm very tightly. Thank God he had been here. She'd done a good job of fighting Sir Peter off, but she'd have been no match for him in the end.

Alex was going to take her inside, return her to her chaperone, make sure that she was safe with her, and then leave.

'Do you—?' he began.

He was interrupted by a sudden commotion at the ballroom door above them and a man shouting, 'Miss Bolton, Sir Peter.'

As Alex looked towards the door Sir Peter launched himself at the lady—presumably Miss Bolton—and attempted to kiss her. Miss Bolton got one arm free and dealt him a forceful blow to the ear, which made Alex smile and Sir Peter howl yet again.

'You will not treat me so when we're married,' Sir Peter panted.

Really? Alex shook his head. Everyone was aware that rogues attempted to compromise young women into marriage fairly often, but Alex hadn't personally witnessed such an attempt before. The commotion at the door was increasing now, and the man who'd just spoken was shouting inside the room about what he'd just seen. Presumably a co-conspirator.

Alex felt his lip curl. He held his hand up and addressed the gathering crowd. 'I have been here the entire time and this man has in no way compromised this lady. Nothing untoward has happened between them.'

'Incorrect,' Sir Peter shouted, apparently a lot braver with a crowd supporting him. 'This young lady has given me her virtue. She is my fiancée.'

The woman in green who'd been with Miss Bolton inside the ballroom pushed her way through the throng and planted herself in front of them. 'Emma, is this true?'

'No, Aunt, of course not.' Miss Bolton's voice was shaking a little now.

'Look at her gown.' Sir Peter's voice was triumphant.

Alex's eyes followed where the man's spindly finger was pointing. The bodice of Miss Bolton's gown was torn, exposing most of her full breasts. It must have been ripped during their tussle. Miss Bolton looked down too, and pulled ineffectually at the fabric, while Alex began to work his arms out of his tightly fitting jacket.

'Miss Bolton and I will be married tomorrow,' Sir Peter announced. 'I have a special licence.'

'Emma, how could you?' her aunt moaned.

'I couldn't and I won't,' Miss Bolton stated.

'Yes, you will.' Her aunt spoke out of the corner of her mouth, as though that would prevent anyone from hearing her. 'You are ruined.' She indicated with her arm towards the crowd at the doors.

'No.' Miss Bolton visibly shuddered.

'Yes.' Sir Peter put his arm around her waist.

She tried to move away and he gripped her more tightly, pulling her further from Alex.

Oh, God. Alex had the strange sensation that he could see, almost feel, two avenues open to him. One, the easy one, where he walked away from this situation. These things were not unheard of in Society, and usually the young lady—the victim—in question wasn't lucky enough to have a saviour to hand. Had he not been here, Miss Bolton would now be affianced to Sir Peter and that would effectively be that.

Unfortunately, Alex *had* been here, and it seemed that he was going to take a second avenue, which he was pretty sure would be hell. It was as though he was observing the scene from a distance and could see catastrophe unfurling but could do nothing to avert it.

'We will be married by the end of the week,' Sir Peter said.

'No.' Alex stepped forward, holding his jacket. 'The young lady is *my* fiancée. Unhand her immediately.'

For God's sake. He was speaking like an actor in a cheap melodrama. And, a lot more importantly, he'd just announced that Miss Bolton was his *fiancée*.

Sir Peter didn't let go of Miss Bolton. Alex took another step closer and glared at him, and the man's grip on her slackened. Alex moved right next to them, clenching his fists, and Sir Peter shrank backwards. Nothing more pathetic than a cowardly bully.

Alex moved in front of Sir Peter and placed his jacket around Miss Bolton's shoulders, his hand brushing the bare skin of her upper arm briefly as he held the jacket so that she could put her arms into the sleeves. He fancied that he felt her shiver as he touched her, and thought he understood why; it felt oddly...what, intimate perhaps? When it absolutely shouldn't.

He shook his head slightly. His mind was going in all manner of strange directions.

She looked up at him, her eyes huge in her small face, and whispered, 'Thank you.'

'My pleasure.'

Which was about as far from the truth as you could get. He was struggling to process what had just happened, but he did know that it was bad, very bad. He'd just announced that they were *engaged*. He had just committed himself very publicly to *marrying* this lady. Marriage. He didn't want to remarry. For his sons' sake, for his own sake, for Diana's memory's sake. But he clearly wasn't likely to have any choice now. He couldn't honourably let Miss Bolton down.

*God.* He wanted to put his head in his hands and swear and swear.

He couldn't do that, of course. It would be rude to Miss Bolton; and many dozens of people were watching them, chattering about them. He wanted to shout about the hypocrisy of the *ton*: the way in which they regarded themselves as above ordinary people and yet fed almost feverishly on others' misery, mob-like.

The hum of the crowd's chatter began to increase, the air practically throbbing with it now. He and Miss Bolton both needed to leave.

He cleared his throat and held an arm out to her.

She stared at his arm for a long moment, and then took it with another whispered 'Thank you.'

He could feel her almost trembling, and reached his other hand over to press hers briefly for comfort. And strangely, for a moment, it felt as though the two of them were banded together against the rest of the world. Which was ridiculously fanciful and entirely untrue. They were complete strangers to each other, and, while it seemed unbelievable that they might indeed soon be banded together in name, they wouldn't be in practice. He would not be having any kind of real marriage with Miss Bolton—Emma—or any other woman. He just couldn't.

He closed his eyes briefly and then began to move towards the house.

And then the woman in green, Emma's aunt, trilled, 'Your Grace,' and sank into a deep curtsey before them.

It cost Alex a big effort not to roll his eyes above her head or snap at her. Now did not feel like the time for social niceties.

As Emma's aunt rose from her curtsey, a thought struck him and he looked down at Emma again, suspicious. Had this entire scene been enacted by her and her aunt to entrap him? Were they in cahoots with Sir Peter? He went very still for a moment, replaying the events of the last few minutes in his mind. No, highly unlikely.

He felt Emma shudder slightly again. No. Unless she was an outstanding actress, this absolutely couldn't be a scene of her making.

'Allow me to escort you home now?' he said to her.

'Thank you. I think that would be for the best. I must apologise. I am not normally so pathetic. I will recover my spirits directly. I must apologise also for your having been dragged into this situation.'

'Not at all,' Alex said with great insincerity.

*God*, he wished he'd left the house by the front doors after speaking to Lady Cowbridge. Or even just danced with Lady Cowbridge's daughter. Although, looking down at Emma's slim shoulders, dwarfed by his jacket, and her elegant neck beneath her dark brown, nearly black curls, he hated to imagine what might be happening to her at this moment if he hadn't been here. Nearly as much as he hated to imagine what was about to happen to both of them.

Barely credible, but he really had just announced to half the *ton* that they were betrothed. As in he really was going to have to marry her, because her aunt was right: she would be completely ruined if they didn't marry.

He shook his head for about the tenth time this evening. After his wife's death in childbirth he'd decided never to remarry. Even just the idea of allowing himself to love again and therefore lay himself open to the possibility of further loss was too painful to bear. And yet here he was.

Although, of course, this wouldn't be a love match. It would be one person helping out another, a marriage in name only. So he wouldn't, in fact, be betraying Diana's memory. He'd have to explain as soon as possible to Emma that this would not be a real marriage. He hoped very much that she wouldn't be too upset by that. If she was, it couldn't be helped, unfortunately.

Oh, God. What if she wanted children?

Why the *hell* had this had to happen?

He nearly groaned out loud, and then realised that Emma was speaking again.

'I wonder if I could possibly impose on you for a further few minutes of your time?'

It was an odd question to ask when they were about to be tethered for a lifetime, in name at least.

He was prevented from replying by Emma's aunt, wreathed in smiles, grasping their hands.

'Your Grace, Emma, I must congratulate you. Such wonderful news.' She half turned and waved to the hordes jostling behind her, almost as though she was seeking witnesses, just as Sir Peter had; and her rather odd turban—green, like her dress—slid to one side of her head.

She pushed the turban back into place, turned again to Alex and Emma, and said, 'I was well acquainted with your mother. I am Lady Morton.'

'How do you do?' Alex said, not bothering to try to smile.

Lady Morton really wasn't going to care whether or not he was happy; her ecstasy would do for all of them. He thought for a moment of his first betrothal—his and Diana's happiness, the sheer bubbling joy that had kept him permanently smiling and laughing for weeks afterwards—and wondered briefly if his head might explode.

Lady Morton began to talk volubly about weddings.

Alex just wanted to leave, get away from this nightmare.

Lady Morton's conversation turned to the miracle it was that her darling Emma had melted the heart of the Ice Duke. Really? The Ice Duke? That was what people called him? For God's sake.

He sensed Emma stiffen beside him and felt instant remorse. This situation was, of course, much worse for her than for him.

Her whole body seemed to heave and he looked at the top of her head more closely. Was she crying? He should get her out of here immediately, give them both a chance to begin to come to terms with what had happened.

'I'd like to escort my fiancée home now,' he told her

aunt, impressed that he'd managed not to choke on the word *fiancée*.

He'd walked the short distance here from his house, so he hoped Emma and her aunt had come in a carriage; it would be much better if they didn't have to walk back now. He should agree on a time to call on Emma tomorrow, so that he could explain that he could be married in name only.

'Of course.' The turban slipped again. 'Do you have a carriage? If not, please take ours. Dear Lady Cowbridge will take me home, I'm sure.'

Lady Cowbridge, who had beaten her way to the front of the scandal-drawn crowd swirling around them, looked as though she'd sucked a lemon. She gave one of the most insincere smiles Alex had ever seen and nodded her acquiescence.

Despite everything, Alex almost laughed out loud. From the looks of her, it would be some time before Lady Cowbridge would be forgiving Lady Morton for her ducal wedding triumph.

Emma squeezed the underside of his forearm surprisingly hard, and he looked down at her again. She must be desperate to leave.

'Good evening.' He nodded around the crowd and then began to walk forward with Emma through the hundreds of ball-goers, all of whom seemed to be attempting to get a close look at the two of them. They were obviously going to be the subject of much gossip for the next few days or weeks. Since there was going to be no way of avoiding the wedding, they should get it out of the way as soon as possible and escape to the country for a long time.

Being taller than most people, he had a very good

view of the fashionables swirling around them. Literally hundreds of people pushing. He caught a couple of snatches of waspish comments and felt Emma's shoulders tense. Glaring at anyone who dared to look directly at him, he tightened his hold on her and they picked up speed across the long room. Eventually, they reached a series of footmen and a butler in the large, marbled entrance hall.

The butler opened the front door to them as their hostess, Mrs Chardaine, pushed her way towards them and dropped into a deep curtsey, tittering as she did so.

'I shall be proud forever that you announced your love affair to the world at my house,' she said, fluttering her eyelashes at him. 'Such a great pleasure.'

'The pleasure is all ours.' Alex didn't smile.

'Thank you so much for a most delightful evening,' Emma said, not looking as if she was smiling very much either.

They finally made it out of the house, down the steps and into Lady Morton's carriage about five minutes later.

Emma sank onto the upholstered bench to the right of the carriage door and Alex seated himself opposite her. This was the first time he'd been able to take a good look at her. She was beautiful, but in a very different way from the current fashion for pale skin and blonde hair. Her skin was the warm light brown he'd noticed before, and her eyes and hair were very dark. She was perhaps a little older than he'd assumed she was, definitely in her twenties rather than in her late teens as most debutantes were. Maybe slightly older than he had been when he'd met and married Diana.

She started speaking almost before the footman had

finished closing the door behind them and Alex had sat down.

'Thank you so much for rescuing me. Obviously I won't hold you to your promise.' She was holding her shoulders square inside his jacket, which swamped her slender frame, and looking him straight in the eye, as though she meant what she said. 'I'll tell my aunt in the morning that it was all a ridiculous mistake.'

Alex felt his own shoulders actually physically relax for a moment at the relief of it, until a voice of reason from somewhere deep inside him shouted that telling everyone it was a mistake wasn't an option.

'You can't possibly do that,' he said. 'You'll be ruined.'

'No.' Her dark curls swung round her face as she shook her head with force. 'To speak distastefully frankly about money, I'm an heiress with a significant fortune. There will be men who are prepared to overlook what happened this evening. There is no need for you to marry me.'

'Yes, there is. You will be ruined otherwise,' he repeated.

'No, I won't. There are any number of impecunious aristocratic men who would be delighted to marry my dowry.' She cocked her head to one side and narrowed her eyes slightly. 'From the little I've seen of you, I would say that you have need of neither a wife nor a fortune?'

He looked at her for a long moment. He felt as though he should actually pretend that he did need one or the other or both.

He wasn't going to pretend.

'Correct,' he said.

'Then I cannot allow you to make this ridiculous sacrifice on my behalf.'

Alex raised his eyebrows. It was unusual for a young

lady to state that she would or would not allow a gentleman to behave in a certain way. Although nothing about this situation was usual.

'It isn't a sacrifice,' he said, the words sounding hollow. 'It would be my very great pleasure.' Oh, God, no. He didn't want to sound as though he wanted their marriage to be anything other than in name. 'That is, I...'

Emma snorted. In a small, very ladylike way, but it was definitely still a snort. 'Absolutely everything about your demeanour tells me that it would be a huge sacrifice and certainly not a pleasure. Clearly neither of us loves the other. I agree that some men, particularly those who have no need to marry for money, might be deterred by the events of this evening from wooing me, but I'm very sure that men like Sir Peter will still be happy to marry me.'

'Exactly. Sir Peter. A middle-aged roué, who would almost certainly treat you badly.' Alex thought for a moment with disgust of when Sir Peter had held Emma in his arms.

Emma opened her mouth and then closed it again, and then visibly drew a breath and said, 'Obviously, Sir Peter would not be my ideal husband. Indeed, I would rather work for my living than marry him, and will do so if necessary. However, I have it on great authority, that of my own aunt amongst others, that I "smell of the shop"—delightful phrase—and that that will already have deterred a number of suitors, but nonetheless my fortune has continued to attract a great deal of attention.'

'I'm sure that the attention is due to your beauty and your conversation,' Alex said with reflexive politeness.

Emma snorted again. 'Much like all the attention you received this evening was entirely due to your broad shoulders and wit rather than to the fact that you are a very rich widowed duke.'

Alex found himself giving a snort of his own—of laughter. 'Fair enough,' he said. 'Yes, I'm sure that you have received a lot of attention, for both good and bad reasons, but I'm not sure that any man with whom you might be able to live happily will now offer for you. You might not, in fact, have the opportunity to meet any more respectable and eligible men because if you don't marry me all fashionable doors might be closed to you. I think that you perhaps underestimate the snobbery of the *ton* and their delighted horror of scandal.'

'I think that you perhaps underestimate my father's fortune.'

Alex shook his head. 'I cannot see that you have any alternative but to marry me.'

'I'm grateful for your concern—indeed I'm very grateful to you for having rescued me from Sir Peter—but I do not feel that my future is any concern of yours.' She picked up her reticule as the coach slowed. 'Thank you again. If I might impose on you just a little longer, I'd be very grateful if I could keep your jacket until I reach my bedchamber. I will ask one of my aunt's footmen to return it to you tomorrow.' She bestowed a brittle little smile on him and moved forward as the carriage door began to open.

Alex frowned. Something was niggling in the back of his mind, something in addition to the big issue, which was that she was clearly doing the wrong thing.

He leaned forward himself and spoke to the coachman. 'My fiancée and I have not yet finished our conversation. Please drive on for another few minutes.'

'Actually, we *have* finished our conversation.' Emma's eyes were flashing as the coach drove off again. 'I would like to go inside now.'

She thumped on the silk-upholstered wall of the carriage with her fist.

'I'm sorry.' Alex banged on the wall with his cane and the coach came to a halt. 'That was very rude of me. I shouldn't have overridden your wishes like that. Could I ask one further question before you go inside?'

He'd worked out what had been niggling him.

Emma pressed her lips together for a moment, as though she was trying not to sigh, and then after a pause said, 'Yes, of course.'

'What did you mean when you said that you'd rather work for your living than marry me, and might do so?'

## Chapter Two

Emma wanted to glare at the duke, get out of the carriage, go inside her aunt's house and up to her bedchamber, crawl under her covers to digest the fact that her prospects had changed so dramatically in such a short space of time, and then come up with a plan. But she owed the duke a huge debt. She was still shuddering every time she recalled that without his intervention she might now be betrothed to Sir Peter and she was truly grateful to him.

She widened her lips into the best approximation of a smile she could manage, and said, 'I meant that I don't *need* to marry because I am very well able to work instead.'

The duke's eyes were narrowed. 'But why should you need to work? What of your great fortune?'

Emma *really* didn't want to talk about this. But, again, she owed the duke a lot, so the very least she could do was be polite.

'My father left me his fortune as dowry on condition that I marry a man from an aristocratic family within two years of his death. If I don't, I inherit nothing. Ironically, I don't even know whether Sir Peter's birth would be acceptable under the terms of the will.'

The duke raised his eyebrows but said nothing.

For some reason, it suddenly mattered to her what he thought of her father.

'It sounds worse than it is,' she told him. 'I'm sure my father truly only wanted the best for me. It's often difficult to know what the best for someone is.'

That was what she'd told herself, anyway, when she'd been *incandescent* with fury when their family lawyer had explained the terms of her father's will to her.

'He was a textiles manufacturer from Lancashire and my mother was the daughter of an earl, whose father cut her off when she met and married my father. Being excluded from her own family's social circle made my mother miserable. My father hired governesses for me and sent me to an exclusive seminary in Bath, because he wanted me to be able to take what he thought of as my rightful place in society. He didn't want me to be as miserable as my mother.'

No need to mention that her mother had been *so* miserable that she'd left Emma's father and gone to live in Paris.

'Except he was very comfortable living with me, so he didn't actually want me to leave until he died.' *So* annoying that her voice *still* wobbled when she talked about losing him. 'So I'm a lot longer in the tooth than the average debutante. In fact, I really shouldn't be called a debutante. Anyway, thanks to his obsession with educating me like a lady, I'm *extremely* well-educated—much better than most ladies, in fact—and so I flatter myself that I would make an *excellent* governess.'

The duke looked at her for a long moment, his eyes

grave. 'I'm sorry to hear about the loss of your father. And to hear about the situation in which you find yourself with regard to marriage.' He paused and then continued. 'But, being brutally frank, I'm not convinced that many families would happily engage a governess who had just been ruined in front of half the *ton*.'

'I would very happily be a governess to a family living in the country.'

He shook his head. 'News travels.'

Hmm. Maybe he was right. Emma swallowed hard. She was *not* going to cry. This wasn't the worst thing that could happen to anyone. She was only twenty-five, which was still quite young if you weren't a debutante. She was healthy; she was resourceful. She would manage.

'In that case, I will approach the headmistress of my old seminary.'

'I imagine that news travels just as quickly to seminaries and the parents of prospective pupils.'

Yes, he was right. She hadn't been thinking clearly. It must be the shock of the events of the evening.

'Fine. There are other options. I could be a housekeeper.'

'Really?'

Honestly. So sceptical. Of *course* she could be a housekeeper.

'Yes.'

'I haven't been involved in hiring a housekeeper myself, but I wonder whether you would be expected to have some experience.'

'I do have experience. I looked after my father and our house for several years.'

'I'm not sure that would be sufficient.'

Emma pressed her fingers to her temples for a moment. 'I'm sure I could find *something*.'

'And I am genuinely not sure you could. Not something palatable, anyway.' He sat back and looked at her for a long moment, his brow slightly furrowed, while Emma fought tears again.

*Why* had she become separated from her aunt for that moment, so that Sir Peter had been able to get hold of her arm and pull her towards the garden? Things had been going perfectly well before this evening. She'd received several depressing proposals from men whom she'd been sure would be difficult husbands, but at least three pleasant, impecunious younger sons of two earls and a viscount to whom she thought she might be able to be reasonably happily married had looked as though they were on the brink of proposing to her.

She'd had high hopes that at least one of them would be so grateful to get his hands on her fortune that he'd agree to her retaining some independence and travelling after their marriage. And if none of them had proposed, she'd been prepared to walk away from her father's fortune and this world, to which she didn't really belong anyway, and work as a governess and hope to save enough to be able to travel when she was older.

It was difficult to comprehend that both options seemed to have been removed from her grasp in one fell swoop.

The duke smiled at her, and Emma suddenly wondered what it would be like to lean, both physically and metaphorically, against his broad shoulders.

'I really believe that your best option now is to marry me,' he said.

The kindness in his green eyes was almost too much

to bear. For a moment, she wavered. Of course, of the options available to her right now, marrying him would be by far the best one, if only she could allow herself to treat another person so shabbily. She couldn't, though, because he clearly had no actual desire to marry her. It was one thing accepting the loan of his jacket and his offer of temporary escape from the predicament in which she had landed; it would be another accepting his offer to spend the rest of his life married to a complete stranger just because he'd been in the wrong place at the wrong time.

A thought struck her. His affections might well be already engaged. 'Are you…?' How to word it? 'Is there not someone with whom you are already acquainted that you would rather marry?'

'No.' He spoke the word so baldly that Emma gasped.

'No,' he repeated in a milder tone, and shook his head. 'No one else.'

She closed her eyes for a second and then said, 'I'm truly grateful to you for all your help this evening, but I cannot accept your very kind offer.'

Ridiculous that it felt more difficult to turn down the clearly extremely reluctant duke than it had to turn down the eleven sincere offers of marriage she'd already refused.

Her aunt had been beside herself about some of those refusals. She might actually expire with anger when she discovered that Emma had refused the duke, and was very likely to refuse to have her to reside with her any longer. She really hoped that her aunt wouldn't ask her to leave immediately. She would need some time to organise employment, and it would be a lot more enjoyable doing that while living in a mansion in Berkeley

Square than in whatever cheap lodgings she would be able to find herself.

Things were going to be dreadful for a while. She'd better end the conversation immediately, or she might actually finish by accepting the duke's offer.

'Thank you. I should now bid you goodnight,' she said.

The duke made no move to open the door. Well, she would open it for herself.

She untwisted her fingers—she now realised she'd been clutching her reticule ridiculously tightly—and reached out for the door handle. It was utterly ludicrous that she actually felt a momentary twinge of sadness at the thought that she would never see the duke again. Maybe it was because he was one of the few people she'd met in London who'd been genuinely kind to her, with no apparent ulterior motive.

As she began to turn the handle, the rumble of his deep voice cut through her thoughts.

'I have a proposal for you. You're right that I have no desire to get married. But I do need a governess for my three young sons. We lost their mother four years ago.' He paused for a moment, as though collecting himself, and then continued, 'Marry me, in name only, and act as governess to my boys. I will settle your entire dowry on you. I think this is a bargain we could both benefit from. You won't be forced to marry a man who might treat you badly, and you'd be financially independent, while I will no longer have to fight off matchmaking ladies who'd like their daughter to be a duchess, and, more importantly, I'll have found a governess for my sons. I've interviewed an extraordinarily large number of unsuitable candidates and was beginning to despair.

Had I had the good fortune to interview you, I would have offered you the job.'

'Really?' Emma hesitated, and then released the door handle and perched back on her seat. 'In that case, could I not just be your governess?'

The duke shook his head. 'I had already thought of that. There would obviously be gossip if the woman who had been announced as my fiancée became my sons' unmarried governess. I do not wish there to be any gossip surrounding my household, for the boys' sake.'

Emma nodded slowly. He was probably right. Wasn't his offer madness, though? Surely he couldn't really be so desperate for a governess that he'd happily marry someone to whom he didn't wish to be married?

The duke cleared his throat and shifted his eyes away from hers before looking back. 'I should point out that in accepting this bargain you would be relinquishing the opportunity to achieve a love union or have children. I would not like any scandal to attach to us.'

Emma nearly gasped out loud again. He *really* didn't want to get married. Unless he just found her particularly unattractive, of course. What he was suggesting sounded like a remarkably unusual bargain. Unbelievable, in fact.

'I don't want a wife, but I really do want a governess,' he said, as though reading her mind.

He smiled at her, a slow, lopsided smile that got to her somewhere deep inside as it grew.

'And I think you'd be wonderful with my children. I have a beautiful dower house on my estate, which is in Somerset. You would be welcome to live in it if you'd prefer your own household.'

Emma shook her head. This was all too much to take in.

'I... Being honest, I really don't know,' she said.

Before her father's death, she hadn't really thought about marriage beyond an infatuation at the age of eighteen with one of the factory managers that had come to nothing after her father had heard of it. He had banned them from seeing each other, and the manager, to Emma's extreme disillusionment, had fallen in with her father's wishes, telling her that he had no option because he couldn't support a wife if he had no employment.

She'd then assumed that, as the possessor of a significant fortune, she would, unlike the vast majority of women, be able to live however she liked after the far distant event of her father's death. By then she'd reflected on how her parents' incompatibility had destroyed their relationship, despite or even because of their mutual love, and had come to the conclusion that the only reason for her to marry would be to have children. And that if she did decide she wanted to marry, it would be to someone whom she liked and with whom she felt she could live happily, rather than to someone with whom she was deeply in love, because, from what she'd seen, passionate love could easily turn to hatred.

Her decision had been made for her by the terms of her father's will, of course. Once she'd recovered from her fury, she'd decided that she would make the best of it; she would hope to find someone pleasant with whom she could rub along quite happily, and hopefully they would have children. Indeed, the majority of her fury had been because it was just so *rude* and overbearing of her father to have dictated to her in such a way.

She suspected that she'd already come to the conclusion before his death that she wanted to have children and therefore wanted to marry. And now, she realised, she really did very much want to have children of her own. Could she give up that opportunity? Or had it already been taken from her because the only proposals of marriage she might receive beyond this cold-blooded, marriage-in-name-only one from the duke would be from men like Sir Peter, and she couldn't bear to marry someone like that?

She'd have the duke's children to care for, of course. Although only as their governess, and if their marriage ended in separation she might not continue to see much of them.

'Perhaps I could call on you tomorrow and you could let me know then, if that will allow you sufficient time to come to a decision?' he suggested after a couple of moments.

'Yes, please.' She really did need some thinking time.

'Excellent.' And there was that smile again.

As he moved in front of her to open the door and descend the carriage steps, her eyes were drawn to the bunched muscles across his shoulders, clearly visible through his shirt.

It was unusual for an aristocrat to have such a developed physique. Perhaps he boxed. His arms looked very strong too. Very…solid.

'Miss Bolton?'

*Oh.* He was waiting to hand her down.

She clutched the jacket tightly as she stood up, to avoid giving him another view of her chest, and moved to tread down the steps. And, goodness, it was difficult balancing when your hands were full of jacket. Her foot missed the second step and she began to sail through the air, one hand still holding the jacket and the other scrabbling against the side of the carriage to save herself.

Within a very short space of time the duke had her,

his firm and also very muscly forearm barely moving as he supported almost her full weight, before righting her with ease and helping her down the remainder of the steps.

She took a final step onto the ground and said, 'I must thank you again.'

She was annoyed to hear a tremor in her voice. It must be all to do with shock and nothing to do with how embarrassingly aware she suddenly felt of the strength in his arm, of how the fabric of his shirt stretched deliciously across his chest, just in line with her eyes.

'Not at all,' he said.

'Mmm.' She looked up at him and saw him swallow. Which made her swallow too. He had a very firm neck, and his hair was just longer than was strictly fashionable, curling a little over his collar. And…she was staring. She was staring at him. He'd saved her from Sir Peter, he'd saved her from falling out of the carriage, and she was staring. And his forearm really was very strong. And she *really* had to stop staring.

And, goodness, she was still holding his arm.

She let go very suddenly, as though it were very hot.

'So, thank you. And goodnight.' Her fake breezy tone sounded utterly ridiculous. 'So, I'll go inside now. Thank you.'

Good heavens, what was happening to her? This was insane.

She took a deep breath and, still clutching the jacket across her chest, moved towards her aunt's house.

'Of course.' The duke moved with her. And now she had nothing to say to him. Nothing. She could comment on how beautiful the still night was. But it wasn't really, nights were usually much more beautiful in the countryside, and also it just felt too mundane and inane a topic following the magnitude of the conversation they'd had inside the carriage. Maybe she could comment on how wonderful the ball had been. No. It hadn't been wonderful; it had been awful.

She glanced up at the duke's face. He was staring straight ahead at the house, his profile stern, apparently not at all tempted to speak either.

They trod side by side across the pavement and up the wide steps to the imposing front door of her aunt's house in continued silence, and it was one of the most excruciating short walks of Emma's life.

When her aunt's butler, Finch, punctuated the awkward silence by opening the door wide for her and bowing her inside, she could have kissed him.

'Thank you so much, Finch,' she said, almost jumping over the threshold in her relief.

Then she stopped and turned round. Obviously, she ought to bid the duke a formal goodnight.

She held her hand out to him. 'Good evening, Your Grace.'

The duke remained motionless for a moment, and then took her hand in his much larger one. And, of course, his hand was firm and strong, like the rest of him. And, *really*, she was almost blushing now. For no good reason whatsoever.

'Good evening.' He inclined his head over her hand, and, finally more in control of herself, she wiggled her fingers. He let her hand go and turned and went back down the steps. And insanely—truly *insanely*—she felt almost bereft, as though she was suddenly adrift in a boat on a choppy lake, with her only oar gone.

She shook her head. Her thoughts were utterly nonsensical. She did feel, however, as though she could do worse than putting herself under the duke's protection. As long as he would truly allow her a high degree of independence.

Three minutes later, she'd exchanged a couple of words with Finch before whisking herself upstairs and into her bedchamber. She was desperate to get rid of Jenny, her maid, so that she could plonk herself down on her bed and just sob for a few minutes at the enormity of everything that had happened this evening. And then she would have to begin to work out whether she should—could—accept the duke's offer.

'You're wearing a gentleman's jacket, miss.' Jenny, who had been with her since they were both very young, more of a companion and close friend than a maid, sounded both scandalised and delighted, clearly expecting a comfortable gossip about the ball.

'My dress tore, and, um, one of the gentlemen there was kind enough to give me his jacket.'

'Indeed!' Jenny raised her eyebrows and waited.

Emma said nothing.

'Did you have a lovely evening, miss?' Jenny picked up Emma's hairbrush.

'I did, thank you.' Emma swallowed a big lump in her throat. 'But I have the headache now. Thank you so much for your help, but I think I'll prepare myself for bed this evening.'

'Lady Morton won't be pleased if you do that.' Jenny wasn't budging. 'She'll think it doesn't befit your station. She already thinks it doesn't befit your station to have *me* to help you.'

'Well, luckily Lady Morton isn't here to witness my

appallingly unladylike wish to nurse my headache alone. So we don't need to worry about her. Thank you again.' Emma held her hand out for the brush.

Jenny looked at her for a while and then gave it to her. 'Call me if you need anything. Shall I take the jacket?'

'Thank you, lovely Jenny, but I'll keep the jacket here until I'm in my nightclothes.'

Emma pulled it a little more tightly round herself. She really didn't want Jenny to see her dress torn as it was. And, to her shame, she *liked* the feel of the jacket about her shoulders and body. It felt...maybe comforting? And it smelled deliciously masculine.

Emma suddenly realised that Jenny would hear all about her engagement from the other servants and be hurt that her mistress, her *friend*, hadn't told her herself.

'I had a very stressful evening. I promise I'll tell you all about it tomorrow morning. Promise. But I just need to sleep now.'

*Sleep.* Ha. She was more likely to be awake all night, wondering what she should say to the duke tomorrow.

'Goodnight, then, miss. If you're sure.'

'I am. Thank you.'

Descending for breakfast had been a mistake, Emma thought six hours later, eating toast and fruit while her aunt talked at both high volume and high speed, with no apparent need for breath, about Emma's forthcoming wedding, wedding dress, wedding trousseau, wedding reception, wedding everything. And it seemed that she was very much looking forward to visiting 'my niece, the Duchess of Harwell'.

When Lady Morton began to talk, with an affected dab at her eye with a napkin, about how delightful it would be to be great-aunt to the duke and duchess's children, Emma felt genuine tears forming behind her own eyelids and decided that enough was enough.

She popped the rest of the apricot she'd been eating into her mouth and pushed her chair back. 'I might perhaps take a walk in the garden square,' she told her aunt.

'Make sure you take a parasol. The February sun can be surprisingly strong,' her aunt said. 'And do, of course, take Jenny or a footman. The future Duchess of Harwell must not be seen walking unaccompanied.'

Emma very much wanted to be alone with her thoughts. 'On reflection, I might instead retire to my chamber and write some letters.'

'As you wish, my dear. What time did you say the duke would be calling this morning?'

'Eleven o'clock.'

'Unfashionably early, but one must make allowances for a man deeply in love.'

Emma managed to smile, and to refrain from rolling her eyes, and left the room to return to her chamber.

Half an hour later, she was thoroughly sick of her circular thoughts.

The whole idea was preposterous. Although in many ways ideal.

She didn't want to marry for love and, if the duke was true to his word—which she sensed he would be—this arrangement would allow her as much independence as she could hope to gain so that she could travel. And being governess to the duke's boys would allow her many of the benefits of motherhood.

But was he just being chivalrous? He clearly didn't need or want a wife. Did he really need and want a governess? And would he really have chosen her for the post? Would she be taking advantage of his kind nature in accepting his offer?

Enough. She should go for a walk. Fresh air was a commodity sadly lacking in London upper-class life, and the stuffiness of the house was making her headache even worse.

If she took Jenny with her, she could take the opportunity to tell her that she was—for the moment—engaged. And if she went now, she'd have time to come back and spend half an hour adjusting her hair and her dress before receiving the duke.

An hour and a half later, Emma allowed Jenny to give a final twitch to the dress they'd decided she would wear to take the duke's call—a primrose-yellow sprig muslin that Jenny said showed Emma's lovely skin and dark curls off very well—and said, 'Thank you. I might just spend two or three minutes alone to compose myself.'

'Of course, miss.' Jenny blinked hard, sniffed loudly, and waved her hand in front of her eyes. 'I'm that pleased for you I'm going to cry.'

Jenny had charged headlong down the 'it's so exciting' path, and Emma just hadn't been able to find the words to say out loud that the duke only actually wanted her as a governess. She *had* told Jenny that she was sure that, should the marriage indeed take place, she and the duke would maintain quite independent lives, and that she hoped to travel to India in due course to visit her grandmother's birthplace, but that had just had the effect of increasing Jenny's enthusiasm rather than dampening it.

'We don't even know that the marriage will go ahead.' Emma didn't want Jenny or anyone else to get excited about something that might not happen. She'd realised that she herself *did* want it to go ahead, because of *course* it was her best alternative, but she just couldn't agree to the duke's proposition if he didn't seem sincere in wanting her as his governess.

'Of course it will, miss. Why wouldn't it? Oh, *miss*. You're going to be a *duchess*.'

Emma did her best to blink back her own tears and to smile through the immense headache that was now throbbing at her temples.

'Indeed,' she said.

Ten minutes later, Emma had regained her composure and was walking in her best seminary-learned stately and composed manner into her aunt's blue saloon.

And there was the duke, directly opposite the door, standing with his back to the marble fireplace, looking straight at her without even the hint of a smile on his very handsome face.

Emma checked over her shoulder and, yes, she really was the person at whom he was looking in such a forbidding manner. It was difficult to believe he was the same person who'd rescued her last night. Now she could understand why people called him the Ice Duke; it wasn't just because he appeared frozen to all the ladies who set their caps at him, it was because he was capable of looking like *this*.

Like a man who was very unhappy at the prospect of going through with the offer he'd made last night.

She was going to have to tell him that, on reflection, she didn't want to accept the offer. She couldn't ruin a stranger's life.

He shifted his position slightly and his broad shoulders seemed to expand even further, filling a good half of the gilded mirror above the mantelpiece. He really was very big. And almost raw in his stern masculinity. It seemed quite ridiculous that he was wearing such tailored clothing; it was like seeing a lion in a dress.

'Emma, my dear?'

Oh, her aunt had been speaking.

'I believe you have not heard a word I said. I will leave you and the duke alone for a few minutes. There can be no need for me to leave the door ajar, I believe, when I understand that you are to be married within the next few days.'

Few days! And the door not ajar! Was her aunt actively trying to ensure that they were even more compromised into marriage?

Well, yes, she probably was.

'Good morning.' The duke's voice was so deep. Emma rubbed her arms to try to dispel sudden goosebumps.

'Good morning.' She took a long breath, feeling suddenly distinctly light-headed and wobbly on her legs. And tearful. But she must *not* cry. It was entirely understandable and to be expected that the duke didn't want to go through with marriage to her, and she should accept it with good grace.

She gestured to the sofas behind her. 'Shall we sit down?' She walked towards the nearest sofa and arranged herself in the middle of it, so that the duke couldn't possibly imagine that she was inviting him to sit next to her.

'Thank you.' The duke sat himself stiffly down on a sofa at right angles to the one she was on.

He gave her a half-smile and cleared his throat.

Emma waited.

He didn't say anything.

And she couldn't find any words.

She should speak immediately. Release him from his obvious agony. It was the only honourable course of action open to her; she couldn't effectively force him to marry her. Maybe it would be better if she stood up again, to signal to him that he should leave.

She rose to her feet and said, 'Your Grace. I'm certain that you are regretting your very generous offer last night. I fully understand, and indeed have no wish to go through with the charade myself. I thank you again for your kindness and bid you goodbye.'

# Chapter Three

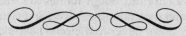

She was all huge dark eyes and riotously curling hair and heaving chest. She was... She was beautiful.

And Alex did not wish to think about that. He'd come here this morning hating the fact that he'd found her attractive nearly as much as he hated the idea of marrying her. He'd been desperately hoping that she'd have decided overnight that she didn't want to go through with it. He'd been planning that, if she *did* repeat that she didn't want to marry him, he'd thank her and suggest that he settle a sum of money on her, to ensure her financial independence, and then walk away hugely relieved.

But now he was with her, and she was saying exactly what he'd wanted to hear, and he knew both that she wouldn't accept any financial settlement from him and that he couldn't stand by and watch the ruination of her life.

It beggared belief that she would genuinely choose near-certain poverty or marriage with someone like Sir Peter over the proposition he'd outlined last night. She was clearly just being stupidly kind in not wishing to hold him to a promise that she'd thought he hadn't wished to make. So he was going to have to persuade her that he genuinely wanted to marry her. Difficult, because he really didn't.

Ignoring convention, he remained seated.

'I do not regret my offer, and I don't regard it as generous,' he said slowly, searching for words that would convince her. 'I would very much like you to be governess to my children. Their names are Freddie, John and Harry, and they are nine, seven and four years old. They're lively, but never malicious. I should warn you that Freddie and John do like to play jokes involving planting large insects in the way of people they think will scream on sight of them, so you should make sure that you don't scream the first couple of times they do it and then they'll stop.'

He was rewarded with a small smile from Emma.

'Have you had other governesses?'

'Six. Or seven. I forget exactly. The boys got rid of all of them, about which I am now delighted, because I know you would be so much better than they were.'

She narrowed her eyes. 'Hmm. Why is that?'

'You fought Sir Peter. You didn't indulge in any kind of vapours. You're clearly very kind. You state your case clearly and succinctly.' Good Lord. If he carried on like this he'd be a fair way to convincing himself that he genuinely wanted her instructing his boys. 'I think you would be an excellent governess.'

He was fairly certain from the way she was half frowning that he'd given her food for thought.

'Also, it would be of great benefit to me to be married, so that matchmaking chaperones no longer hound me. I really would be deeply grateful if you would marry me.'

She looked at him and swallowed, but didn't speak.

'I feel as though I am fortunate that fate threw us together yesterday evening,' he said. 'Our marriage could be the perfect solution for both of us.'

He was pretty sure that it would be a reasonable solution to *her* problems, anyway, as long as she didn't mind too much not having children. He was also pretty sure that he was doing a good job of sounding sincere.

'Really?'

'Absolutely. Please marry me? According to what we agreed last night?'

'*Definitely* really?'

'Definitely really.' Alex dug deep inside himself and produced a smile.

'I...' She drew a deep breath and then said, 'Thank you, Your Grace. If you're certain that you will benefit from our arrangement, then I in my turn am deeply grateful to you and I accept your offer.'

*Good. But also terrible.*

Alex shoved away the many negative thoughts jostling for prominence in his mind and focused hard on the fact that he was doing the right thing.

'Thank you.' He stood up to join her; he felt as if he ought to, now that they'd come to an agreement.

'No, thank *you*.' She had her hands clasped together, fingers locked so hard that her knuckles were whitening. Alex stood a couple of feet away from her, wishing that he'd remained seated and very conscious of his own hands hanging loosely by his sides as he watched hers clasping even harder.

'So.' He cleared his throat yet again. 'Would you be happy for me to make all the arrangements for the wedding? And would you be happy to travel immediately afterwards to my estate in Somerset?'

Emma nodded. 'Yes.'

'That's wonderful.' He choked slightly on the word *wonderful*. 'Perhaps in a week from now?'

He was going to have to journey back to Somerset for a night or two, to explain to his sons that they'd be having a new governess and that she would be called the Duchess of Harwell. Thank God they were too young to understand about things like marriage and stepmothers.

'Perfect.' She smiled a tight little smile that didn't reach her eyes. The miserable smile pierced his own misery and on impulse he reached forward and took her clasped hands in his.

'We can make this work to both our advantages,' he said. 'We really can.'

'I hope so.' Her hands relaxed slightly, and she allowed him to hold them separately in his. Looking down at the top of her dark head, he felt a surge of sympathy for her.

'I'm so sorry this has happened to you,' he said.

She looked up at him, tilted her head slightly to one side, raised her eyebrows and said, 'Although to hear you speak it couldn't have worked out better for you, because you need me as a governess.'

Honestly. So cynical.

'I do need you as a governess.' He smiled blandly at her. He'd suddenly wanted to make that clear, because there was something about her dark liquid eyes, the way she was looking at him, that had him feeling things he hadn't felt for a long time. Physical things, though, not emotional. And, rationally, that didn't matter. Physical attraction he could deal with. What he couldn't deal with ever again, and wasn't going to, was falling in love with someone.

Images of Diana struggling and then fading after giving birth to Harry, her coffin at her funeral days later and his three motherless sons flashed into his mind. The loss of Diana... He never wanted to experience pain of that magnitude again.

The saloon door rattled and began to open and the darkness cleared from his head. Good Lord, he and Emma were still holding hands.

Emma snatched her hands from his, as though they'd been doing something they shouldn't, and took a couple of steps away from him, turning to face the door and smoothing her skirts with her hands as she did so.

'Your Grace, Emma.' Lady Morton swept into the room, beaming. 'Do forgive my interrupting you. I come bearing wonderful news. The Bishop of Locke is able to marry you on Wednesday.'

'But today is Saturday,' Emma said. 'That's only four days away.'

'Fortunately, Madame Gabillard is able to fit you in this afternoon, and will work tirelessly on Monday and Tuesday to prepare dresses for your honeymoon. I had thought of a wedding dress similar to Princess Charlotte's silver one last year, but we don't have time for that, so I think the cream gown with silver overlay—the one that you were planning to wear to the Castlereaghs' ball, dear. The wedding breakfast is easily arranged. My own household will be able to prepare it with only a little additional help, and we can host it either in our ballroom here or in the duke's. I've already spoken to Tubbs about flowers. We will send invitations directly. The Duke and Duchess of Harwell will be forgiven for inviting their guests at such short notice. The breakfast will be very well attended.'

Alex drew breath, not sure which of the woman's false assumptions to tackle first. 'That's very kind, but I am able to make my own wedding arrangements,' he told her. 'I have business to undertake before the wedding. We are planning to marry next week. And—'

'Your Grace.' Lady Morton sank into a deep curtsey. Too deep. She wobbled alarmingly and panted, 'Emma.'

Emma and Alex both hurried over to her and hauled her up with an arm each. Lady Morton righted herself, but didn't let go of their arms, so that the three of them were standing in an uncomfortably tight circle.

'Thank you. I do not wish there to be any scandal attached to my niece, Your Grace. As her guardian, I must request that you marry as soon as possible.'

'One week is hardly a long engagement, Aunt,' Emma said.

'I must insist.' Lady Morton's voice was suddenly steely, and so was her grip on their arms. Alex looked down. Red marks were actually appearing on Emma's skin.

'Your Grace? I presume that, like most young men who have just got engaged, you are eager to enter into marriage as soon as possible. Wednesday.'

'I... Yes, of course. However, I have important business to undertake first.'

'I'm sure that as your wife, Emma will not prevent you from undertaking any important business. Although I trust that it is not of a delicate nature.' She screwed up her face and waggled her eyebrows.

'Aunt!' gasped Emma.

'No,' Alex almost snapped. 'It is not of a delicate nature.'

Not the kind of 'delicate nature' Lady Morton was

obviously implying. He hoped that marriage to Emma wouldn't mean that he had to spend much time with her aunt. He looked at Emma, who was clearly trying not to laugh, and to his surprise found his own lips twitching a little.

Lady Morton was squaring her shoulders, blatantly prepared to fight for Wednesday. He supposed he could explain to his sons after the marriage that they had a new governess. And...stepmother. He felt his entire face tighten. The word 'stepmother' was all wrong. As though he was being disloyal to Diana.

'Wednesday?' Lady Morton still hadn't released her grip on their arms.

'I'd be delighted,' Alex said after a long pause.

'Wonderful.' Lady Morton let go of their arms and reached up to pat his cheek, while Emma, half laughing and half grimacing behind her, mouthed, *Are you sure?* at Alex.

He nodded at Emma and took a step backwards, away from the cheek patting.

'Thank you for making the arrangements with the bishop and the church. I will visit the bishop myself to finalise preparations. And thank you for the offer of planning a wedding breakfast. Emma and I have, however, decided to leave for Somerset immediately after the ceremony finishes, and will not therefore be holding a breakfast.'

He wasn't going to refer to her mention of a honeymoon.

'No.' Lady Morton shook her head decisively. 'There must be a breakfast. Many of my friends are extremely desirous of attending and wishing you well.'

'I'm so sorry, Aunt.' Emma looked as desperate as he

felt to avoid a breakfast. 'The duke and I have to leave immediately once our nuptials are completed. He has urgent business in Somerset.'

'Sounds like a complete faradiddle to me.' Lady Morton plumped down onto the sofa on which Emma had just been sitting. 'However, if I can't persuade you, I can't. We shall have the wedding breakfast without you. Should I have the bill sent directly to you?'

Good Lord. Outrageous. Alex couldn't help smiling again at her effrontery, though.

He glanced over at Emma, whose eyes were dancing.

'Absolutely,' he said. 'And now I must take my leave of you. I have much business to attend to before Wednesday.'

'Outmanoeuvred. I'm sorry,' Emma whispered as he bent his head to kiss her hand.

He smiled at her and bowed at her aunt.

As he left, he heard Lady Morton say, 'You need to marry him as soon as possible, Emma, so that he can't escape.'

'*Aunt.*'

Almost exactly four days later, Alex was standing at the front of St George's Church in Hanover Square with his younger brother, Max, and the Bishop of Locke, waiting for Emma and trying very hard not to remember that the last time he'd stood waiting in this exact spot in a church he'd been waiting for Diana.

'Nervous?' Max nudged him, grinning.

Alex summoned a smile from somewhere, and said, 'Ha, yes.'

He really wasn't enjoying deceiving Max, but he'd been so happy for him, and Alex had been so pressed for time, that in the end he'd just gone along with Max's pleasure that he'd finally met someone new. Max was bound to hear a fuller version of the gossip surrounding the betrothal soon, and then Alex would explain. When he'd come to terms with it himself.

Max nudged him again as the door at the back of the church opened and Emma entered on the arm of a thin, older man. Perhaps an uncle.

'She's beautiful,' Max said in Alex's ear.

Alex nodded. Objectively speaking, yes, she was. The simple pale blue dress that she was wearing set off her slim figure and dark beauty perfectly. Although hadn't her aunt mentioned silver? Maybe Emma had put her foot down. Her hair was done in ringlets, falling down her neck, and she had a hint of colour in her cheeks.

It wasn't her beauty that caused Alex's heart to clench, though, it was the fact that, in contrast to when he'd last seen her in her aunt's drawing room, trying not to laugh about her aunt's outrageous behaviour, now she could barely meet his eye.

And the fact that when you'd been through a *real* marriage once, one like this felt all wrong.

He turned to face the front, suddenly almost overcome with misery.

Max squeezed his arm and whispered, 'Diana would have wanted this, you know.'

No. She really wouldn't have wanted him to enter a loveless union.

'Thank you,' Alex croaked.

Damn Max for being at least partially intuitive, knowing he was thinking about his first marriage. And damn this whole hellish situation.

Emma took her place at his side and he painted a

smile on his face before looking down at her. She was staring straight ahead, almost unnaturally motionless. God, he was self-centred. This was no worse for him than it was for her. In fact, it might be a lot worse for her than it was for him. From what he'd seen of her, she didn't strike him as a woman who was particularly desperate to be a duchess, and that was essentially all he had to offer her.

'This won't take long,' he whispered.

'I know.' Her voice was a lot steadier than his. She still wasn't succeeding in meeting his eye, though.

The bishop hurried through the service at a remarkable pace. Alex couldn't work out whether he was just bored with repeating the same lines yet again, or whether Lady Morton had warned him that she thought there was a danger of the groom absconding.

And soon they were at the main part of the ceremony. The part from which there was no going back.

'With this ring, I thee wed.'

For the second time since he'd met Emma, Alex had the sensation that he was watching this experience from afar, as though it wasn't really him doing the actual getting married. Emma's hand was very cold, so cold that it was easy to slide the ring onto her finger, despite the fact that her hand was shaking somewhat.

They offered each other lips-pressed-together smiles and a few minutes later the service was over and it was time to walk down the aisle towards the outside world as man and wife. They looked at each other, and then Alex held his arm out because for the moment they clearly had to behave like a normal couple. After a moment's hesitation, Emma took his arm lightly and they began to process down the aisle.

Alex was acutely aware as they walked that Emma was holding herself stiffly away from him, nearly as stiffly as he in his turn was holding himself away from her.

And finally, after what had felt like an extraordinarily long walk—that aisle must be a lot longer than the average—they were outside the church.

'I shall miss you so much, my darling Emma.' Lady Morton hugged her niece, before almost shoving her into Alex's chaise.

'I'll miss you too, Aunt. Thank you for everything,' Emma said as Alex handed her up into his curricle.

Alex winced as Lady Morton squeezed his cheek and said, 'Enjoy yourselves tonight,' before he jumped up next to Emma. He would have laughed under any other circumstances.

The door closed behind them and here they were, together, alone, the two of them, complete strangers, newly married in name only, trapped together on a lengthy journey.

Thank the Lord Alex had his horse excuse ready.

'Beautiful weather today,' Emma said as she arranged herself in the corner of one of the seats.

Alex sat down on the other seat in the opposite corner.

'A lovely day for a journey,' she added.

'Indeed. But somewhat chilly. There are blankets here, and I've asked my housekeeper to prepare a foot warmer for you for the journey. She should have it ready when we get to the house.'

'Thank you. The current fashion for wedding garb is sadly lacking in consideration for a lady's comfort. But I'd assumed we were leaving London immediately?' Emma's luggage had already been collected by one of Alex's grooms from Lady Morton's house.

'We are.' Alex cleared his throat, suddenly feeling a little...not rude, maybe awkward. 'But I'm going to ride alongside the chaise. The only way to get my horse home.' Not precisely true. If he'd really wanted to travel inside the chaise he'd have trusted his head groom to ride Star, his horse. 'We're going back to the house so that I can ride from there.'

'Oh, I see. That makes great sense. And I'll be able to read my novel without having to make polite conversation with you.' She twinkled at Alex and surprised a laugh out of him.

A few seconds later, they drew up outside his house.

'We'll stop for luncheon and a break for the horses at around one o'clock,' he told her. 'If you can drag yourself away from your book, of course.'

She smiled at him and he nodded—a little awkwardly—and then opened the chaise door. Maybe he should travel inside the carriage with her. It would be more polite and his riding separately might give rise to gossip. No. He didn't want to spend too much time with her. He really didn't want to get close to a woman again.

## Chapter Four

Emma found herself staring at the door that the duke had just closed behind him. It might be a metaphor for his clear signal that he planned to keep her closed out of his life as far as possible. That was completely understandable, of course, but, if she was honest, her spirits, which had not been high when she'd woken up this morning—her wedding day for goodness' sake—were now dragging even lower.

A journey spent in splendid isolation in this luxurious, velvet-upholstered carriage was going to feel very long, and a life spent in splendid isolation in the no doubt luxurious ducal castle would also feel very long.

Well, she would just have to make the best of it. She would have the duke's sons to care for, and he might accept her help in visiting tenants, and hopefully she would be able to make some local friends. And maybe, in time, despite his obvious reluctance, she and the duke might become good friends.

And now, at least she had time to read her book. She'd told the duke that she would be pleased to have some time to read—she'd even managed a little joke, of which she was very proud. She felt as though it was good to maintain one's dignity when one's husband had effectively told one that he didn't wish to share one's company at all. And she *was* pleased, actually, to have some peaceful reading time after the past few days packed morning to night with wedding preparations for a wedding neither of the two participants had wanted.

A few minutes later, she slapped the book closed, narrowly avoiding slamming her finger in it. It really was impossible to concentrate when out of the corner of her eye through the window she could see grooms, maids, all sorts of people bustling about, getting Alex's horses ready and finalising the packing of other carriages containing valises, trunks and servants.

It felt quite ridiculous, being incarcerated here by herself, so she was delighted when there was a knock on the door.

It was Jenny.

'The duke suggested that I travel with you, miss, oh, my goodness, *no*, Your *Grace*.' Jenny was practically bouncing on the spot, looking as though she was going to burst from excitement.

'Oh, *miss*.' Her eyes were saucer-like. 'Look at all the velvet. This is going to be *wonderful*. I'm so glad you're a duchess now.'

Hmm. It was kind of the duke to have thought of Emma's comfort, but maybe there was something to be said for isolation after all. Perhaps a journey alone would have been a good time for her to have begun to digest the fact that this morning she'd got married, when a week ago she hadn't even met the duke.

Jenny stopped bouncing and said, 'Would you *like* me to travel with you?'

Emma looked at her. She really didn't want to hurt

her feelings, and solitude *was* boring, and she could always pretend to bury herself in her book if she didn't want to talk. She was also likely to have a fair amount of time by herself over the coming weeks and months if the duke was intent on avoiding her, so she should probably take any company she could get.

'That would be lovely, Jenny.'

Jenny bounced herself into the chaise and took up residence on the opposite bench, while Emma tried not to find it annoying that so many people were pleased about her marriage.

'I've never been to Somerset before, miss.'

'Nor have I.'

'How long do you think it will take to get there?'

'I don't know.' Emma frowned, not pleased that she was so much at the mercy of the duke's whims. He had, of course, shown her nothing but kindness, but she would have liked to have had an idea of exactly where they were going and how long the journey would take.

She caught a glimpse of him out of the window, moving in their direction. He'd changed into riding wear, which showed off his strong physique marvellously well. Emma felt herself begin to smile in anticipation of him coming to speak to her again. She looked at the door, expecting him to knock, or open it. And...nothing.

And then the chaise jolted and began to move. Without another word from the duke.

Jenny actually clapped. 'Oh, miss, *Your Grace*, this is so exciting, isn't it?'

No, it really was not. More...profoundly depressing.

'Yes,' Emma said. 'I think I might read my book, if you don't mind.' She pulled it out of her reticule.

'Of course, *Your Grace*.'

This *Your Grace* thing was going to become annoying very quickly.

'You may continue to call me "miss" if you wish, Jenny.'

'Oh, no, miss, Your Grace, I couldn't do that.'

Emma smiled at her and shrugged internally. It probably wasn't going to be the worst thing about her new life.

The morning was long. Emma divided her time between trying to read but failing to turn more than a handful of pages—normally she was a voracious reader—and trying to look at the scenery and possibly catch a glimpse of Alex out of the window without catching Jenny's eye and having to talk. And, of course, just *sitting* the entire time. Frankly, doing absolutely nothing while feeling quite passionately irritable about life in general was exhausting.

When the chaise drew smoothly to a halt in a yard in front of an inn, Emma found herself almost beaming in delight. Luncheon. Something to *do*.

There was a knock at the door and it was pulled open.

'I hope you don't mind my intruding.' The duke's head and shoulders appeared inside the carriage and suddenly it felt significantly smaller. 'We stop here for luncheon.'

Emma regarded him, her head slightly on one side. Her husband. Her *husband*. How...odd.

As she had observed, his broad shoulders and sheer solidity showed off his riding wear to perfection, and the austere simplicity of his clothing was also perfect. It made one think very disparagingly of the frivolous frock coats worn by more foppish men.

Objectively speaking, he did look good.

Subjectively speaking, though, he was annoying.

He seemed to have literally no concept that she might not want to stop here, and that he should have asked her whether she would *like* to stop. Why should men make every single decision, from whether or not they should travel together, to when they should stop on the journey? Obviously she should be grateful to Alex—and she *was* grateful to him—but literally everything other than the fact that they'd got married in the first place seemed to be on his terms. Of course, it was the way of the world that men made all the decisions, but why should it be that way?

'Is this the only inn on our route? I'm not particularly hungry yet.' Emma realised immediately that she was starving. She also sensed Jenny twitching on the opposite side of the chaise; she was probably hungry too.

The duke looked at her. She really wished she could read the expression on his face.

'We need to change the horses here,' he said. 'The next good inn is twenty miles distant. If you'd prefer to wait until then to eat, we can, of course, do that.'

'Thank you.' Emma smiled at him while her stomach growled. Apparently she'd just bitten off her nose to spite her face.

The duke hesitated briefly and then said, 'Jenny, I wonder if I could have a moment alone with Her Grace?'

'Of course, my lord, Your Grace.' Jenny almost fell out of the chaise in her haste to comply, and was only saved from falling flat on her face by the duke catching her arm.

Emma's mind immediately went to when he'd caught *her*, the evening they'd met, and a shiver ran through her entire body.

Once he had Jenny solidly on her feet outside the chaise, the duke put his head through the door again and asked, 'Would you mind if I joined you inside the chaise for a moment?'

'Of course not.' Emma moved her skirts out of his way, taking her time to allow her suddenly uneven breathing to settle.

Being alone in here together seemed very...intimate. Especially since Jenny would probably be watching them from a discreet distance—or possibly not so discreet. It felt much more intimate than it had the evening after the ball, because she'd been far too stressed then to think about the intimacy. Since they were now man and wife, they might be expected to be in any number of intimate situations, of course.

A lot of women would be sad in her position— desperately sad—about the fact that they wouldn't be engaging with their husband in the most intimate situation of all. But, other than the fact that it meant that she wouldn't be having children of her own, Emma was fortunate in being perfectly happy about that. *Perfectly* happy. Really. She had no particular desire to engage with the duke in that kind of thing at all. Really.

The duke pulled the door closed behind him and took the seat opposite her, where Jenny had been sitting. Emma swallowed. Each time she'd seen him, she'd been struck by how *large* he was. Right now, it seemed as though he was filling the entire chaise, which previously had seemed extremely roomy for two people.

He cleared his throat. 'I've been thinking. Obviously, for our own reasons, neither of us wishes there to be any gossip about our relationship.'

Emma inclined her head, her throat suddenly tight with an emotion she couldn't name.

'During our journey, therefore, I think that we should eat our meals together—in a private room, if possible, as that will be expected of us—and sleep in adjoining bedchambers.'

He was clearly right. And frankly, after the boredom of the journey so far, Emma realised she would welcome conversation with him over their meals. And they ought to get to know each other a little better, given that they were, effectively, co-conspirators.

There was no reason whatsoever for her to feel a little hot at the thought that they would have adjoining bedchambers for a night. Or two nights?

She really wanted to know how long the journey was going to be. During luncheon would be an ideal time to question him. There were a lot of things she'd like to know about her future life.

'I agree,' she said.

'Still not hungry?' he asked.

Emma wondered if he'd actually heard her stomach rumble.

'I have just this moment become a little hungry. Perhaps it would make sense to luncheon here after all.'

Enough was enough when it came to her asserting her right to eat when she wanted to.

The duke bowed his head.

Emma was fairly sure he was hiding a smile as he did so, which should have been annoying, but made her smile too.

The ducal crest and servants had worked a lot more magic than the mere greasing of palms that Emma's father had been able to do when he had travelled as a plain mister, however rich. The landlord of the inn and his staff were all bowing so low Emma was surprised they didn't lose their balance.

'Our best private dining room is at your disposal, Your Grace.' Had the landlord bowed any more deeply his ample stomach would have been dusting the ground, and had his smile been any broader his face might have split.

'Thank you very much.' Emma and the duke spoke as one, and then glanced at each other as one, which shouldn't have pleased Emma as much as it did. Given that her life had just taken a huge turn for the unknown, though, there was something nice about feeling that the two of them might occasionally be... She didn't know quite what. Maybe a team?

The two of them made *very* small talk—exclaiming over the delightful cottage garden they could see from the window of the dining room and commenting on the carved panelling in the room—until the table had been laden with more food than two adults with even gargantuan appetites could possibly eat and the landlord had bowed himself out of the room a final time.

'Can I help you to some of these sweetmeats?' The duke looked as though he was going to continue with the small talk.

'Yes, please,' said Emma, not even looking at the dish. While she had him with her, she had questions for him that were a lot more important than sweetmeats. She passed him her plate and said, 'Could I possibly ask you a few questions?'

'Of course.' He inclined his head.

'Firstly, could I ask what my duties as governess will be?'

'Duties?' The duke spooned three choice sweetmeats onto her plate and looked around the table at the other food, as though she hadn't just asked a very important question. 'No duties. As I said before, I'd be extremely grateful for your help with the boys, but I can't possibly ask you to take on formal duties. If you're happy to be involved in their care, or indeed take charge of it, I'd be delighted, but, equally, if you don't feel that you wish to be involved, I will look for another governess. If you do wish to be involved, then of course we can discuss matters of import, for example the hiring of tutors and a broad timetable. Buttered cauliflower?'

'No cauliflower, thank you.' Emma was fast losing her appetite, not something that happened to her very often. 'Was your professed need for a governess perhaps an invention?'

He placed three cauliflower florets very carefully on his own plate before looking up at her. 'It wasn't an invention. I do need a governess for my boys. I find, however, that I cannot possibly instruct *you*. You're—' he waved a fork at her '—you. *You*. The Duchess of Harwell. *You*.'

'I'm only the Duchess of Harwell because you were forced to marry me, and the only reason I agreed to your sacrifice was that you told me that you needed my help.'

Emma cut one of the sweetmeats in two, hard, her cutlery clattering against the plate, and sniffed as quietly as she could. Tears and anger were battling inside her, and she didn't wish to give in to either of them.

'I would like to help with the boys. If you would like me to.'

She'd believed they'd had a bargain, but it seemed that he'd completely hoodwinked her. He'd clearly just told her that he needed her help to prevail upon her to accept his offer. Out of kindness, of course. And she'd allowed herself to believe he needed her help because she'd *wanted* to believe it, because it was her best option. Really, she'd hoodwinked her*self*. Also, she couldn't *make* him allow her to help with his children—and indeed she didn't want to press her services where they weren't wished for—but if she couldn't help with them, what was she going to do with herself all day, every day?

'Yes, of course, and thank you. But not as an employee or a servant or social inferior of mine in any way. I didn't mean that I can't instruct you because you're a duchess now; I meant I can't instruct you because you're *you*, Emma, the person you are. I plan to settle your dowry on you so that you can live in any manner or style you like. As I mentioned before, there's a dower house on the estate to which you may wish to remove in due course. You would be very welcome to have it refurbished to your own specification.' He smiled at her, apparently unaware that she was now... Well, she didn't know what she was, but it wasn't good. She was either furious, or desperately miserable, or both.

'We had a bargain and I intend to stick to my side of it,' she told him. 'I would very much like to help with the children. Perhaps I could also help you in visiting tenants who might be in need?'

'Certainly. Thank you.' The duke busied himself with the food on his plate while Emma blinked back another few tears. She was, of course, being ridiculous. There was no reason for her to feel tearful; this was hardly the worst thing that had ever happened to anyone. Many of the debutantes she'd met in London would be ecstatic to be in her position now, setting aside the fact that they wouldn't be having children of their own. Really, she was very lucky.

She loaded a second mouthful onto her fork.

'These sweetmeats are quite delicious,' Emma said eventually, into the fairly long silence during which they'd both...chewed their food.

Oh, the romance of this wedding day. She didn't want a passionate love match, but this... This wasn't how she would ever have imagined her marriage to be.

'Yes, they are.' The duke's conversation was as scintillating as hers.

There was more chewing from both of them, and then he said, 'You said you had more than one question for me?'

Oh, yes. *Would you mind if I travelled to India to explore my grandmother's birthplace if I'm not going to have anything else productive to do with my time?*

No. Maybe not a conversation to have until she'd gauged how conservative he was.

'Yes. I wondered how long our journey to Somerset will be?'

'Assuming that no unforeseen incidents occur, I hope to arrive tomorrow evening. One night at an inn, therefore.'

'Wonderful.'

And then they lapsed into near silence for the remainder of the meal, any conversation revolving entirely around the food—which was nice, but not outstandingly so, although any deficiencies in quality were made up for in extreme quantity.

After what felt like a long silence-filled time later, which turned out to have been perhaps twenty minutes, the duke said, 'If you don't mind, I feel that it might be better for us to be on our way sooner rather than later, so that we arrive at our staging inn this evening well before nightfall.'

Emma gave him a big smile in relief that the meal was at an end and in response to the fact that he'd asked, rather than told, her about their departure.

'Of course.'

An extraordinary number of people seemed to have gathered in the inn's entrance hall to witness their departure. During the extreme bowing and curtseying that ensued, a woman stepped forward and introduced herself as the landlord's wife.

'I'm so sorry that I wasn't here before, Your Grace,' she addressed Emma. 'I was shopping in the town. Praise be that I got home in time to see you.' Goodness. The allure of a duchess.

'Indeed.' Emma smiled at her.

'I wondered—' the woman must have thighs of steel; her curtsey was remarkably low and yet still steady '—whether Your Grace would like to see my kittens?'

'Kittens?' Was that a euphemism for something? Or a country word?

'Baby cats, Your Grace.'

Emma laughed. 'I'm so sorry. You must think me quite odd. I hadn't realised what you meant. I'd love to see your kittens.'

'And then we must be on our way,' the duke said.

Emma turned to look at him, one eyebrow raised. He might be reneging on the governess part of their bargain; he was *not*, if she could help it, going to renege on giving her autonomy.

'If you don't mind,' he clarified after a pause.

Emma smiled. 'I'm sure we can spare a few minutes,' she said, 'and then I think we'll need to leave.'

'Oh, my goodness. They're adorable,' she breathed a couple of minutes later as the landlady opened a stable door for her. 'How old are they?'

'Two months, Your Grace.' The landlady dropped into yet another curtsey. Emma really wished she could ask her to stop curtseying, but she was fairly sure the woman would be offended. It seemed as though she was going to have to get used to being curtseyed to.

She bent down and then knelt on the straw next to where the kittens were lapping from a bowl.

'Your dress, Your Grace. If I might be so bold.'

'I'm sure it won't be damaged. This straw looks very clean.'

And it was her wedding dress, but her wedding had been a complete fake and she knew that she would never wear the dress again, because today was not a day that she was going to want to remember.

'May I?' She indicated one of the kittens, which had finished drinking.

'Please do.'

Emma reached forward and picked the kitten up, stroking its silky fur. The tiny creature mewled and arched into her.

'It's beautiful,' she said.

Today was a very lonely day, and it seemed that her life might be quite isolated from now on. Her new husband clearly had no interest in any kind of friendship with her, and she could already see that the vast majority of people she met were going to be very interested in her, but not actually in *her*, just in her persona as a duchess. Even Jenny, whom she'd known for over a decade now, was trying to treat her differently now she was a duchess.

It felt wonderful for another living creature to wish to cuddle into her, as the kitten was doing, for no reason other than that they were fellow creatures.

She picked up a piece of straw and tickled the kitten with it, and soon they were playing together. For a few moments she forgot that she'd got married and just enjoyed the kitten.

And then a large shadow appeared above her and she heard the duke say, 'I'd like to leave now, if you're ready.'

No, she wasn't ready, but she might never be ready, and of course it would be better to arrive at the next inn before nightfall.

'Of course.' She carefully picked up the kitten and with great reluctance placed it back with its mother. Now she needed to stand up. She looked around. There was nothing to hold on to. She was going to have to scramble to her feet by pushing herself up from the ground, which she wouldn't mind at all without an audience, but as it was...

The duke stepped forward and held his hand out to her. Yes, that was clearly her best option. A bit of an analogy for her marriage to him, really.

'Thank you.' She took his hand and found herself almost flying to her feet.

The duke loosened his fingers on her hand, as though he was going to let go, and then re-tightened his grip and drew her arm through his. Of course: he'd done it to avoid gossip, which they'd agreed they both wanted to do, so she smiled up at him in her best wifely manner, actually a very easy thing to do, because he did have a lovely face when he wasn't doing his stern Ice Duke thing.

He was looking at her, and smiling back at her, and Emma felt her entire body bask in the smile even though she knew it was fake.

'Your Grace?' The landlady was scrape-the-ground curtseying again. 'If I might make so bold? Would Your Grace like to take the kitten? It will be very difficult for us to find homes for them all.'

Emma realised immediately that she'd *love* to take the kitten. She looked back up at the duke, who rolled his eyes slightly.

'Is it practical to transport a kitten from here to Somerset in the chaise?' he asked.

'Oh, yes, Your Grace. We can provide a box and bedding and food and milk.' The landlady was nodding emphatically.

'I'd love to,' Emma said, ignoring her new husband's raised eyebrows. 'I wonder... Would it be lonely without a sibling?'

'Probably,' the duke said, rolling his eyes more, but smiling. He turned to the landlady. 'You must allow me to pay you for the kittens.'

'Oh, Your Grace. I couldn't.' She already had her hand held firmly out. 'Thank you.'

In the end they took three kittens, and Emma's mood had lightened considerably at the prospect of something to do and the company the cats would provide.

'People are certainly very interested in the movements of the Duke and Duchess of Harwell,' Emma murmured as she and the duke stood in the courtyard while the landlady gathered together necessities for the kittens.

More people than she'd imagined the inn even held had assembled to see them off.

'They are.' He didn't smile. 'I appreciate the many advantages of my station, but it would take a better man than I to enjoy that side of my life.'

Emma felt strangely comforted from knowing that he didn't love this weird adulation either.

'It's better at home in the country, though. People get used to your title and possessions, and to some extent start treating you as the person you are, especially the household retainers who've been with our family for many years, and some of my tenants, not to mention friends.' He looked down at her. 'Are you sure you're happy to travel in the chaise with the kittens? It could be very difficult. And possibly smelly.'

Emma laughed. 'I'm very happy to,' she told him.

'Have you spent much time with cats?' he asked.

'No.' She could see his lips twitching. 'What?'

'Nothing,' he said, smiling blandly.

A few minutes later, as she sat in the chaise and watched him ride off, she realised that she was almost looking forward to seeing him later, when they stopped for the evening.

# *Chapter Five*

As Alex strode away from the chaise in the direction of his horse, he could have sworn he heard a little squeak, possibly of pain, from Miss Bolton—Emma, the new duchess, how to think of her?—in the interior of the chaise. Maybe one of the kittens had scratched her.

He wondered how long it would be before she'd be seriously regretting her impulse purchase. He was fairly sure that unless the cats were lulled to sleep by the movement of the vehicle they'd play merry hell with her. So much so that he was almost tempted to travel in there with her, just to enjoy the spectacle.

Not that tempted, though. He really didn't want to get too close to her, and he always enjoyed riding.

Mid-afternoon, he saw ahead of him, on a long, straight stretch of road, a broken-down stagecoach, half tilted into a ditch, with passengers struggling to disembark and trunks and bags strewn across the road. Reining in his horse, he stopped and dismounted, looping the reins around a tree and securing them before heading over towards the coach to help passengers out.

A few minutes later, working in his shirtsleeves, he heard another carriage come to a halt and realised that it was his own. Shortly after that, Emma was standing next to him on the dusty road, asking what she could do to help.

'You would be best placed by returning to the chaise and continuing your journey,' he told her. 'This is no place for a gentlewoman.'

There were some extremely angry people using some extremely fruity language not far from them, and Alex had already had to wade in to prevent an argument coming to serious blows.

'I am an adult, not a baby, nor a Bath miss. Some of these people are clearly in distress. Why would I not help?'

Alex tried very hard not to sigh out loud, and was pretty sure that he'd succeeded.

'Obviously you *can* help,' he said, 'but a duchess is always a target for thieves and vagabonds, and the stagecoach is not a particularly—' he sought for a polite word '—*exclusive* mode of travel. It is entirely possible that one of the passengers might seek to relieve you of some of your jewellery, for example.'

'Then I will shoot them.' She said it so calmly that he really couldn't tell whether or not she was joking. It *sounded* like a joke. Because obviously she *wasn't* going to shoot anyone. Except... He'd already noticed that when she was joking there was a little quirk to her lips. And the quirk was not there.

'Just through the fleshy part of their arm or leg, obviously. I wouldn't want to kill them.' She patted her reticule. She really didn't seem to be joking. Did she have a pistol in there?

'My father, while not a duke, was an extremely wealthy man, and he wished to ensure that his only daughter was protected.'

This time Alex did not succeed in not sighing out loud. 'I'm not sure that a shooting, even just through the fleshy part of someone's limb, would help any of us. And there would, of course, be the risk that your aim faltered and greater injury occurred.'

'It would not falter. I was taught very well and I have an excellent aim.'

'Real-life situations are not the same as practice ones, though,' he pointed out.

Why was he even engaging with her?

'True,' she said. From over her shoulder.

Because, totally ignoring Alex's wishes, she was on her way to speak to some female passengers, who were sitting by the side of the road.

He'd already noticed during their stop at the staging inn, when she'd blatantly pretended that she wasn't hungry just to make a point, that she was clearly not planning to allow him to tell her what to do in any way. Which, of course, was completely understandable, and he didn't *want* to tell her what to do. Most of the time, anyway. Right now, he would very much have appreciated her doing what he'd asked.

He nodded at two of his grooms, both of whom immediately moved towards Emma. Their mere presence would protect her, and he, of course, would be constantly looking over his shoulder to check that she was all right.

To give her her due, she really did help very enthusiastically, and her presence did, to some extent, quieten people down, partly because so many of them were watching her open-mouthed. His grooms did a very good job of intimidating the livelier of the little crowd, and it was not long before Emma had managed to calm a woman who'd been having full-blown hysterics.

Soon Emma was sitting in a little group of other women, talking away about their children, from what Alex could hear, and very quickly it was as though they were fast friends. He'd better just hope they didn't have any kittens or other animals to sell her.

When the stagecoach was eventually righted, and its broken wheel shaft mended—Alex hadn't felt he could leave before that—he joined Emma in bidding farewell to all her new friends.

'I'll try that new recipe, Your Grace,' said an older woman dressed in a voluminous grey dress and wearing a large, bright yellow hat.

'You'll be delighted with the results, I'm sure,' Emma told her.

Alex nodded at all the women and then said, 'I believe that the stagecoach is ready to depart, and we should be on our way too.'

'She's a lovely duchess,' the lady in the yellow hat told him.

Alex nodded. It did look as though she was going to be. And, to be fair to Emma, she *had* helped, and there had been no unpleasantness nor any problems. Perhaps she genuinely would be able to look after herself with a pistol as well. It certainly seemed as though she was a woman who should not be underestimated.

He nodded and smiled at the woman. 'I agree.' He held his arm out to Emma and she took it, and they made their way back to the chaise, where her maid had been patiently waiting with the kittens.

'You should take a short walk to stretch your legs, Jenny, before we set off again,' Emma told her.

'Thank you, Your Grace, if you're sure.' Her maid smiled broadly at her, and Alex reflected that there was a fighting chance that even his famously prickly housekeeper might like Emma.

Once Jenny was out of earshot, Alex leaned in so that no one else could possibly hear, and said, 'You should keep that pistol very much out of sight. And be careful.'

As he leaned, he caught Emma's scent, which reminded him of summer, and something sweet, and made him just want to keep on standing close to her.

That didn't feel right, so he took a step backwards, which gave him an excellent view of the little flash of anger in her eyes as she said, 'Should I *really*? Thank you so much for your sage advice. I was planning to wave it around and, indeed, hand it to any aspiring highwayman on a platter to help him with his job.'

Alex laughed. 'Fair enough. I'm sorry. Perhaps I sounded a little patronising there?'

Emma raised an eyebrow.

'*Very* patronising,' he said. 'My apologies.'

'Thank you.' She nodded at him and entered the chaise, immediately bending down to speak to the kittens, sounding a lot happier to be talking to them than to him.

'I'd planned to stop near Andover, at a good staging inn that I know. Would you be happy to spend the night there?' he called into the chaise in the interests of harmony; in an ideal world he and Emma would be on good although distant terms.

She turned to look at him, cuddling a kitten, and bestowed a wide smile upon him, which transformed her face from very pretty to...extremely beautiful. Objectively speaking.

'I'd be happy to, thank you.' And then she turned back to the kitten.

'Excellent, then. So...have a good journey,' he said to her back.

'Thank you. And you,' she said over her shoulder, one eye still on the kittens.

*Excellent, then.*

Alex arrived at the inn at which they were spending the night a little before Emma. He took his horse round to the stables, and then returned to the yard in front of the inn to wait for her, so that they could enter the building together.

When the chaise drew up, he moved forward to open the door, interested to see how Emma and Jenny had fared with the kittens.

'Pleasant journey, I trust?' He held out his arm to Emma so that she could descend the steps.

'Delightful,' she said, smoothing her somewhat dishevelled hair as she reached the ground.

'Did you get a lot of reading done?'

'We were both somewhat occupied with the kittens,' she said, with as much dignity a woman with straw in her bodice and scratches on her arms could produce. Alex laughed out loud as Emma continued, 'I shall enjoy reading my book this evening instead.'

'Not planning to share your bedchamber with the kittens, then?'

'Jenny has very kindly volunteered to find a place for the kittens to stay overnight, perhaps in the stables. They are *truly* delightful.'

'But?'

'Very lively and not yet trained. Although *certainly* delightful.'

As Alex laughed again, he was interrupted by his head groom, who had a question about one of the horses.

'Forgive me,' he said to Emma, handing her over the threshold into the inn. 'I'll return to you very soon.'

When he got back, Emma had her back to the main door into the inn's reception area and was engaged in conversation with a little group of other travellers, who all appeared from their attire to be members of the *ton*. He could see from the way she was holding herself that she wasn't enjoying the conversation.

When she'd been chatting to the stagecoach travellers, he couldn't have said precisely how, but she'd looked relaxed. Now, her shoulders were just a little frozen, and her head was angled to one side in a slightly unnatural-looking manner.

'Indeed, you played your hand remarkably well,' one of the other ladies in the little group said, accompanying her words with a titter.

Alex thought he recognised her as one of the many women who'd been thrown, or had thrown herself, in his direction during the course of the last few weeks.

'Did you have any accomplice beyond your aunt?' she continued.

'Perhaps Sir Peter was the accomplice,' mused another of the ladies in the group.

This one bore a strong resemblance to the first one— in both looks and apparent nastiness—and accompanied her words with a gloved finger to her chin and an artful tilt of her head, as though she was thinking.

Emma visibly stood a little taller, as though she was

bracing herself, and her voice was a little higher than usual when she said, 'I'm afraid—'

Alex strode forward before she could continue—because really there was nothing she could conceivably say in response that would improve the situation—and slid his arm around her waist, sure that the only effective way of shutting down this gossipy cattiness was to demonstrate, if he could, that their union was at least some way towards a love match.

As he pulled her in, tight against his side, she gasped and looked up at him. From nowhere, he was struck by the thought that she fitted very well against him, as though their two bodies might have been made for each other. As might many people's, though, actually. That was just human biology.

The two women and their companions—an older woman whom he recognised as Lady Castledene, presumably their mother, and two men, perhaps brothers—were all looking at him and Emma appraisingly.

Alex really did not appreciate the way they were doing so. If they wanted something to appraise, he was going to *give* them something to appraise.

He dropped a kiss on Emma's forehead, catching that delicious scent again, and squeezed her waist a little more tightly. Her curves really did mould very well against his side.

'Your Grace.' Lady Castledene had produced a sycophantic smile and was curtseying very deeply. 'I do hope that you find yourself...well.'

She rolled her eyes, just very slightly, in Emma's direction as she spoke. Emma stiffened and Alex glared. How *dare* this woman imply...well, the truth. Yes, obviously it was the truth, of course he wouldn't have married Emma or anyone by choice. But how *dare* she be so rude to Emma? And in front of him. Emma was a good person, and Alex was going to do everything he could to prevent her becoming a social pariah.

He wanted to be extremely rude to Lady Castledene and her party, but that probably wouldn't be the right approach, given that they probably didn't realise he'd overheard the last part of their conversation before he'd joined them.

'Yes, very well, thank you,' he said, continuing to grip Emma's waist very tightly. 'I count myself a very fortunate man and am greatly looking forward to taking my wife home to begin our honeymoon.'

He pressed his lips again to Emma's hair, which felt odd, given that they really were not man and wife in the conventional sense, but was no great hardship, because that scent was just...*tantalising*. It drew you in.

He looked Lady Castledene in her narrowed eye and smiled. It really shouldn't be too hard to convince people that he was happy to be married to Emma. By anyone's standards she was a beautiful woman, and she was known to be an heiress, and the *ton* was a hugely shallow environment. They—*he*—just needed to brazen things out.

'Indeed.' Lady Castledene produced a smile of her own, very tight-lipped, and added, 'We must wish you well, Your Grace.'

She'd actually managed to turn her body so that it was as though she was speaking only to Alex and not to Emma.

'Thank you.' Alex bowed his head, shifted himself and Emma a little, so that they were both facing the group, and said, 'We're both very grateful for your good wishes.'

'We enjoyed your wedding breakfast, but were concerned that something might be amiss when we saw that you weren't able to attend yourselves.' Lady Castledene gave him a smug *How will you trump that?* smile.

'We wished to return home to the children as soon as possible. The only thing that's amiss is that the journey is long, so we haven't yet been able to be alone to begin our honeymoon,' Alex said.

Thank God they wouldn't know that he'd chosen to travel separately from Emma today. In hindsight, that had been a mistake from a gossip perspective.

'If you'll excuse us?' He removed his arm from Emma's waist and took her hand, linking his fingers through hers, and tugged her gently towards a doorway through which he could see his man, Graham, indicating, presumably, the private dining room that had been arranged for them.

He kissed the top of her head again as they went through the door, as Graham made a discreet exit.

Alex waited until the door was firmly closed before releasing Emma's hand and walking round to the other side of the table that had been laid for them to pull her chair out for her.

'Thank you,' she said as she sat down. 'And I must thank you also for rescuing me. Again.'

Alex shook his head. 'I'm only sorry that you had to experience that.'

'It wasn't a great surprise,' Emma said, taking a small bread roll from the basket he was holding out for her. 'I've met those women before on several occasions, and they had a lot to say about my father's origins.'

'I'm sorry.'

'Really, there's nothing to be sorry about. There are nice people and not-so-nice people everywhere, and I don't think I'm the only woman not to have loved her Season. There might be a particularly large amount of venom amongst the *ton*, but I always feel that one of the reasons so many of them engage in such awfulness is that they just don't have enough to *do*. I can't imagine a lot of people thriving in that environment.'

'I think you're right.' Alex broke off a piece of his own bread roll. 'Although, in fairness, I did have a lot of fun during the Season when I was young.' He paused for a moment as he was hit by a memory of meeting Diana, then collected himself and continued. 'But men have boxing and horses and financial affairs with which to busy themselves, in addition to all the social events.'

'Indeed. Whereas for women there's only gossip, shopping and visits to the dressmakers. And perhaps it isn't so enjoyable for slightly older men?'

'I certainly didn't enjoy *this* Season,' Alex agreed.

'Partly because you were being hounded by fortune-hunters such as myself?' Emma said.

'Exactly.' He smiled at her. 'That plan you hatched with Sir Peter and your aunt was *fiendish* in its ingenuity.'

'I know. We are geniuses.' Emma paused. 'Joking aside, I'm going to apologise and thank you one more time.'

Alex shook his head. 'Don't. We both know that neither of us would have chosen this, but I'd like to think we can make things work adequately for both of us.'

He was beginning to think that he was going to be able to cope reasonably happily with Emma being in his life. It was a positive sign that they could already laugh together about how they'd been compromised into this situation. He wasn't sure it was going to be so good for her, though. She obviously didn't have a single friend in Somerset and, going by the way she kept chatting to people, she was sociable and would be lonely if she was ostracised by the neighbours.

'I wonder whether, with your permission, it might be sensible to demonstrate our mutual affection a little more in front of those people.' Good Lord. He'd just had the thought that it might be a good idea to *kiss* her in front of them.

'They are some of the most gossipy of all the gossips,' Emma said. 'Maybe we ought to. If you think it wise?'

'Probably.'

Good Lord again. He didn't even *mind* the thought of kissing her, since there was going to be a good reason for it. If it happened. It might not happen. They might not see them again.

Maybe they should change the subject.

'What do you know of Somerset?' he asked.

Dinner was pleasant. Emma was very interested in the history and geography of the south-west of the country, and had interesting knowledge to impart on Lancashire and the rest of the north-west, an area that Alex had never visited.

They whiled away the time with amiable conversation, which at times even led to proper laughter on both sides.

'So, the pistol?' he found himself asking some time later. 'Your father deemed it important to educate you at a seminary for young ladies…and also to teach you to shoot?'

'Yes, indeed, and to fence. And to assist him in the

running of the factories. I learned about the machinery, the different fabrics, and the economics behind the business. My father taught me as he would have taught a son. He was very forward-thinking.'

'Indeed.'

Not so forward-thinking that he hadn't tried to force his daughter into marriage with an aristocrat, whether she wanted it or not.

'Other than in regard to his ideas on marriage, of course,' she said, as though reading his thoughts. She paused, and then asked a little hesitantly, 'And you…? Were you very young when you got married?'

'Yes,' he said. 'Twenty-three.'

Emma smiled at him and tilted her head a little to the side, as though expecting or hoping for elaboration. He wasn't going to elaborate. He couldn't talk about Diana this evening. He might become uncomfortably emotional.

He reached for the pitcher between them and said, 'Would you like more wine? I find this a very tolerable red. If you enjoy wine, you will be pleased to hear that we maintain a large cellar at the castle.'

He began an anecdote about smugglers on the Somerset coast, and before long had Emma laughing and the conversation moved far away from any further questions about his late wife.

'Would you like another drink?' he asked Emma some time later, when they'd agreed that the inn's cook was very good but that they could neither of them eat any more.

'No, thank you. I think…' She looked at him, as though trying to gauge what he'd like her to say. 'I think

I might perhaps go to bed now. Unless you'd like to stay downstairs a little longer?'

'Now is perfect for me.'

But he was thinking of the oddness of their going upstairs together, and from her suddenly more reserved demeanour it looked as though Emma was too.

They moved towards the door together—very politely, barely speaking—and Alex opened it for Emma to pass through.

As luck would have it—as though the woman had been listening out for them—the door opposite them opened precisely as they were leaving the room, and one of Lady Castledene's daughters came out.

'Good evening,' she said.

'Shall we?' Alex said into Emma's ear.

'Yes,' she whispered.

He reached his arms around her waist from behind and turned her towards him in what he hoped was a convincing show of husbandly ardour. Then he leaned down to kiss her on the lips, one eye on the woman opposite, whom he was pleased to see was now outright staring at them.

He lingered in the kiss for a moment, wanting to ensure that he looked suitably enthusiastic, and moved his hands to cup Emma's face, because that was what you did when you were kissing someone passionately.

The kiss was as chaste as a kiss on the lips could be, and purely for show. And then...

And then he became aware of the softness of Emma's lips, smelled that frankly almost intoxicating scent again, and felt his entire body begin to respond to her nearness, to the sensation of her lips under his, his hands on her face. He found himself moving his hands into her thick hair, holding her tight against him, enjoying—*really* enjoying—the way she was beginning to open her mouth to him.

Their tongues met, and explored, and almost danced together, and then he lost awareness of their surroundings, deepening the kiss ever more, conscious only now of Emma, and the way it felt as though his entire body were aflame.

She tasted wonderful. Sweet, tempting, in a different way from Diana.

*Diana.*

He didn't want to enjoy kissing a woman he *knew*. And he didn't just *know* Emma, she was his *wife*. He didn't want to become close to her and then lose her. One terrible grief in a lifetime was enough.

He could feel himself freezing, his hands, body, mouth now unnaturally still. Emma was clearly sensing his stillness too; she herself had stilled and withdrawn slightly.

He opened his eyes, which he must have closed somewhere along the way, and, yes, that damned woman was still standing opposite them, still staring.

Well, they'd been at it long enough now, he judged, for it not to look odd if they stopped.

He drew back slowly, keeping an arm around Emma, and coughed.

'Good evening,' he said to the lady.

She might still gossip about Emma having compromised him, but she would be less able to describe him as an unwilling participant in their marriage now.

She flushed a deep red and whisked herself back inside the room out of which she'd come. Which was ideal, because it made Emma look up at him with pure glee on her face, which made him laugh, which made what could have been a very awkward post-fake kiss moment much less awkward.

He held out his arm to her again and they headed over to the inn's staircase.

'Your Graces.' The landlord had emerged from nowhere—he must have been waiting for them so perhaps he'd witnessed their kiss too—and was bowing. 'Allow me to escort you to your chambers.'

And up the stairs the three of them went.

Alex's man was waiting outside his room and Jenny was outside Emma's, a little further along the corridor.

'Thank you so much,' Emma said to Jenny. 'But I think I can prepare myself for bed this evening.'

'Oh, no, Your Grace, I need to help you.' Jenny swivelled her eyes in the direction of Emma's door, clearly keen to be involved in her wedding night preparations.

Alex had to try hard not to wince.

'Really, Jenny, there is no need. Thank you, and I'll see you in the morning.' Emma's voice was impressively steely; if she used that voice on Alex's sons they might even do as they were told.

As Jenny left them, followed by Alex's man and the landlord, Alex opened the door to his chamber and held it so that Emma could go in ahead of him.

She walked straight into the middle of the room and then turned to face him as he closed and locked the door.

'I think we should lock your door too,' he said, very quietly, in case any of the apparently many interested parties were listening on the other side of the door.

He looked at the bed. He was going to have to remember to make it look as though they'd both been in it for at least a portion of the night.

Emma was looking at the bed too. 'I'll take great care to make my bed in the morning so that no one can tell that I slept in it,' she said. 'Fortunately I don't toss and turn at night.'

Alex really didn't want to think about Emma in bed, in her nightdress. Perhaps her maid had put a wedding night gown out for her. Well, of course she would have done.

He swallowed. This was not going the way he'd planned; he didn't want to be having thoughts of this nature about Emma. Time to bid her goodnight and force his thoughts in a more sensible direction.

## Chapter Six

'Excellent,' the duke said.

'So, goodnight, then,' said Emma, trying hard not to stare at his face, his chest, his...everything.

For the last few minutes, since their amazing kiss downstairs, she'd been struggling not to think all manner of things she shouldn't.

Why had he seemed so lost in the kiss and then suddenly frozen?

What might have happened next if they'd been alone in a room together?

How would she have felt if it had continued?

Would it ever happen again?

She hoped not, obviously. Really, she did. Although it *had* been very nice.

The duke swallowed again and Emma realised that she was staring at his strong neck, the movement of his Adam's apple, his jawline, those firm lips that had only a few minutes ago been against hers...

'Goodnight,' he said. 'Sleep well.'

His eyes slid to the wide bed to the side of them as he spoke, and Emma's followed his, and now she was swallowing, too, as her mind went in all sorts of directions about what a normal wedding night with him might have entailed.

'Thank you. And you too,' she said, and stepped forward, fast, to get herself into her own bedroom and stop having these ridiculous thoughts.

She put her hand on the door handle and turned. Nothing. She jiggled a bit. It was locked.

'Um. Your Grace. Alexander.' How should she address him? She turned to face the duke, to discover that he was already searching for a key, along the mantelpiece and then on the shelves in the corner of the room at the end of the wall the door was in.

'Call me Alex.' He opened two drawers in a little table in the corner and closed them again. 'It must be here somewhere,' he said.

Emma squared her shoulders; it was hard not to feel put out that he sounded *quite* so desperate to get rid of her. Although he was probably tired after his long ride today. And perhaps he wanted to be alone—as she did, she reminded herself—to digest the fact that for better or worse they, two complete strangers, were now legally bound together.

As the duke—Alex—reached for a high shelf, she saw the muscles in his shoulders flex, and shivered, remembering how he'd looked earlier today when, in his shirtsleeves, he'd been working with the coachman and coach hands to right the stagecoach.

And she'd been pressed right up against all that muscle and hardness earlier, when they kissed.

For the first and last time, obviously.

'I can't find a key anywhere.' Alex turned round, put his hands on his lean hips and scoured the room with his eyes. 'This is ridiculous. It must be an oversight.'

'Perhaps we should go and ask for it.'

'I doubt people would expect us to have noticed yet.'

Emma nodded. It was true. They would be expected to be otherwise engaged. Kissing and…more. You couldn't grow up in the country, even with a father as protective as hers had been, without gaining a certain amount of knowledge of the way intimacies worked. And you really couldn't spend several hours in a chaise with Jenny on your wedding day without gaining further knowledge on the subject.

Five minutes' more fruitless searching convinced them both that there was no key to be found.

'Right,' said Alex, hands on hips again, 'we need a plan. You can sleep on the bed and I'll sleep in this chair.'

Emma slightly wanted to cry at the ridiculousness of their supposed wedding night and she *really* wanted to use the chamber pot, and she didn't want to do either of those things in front of Alex.

'I know what we could do,' she said, finally summoning up some clear thought. 'If you went round to my chamber via the corridor, perhaps with your boots off, that would look, um, intimate, husbandly, and you could perhaps, if you don't encounter anyone, just stay in there while I stay here?'

'You're right. Panic was clearly addling our brains.' Alex took his boots off, and then also his jacket, while Emma focused on a picture on the wall, again not wishing to look as though she was staring at him, particularly because she actually *did* want to stare.

'Yes, I think the best thing would be if I stay in there and then return in the morning. Perhaps we can swap then, to get dressed. Right. I'm off.' He did an exaggerated tiptoe towards the door, which made her laugh through the misery that had suddenly threatened to engulf her.

'You look as though you're an actor in a farce,' she hissed as he poked his head out of the door and looked left and right.

'This *is* a farce,' he whispered, and then made a dash for it, closing the door behind him, while Emma tried not to reflect on the fact that many a true word was spoken in jest.

Alex had just referred to their situation as a farce and...that did not feel good. Even though it was true.

She looked at the closed door for a moment and then shook her head. There was no point standing here feeling maudlin about her new life situation. Things could be worse.

She looked over at the bed. Things could be better, actually. Practically speaking, she didn't have a nightgown, or her hairbrushes, or *anything*. She'd very much like her book, at the very least, because she didn't feel as though she was going to sleep easily tonight.

She walked over to the bed and thumped down in the middle of it, then sniffed and wiped under her eyes with her forefingers as a couple of tears trickled out. She shouldn't be feeling this miserable. Tonight wasn't going to be wonderful, but once they arrived in Somerset things would be much better.

She flung herself backwards and wriggled herself into the very comfortable bed. She needed to cheer up immediately. This really wasn't the worst it could have been; it was in fact far better than it might have been. Of *course* she could be happy in a marriage with Alex without intimacy. It would just be like living with a friend. She might, for example, have been dealing with Sir Peter's husbandly advances right now. Or already on her way to living in penury. And this bed was *so* comfortable.

Hearing a clatter at the connecting door, she raised herself on one elbow. And then Alex walked through the door, saying, 'Surprise. The key was in the other side.'

'Oh. *Oh*. I can't believe we didn't think of that.'

'That's panic for you.'

'Well, thank goodness.' Emma gave up on trying to sit up from where she was—the bed was so soft that she'd sunk too far down to be able to get herself straight up—and turned onto her side, trying to ignore the fact that this was remarkably undignified.

As she turned, Alex's legs and—she gulped—more appeared in front of her, and he put his hand out.

'Thank you,' she said.

He hauled a little too hard and she almost flew off the bed, landing against his hard chest. He let go of her immediately and took a step backwards, clearly extremely eager not to touch her at all if he didn't have to.

'I think I misjudged your weight.' He smiled the slightly twisted smile she was already coming to recognise as very particular to him.

'Yes.' And suddenly she was so tired of this day. 'Goodnight, then.'

'Goodnight.'

Once she was in her own room, she locked both the door to the corridor and the connecting door and then lay down on the bed, the events of the day jostling in her brain.

The 'I now pronounce thee man and wife' moment featured heavily, and so did the acquisition of the kittens, of course, as did the true nastiness of Lady Castledene and her party. But the thing that she couldn't stop thinking about the most was the kiss. Or The Kiss, as she was fairly sure she'd think of it in her mind for evermore.

She'd kissed a few men before, including a couple of the men who'd proposed to her—while she'd decided that she didn't need or indeed *want* to be in love with the person she married, she'd thought it would be better to *like* them, both emotionally and physically, so she hadn't been averse to a little experimentation—and none of those kisses had been anything compared to the one she'd shared with Alex.

And it hadn't even been a proper one; it had only been for show.

It might be the last time she ever kissed a man.

After several hours tossing and turning—she was going to have a *lot* of work to do before she left the room in the morning to make her bed look un-slept-in—Emma was finally in a very deep sleep when she was woken by what she realised was a persistent tapping on the connecting door.

She dragged herself out of bed and walked over and opened it, putting only her head round the edge, so that Alex wouldn't see her in the embarrassing wedding-night nightgown her aunt had had made for her and Jenny had put out for her to wear last night.

She'd worried a lot during the night that she'd been too enthusiastic when Alex had kissed her, and she really didn't want to look as though she was throwing herself at him when he clearly had no interest in her.

'I'd very much like to leave as soon as possible,' Alex told her. 'If that's all right?'

'Of course. I'll be ready as soon as I can.'

Maybe she should make the bed very carefully and

then call for Jenny, she thought as she closed the door. Or maybe that would be too risky. Maybe Jenny would be able to tell, somehow, that they hadn't...

Yes, she should probably dress herself.

Living a life of deception was going to be ridiculously complicated. She and Alex should probably find a way of her removing to his dower house as soon as possible.

Fifteen minutes later, she was extremely hot from trying to do up all her buttons. She was never going to manage to look suitably duchess-like without help from *someone*. The question was: should that someone be Jenny...or Alex?

She walked back to the bed that she'd spent ages smoothing down earlier, and then looked around the room. Going by what Jenny frequently had to say about all sorts of people from all walks of life, she had a very strong nose for lying and also for anything to do with marital or extramarital relations. She'd probably have a strong nose for a lack of marital relations too.

Sighing, Emma walked over to the connecting door and knocked, before opening it slightly. Alex was sitting on the chair in the room, putting his boots on.

'Good morning. I wonder if you could help me finish dressing? I thought that might be best, just for today.'

'Of course.' Alex stood up, one boot on and one boot off. 'As you will see from my footwear, I also decided that today it would be best to dress myself, and am also struggling.'

Emma laughed. 'I imagine that your man and Jenny would both be delighted to know that they're genuinely indispensable. I'm sure you'll be able to do my buttons up, but I wouldn't let you loose on my hair, and I have literally no idea how anyone gets someone's foot inside boots that fit as tightly as those.'

'I know. Graham is a true genius.' Alex moved towards her. 'Where are these buttons?'

Emma felt suddenly breathless, as though her dress was too tight, which was ridiculous, given that it wasn't even fully done up yet.

'Just at the top, at the back.'

She turned round for him and lifted her hair out of the way. How was it that she was fully dressed and was indeed asking him to dress her *more*, and yet felt almost naked at this moment?

She sensed Alex move closer to her and lift his hands towards her neck. She could barely breathe. He took the fabric very gently and tugged at it a little. The room was completely silent other than the sounds of their breathing—such as it was in Emma's case—and the very faint rustle of the silk as Alex tried to do up the buttons.

'This is a lot more difficult than you would think.' Alex's breath skimmed across her skin as he spoke. Clearly, he had his head bent close to her so that he could see what he was doing, and Emma was sure that the tiny hairs on the back of her neck had risen.

'Jenny's obviously a genius too.' Emma cleared her throat to get rid of the croak that her voice suddenly contained.

'Would you mind if I...?' Alex's voice was croaky too now. 'If I moved your hair a little further?'

'Of course not.'

Emma was braced for the contact, but she still almost jumped a mile when Alex's fingers brushed the skin at the base of her neck as he carefully lifted her hair. She was remembering now how he'd thrust his fingers into her hair during their kiss last night.

'Nearly done,' he grunted.

Emma was struggling not to close her eyes and just melt into the feeling of his fingers against her when suddenly she felt actual pain. *'Ow,'* she squeaked.

'Don't move.'

He tugged some strands of hair very gently, and, *oh*, his fingers against her scalp and her neck felt good.

'You have some hair caught in a button. I am *really* not good at this.'

'Mmm,' Emma said.

He was wrong. He *was* good. *So* good. His fingers were gently moving more of her hair now, and she just wanted to lean into his hand. If she just took a step she'd be leaning against his very solid chest, too, and…

And… What was she *thinking*? He was literally doing her buttons up for her, very incompetently; and this wasn't a matter of *intimacy*, it was just a matter of expediency.

His fingers were still working at her neck and it was utter torture. In a very blissful way.

'This time I really have finished.' His voice sounded heavier than usual. He stepped backwards and Emma turned round, suddenly incredibly self-conscious for no good reason at all.

'Thank you so much.'

The hairs at the nape of her neck were going to be standing on end for hours to come at the memory of how he'd touched her there, she was sure. She was struggling to remember what time of day it was, even. *Breakfast.* It was breakfast time.

'Should we perhaps go below stairs for breakfast now?' she suggested.

'We should. As soon as I've wrestled myself into my other boot.'

'I'd like to offer to help, but I've no idea what I could do.'

'I'll be fine.' Alex sat down again and inserted his foot into the boot. 'I'm a grown man. Of course I can dress myself. How hard can it be?'

Very hard, it seemed.

Emma gave up on politeness quite quickly and laughed and laughed, which was an excellent way of recovering from his doing up her buttons.

Finally properly booted, Alex stood up and shook his head at her. 'I'm not sure people are going to expect the Duchess of Harwell to behave with such a lack of decorum.'

'I'm not sure people would expect the Duke of Harwell to be so incredibly incompetent at putting his own foot into a boot.'

They smiled at each other and then Alex said, 'Right. Breakfast.'

'Your Graces.' The landlord was bowing almost as low as had the man at the inn where they'd stopped yesterday at midday. 'I must apologise. I didn't realise you would be descending so early in the day for breakfast. Allow me just a minute or two to make a private room available.'

'Do you mean that you're going to ask someone to leave a private room?' Emma asked.

'Yes, Your Grace. I'll make sure that they're quick.'

'No, please don't.' Emma was horrified: this felt awful. It was a good reminder that she was going to have to be on her guard constantly to ensure that other people weren't frequently inconvenienced just because she was a duchess. 'We can very well eat in the public room.'

'But Your *Grace*. You're...' The landlord gave a hand wave in her direction that clearly meant *You're a duchess*. 'You're newly married.'

'Even so, we cannot be the cause of the ruination of others' breakfasts.'

'And we will have many other breakfasts together, just the two of us, once we reach our own home,' Alex said, so soulfully that Emma nearly laughed. 'My wife and I are indeed very well able to sit in the public room. I see that there is a table free there.'

He held out his arm to Emma and turned towards the table.

'Very good, Your Grace, if you're sure.'

Settled at the table in the public room, Alex broke his fast with ale and steak, while Emma chose a selection of fruits and some toast. They filled the first few minutes of their meal with low-voiced small-talk, about the journey to come and the Somerset climate, until very suddenly Alex leaned in and said, 'The Castledene party—and they are staring.'

Emma's hands were empty, and he reached across and took them in his and drew them towards him.

Emma said, *'Oh,'* and then tried to change it into something that sounded more amorous than surprised. *'Ooh.'* No, that just sounded odd.

'Ooh?' Alex whispered, still holding on to her hands.

'I was trying to sound amorous.'

When he was looking at her in that half-laughing way, it wasn't actually very difficult to imagine feeling amorous. In a purely physical way, obviously.

Alex squeezed her hands, then let go of them and picked up his cutlery again. 'They definitely noticed.'

'You look very smug.'

'We're excellent actors.'

'Oh, yes, we are.' Emma batted her eyelids at him and pouted, and he grinned at her. This acting thing really wasn't that difficult with someone who was as easy to be with as Alex. She'd found it a lot more difficult to pretend that she enjoyed the company of most of the men her aunt had been so desperate for her to get to know earlier in the Season.

She heard a loud throat-clearing behind her, and glanced over her shoulder as one of the Miss Castledenes stared at her for just a second too long—clearly on purpose—and then dropped her eyes without smiling.

She turned back to Alex and almost gasped at the way his eyes had become like flints and his lips had tightened to a thin line. His Ice Duke demeanour again. She hoped that he'd never look at *her* like that.

'Bordering on the cut direct,' he said. 'I will *not* have you treated like that.' He put his cutlery down, took her hands in his again, and said in a low voice, 'We should have thought of this before, but I suppose we've been caught up in too much of a whirlwind. We should concoct a story about how we first met.' He smiled at her. 'We were, of course, secretly courting before the ball at the beginning of the week.'

'Oh, yes. And we kept our mutual affection secret because we sensed that it was something perfect and we didn't want to risk it being spoilt by too much attention.'

'Yes, our love was pure and strong, but also delicate and fragile.'

'Alex, you should try your hand at poetry. I think you would be competition for Byron himself.'

Alex laughed and then, making his eyes very wide, said, 'I'm not a natural poet. It is you and you alone who brings this out in me. It has been so since the first moment we laid eyes on each other.'

'Across a crowded ballroom?'

'Certainly not. Nothing so mundane. We were...' He stopped and frowned, and then said, 'Um, what *were* we doing? We didn't meet at a ball or any other kind of party, did we? Because people would have seen us. And obviously talked.'

'Don't you remember?' Emma said, struck by a brainwave. 'You were my knight in shining armour. I was riding early one morning with my maid when my horse ran away with me and I was saved by you on your horse. As we were riding alone, neither of us knew who the other was, and neither of us wanted to reveal our true identities, but we both knew that Cupid's arrow had immediately struck and that we should keep our pure, strong but delicate and fragile love to ourselves for the time being, especially as neither of us was sure that Society would approve the other as an appropriate match for us. We then met surreptitiously in a variety of secret locations. We were on the brink of announcing our love to the world when Sir Peter forced our hand by attempting to compromise me. We are now, of course, deeply grateful to him, as we might otherwise have ended up waiting longer to marry.'

'I like that,' said Alex, nodding approvingly. 'Have you perhaps invented a big lie before? You're very good at it.'

'Never.' Emma shook her head. 'But I agree that I do seem to have a great talent for it. I'm pleased to have discovered it.'

'Yes, I'm sure it will stand you in excellent stead on any number of future occasions.' Alex squeezed her hands again and then let go. 'I'm still hungry. I can't keep holding your hands because then I can't eat.'

'Is not love alone enough to sustain you?'

'Love and just a little more of this steak, purely because it really is delicious and I don't want to offend the landlord. And I have a long way to ride today.' He took a mouthful, and then said, 'Actually, I ought to ride in the carriage, I think, if you don't mind. Just for the first part of the journey.'

'Yes, you're probably right.' Emma eyed Miss Castledene, who was now staring at them from across the room. 'I almost want to *slap* that woman.'

Alex nodded. 'Indeed. So, we're agreed about me coming in the chaise with you for the start of the journey? I wonder if it might be better for Jenny to travel in one of the other carriages at that point.'

'Definitely.' If Jenny was with them they'd have to play-act all morning. 'But we can still have the kittens with us.'

'Really?'

'Really. They're adorable.'

And they would also be something to concentrate on instead of Alex, because this was suddenly feeling too much again. It was confusing. Currently, they were trying to demonstrate to everyone that they were a normal married couple to avoid gossip. How and when were they going to stop that?

She wanted to ask Alex, but she wasn't sure how to

broach it. Maybe it would be easier once they were in Somerset. They would settle down, the staff would learn that they weren't a particularly amorous couple, and everything would become easier. *Hopefully.*

A few minutes later, Alex had finished demolishing his steak and was sailing past the Castledene group with Emma on his arm.

'I shall look forward to calling on you in London, Your Grace,' said the younger Miss Castledene to Emma, who nearly gasped out loud at her effrontery.

How could anyone go from that level of rudeness to pretending to be friends with someone mere minutes later? Lady Castledene and her older daughter were both nodding vigorously.

'I shall look forward to receiving you,' Emma said, and almost achieved a real smile. Really, her acting skills were superb, if she said so herself.

'I think it worked,' Alex said as they got into the chaise.

'Really?' Emma wasn't so sure.

'Well, of course. People will hate you for a while, because you snaffled a duke, and there are never that many of us available on the marriage mart at any given time. But once they've come to terms with the fact that you are the new duchess, and as long as no gossip attaches to you and you are seen to be regarded highly by me, they will all endeavour to be your friend and invite you to everything.'

'How delightful,' Emma said. 'I look forward to a lifetime of fake friendships.'

'Indeed.' Alex smiled at her and Emma smiled back—

a real smile—and then they both fell silent, and she remembered that they were near strangers, bound together only by their farcical marriage.

## Chapter Seven

Alex would never under normal circumstances choose to travel in an enclosed space with three cats, but it was actually a relief when his groom deposited Emma's kittens with them.

His plan to remain aloof from her had very much not gone to plan during their stay at the inn, and he was keen to withdraw a little, but he didn't want to be rude, and it wouldn't be particularly pleasant for either of them to travel entirely in silence—unless Emma was actually engrossed in her book for hours on end—so the kittens would be a welcome diversion.

He settled back into his corner of the chaise, unable to help smiling as Emma immediately started cooing over the kittens and tickling and playing with them.

He really did need to remember to maintain a distance between the two of them. He'd enjoyed their kiss far too much—indeed, he might easily have gone a lot further had they been alone—and during breakfast he'd found himself furious on Emma's behalf that the Castledenes were being so insolent to her.

Apparently, he'd already started to care a little for her.

As a friend, he supposed. You didn't enjoy kissing your friends, though. Well, maybe you did when the friend was such an attractive woman. It had probably been just a natural physical reaction.

It was fortunate that they'd be arriving in Somerset by the end of the day. He'd switch to his horse again well before that, too.

He'd better remember to agree with Emma in advance of the horse change where they were going to stop for their luncheon; there was no point annoying her in that regard again.

'You're beautiful,' Emma told the kittens, for about the twentieth time.

Alex laughed. 'You're spoiling them.'

'I'm not. I'm just stating facts.' She kissed one of the kittens on the nose and it purred contentedly. She and the kittens did make a lovely picture together as she played with them, her thick, silky, dark brown hair falling over her face and their tiny black bodies.

'Are you enjoying travelling with them?' he asked as she got one of the kittens into the box they'd brought for it in the nick of time.

'Of course,' she said.

When the kitten had finished its business, she picked it up and deposited it with its siblings in their bed, shut the basket, then leaned back against the bench and closed her eyes for a moment, the picture of exhaustion.

'You know, I would never have guessed that you hadn't been familiar with cats before.'

Emma ignored him. 'We might need to stop and change their straw.'

Alex sniffed. 'Sooner rather than later, do you think?'

'Probably.'

'I knew you'd soon think better of having them as travel companions.'

'No, they're delightful. I think they could do with a sleep, though. They're very young.'

'Of course.'

She narrowed her eyes at him. 'Are you laughing at me?'

'Yes, I think I am.'

'Hmm. Well, if you don't mind, I think I'm going to read my book now.' She made a great show of pulling it out of her reticule, before shooting him a cheeky little grin, at which Alex could do nothing other than smile.

He couldn't help noticing that she didn't turn a lot of pages while she was supposedly reading. But he shouldn't talk to her. He was supposed to be remaining aloof. It really was very boring, though, just sitting doing nothing. This was why he'd always rather ride.

'What are you reading?' he asked eventually.

'A book called *Emma* by the author of *Pride and Prejudice*.'

'Oh, yes.'

Diana had read and enjoyed that. He took a deep, slow breath to dispel the unwelcome dark thoughts that often still washed over him when he was reminded of his loss, and then raised his head to find that Emma was looking at him.

'Are you all right?' she asked.

*No. Not really.*

It was odd when your new wife—Emma *was* actually his wife—reminded you of your late one. Especially when you'd had no wish to marry the new wife.

'Just a...difficult memory. My late wife enjoyed those books.'

He frowned. He hardly ever mentioned Diana, and certainly not to near strangers, but, oddly, he could almost imagine talking more to Emma about Diana, telling her what an avid reader she had been, and even how much he missed her. It was as though over breakfast they'd breached the barrier between mere acquaintance and the beginnings of a friendship, which was not what he'd been planning.

'I'm so sorry; it must be very difficult. You must miss her hugely.'

Alex swallowed hard and nodded. 'Yes. Thank you.'

They both lapsed into silence, and it was a relief when they arrived at the next inn. Firstly, because the cats' straw really did need to be changed, for the comfort of their travelling companions, and secondly, because it gave Alex the opportunity to switch to horseback. It was unsettling, talking so much to Emma.

'So we'll meet in about an hour and a half for luncheon,' he confirmed with her before they set off again.

The inn at which they'd agreed to stop was a small one, which Alex hadn't used before, his favoured one being closed for refurbishment following water damage, and it didn't contain a private room. It also didn't contain any guests whom either of them knew personally, so they were able to sit down in the public room without incident.

'May I ask a few more questions about life in Somerset?' Emma said.

'Of course.'

'I presume that your household is a large one?' she asked, once the landlady had placed a steaming rabbit stew in front of them and apologised for a second time that she didn't have any more elegant fare for them, and Emma had reassured her for a second time that there was nothing that she wanted more at this moment than rabbit stew.

'Yes, I suppose so. Yes, it is.' Alex hoped Emma wasn't going to try to work the conversation round to Diana again. He took her plate and picked up a ladle. 'Are you hungry?'

Emma looked into the tureen, where there were a few lumps of something that was presumably rabbit in a thin broth with blobs of grease floating on the top.

'Just a little,' she said. 'It looks delicious, but I ate very well at breakfast.'

Alex nodded, also strongly tempted to rely on his breakfast to see him through until dinnertime.

'So, your household?' Emma prompted, staring at the three twisted pieces of meat and the oily liquid he'd placed in her bowl.

'You'll meet my—*our*—housekeeper, Mrs Drabble, when we arrive.' Alex was surprised to note that he didn't particularly mind the thought of sharing his staff with Emma. 'She's a wonderful housekeeper, but notoriously difficult. If you ask…' His words petered out as he thought that the best person for Emma to have asked about Mrs Drabble would have been Diana.

'Your late wife?' Emma supplied after a pause. 'I'm so sorry.'

'Thank you.' Alex turned his attention to his stew to hide his emotion, and unwisely took a large mouthful.

He was still chewing some time later, grateful that Emma hadn't said anything further about Diana, when she leaned forward and said in a low voice, 'Will I also meet your chef?'

'Emma. What are you implying...?' That this food was the most inedible he could remember tasting in years? There were many advantages to being a duke, and one of those was that he was nearly always served well-cooked meals made from high quality ingredients.

She twinkled at him, and he laughed around the piece of gristle he was *still* chewing.

When he'd eventually swallowed it, he pointed his knife at her plate accusingly. 'Have you had any?'

'Yes.' Emma nodded. 'You gave me a large portion, which I've very much enjoyed, but having had an equally large breakfast, I find myself unable to finish these last three morsels.'

'You're already utilising your newfound talent for invention,' Alex said. 'I'm impressed.'

'Thank you.' She beamed at him and he laughed again.

They passed the rest of the mealtime in inconsequential chatter, before setting off in good time to arrive in Somerset before dark, Emma in the chaise and Alex riding at a safe distance from her far too beguiling presence, but close enough to keep an eye on her entourage.

Once they were within striking distance of the castle, and Alex was sure that he was no longer required for Emma's protection, he rode ahead in order to arrive well before the carriages. He wanted both to welcome Emma—while this situation hadn't been his choice, it hadn't been hers either, and it was clearly the least he could do—and, more importantly, greet his sons and explain to them that there was a new member of the household.

'Papa,' hollered Freddie, the oldest, tearing across

the great hall towards him, followed by his two younger siblings.

Alex swept the three of them into a huge bear hug and just stood there, holding them tightly for a while. He hated the fact that he'd had to be away from them, and he hated the fact that he was about to foist upon them a new— God, *what*? Stepmother? Governess? Temporary house guest before she moved to the dower house?

He couldn't believe that only a few hours ago he'd been sitting merrily eating with her and laughing about rabbit stew. He should have been thinking about the impact her arrival might have on his sons. And last night... he'd only been thinking about Emma.

All wrong.

'Did you bring us presents?' asked Harry, the youngest.

Alex laughed. 'Excuse me, young man. You should be pleased to see me, not wondering if I have presents for you.'

'I am pleased to see you, but did you bring me a present?' Harry said.

'I might have a little something in one of the coaches when they arrive.' *Oh, yes, and also a new duchess.* 'Boys, there's something I need to tell you.'

'Is it a bad present?'

'No. The presents are *splendid*.'

They were. He didn't like the idea of spoiling them any more than the sons of dukes were by the very nature of their birth going to be spoilt, but on this occasion he'd taken some time the day before his and Emma's departure from London to buy a life-sized rocking horse, which he had to acknowledge was entirely a guilty purchase.

'I need to let you know that I have...'

He looked at them. Freddie and Harry favoured him, but John, his middle son, was completely Diana. Their mother. Whom he could not and did not want ever to replace. He couldn't describe Emma as their stepmother, or his wife. He just couldn't. He had to, though, because she *was* his new wife. Legally.

'I have married someone. Her name is Emma and she's very nice. I think you're going to like her. She's going to spend a lot of time with you, a bit like a governess would. So you won't need another governess. For now, anyway.'

John and Harry both nodded, but Freddie said, 'That's strange. Will she be called the Duchess of Harwell? Like Mama and Grandmama?'

'Er, yes, she will. She is...' Alex cast around in his mind for some words—good words—to make this sound better. 'It's just a name,' he said eventually. 'The Duchess of Harwell. Like there are three grooms called Mikey.' The boys had always loved that coincidence. 'Now there's another Duchess of Harwell. Because I, er, married her. So I'm the duke and she is the duchess.'

Excellent avoidance of the words *wife* and *stepmother*.

John and Harry nodded again, but Freddie shook his head. 'That does *not* make sense,' he said.

Correct. It did not.

They were interrupted by the sound of carriages outside.

'And here's the carriage with your present in it,' Alex said.

And here was Emma too. God, he was a coward.

In his defence, this was not an easy situation, and it was not one he'd wanted or planned *and* he'd only had a few days' preparation for it. However, Freddie's furrowed brow and look of suspicion were causing his stomach to twist uncomfortably.

He'd had the whole journey to prepare for this. He should have practised how he was going to tell them.

He realised as he went outside with the boys that, despite the advanced hour of the day, Mrs Drabble had what looked like the entire household lined up to welcome Emma—or to gawp at her and take an immediate dislike to her.

If he'd had any space left in his heart to pity anyone beyond his sons, he'd have been feeling very sorry for Emma right now.

Alex looked at his boys and then he looked at the chaise. He didn't want to betray or upset the boys by appearing to be too close to Emma. But he also didn't want to let them down by setting them a bad example.

He pressed his fingers to the bridge of his nose for a moment—he was beginning a thumping headache—and then moved forward to open the chaise door and hold his arm out to Emma.

'Thank you.' She leant on him only very lightly, and then almost immediately let go, and walked over to his butler, Lancing, and Mrs Drabble, at the head of the line of servants, directing a bright smile at them and holding her hand out.

As Mrs Drabble bobbed the tiniest of curtseys without meeting Emma's eye, Alex realised that he was almost holding his breath.

'I'm so pleased to meet you,' Emma said. 'I'm afraid that, although I ran my father's household, I have no experience in running a household of this exact nature and will need to rely heavily on your expertise.'

Having known Mrs Drabble for over twenty years,

Alex knew a chink in her armour when he saw one, and she definitely twitched—in a good way—before returning to her *'It'll take more than that to win me over thank you very much'* stance.

'Indeed, Your Grace,' she said, moving her eyes to Emma's face for the merest of moments before resuming her stare over her left shoulder.

'That was a long journey,' Emma said, for all the world as though Mrs Drabble wasn't being stunningly unfriendly. 'I wonder whether, after I've been introduced to the household, you would be able to show me to my chamber so that I might freshen up before dinner?'

'Of course, Your Grace.' There was that little twitch from Mrs Drabble again.

There was a scuffle from behind Alex, and he looked round to see John with Harry in a headlock.

'Boys,' he said in his deepest, sternest voice.

John let go, and Harry aimed a kick at him as he did so. Freddie was standing a couple of feet away from his brothers, glaring in the direction of Emma. Alex swivelled his eyes between them all and sighed internally. In time, Emma might perhaps be able to perform the miracle of winning Mrs Drabble over, but would she be able to win the boys over?

That would probably be a miracle too far for anyone.

'I should introduce you to my boys,' he said to Emma, who whipped straight round, almost overbalancing.

'I'm so sorry,' she said, moving towards them, her arms outstretched. 'I didn't see you there in the dusk.'

John and Harry immediately stood behind Freddie and looked at him, as though to see how he was going to react. And Freddie... Well, it was almost like looking in a mirror. Alex had glimpsed himself from time to time in lavishly mirrored ballrooms when faced with someone to whom he really didn't want to talk, and knew that he did the same straightening of the shoulders and complete lack of facial expression.

'How do you do?' Freddie barely moved a muscle as he spoke, but then held his right hand forward.

Emma diverted her outstretched arms—clearly intended for a hug—into shaking hands with Freddie. As they shook, the merest hint of distaste—a tiny curl of the lip and very slightly raised eyebrow—crossed Freddie's face, before he withdrew his hand just a fraction too quickly.

If he hadn't been torn between deep misery on behalf of his sons, mortification at Freddie's rudeness and sympathy for Emma, Alex would almost have been impressed. As it was, he felt as though he ought to try to improve the situation.

He took a step forward and put his arm around Freddie's shoulders, just as Emma said, 'I can't imagine that you want to waste any time talking to me when your father is just home after his stay in London. You must have so much to tell him. Why don't the four of you spend some time together while Mrs Drabble begins the mammoth task of introducing me to the house?'

She looked at all of them with a very bright and, to Alex's eyes, very forced smile, and then continued, 'In fact, I am very tired after such a long journey. I wonder if my dinner might be brought to me in my chamber just for this evening, after you've shown me around a little, Mrs Drabble? If that wouldn't inconvenience anyone too much?'

Freddie's shoulders relaxed very slightly, Mrs Drabble's

mouth twitched at the corners, as though she was on the brink of smiling, and Alex almost wanted to hug Emma.

He barely saw her again for the rest of the evening, other than a couple of glimpses of her rounding corners with Mrs Drabble and occasional snatches of her voice in conversation, and spent an enjoyable time immersing himself in the world of his children again, eating supper with them in their nursery.

Freddie didn't mention Emma at all, and neither did John or Harry. Instead, they filled him in on the dam they'd been building in a little river to the west of the estate, and the fish that they'd seen in the river, and the big fight that John and Harry had had, during which John had made Harry's nose bleed and after which Mrs Drabble had given Harry an extra custard tart to make him feel better.

It was the best evening Alex had had since before he'd left for London. In fact, now that he was back here, it was almost possible to believe that the entire marriage was a nightmare that had never really happened, until—weary after last night in the inn tossing and turning thinking about Emma, their situation and their kiss—he took himself off to bed and looked at the connecting door between his and Emma's suites and began to think, really hard, about the fact that she was just on the other side of the shared sitting room that that door led to. Probably in her nightgown.

*God.*

After another less than optimal night's sleep—hopefully he'd get used to Emma's presence in the house quickly—Alex was up early to break his fast before Emma could feasibly be expected to be awake, let alone ready to descend for her own breakfast. He'd see the boys and then take himself off on business around the estate. There was always more business in which he could involve himself, so it wouldn't be difficult for him to be so busy with his work and the boys that he would have little time to spend with Emma.

By the evening, his mood had calmed. Once they'd got used to the situation they would easily be able to achieve an amicably distant marriage; many aristocratic couples managed it. They could establish a routine similar to the one they'd had today, and then Emma would move to the dower house, and all would be well. She would essentially be just another pleasant person whom he knew and saw for short periods reasonably regularly. He was surrounded by people all the time, after all.

Before going to see the boys while their nurse began their evening routine, he sat down at his desk to write a quick note to let Emma know that he would unfortunately not be able to dine with her this evening. He'd contemplated sending her a message via Lancing, but that had seemed a little rude.

Oddly, it was difficult to find exactly the right words.

He screwed up the fourth piece of paper he'd started and dipped his quill into the ink for perhaps a tenth time. What was wrong with him? All he needed to say was that he was paying a long overdue visit to a neighbouring friend. There was nothing wrong with that. They'd agreed that they would lead separate lives. He hoped she wouldn't be lonely, though.

He looked at the stack of invitations to one side of the desk. Perhaps they should accept a few of those, sooner rather than later, and attend them as a couple, so that Emma had the opportunity to make friends in the neighbourhood.

It wouldn't be a problem attending dinners and dances together; it would be very different from spending time together at home.

Back to his message to Emma. What should he say?

Eventually he finished the two-sentence note—time spent on it approximately two minutes per uninspired word—and rang for Lancing to pass it to Emma, telling him that he was unavoidably required to go out this evening.

Lancing looked at him for maybe half a second longer than would have been usual and then said, 'As you wish, Your Grace.'

He was without question criticising Alex for not staying at home with his—no, Alex couldn't even *think* the word 'wife' without qualification—with Emma. This was the problem with devoted lifelong retainers. Obviously they were wonderful most of the time, but sometimes, when you just needed a bit of privacy and no criticism for your actions, you could do without them. Much like certain members of your extended family, really.

'Thank you,' he said firmly, and Lancing gave him another slightly too long look before leaving with the note.

The boys were eating their dinner when Alex reached the nursery. Emma was sitting at the table with them, helping Harry cut up his food, while Freddie and John both sat somewhat unnaturally far from her.

'Good evening,' she said to Alex, standing up. 'I hope you've had a good day. I will leave you to spend some time with the boys and bid you goodnight.'

'Goodnight,' said Alex, feeling guilty that he was effectively abandoning her to an evening of solitude.

Once she'd left the room, the boys, as always, had a lot to say—or shout—about what they'd been doing today. And Alex, as always, wondered if he should be making a better job of fatherhood.

Perhaps Emma would be able to instil a little more discipline into them, while not squashing their personalities. It was a difficult balance, and one that he didn't feel he'd achieved very well, because his main aim since they'd lost Diana the day Harry was born had been to make them feel loved, with no great regard for anything else.

'Emma took us for a walk,' Harry told him.

'She knows a lot about frogs,' John said. 'And she wanted to know about our studies and what we like doing best.'

Freddie didn't say anything for a while on the subject of Emma until, when pressed by John, he conceded that she wasn't the worst governess they'd ever had and did know a lot about animals.

'But she won't stay. They never do.'

Alex hadn't understood until he had his children quite how much being a parent could break your heart. Telling his children that they'd lost their mother and seeing the anguish of the older two had magnified his own grief immeasurably. Right now, he just wanted to hug all three of them. He also wanted to reassure them and tell them that Emma *would* stay, because she was different from the many governesses who'd left because they... Well, he hadn't *married* them. Difficult to put that into words, though, without discussing things best left undiscussed.

'You know you're the best three sons in the world?' he said instead.

'So can we have extra pudding?' John asked.

\* \* \*

Two hours later, Alex, seated in front of a fire in the library at the great baronial hall of his friend and neighbour Gideon, Viscount Dearly, reflected again that it was good to see Gideon. They'd known each other since they were in leading strings, as their estates backed onto each other and their fathers had been friends, and then they'd been to both Eton and Oxford together; and they shared the same sporting interests and genuinely liked each other. It was a real relief after all the fakeness and plotting and, frankly, nastiness of a London Season, followed by his surprise marriage, to be home relaxing with his closest friend.

Until, inevitably—as he should have realised it would—the conversation turned to the rumour Gideon had heard about Alex's marriage.

'It's actually *true*?' Gideon said.

His incredulity wasn't surprising. Under normal circumstances there would have been no possibility of Alex's marrying without Gideon being involved.

Alex nodded. He didn't have any words. He couldn't say *Yes* without qualifying it with *unfortunately*, but that felt incredibly rude and something else—disloyal, perhaps, to Emma.

'Congratulations?' Gideon raised an eyebrow.

Alex didn't twitch. 'Thank you.'

'Please don't feel that you have to say anything, but if you do wish to talk, you know I'm the soul of discretion.'

That was true. Gideon was an excellent person in whom to confide. He was not only very discreet, but also very understanding and supportive. Perhaps that was why Alex had decided to come here this evening, he thought. Had he subconsciously wanted to talk about it?

'You got married only a couple of days ago and yet you're here with me this evening. Rumour has it that the young lady's aunt forced you into the marriage?'

Alex looked at Gideon's wide, so familiar, and currently very concerned face. And then he thought of Emma's face, and the way she looked when she was laughing, or smiling, or had concern in her eyes. Funny how you could quickly get to know someone quite well. And, God, what was he thinking? He really did *not* know her well. He couldn't betray her, though, even to his oldest and dearest friend.

'No, her aunt didn't force me into it,' he stated. 'I...'

Gideon said nothing; he just poured them both more brandy.

Alex really did want to talk about it, he realised, but he didn't want to say anything bad about Emma.

'Basically, I saw Sir Peter Fortescue trying to compromise her into marriage. He managed to tear the bodice of her dress and summon a huge crowd of people to witness the whole thing. She would have been ruined if she hadn't finished the evening betrothed, and I couldn't abandon her to that fate. So I asked her to marry me.'

'I see.' Gideon nodded. 'And that was that?'

'It actually wasn't. She tried very hard to refuse me. She's an extremely honourable woman. One of the few young ladies I've met who wasn't desperate to become a duchess, and she didn't want to see me trapped into a marriage she knew I didn't want. I had to convince her that I needed her as governess to the boys.'

'And do you think you could be happy with her?'

'No.' The answer shot straight out of Alex's mouth. 'I will never be happy with another woman. I don't want to be.'

'Because?' Gideon stared. 'Oh. You're scared of losing someone again.'

Alex nodded, not surprised by how perceptive he was.

'I'm sorry. That's a very difficult situation.'

Alex nodded again. And then he said, 'A game of piquet?'

Because now he'd told Gideon everything—pretty much everything anyway—and why was he thinking about their kiss at the inn again—there was nothing more to say.

*Difficult situation* summed it up well.

# Chapter Eight

Having visited the kittens in the stables, and then eaten a lonely dinner, Emma plonked herself down in the chair at the writing table in the very lovely boudoir that Mrs Drabble had informed her was now hers. She pulled open the drawers to each side. They were filled with paper, envelopes, quills, ink, everything a duchess might need for her correspondence.

Had they belonged to the last duchess?

What had Diana been like?

Emma was never going to be able to compete with her in anyone's affections. She didn't *want* to compete with Diana, and she didn't *want* a marriage filled with grand passion, but she *did* want to be held in at least a modicum of affection by someone in her new life, or she'd have a very lonely existence.

She took out a piece of paper. Sitting by herself doing nothing wasn't going to do her any good, and writing to someone would engage her mind. Perhaps she'd write to her great friend Lily, whom she'd met at her Bath seminary and with whom she'd maintained a regular correspondence ever since, through Lily's marriage to a very respectable squire who resided in the county of

Hampshire and her subsequent speedy production of three little girls.

Perhaps she could go and visit Lily. Hampshire was nearer to Somerset than London, and a duchess could certainly travel without her duke as long as she took a maid and a footman.

A few minutes later she put her quill down. She didn't have the words now to describe to Lily her meeting with the duke and subsequent marriage to him. She *should* write to her soon, in case Lily heard about the wedding and was hurt that Emma hadn't told her herself, but it wouldn't make any difference if she left it until tomorrow.

She would do some embroidery. She'd brought with her the slippers on which she'd been working at her aunt's. Maybe she should get those out.

She hated needlework. She'd been embroidering these slippers since the beginning of the Season and had accomplished very little. There were advantages to being a duchess, and one of them had to be not doing embroidery very often.

She would read instead. Maybe she'd go and sit in the shared sitting room between her bedchamber and the duke's and read there before getting into bed. It would be too depressing to sit in her own chamber for the entire evening. She'd better allow Jenny to help her into another one of the bridal nightgowns she had, and then tell her she wouldn't have any further need of her services tonight.

Jenny insisted on brushing out Emma's hair and arranging her near-transparent nightgown just so, for Emma's imagined night-time encounter with the duke. When she'd finally finished, Emma locked her bedroom door, hauled a robe around herself and went into the sitting room, locking the door from there to the corridor outside too. She really didn't want to see Jenny again this evening. It was too wearing—and if she was honest, also depressing—parrying all her comments about what Emma and the duke would be getting up to tonight.

She tried very, very hard and eventually managed to concentrate a little on her book, to the extent that she even turned some pages and became quite interested in what might happen between the book's heroine, Emma, and her neighbour Mr Knightley. Normally, she absolutely adored this author's writing, but she wasn't in the mood for reading this evening.

She could just go to bed. She wasn't at all tired, though. Maybe she should start again from the beginning of the book and concentrate better this time.

She was still awake, curled up in the corner of the sofa, when sounds from the duke's chamber alerted her to the fact that he must have returned home and retired for the evening. She'd better go and get into bed immediately; it would be mortifying if he came in here and found her, as though she'd been waiting for him, when he so clearly didn't want to see her this evening.

Perhaps he didn't want to see her any evening. That was a lowering thought, although it was of course exactly what they'd agreed.

In her haste to jump up, she caught her foot in the end of her robe and tripped and fell onto the floor. As she picked herself up, the connecting door into Alex's chamber opened and he appeared in the doorway.

'It's you,' he said. 'I just wanted to see what all that clattering was.' He moved forward and unnecessarily held out his hand to her.

'Thank you,' Emma said, not taking the hand. She

didn't want to look as though she was desperate for physical contact with him. 'I tripped. I was reading in here.' She held her book up as though it was evidence. 'And now I'm going to bed. Goodnight.' She put her hand on the sofa to lever herself up.

Alex took a step backwards and said, 'I trust that you are unhurt?'

'Yes, indeed I am.'

Now that she was back on her feet, trying not to wince at where she'd landed heavily on the side of her bottom—she'd have a big bruise there in the morning—she could see that he was struggling to keep his eyes on her face. They kept straying down to her décolletage. She looked down and realised why. Her *robe de chambre* was open and the frothy lace at her bosom had fallen down, so that her nightgown was far too low, only very barely skimming her nipples, and, in fact, it was so close to see-through that she might almost be naked.

Her entire body suddenly felt warm, and all she could think about was the way his eyes were on her and the look of appreciation in them. The room was cooling now, and the air on her skin, together with his gaze, almost made her feel as though he was touching her.

He swallowed and she took a deep breath. Suddenly, she realised that she was standing still, half-naked, being gazed at by a man who, while he *was* her husband, had explicitly stated that he did not wish to engage in husbandly activities with her.

She whipped the robe around herself, making sure that it covered her up to her neck, and said, 'So, goodnight.'

If there was one tiny note of satisfaction in the incident, it was that Alex's voice was definitely hoarse when he replied, 'Goodnight.'

\* \* \*

Emma struggled to get to sleep because it was very difficult not to think far too much about both her boring evening—the first of many to come, presumably—and Alex's eyes on her body in her nightgown.

She was still eating a relatively late breakfast when Lancing informed her that His Grace would be grateful if she would go and see him in his study when she was ready.

'Thank you so much for coming,' he said when she entered the room.

It suddenly felt very similar to the occasions during her teenage years on which she'd been required to go and see the head of her seminary, when she'd behaved in a manner 'unbecoming to a young lady of quality', in the head's words, for misdemeanours ranging from running in the garden to giggling with Lily during lessons to exchanging notes with the very attractive piano master.

Emma was not going to enter into a head-of-seminary-versus-naughty-schoolgirl relationship with Alex, so instead of standing in front of his desk, which was what he seemed to be expecting, she took a seat in a comfortable armchair to one side of the desk, so that he was forced to turn to look at her.

'Not at all,' she said when she was comfortable in the chair. 'Did you have something you wished to discuss with me?'

'Yes. I wanted you to know that I've asked my man of business to settle on you formally the fortune and other assets comprising your dowry, so that whatever might happen to me you will be financially independent for life.'

'Thank you.' Emma realised that she wasn't at all surprised; Alex had already demonstrated himself to be both kind and a man of his word.

'Also, I thought you might like an introduction to the estate. If you would like, I could drive you around it this afternoon.'

Emma genuinely couldn't imagine anything she'd rather do today. She needed to get to know her surroundings, and during their journey from London Alex had proved to be a very pleasant companion. He would, of course, be the ultimate expert on his own land, and she certainly didn't wish to spend any more time than she needed to alone.

'I'd like that very much,' she told him.

'Excellent.'

And then he didn't say anything else, which gave her the impression that, much as when her seminary headmistress had finished telling her off each time, she was being dismissed.

She didn't want to be dismissed. Obviously, Alex had been extremely kind to marry her, and this situation was not of his choosing, and she had gained a lot from it while he had gained nothing, but they were still going to have to find a way of dealing with each other with which they could both be reasonably happy. And Emma could not be remotely happy if Alex treated her as though he was in charge.

'Would two o'clock be acceptable for us to set off?' she asked.

'Yes, I...suppose so.' He seemed like an inherently kind and decent man who had, however, fallen into the way of being a duke and got used to things being on his terms, including what time they might set off anywhere.

She beamed at him. 'Perfect. Well, if you'll excuse me, I need to go and see the boys now.'

Emma was ready, in one of her smart new pelisses, a dark green velvet one, covering a pale grey walking dress in worked muslin, also new, in good time for their drive, and arrived in the castle's great hall at the same moment as Alex, who was wearing a greatcoat, which showed his shoulders to excellent advantage and made him look very, well, big.

'Good afternoon,' she said, trying to ignore the shiver that just seeing him seemed to have caused.

That kiss had a lot to answer for.

'Good afternoon.' He did have a very nice voice. Deep and kind of...*throbby*. In a very alluring way.

For goodness' sake. She was losing her wits.

'I have had my curricle brought round to the front,' Alex said, indicating the door ahead of them.

'Thank you,' Emma said, and they walked out of the castle together, for all the world like a normal couple.

'I'll take you out in a gig another day, so that we can go cross-country, but today I'd like to give a recently acquired pair an outing,' he said, holding his arm out for her as they descended the wide steps down from the castle's main entrance.

'How exciting to see a new pair being put through their paces,' she said, wondering if there was any chance that he'd allow her to drive for any part of this afternoon.

Alex handed her up into the curricle and gave her a blanket for her to wrap around her legs, before leaping up himself and taking the reins.

He was a good driver, Emma noted as they set off. Fully in control, but not forcing his horses in any way.

He was also a man who knew and loved his land, it seemed.

'There's been a settlement here since the turn of the twelfth century,' he told her as they skirted the nearest village after he'd—very proudly—pointed out the school he'd had built and told her that the village girls as well as boys were educated there.

'We're heading up towards some of my farming tenants now. The earliest farmers here were Normans. The land's particularly good for sheep and wheat, but we farm as great a variety of crops as we're able, for the nutrition of the soil and the health of the crops.'

He definitely had his tenants' interests very much at heart. The properties that she saw were all well-maintained, and Alex had a lot to tell her about the hospital that he'd had built over the past few years. He was also very enthusiastic about agriculture.

'I presume that there must have been a revolution in farming techniques with the invention of so much new machinery in recent years?' Emma asked.

'Yes, very much so. My own father, as a landowner, was resistant to it, as are some of the farmers. Others worry that the introduction of mechanised labour will result in the unemployment of workers. But my view is that it's very much a good thing—and indeed we've seen that workers' activities are now merely diverted to other uses relating to crop rotation and field enclosures, for example, which expands our economy rather than causing unemployment.'

Emma nodded. 'It's similar in the textiles industry. My father was a very early adopter of new machinery and practices, and we intend to continue that in the factories. We have adopted additional security in case the Luddites' attacks spread to our region.'

'*You* intend to continue that? *You* have adopted additional security measures?' Alex asked, without looking at her, concentrating on negotiating a tight bend in the lane.

'The manager of the factories—my cousin—asked me to continue advising him by correspondence. He and I worked closely together before my father's death. I would like to visit the factories and the villages where the workers are housed from time to time. My father was quite devoted to his employees and ensured the safest possible working conditions and good pay for them, and my cousin and I intend to continue similarly. I am very grateful to you for settling my father's assets on me so that I might continue to be involved in a more formal manner.'

'It sounds as though you and I might both benefit from an exchange of information in our different ventures.' Alex turned his head briefly to smile at her before refocusing on his driving.

'Yes, I think we might.'

Emma had to admit to herself that she was impressed at Alex's ready acceptance of her intention to continue her involvement in the running of the factories. A lot of men would have been horrified by her links to trade, and by the fact that she, a woman, thought she had anything of an intellectual or managerial nature to offer.

Maybe he would be open-minded enough to allow her to drive him.

'I was thinking of buying myself a carriage,' she said. 'Perhaps a phaeton.'

'Indeed?'

'Yes. I drove a lot in Lancashire and missed doing so while in London. I love driving.' She paused for a moment and then said, 'Today is a very good day for driving.'

Alex slowed his horses and looked at her. 'Are you suggesting that you'd like to drive now?'

'Yes.' Emma smiled at him.

He didn't look as though he was keen to hand the reins over. 'This pair are particularly lively,' he said. 'And strong. And this is a curricle.'

'And I am a good driver,' Emma said.

'Although unpractised in recent months. Have you driven a curricle before?'

'Yes, I drove my father's curricle, on his instruction, and while I *am* unpractised in recent months, I was so practised before—over many years—that I don't think the lack of recent practice will have made any discernible difference to my skill.'

'Really?'

'Yes.'

Alex turned to study her again for a moment. He didn't say anything for a few seconds, and they both sat and looked ahead at the horses and the lane in front of them.

Then he said, 'I'll take you to a quiet, straight length of road and you can drive. I must warn you again, though, that these horses are wonderful, and very well-matched, but require an experienced and strong driver.'

'Thank you—and thank you for the warning. However, I think we and the horses will survive my driving very happily.'

When they got to a part of the road that Alex told her he judged to be a suitably easy place to drive, he handed her the reins.

Emma found herself smiling just at the feel of them

in her hand again. She moved her fingers very lightly, to get the measure of the horses, how they would respond. They did indeed feel very lively, and very well-matched. She would of course have expected nothing less of Alex's horses.

Once she was sure that she was ready, she set off. Soon she increased their pace, conscious the entire time of Alex hovering very close to her, clearly not at all confident that she could handle his team.

'You drive well,' Alex said after a few minutes.

'Why, thank you,' Emma said, slowing very slightly for a corner. 'You will note, however, that while I do think that you drive very well, I did not comment on your driving as I did not wish to patronise you.'

'You will perhaps have noted that most men of the *ton* do drive but the majority of women do not.'

'Well, I told you that I am a good driver.'

'And you are.' He nodded. 'Very good, in fact,' he added as Emma negotiated a sharp double bend in the road at speed.

'You are a very good driver too.'

'Er, thank you. I feel I should perhaps apologise for prejudging your driving.'

'Not at all.' Emma accompanied her words with her best sarcastic eye-roll, all the while focusing on the horses and the road, and Alex laughed.

They had come to another more open, straight section of road, and Emma increased their speed again.

'I might have been a little patronising before,' said Alex, 'but now I'm not being patronising. I'd say this to anyone—man or woman—you're driving so well that I'm literally relaxing in my seat. That is not something that happens when anyone else drives me. In fact, it's very rare that anyone *would* drive me. Not even my best friends, all of whom are good drivers. And, as I say—and as you are obviously aware—these horses require an experienced handler. I care very much about my horses, and I would not like anyone to job their mouths. Before you drove, I obviously had no idea whether or not you were any good, other than your clear belief that you were.'

Emma laughed. 'I'll take that as a compliment. Thank you for trusting me enough to allow me to drive them in the first place.'

'If I'm honest, I was prepared to take the reins if necessary.'

'Oh, really? I didn't notice you hovering and breathing down my neck at *all*.'

Alex laughed again, Emma gave him a sideways smile, and then he said nothing about re-taking the reins himself, and she drove all the way back.

Jim, the head groom, came running out as they came into sight. 'Are you injured, Your Grace?' he shouted.

'I'm very well, thank you, Jim,' Alex called. 'He's never seen anyone drive me before,' he told Emma, 'so he naturally assumed that a disaster had befallen me.'

'It seems I must thank you again.'

'Not at all. I was merely trying to compliment you again without patronising you. And, yes, I do think you should buy your own carriage. And horses. Should you like to arrange the purchases yourself, or would you like to discuss them with me? Or you will be very welcome to drive any from our stables here.'

'That's very kind.' Emma hadn't felt this contented for months. 'I believe that I should draw on your local expertise.'

'At your service.' Alex gave a mini salute and she laughed. 'Do you also ride?' he asked.

'I do ride, but only very averagely,' Emma said, rising with reluctance to alight from the curricle.

'You know, I begin to think that little about you is average.' Alex held his arm out for her and she took it lightly.

'I'm going to take that as another compliment,' Emma said.

'It is.' Alex smiled at her and she felt even more contented than she'd felt a couple of minutes ago, if that were possible. 'Now, I hope you don't mind, but I have some more papers to look through before I go to see the boys. I thought I might eat with them in the nursery this evening.'

Oh. A very clear message that for the second evening running he wasn't going to eat with Emma.

And just like that, her mood deflated.

She had her pride, though. 'Perfect,' she said. 'I'm very tired and thought I might take my supper in my chamber again.'

'Ideal. I will see you tomorrow, then.'

'Indeed.'

And so, after what had felt like a wonderful afternoon, she walked inside to begin another miserable evening.

## Chapter Nine

Alex felt extremely guilty watching Emma go. He shouldn't abandon her like this.

On impulse, he called out to her. 'Emma. Why don't you join the boys and me in the nursery for supper? If you like?'

She stopped, and even from a distance he could see that her shoulders grew a little rigid, and then she turned round to face him.

He moved closer to her so that he'd be able to hear her response, as she said, 'Thank you, but I do not wish to intrude on your time with your boys.'

Alex opened his mouth to tell her that it wouldn't be an intrusion. Except that wasn't true and he couldn't say the words because he was obviously going to put the boys' happiness above Emma's, and he was fairly sure that they benefited from time alone with their only parent.

He could see her features settling into what looked to him to be a careful mask, to hide any emotion she might be feeling. He recognised it because he often wore such a mask himself. And he realised that he couldn't do this to her. On the occasions he'd seen her with others she'd seemed very friendly. He couldn't consign her to loneliness every single evening.

When he'd asked her if she'd like to go for the drive today it had been because he'd felt—had known—that he had a responsibility to ensure her happiness as far as he could, without engaging too closely with her. The drive had been perfectly enjoyable; it wouldn't be a terrible hardship to eat dinner with her two or three times a week.

'I realise that I am not yet particularly hungry,' he said. 'I don't think I will eat with the boys, therefore, but will instead take dinner in the dining room later on, after I've spent some time with them in the nursery. Would you care to join me?'

Emma was standing very still, clearly reflecting. After a few seconds, she said, 'I'd enjoy that, thank you.'

'Excellent. I'll see you then.'

She came down for dinner wearing a pale pink dress that he didn't think he'd seen before, and against which her dark hair and light brown skin looked very beautiful.

'I believe that Martin—I presume you've been introduced to our chef—has produced some particularly delicious dishes for this evening,' he said.

It felt important to keep the conversation on mundane matters, because he'd been enjoying her company far too much and had struggled greatly to banish from his mind the image of how she'd looked last night in her nightgown. He needed to regain some self-control.

'I look forward to tasting them.'

As they finished bowls of velvety chestnut soup, Emma said, 'The boys are wonderful, a credit to you.'

'Thank you.' Alex smiled at her and then, almost to his own surprise, added, 'Much credit must go to their mother, for her influence in the early years with the older two.'

Where had that come from? He didn't usually choose to mention Diana.

Emma nodded. 'Tell me about her? If you'd like to?'

Alex knew that he didn't have to reply—knew that although she would be interested in his answer she would understand if he chose not to say anything—but, actually, found that he did wish to tell her.

'She loved our children. She loved dancing. She loved to laugh. She loved playing backgammon. She hated apples, of all things. And she was beautiful. And funny.' He felt a little choke in his throat and clenched his jaw.

'She sounds wonderful. I'm so sorry for your loss.'

'Thank you.'

Oddly, Alex felt as though some of the emotion washing over him was due to the sincerity in Emma's regard, not just his bereavement.

He really should try not to become too close to her.

He did his best to keep the conversation on food, a potted history of his family and questions about Lancashire for the remainder of the meal, and, other than a couple of occasions on which Emma caused him to laugh out loud, it wasn't particularly different from making mild conversation with a pleasant acquaintance. He could certainly do this, remain emotionally and physically aloof from her while being polite and not ignoring her. He hoped that they could rub along very happily together like this.

After Emma rose from the dinner table, Alex had half a glass of port in boring isolation, and then went to join her in the drawing room, just to bid her goodnight out of politeness.

She was sitting next to the fire, her dark head bent over some embroidery. It was a slightly incongruous picture, in that it was difficult to imagine someone as energetic and vibrant as he'd learnt that Emma was spending hours with a needle.

'What are you making?' he asked politely.

'Gentleman's slippers,' she said, holding up the one she was working on. 'They were initially intended as a gift for my uncle, but since they aren't going to be worthy of parcelling up and sending by post I think they might have to be for you.'

'That is very kind,' Alex said, stunned.

So far in their acquaintance she'd demonstrated herself to be very competent at a wide range of things, everything he'd seen her do, in fact. Until now. She was *not* a gifted embroideress.

'They are...' Good God. Would he have to *wear* them? 'They are, sadly, relatively small.' Thank heavens. 'Sadly, I have very large feet.'

'Oh, don't worry.' Emma bestowed a sunny smile upon him. 'I'm sure that with my needle skills I'll be able very easily to alter them to fit you. I could perhaps sew an extra piece on the end.'

She *had* to be joking. She looked deadly serious, though.

'Thank you,' he said while she continued to sew, very slowly and, to Alex's eye, very unevenly.

'Perhaps a brocade strip,' she said, eyeing his feet.

'Wonderful.' Alex shifted slightly in his seat. How was it possible that, while sitting opposite a woman mangling a pair of slippers that she was threatening to make him wear, all he could think about was the fact that she was looking at his feet, and how she might look at the rest of him? Really, how was that possible?

She raised her eyes to his and smiled at him. 'You're genuinely scared, aren't you?'

'I'm not scared,' he said.

She leaned towards him and he leaned forward too, in a reflex action.

'I'm not going to make you wear them,' she said.

'I knew that,' he told her.

Emma laughed, a lot, and then Alex laughed a lot too. 'I might have been worried for a minute,' he admitted eventually, which made her smile in a very victorious manner, and that made Alex smile too.

And now neither of them was speaking, nor smiling. They were just looking at each other. Alex could see the rise and fall of Emma's chest, a tiny pulse beating at the base of her delicate neck. She moistened her lips, the lips that he'd kissed two nights ago in the inn.

*No.*

His mind was going to places it really shouldn't, and if he wasn't careful he might act on his thoughts.

'I think that, if you don't mind,' he said, 'I will retire now.'

It should be up to Emma to decide first to retire, but two people who'd just become legally married shouldn't have to stand entirely on ceremony with each other.

'Indeed,' she said immediately, 'I too am tired.'

They didn't speak at all as they went upstairs together. When they reached the corridor outside their rooms, Alex indicated their shared sitting room with a small nod of his head, and Emma nodded in response.

He opened the door and held it so that she could pass

inside the room, before closing it behind them. Emma had come to a halt a few feet away from the door and was standing looking at him, her hands clasped in front of her, her chest rising and falling more rapidly than usual.

Alex wanted to go straight to bed. He didn't want to be seduced into doing something ill-advised, or even just to be thinking ill-advised thoughts, like how much, all of a sudden, he wanted to kiss her plump lips, pull her against him, make her moan with desire for him, begin to sate his own physical desire for her.

He didn't want to think about that at all.

Emma bit her lip, and then lifted a hand and pushed back a ringlet that had escaped the ribbon holding back the rest of her curls. The ringlet fell forward again. As though propelled by an unseen force, Alex stepped towards her and, very gently, tucked it back into the ribbon, his hand brushing the softness of her cheek as he did so.

He wasn't gentle enough; apparently the hairstyle was quite fragile. His fingers had dislodged the ribbon and now her hair tumbled around her shoulders.

And it was as though his fingers had a mind of their own. He *should* have taken a step backwards and bidden Emma goodnight, but instead he found himself running his hands through her curls, then tugging her hair very gently and cupping the back of her head. And then, as though some invisible cord was pulling him, he was reaching down to brush her lips with his.

Emma sighed against his lips, and the small sound was the undoing of him. He kissed her again, lightly, and then deepened the kiss, parting her lips with his tongue. Emma sighed again, then ran her hands up his chest and around his neck. She was soft, pliant, warm, eager, *perfect*, against him.

He wanted more of her, he wanted to lift her, carry her into his room, place her on his bed...

The marital bed.

He didn't want a real marriage with her. What if she got pregnant? Died in childbirth as Diana had? He didn't want to do that to another woman. And, for himself, he didn't want to grieve again.

As images of the aftermath of Diana's death crowded into his mind, he let go of Emma.

He heard her say, 'Oh,' and dragged himself back to the present.

'I...' He looked at her, beautiful, with her tumbled hair and swollen lips and still half-closed eyes. He wanted to say something nice to her, not hurt her feelings in any way. But he didn't have the right words.

She opened her eyes slowly and smiled uncertainly at him. He found himself shaking his head very slightly. Her smile dropped and she pressed her lips together. She looked...shocked. And—from the way she was now wrapping her arms around herself—maybe as though she had realised that he was shutting her out and was trying to protect herself.

God. He really didn't want to hurt her. But, however much he wanted to say something, he just couldn't talk now.

'I'm sorry. Goodnight.' He took the few steps necessary to enter his chamber and closed the door firmly behind himself without looking back.

That should not happen again.

He made sure that he breakfasted early in the morning, having noticed that Emma was not a particularly early riser. There was no point in laying himself open to disturbing thoughts—any kind of temptation—when he didn't have to. Sharing his meal with a newspaper rather than Emma was a much better way of spending his time.

He went up to the nursery after he'd finished eating. A few minutes after he'd sat down with the boys, Emma came into the room.

'Good morning,' she said.

All three of the boys' heads shot round and they all chorused, 'Good morning,' very over-eagerly.

Alex frowned.

'I hope that none of you are scared of spiders,' Emma addressed the boys.

Harry immediately giggled, and Freddie kicked him under the table. Alex opened his mouth to reprimand him, but Emma was still talking.

'If so, you'd better be very careful because there were a lot in my bedchamber last night.'

Harry giggled again.

Alex glared at him The boys were clearly involved in this, but maybe he should speak to them when Emma wasn't there.

'I'm so sorry,' he said. 'I'll call Mrs Drabble immediately.'

'There's no need,' Emma told him. 'I got rid of them all myself out of the window. Fortunately, I'm not at all scared by spiders. Indeed, I like them, and count myself quite an expert on the different varieties we have in England.' She sat down next to John and put a monogrammed handkerchief down on the table in front of him. 'I believe that this is yours.'

John's eyes widened and he said, 'Oh.'

'I must tell you,' Emma said, 'that it would be polite to thank me for the safe return of your property. Something else I must tell you is that I now have a spy watching my door. One further thing: if any other small creatures should find their way into my chamber, assisted by anyone, I might lose my temper. And I am *fearsome* when I'm angry.'

She smiled sunnily at the boys, and as one they all shrank backwards.

Alex nodded, impressed. *Masterful*, he mouthed at her. She turned her still-sunny smile on him and he couldn't help laughing.

'I'm going to leave you all to it now,' he said, 'and I shall look forward to hearing whether or not any of you make Emma angry.'

As he closed the nursery door, he decided that he would have a polite dinner with Emma this evening, but other than that would not see her today.

Later, as he was eating a quick luncheon in the library, Lancing brought him a note from his aunt—his late father's older sister—informing him that she would be visiting that afternoon as she was desirous of meeting the new duchess, of whose existence, she wrote, she would have liked to have been notified by Alex.

Alex in turn sent word to Emma, and then, reckoning that he had two clear hours, took himself off to the stables to discuss possible horse purchases for Emma with Jim.

Almost exactly two hours later, Alex and Emma were waiting together in the grand saloon next to the castle's great hall when they heard the unmistakable noise and bustle of an arrival.

Lancing flung open the doors and announced, 'The Countess of Denby.'

Alex watched Emma as his aunt walked slowly into the room, wanting to see her reaction. His aunt was an elderly woman and, having embraced and apparently loved the elaborate fashion of the later eighteenth century, had made no concession to the less ostentatious modes of dress favoured by women for the past thirty years.

It wasn't every day that you saw a lady dressed for a country afternoon call in the enormous panniered skirts and huge wigs that had characterised pre-French Revolution fashion, but Emma barely twitched at the spectacle before her and walked forward and took his aunt's outstretched hands.

Alex was impressed; most people reacted more overtly to his aunt on first meeting her.

'Good afternoon, young lady.' His aunt had no regard for convention, and in Alex's experience it was highly unlikely that she would treat Emma as anything other than a much younger lady to whom she would offer a great deal of probably unwanted and possibly incorrect advice.

'Good afternoon.' Emma smiled at her.

'I need tea.' Alex's aunt strode forward, her immense skirts rustling around her, and arranged herself on a sofa in the middle of the room. 'Sit near to me, girl. Alexander, where's that butler of yours? Tea!'

'Of course, my lady.' Lancing had materialised out of nowhere.

Alex was sure that his household, led by Lancing, would magic up all manner of sandwiches and cakes very quickly.

'So what's this I hear about you compromising my nephew into marriage?' his aunt asked Emma, who frowned only a very tiny bit before producing what might almost have passed for a serene smile.

'It's nonsense,' Alex said. 'Emma and I met in Hyde Park and fell almost immediately in love, but kept our relationship secret for a while.'

'Sounds like a complete faradiddle to me,' his aunt boomed, adjusting her ear trumpet. 'But so does the compromise story.' She poked Emma with the black fan she'd been holding. 'I like the look of you. I don't see you behaving badly.'

'Thank you,' Emma said.

'What?' Alex's aunt turned the ear trumpet again.

'I said thank you,' Emma said loudly.

'You have a very quiet voice. Now, tell me about your family. I knew your mother. Bad business when she ran off with your father.'

Emma replied slowly, and loudly, repeating herself when asked, answering an extraordinary number of questions, smiling throughout, even in the face of some quite remarkable incivility.

'So your grandmother was Indian? Your beauty is very unusual. Quite out of the common way. I like it, though.' Alex's aunt smiled at Emma, as though bestowing upon her an enormous favour rather than enormous rudeness.

Emma said, 'I'm honoured,' sounding as though she was trying not to laugh, which was a relief, because a lot of people would just have been offended.

Alex stood up, though. Enough was enough.

'Would you care to take a turn about the gardens, Aunt? And see the boys? Your great-nephews would be delighted to see you.'

'How old are they now?' his aunt asked, not moving from her sofa.

'Nine, seven and four.'

'No,' she said. 'Too young. I don't like young children. Perhaps the oldest. Frederick. Perhaps not, though. I've been feeling rather bilious recently.'

'The garden, then?' Alex persisted.

'No. Too cold. I have my own gardens, you know. One garden is much like another. Sit down, young man.'

'Of course,' Alex said.

He glanced at Emma out of the corner of his eye. She was definitely struggling not to laugh now, which made him smile. A good thing, he realised, because normally an hour into a visit from his aunt he'd be feeling irritated, at best.

'I'm tired,' his aunt said abruptly. 'I think I'll have to spend the night here with you.'

Alex's eyes swivelled straight to Emma's. She was looking as horrified as he felt. Neither of them spoke for a moment, and then Emma, projecting her voice magnificently, said, 'Oh, how wonderful. You'll be able to see the boys properly. We always eat dinner with them in the evenings.'

'They should be in the nursery.'

'I'm afraid that Alex is a very modern parent, and I, of course, follow his...lead. We cannot consign them to the nursery.'

'Help me up,' Alex's aunt said to him. 'I must leave before it gets dark.'

'Masterful again,' Alex whispered to Emma over her head.

'Masterful what?' his aunt asked.

Alex stared at her. Was she in fact not really deaf? Or had he just been unlucky?

'It's been so wonderful to meet you,' Emma said, diverting his aunt's attention in—yes—a masterful manner.

She offered her arm to the older woman, and they passed out of the room together.

'I can only apologise,' Alex said to a laughing Emma, when his aunt's eighteenth-century landau had passed out of sight.

'Not at all. I'd like to think that if I become old and infirm I shall take advantage of it in exactly the same way. I'm sure she has a kind heart.'

'I think it might be your own kind heart imagining the same in her.' Alex smiled at Emma and tried to imagine her old, infirm and rude. She'd still be beautiful if she became old and, please Lord, she would indeed attain old age, unlike Diana. God. He forced his thoughts away from Diana's early death and tried to recapture his previous train of thought. Infirm, that was it. Well, that wasn't a particularly pleasant thought either: he'd hate to think of Emma becoming infirm. He turned his mind to rudeness: it was impossible to imagine Emma becoming rude.

'Perhaps we should indeed both eat with the boys this evening?' Emma suggested. 'So that we didn't take their names in vain.'

Alex nodded, relieved to have his thoughts diverted from hoping that nothing would befall Emma and that she would indeed become an old woman in due course. 'I think you're right.'

He began to regret agreeing to her suggestion within minutes of the meal starting. John and Harry seemed to have thawed dramatically towards Emma, but Freddie, well, Freddie was behaving as though he'd inherited his social skills from his great-aunt.

'I don't want to sit next to Emma,' he began.

'I'm very happy to sit here.' Emma sat down between John and Harry.

'Did you enjoy your walk with Nurse this afternoon?' Emma asked.

'Better than walking with you,' Freddie muttered.

Alex opened his mouth to tell him to apologise immediately, but Emma hurriedly began to talk to John and Harry about frogs and tadpoles. She lifted her eyebrows and indicated Freddie with her eyes, all the while smiling and continuing to talk to the other two, and eventually Alex deduced that she thought he should talk to Freddie.

When they'd finished eating, Emma pushed her chair backwards and said, 'I'm quite exhausted by my busy day today. I'm going to retire to bed now.'

Perfect. If they retired to their chambers at different times, there should be no danger that Alex would succumb to temptation and kiss her again.

'I'll see you in the morning, boys. Alex, I wonder if I could speak to you for a moment outside before you read together?'

'Of course.' Alex stood up and followed her outside. Perhaps she was going to tell him that she couldn't bear to look after the boys any more. He really hoped that wasn't it. 'I'm so sorry about Freddie's rudeness. I'm going to have a very firm word with him now.'

'Without wishing to dictate to you about your children, I'd like to say that I really don't think you should tell him off,' Emma said. 'I think something's happened. I think you ought to ask him what's wrong. When he's on his own.'

Not at all what he'd been expecting her to say. Alex reflected for a moment; maybe she was right.

Half an hour later, as John and Harry were engrossed in a game of sticks, Freddie suddenly blurted out, before Alex had had the opportunity to ask him anything, 'So, are we going to get another baby in our family?'

Well. It seemed as though Emma was right; Freddie didn't sound happy.

'No,' Alex said cautiously. 'Did someone tell you that we would?'

'Mikey said.'

Damn. If Freddie was going to visit the stables, why couldn't the grooms just have done their usual swearing and letting Freddie throw fallen orchard apples and ruin the head gardener's prized ornamental lawn?

'No. We are not,' he said firmly.

'But Mikey said when people get married, like you and Emma, they usually have babies.'

Alex frowned, realising all of a sudden just how carefully he was going to have to tread in setting an example for his children. He wanted them to experience strong, loving marriages as adults, the kind he'd had with Diana and his parents had had. So it wouldn't be good if they witnessed him and Emma in a soulless marriage. But he couldn't allow himself to develop feelings for her, both for his own sake, in case something happened to her, and for the boys, because he couldn't have them thinking that their mother had been replaced.

Should Emma perhaps move to the dower house sooner rather than later so that any gossip could happen and be overcome? And so that the boys would understand that this was a different type of marriage from the one he'd had with Diana? Or should he work hard to get over the ridiculous physical attraction he knew he felt towards Emma? Get used to the fact that they had adjacent bedchambers and be friends with her while she remained in the house?

Whichever, they should begin to attend social events together, so that he could signal to people that, whatever their living arrangements might eventually be, he expected her to be treated as his duchess socially, and so that she could make some friends with whom she could remain friendly in the event that she did move to the dower house.

He had an idea. They should go to a ball, or a dance, and he would dance with her. That would serve a dual purpose. It would send a strong signal—the entire neighbourhood was aware that he wasn't a keen dancer, and indeed had almost never danced with any woman other than Diana—and Emma would meet some of the other ladies who lived locally.

In the meantime, he needed to address this issue, and now John and Harry were listening too.

'Not everyone has babies,' he told the boys. 'Instead of having babies, Emma and I will…dance.'

What? What was he talking about? And why had he just imagined holding her in his arms on a dance floor and liked what he'd imagined?

'Emma likes dancing,' John said.

'How do you know?' Alex asked, surprised.

'She told us in the apple orchard yesterday. And then we danced, and we laughed and laughed,' John said.

'I like Emma,' Harry said.

Damn, this was complicated.

The next day, thinking while he breakfasted alone that he would ask Emma over dinner that evening if she'd like to go with him to some local dinners and dances, Alex realised that they were already falling into a pattern of not really seeing each other during the day, but having dinner together in the evening. If he was honest, the companionship was pleasant. If he could just get over his physical attraction to her—which he was sure he would in time—they could rub along more than happily, from his side, anyway.

'I'd love to,' Emma said, when he broached the subject that evening as they both tasted a particularly good turbot and gooseberry dish.

'Excellent. We have an invitation to a dinner dance tomorrow evening, with some neighbours who live about ten miles away. I think several amongst my acquaintance will be there and think you might enjoy it.'

'That sounds wonderful.'

## Chapter Ten

'The Duke and Duchess of Harwell,' said a footman, flinging open double doors as though he was auditioning for a role in the royal household rather than announcing guests at a country squire's evening dance.

Emma smoothed the skirts of her gauze overdress for the third time since they'd left their carriage.

'You look immaculate,' Alex told her, and put his arm out for her to take. 'Beautiful, in fact. Nothing to worry about.'

Emma tried not to grimace at him. She'd never felt like this in London, but in London she hadn't really cared. Now, though, she felt as though this mattered, since she was likely to be seeing these people regularly, and she'd like to have some local friends.

They took a step forward together, and Alex said a resigned, 'And *smile*,' into her ear, while doing a big, obviously fake, smile of his own, which *did* make her smile as they entered the drawing room, interested eyes watching them from all angles.

He stayed with her and introduced her to almost everyone in the room, for all the world like an adoring new husband. Quite a contrast to how he was at home. There, while he was unfailingly polite—and indeed thoughtful in a number of his suggestions to make her life more comfortable, including taking dinner with her, showing her around the estate in his curricle and accepting the invitation to this dance to enable her to meet their neighbours—he clearly didn't want to spend a lot of time with her.

Which, of course, she was completely happy with. Neither of them had wished to marry the other, and they'd been clear that their marriage would be a bargain that did not include close friendship or anything more intimate. And Alex's behaviour since the second of their two kisses had made it very obvious that he didn't wish anything intimate to happen between them again.

If she was honest, Emma was still struggling not to be upset—deeply hurt, in fact—that Alex clearly regretted their quite earth-shattering second kiss, and was finding it difficult not to be spine-tinglingly aware of him whenever he was anywhere near her. But she must not complain, not even just internally. Alex had been completely open with her from the beginning and this was the bargain they'd made.

'And this is my oldest friend, Gideon,' Alex said, as a large man with red hair and a smile almost as wide as his very broad shoulders shook Alex's hand vigorously.

'Delighted to meet you.' Gideon bowed and then said, 'May I have the pleasure of a dance with you? Only so that I can tell you scurrilous stories about Alex, of course.'

Emma laughed, immediately liking him. 'I'd be delighted.'

'If we're allowed to dance with the duchess, I'd like

the honour of staking my claim now,' another man said, and within a minute or two they were surrounded by several men, all wishing to stake dancing claims.

To Emma's surprise, Alex didn't relinquish her hand, but remained at her side throughout the clamour that ensued, and then raised his voice just slightly, so that the other men fell silent, and said, 'My wife isn't available for the first dance; that pleasure is mine.'

Emma nearly squeaked out loud at the thought of dancing with Alex. Firstly, it was deeply unfashionable for a married couple to dance, even at a private party like this, so it would be a strong signal to the assembled guests that Alex was a devoted husband. And secondly, if she was honest, she'd already imagined dancing with him last night, when she'd been struggling again to get to sleep, thinking about their kisses and him in his bed two doors away from her. But she hadn't expected *actually* to dance with him.

She realised now that when she'd imagined dancing with him she hadn't done him justice. Resplendent in simply cut, sombre-hued and yet glorious evening wear, he eclipsed every other man here tonight. He could be the worst dancer in London, and yet it must feel like an honour to be on his arm, because he *looked* like the best dancer a man could be.

'If the duke and duchess are to dance together, then the first dance must be a waltz,' announced Lady Felicity, the squire's wife. 'Followed by a series of quadrilles and a *danse espagnole*. You will find us bold in this county, Your Grace.'

'Indeed,' said Emma, torn between a giggle exacerbated by the loud grumbles from several disgruntled misses who would now not be able to join the first dance of the evening, as they didn't yet have permission to waltz, and thinking, *Oh, my goodness, I'm going to waltz with Alex.*

The string ensemble at the end of the room struck up and all the women who were dancing stepped into their partners' holds.

Emma had waltzed many times before—her aunt had ensured that she got the permission of the Almack's hostesses early in the Season—and her emotions had ranged from annoyance, or even disgust that she had to dance with a particularly unpalatable partner, through mild irritation, or pity that a perfectly pleasant man was an incompetent dancer, to enjoyment of a partner who had the winning combination of good conversation and competent dancing skills.

She had never once felt any kind of a stomach-flutter or *tingle*. Now, though… Now it was as though all her senses were coming alive for the first time.

As Alex held her right hand lightly in his left, with his other hand skimming the small of her back, it was as though every nerve in her body was attuned to where his body was and where they might touch as the dance progressed. She could smell his deeply masculine scent, sense the rise and fall of his chest almost brushing her own chest, feel the warmth and hardness of his body so close to hers… On the face of it, he was far too tall for her, but somehow it felt—from her perspective, anyway—as though they were the perfect match physically.

They were completely silent as they moved, but the silence wasn't awkward; it was as though their movements were doing the talking. The way they were dancing felt both deliberate and yet entirely natural, as though they couldn't help themselves giving in to the music.

It was wonderful.

Emma loved it when they moved slowly together in the slow parts of the dance, and she loved it when they danced in perfect time with each other in the faster parts.

She only realised the music had stopped because of the sudden movement and chatter around her of others stopping their dance and then leaving or joining the dance floor.

She looked up at Alex. He was still holding her hand and her waist, and was gazing down at her with partly closed, glazed eyes.

He began a slow smile, which Emma felt right to her centre, and suddenly she was feeling hot and as though her insides were liquid and as though she could barely stay standing without the support of Alex's arms.

'I...' he began. And then suddenly Gideon was next to them, and Alex stopped talking. Emma *really* wanted to know what he'd been about to say. Probably nothing... but maybe something.

'And the next dance is mine, I believe,' said Gideon with another of the broad smiles Emma was already beginning to expect from him on the strength of less than one hour's acquaintance.

'Um.' Alex pulled his eyes from Emma's and turned them to Gideon with what looked like a big effort. After a long moment, he said, 'Of course.'

'Thank you for the dance,' Emma said, and then thought how utterly ridiculous that sounded, given that he was her husband. Legally, anyway.

'I enjoyed it,' Alex said, very simply, and Emma's cheeks warmed as Gideon led her away.

\* \* \*

Gideon was a very good conversationalist, with all sorts of harmless gossip and useful, often funny information to impart. He was a perfectly good dancer into the bargain, and yet Emma found herself a little distracted throughout their quadrille.

At one point, during another dance, she realised that she was looking away from her temporary partner, Sir Robert—the squire, and their host for the evening—in an attempt to see where Alex was.

She snapped her head back and beamed at the squire, and said, 'Oh, *indeed*,' in response to his comment on the beauty of an apple orchard in full bloom.

She did love dancing, and she did enjoy the fourth and fifth dances, with the squire's younger son and the single and very charming Viscount Bagley respectively, but it was as though they were just rehearsals for the sixth dance, which—almost scandalously, really, given that they were a married couple—she'd agreed would be with Alex.

And when he made his way to her side the second the dance finished, she felt her whole body lightening and a big beam beginning on her face. Alex was smiling too, seemingly oblivious to the people around them. If she hadn't known better, she'd have thought he was genuinely very pleased to see her. He was clearly a very good actor.

Someone was clearing his throat next to Emma and she gave a start, then realised to her horror that it was her last partner, Viscount Bagley. This was awful. She was behaving like an infatuated debutante, ignoring everyone around her other than the subject of her dreams. What was *wrong* with her this evening? It had to be the shock of their very sudden marriage catching up with her.

The one saving grace was that the viscount was so charming, good-looking and reputedly rich that he must be fawned over by the majority of his dance partners, and his feelings would surely be robust enough to cope with Emma's distraction.

'Thank you,' she said to the viscount, who was now bowing deeply over her hand.

'I very much enjoyed our dance,' he said, still holding on to her hand.

Alex cleared *his* throat, and Emma and the viscount both looked up. Alex's face held a remarkably forbidding expression all of a sudden, and the viscount dropped Emma's hand very quickly. Then, quite ridiculously, Alex immediately took it.

Emma really wanted to tell him that he was over-acting, looking not so much like a fondly loving husband as a jealously obsessive one. If she was honest, though, she was thoroughly enjoying the over-acting. In fact, she was thoroughly enjoying the entire evening.

Still holding her hand, Alex moved with Emma towards the middle of the dance floor to join the next quadrille set.

'Your husband is clearly besotted,' their hostess trilled, dragging Gideon past them. 'I can't remember the last time he danced. Probably not since the last time he danced with Diana.'

She bestowed a huge smile upon the two of them and Emma decided that she had very large teeth and she didn't like her. Really, who would bring up someone's late wife at a moment like this?

'Ignore her,' said Gideon to Emma, just before the

squire's wife dragged him off. 'She had high aspirations for her sister to marry Alex. It's jealousy.'

It might be jealousy, but it wasn't particularly nice to know that, in addition to everything else he'd been forced to do on her behalf, Alex was now being forced to dance when he clearly didn't want to.

She looked up at him and said in a low voice, 'Please don't feel that you have to dance with me.'

'I enjoyed our first dance and I'm looking forward to this one.'

'Really?'

'Really.' He spoke into her ear, so that only Emma could hear him. 'Lady Felicity said that entirely to make you feel uncomfortable. It seems a lot of people are a little jealous of a new duchess. I've been enjoying dancing with you. But even if I didn't, it wouldn't hurt me, would it? So, you shouldn't feel guilty. And I did enjoy it. And apparently I'm talking in circles.'

He smiled at her, and she laughed and said, 'Thank you. And it is true. Dancing twice in an evening is not the biggest hardship for even the most hardened of anti-dancers.'

Certainly it was nothing in comparison to getting married when you didn't want to.

A couple of seconds later, she was whisked into the start of a very energetic country dance. And, *oh*, the gorgeous anticipation of knowing, as she was twirled around by a succession of partners, that she would end up holding Alex's hand again. They smiled, they laughed, they danced in perfect time together, and for the duration of the dance it was bliss.

'I really did enjoy that.' Alex was still laughing slightly, as they all had been, at the antics of a couple of the other men, which had annoyed Lady Felicity considerably, going by her pursed lips and wagging finger.

'A final quadrille set,' announced Lady Felicity, 'and then we go next door for supper. I've planned the night along London lines, Your Grace—' she nodded at Emma '—so that you will feel at home.'

'Thank you so much,' said Emma.

'I'll be back to escort you.' Alex smiled at her as she accepted the arm of her next partner, a very pleasant-seeming man named Mr Scott, and moved away from her to join the squire and another man in the corner of the room.

Emma spent the entirety of the next dance wondering whether Alex would stay with her throughout supper and feeling annoyed that she couldn't stop thinking about him.

When the dance ended, Alex was nowhere to be seen.

'Allow me to escort you?' Mr Scott asked.

'I...' Emma couldn't believe how disappointed she felt. She should really stop this. She and Alex had a non-romantic arrangement and this evening he was doing her a huge favour and she should remember that. 'Thank you.'

'Emma. Scott.' Suddenly, Alex was bowing in front of them, and equally suddenly Emma felt as though the evening had brightened. This truly was ridiculous. She almost wanted *not* to go with Alex, just because she shouldn't be feeling like this. Also, though, she really wanted to go with him.

He held his arm out to her and she took it, and within a short space of time they were seated at a small table in the room next door with two other couples.

'I'm going to perform the introductions again,' Alex

said. 'You met so many people earlier that I'm sure you won't have retained all their names.'

'I'm Letitia,' said the lady nearest to Emma. 'I'm Gideon's sister.'

Emma could see the resemblance—the same hair colour and the same ready smile—and liked her as much and as quickly as she'd taken a liking to Gideon.

'And I'm Maria.' The other lady leaned round her husband and grinned at Emma.

'Or Lady Merrick. As you can see, she's a complete hoyden,' Letitia said, smiling at her friend. 'Well, we both are, but it's all right because we're both respectably married. Like you. So, tell me, have you fallen foul of Lady Felicity yet? She was *desperate* to get her sister married off to the duke, which was never going to happen, because she's one of the rudest people anyone's ever met, and Alex is *not* rude, although he does live up to his Ice Duke name when he's annoyed.'

'I'm not rude? Did I hear you say that?' Alex was grinning at all three of them, looking about as far from icy as the sun.

Supper time flew by, and by the end of it Emma genuinely felt as though she had new friends in Letitia and Maria. Which, of course, she realised, had been Alex's design in escorting her into supper and ensuring that they sat in that group. Again, she couldn't fault his kindness.

'Don't dance every dance if you haven't already committed to doing so,' Letitia said to her as Lady Felicity urged them to return to the other room to continue with the dancing. 'Sit at the side with us and have a good gossip. It's one of the advantages of being sensible married women.'

'Sensible!' scoffed her husband, smiling at her good-naturedly.

Never mind the music, Emma wanted to dance at the thought that she had these lovely new friends.

Letitia and Maria were as good as their word in terms of gossiping by the side of the dance floor, and within fifteen minutes Emma had heard excellent stories about almost everyone in the room.

She was enjoying herself so much that when Alex approached her to ask her to dance Lady Felicity's much-trumpeted *danse espagnole* with him, she was almost annoyed. Not entirely, though: the idea of a third dance with Alex was extremely enticing.

'Three dances in one evening?' Lady Felicity remarked very loudly as they passed her. 'I declare you have your husband quite under your thumb, Your Grace.'

'Not at all.' Alex had a touch of the Ice Duke in his tone all of a sudden. 'My wife was enjoying a comfortable cose with her friends, but I begged her to dance with me again.'

'That was satisfyingly fierce of you,' Emma said as they took their places.

'She was very rude.'

'True. Thank you for introducing me to your friends. They're lovely.'

'I thought you'd like them.' He produced an exaggerated look of smugness, which made Emma laugh. And they laughed together through most of the dance, which Emma thoroughly enjoyed.

'I did not realise that it was now acceptable for married couples to dance thrice together in one evening,' the vicar's wife, Mrs Hardy, said very loudly to her husband, just as the dance finished.

Apparently complaints about marital triple dancing were the order of the evening.

'Ignore her,' Letitia said, materialising at Emma's elbow as Alex moved away. 'She had designs on Alex herself a few years ago, and is still put out that he did not succumb to her lures.'

Goodness. No wonder he'd felt hounded by matchmakers.

'And as for a married couple not dancing three times together when we all know what they do in the privacy of their own bedchamber...'

'Letitia!' Emma was trying to laugh, but all of a sudden she felt completely deflated. How would this relationship of hers and Alex's develop? Would they be pretending like this for ever? When she was forty and childless, and had never had intimate relations with a man, would she still be pretending? Suddenly, she just wanted to leave, go home—if the castle could be called her home—and go to bed. Clearly alone.

As if by magic—or maybe just through excellent observation or a coincidental sudden desire to go home himself—Alex reappeared in front of her.

'Are you ready to leave, Emma?'

'Yes, indeed. I find myself very tired this evening. I think perhaps all the country air has exhausted me.'

'That or the fact that it's three o'clock in the morning,' Alex said.

They said their goodnights and thank-yous, and then Alex led the way out to their carriage, holding Emma's arm in what felt like an extremely *polite* way. Especially when she could make out Letitia and her husband getting into their own carriage ahead of them, definitely being a lot more tactile in a much less polite but much more romantic and lovely way that demonstrated an easy and close affection.

Emma swallowed a sigh and sat down on the forward-facing seat of the carriage, slightly to one side in case Alex might be tempted to sit next to her. He sat down opposite her, right in the middle of the seat. Of course.

'Did you enjoy the evening?' he asked as they set off.

'Yes, thank you, very much.' Most of it, anyway, apart from the references to Diana and the reminder just now that he and Emma would never be more than friends. 'Did you?'

'I did, thank you. Despite the scandal I have caused by dancing with you three times.' He smiled at Emma. 'You seemed to get on very well with Letitia and Maria.'

'Yes, I did. I plan to call on them this week.'

'Very good.'

Clearly, he'd been feeling guilty about leaving her to her own devices during the day, and had hoped to provide her with some friends by introducing her to their neighbours, which was very kind of him.

A few minutes later, they were still chatting about the evening and some of the neighbours—Alex had a very good story involving the vicar, a croquet mallet and some cheese, which made Emma almost snort with laughter in a very unladylike fashion—when the carriage drew to a sudden halt.

Emma flew forward from her seat and put her hands out to save herself. They met a solid wall of chest, and she was saved from being flung any further by Alex's hands gripping her arms.

'Ermph,' she said into his chest.

'Are you all right?'

Was she? Yes, except she felt slightly as though she'd lost her wits. All she could think of was the muscly hardness of his chest and the way she was pressed up against him, almost sitting on his lap.

'Yes, thank you,' she managed to say.

'Good.'

Alex let go of her arms and put his hands on her waist and moved her very gently to the side while Emma fought with herself not to give in to the temptation of sinking right into him as he held her for this moment in time.

'I should check that all is well,' he said after a second.

'Of course!' Emma moved away fast. He'd clearly been experiencing *no* temptation, and just as clearly was *not* still thinking about where their bodies had just touched and feeling almost singed by the contact.

The coachman appeared at the door of the carriage just as Alex opened it. 'A deer in the road, Your Grace.'

'Did you hit it?'

'No, Your Grace, we stopped in time.'

'Excellent. Thank you.'

Emma moved back to her side of the carriage as the door closed and then they sat in silence for a few seconds until, slightly desperate to break the tension that seemed to have sprung up between them, she said, 'Do you have many deer on your land?'

And they passed the rest of the journey determinedly talking about livestock.

When the chaise drew up at the castle's main entrance, Alex descended first and then helped Emma down. He thanked the coachman and then led Emma towards the front door, still with her hand tucked through his arm.

'The stars are amazing.' Emma pointed upwards with her free hand. 'That was something I missed in London. Every night in the countryside I think how magical they are. Look. Argo Navis is so clear tonight.'

'I'm impressed. I don't think I could have named that one.'

'I've always loved the constellations. Which is a good thing, given that I'm educating your boys.'

'Very true.' Alex nodded, and then smiled at her. They'd reached the steps up to the wide front doors. 'I hope Lancing has gone to bed,' he said in a low voice. 'I always tell him and Graham not to wait up for me on occasions like this, but I appear to have little authority in my own home, because they often completely ignore me.'

Emma laughed. If there was one person who, apparently effortlessly, seemed to have a lot of authority, it was Alex. And not just because he was a duke, but because he was *him*.

Her arm was still in his as they went into the empty hall together.

'I see Lancing has abided by your wishes,' Emma whispered.

'Indeed. He's left a candle for us here, look.'

One candle. For them to share. Emma suddenly felt very tired. This pretence was…hard. Although clearly she shouldn't complain, even inside her head, because if Alex hadn't married her who knew what she might be doing now? Almost certainly something worse than pretending to be sharing a bedchamber with a very attractive man.

Alex picked the candle up, and Emma realised that she was still holding his arm.

'Are you ready to go upstairs?' he asked, and she nodded, not sure whether or not to pull her hand away.

In the end she didn't, and they began to move towards the staircase together.

The darkness licking around them, the shapes of furniture and paintings distorted by the candle's flickering light... All of it would have felt eerily intimidating without Alex's solid presence beside her. Emma found herself wanting to continue to hold his arm, just to reassure herself that he was there apart from anything else. She'd always hated the darkness. And, yes, of course it was just *nice* being arm in arm with him.

'We should probably enter our sitting room together, rather than going into our bedchambers separately from the corridor.' Alex's whisper brushed her ear, and she shivered. 'Walls have ears. Well, eyes.'

'You're right,' she whispered back, hoping that her voice wouldn't vibrate as much as her body seemed to be doing.

They carried on up the stairs in silence, arm in arm, Emma almost breathless from her awareness of Alex next to her.

When they finally reached the top of the stairs, rounded the ornate newel post at the top of the banisters, walked along the corridor and arrived in front of their sitting room door, it was almost a relief to be able to let go of him.

Emma removed her arm from Alex's and took the candle from him so that he could open the door quietly, to avoid waking the rest of the household, and in they went.

'So neither Jenny nor Graham waited up for us,' Alex said, once he'd closed the door.

'No.' Emma cleared her throat to get rid of the croak that had come from nowhere. 'No.'

She and Jenny had fallen into a routine where Jenny helped her get ready for bed—usually into a frothy confection of a nightgown with which Jenny presumably imagined Emma would impress Alex—and then left Emma for the night. Emma was sick and tired of all the night-time pretence, and thoroughly relieved that Jenny wouldn't be there tonight.

'So.' Alex cleared his own throat. 'Goodnight, then.'

'Goodnight.'

Neither of them moved.

Then Alex said, 'I should, that is to say, would you like me to light your candle with this one? Or perhaps you'd like to light it yourself?'

'Of course. Thank you.' Emma took the candle from him. Their fingers brushed as she did so and she nearly dropped it.

'Can you manage?'

'Yes! I don't know what happened there. Very clumsy of me. I'll bring it back directly, so that you may use it in your own chamber.'

It took her three attempts and a further near-drop of the candle before she had her own properly lit. Alex was having the most extraordinary effect on her this evening.

'Done,' she said as she returned to the sitting room.

Alex was at the window, looking out into the moonlit garden.

'It's beautiful in the moonlight, isn't it?' she said.

'It's beautiful at any time. Although I don't really feel

as though it's my land, rather that I am a custodian of it for future generations, and I feel very fortunate.' He turned and walked towards her to take the candle. 'We really should bid each other goodnight now that you have your candle lit; it's very late. Almost time for an early breakfast, in fact.'

'Yes.'

Again, neither of them moved.

Alex looked dark, brooding, very serious in the candlelight.

'You...' Emma began, and then stopped, not sure what she had been trying to say. 'Thank you for this evening. I very much appreciate your kindness in introducing me to your friends and in demonstrating to everyone that we—'

'You have nothing to thank me for.' His voice was rough.

'No.' She wasn't really sure what she was saying because all her focus was on his face lit by the candle between them, the shadow of his beard growth, the *size* of him standing there in front of her.

Alex took the candle and placed it on a chest to one side. 'We don't want to get burnt.'

'No,' Emma said again.

She might not get burnt by the candle, but she felt as though she was being burnt by *something*. She could feel heat in all sorts of places.

Alex took a step closer to her, and she moved closer too, taking a deep, shuddering breath as they drew together. Memories, images from when they kissed at the inn, were playing in her mind now.

'I enjoyed our dances,' he whispered.

'Me too.' Emma was whispering as well.

Alex was so close now she could barely breathe from anticipation.

He lifted one hand and very gently traced a finger down her cheek. 'You look beautiful in that dress.'

Emma couldn't speak. All she could do was smile and tilt her head up towards his. He was going to kiss her again, and it was going to be the perfect end to a wonderful evening.

# *Chapter Eleven*

Alex allowed his fingers to wander down the smooth skin of Emma's cheek and to trace the shape of her lips. So soft, so beautiful. The tip of her tongue peeped out and she moistened her lips, and he felt a shudder throughout his entire body. He found himself moistening his own lips in response, and leaning his head nearer to hers.

Their mouths were less than an inch apart now, and they were edging ever closer to each other, heads tilted one way and then the other, mirroring each other like two pieces of a puzzle that were about to fall into place.

He could feel the anticipation building inside him. He knew from their first two kisses how Emma's lips tasted, how well she fitted against him, and he was desperate for more.

Their lips were so close now that he could feel her breath against his mouth. She murmured something unintelligible and suddenly he pulled her against him into a hard kiss. She gave a deep shudder and returned the kiss, threading one arm around his neck, pressing her other hand tight against his chest.

Holding her against him with one arm and continuing

their kiss, ever deeper, he ran one hand from her hip to her waist, and then up to the swell of her breast, feeling her shiver as he touched her. He nipped her lower lip with his teeth and then allowed his thumb to skim her hardened nipple through the fabric of her dress and felt her shudder again against him.

Damn, he wanted her. He wanted to taste all of her, feel her softness against his hardness, explore her body, work out what made her come alive, make her shudder and shiver again, be entwined with her, enter her, be as one with her.

As one with her.

Like man and wife.

Like he had been with Diana.

He stilled. He couldn't do it.

It wasn't even the thought of betraying Diana, because it wasn't a betrayal, was it? She was gone and she'd have wanted him to be happy.

He dropped both his hands and lifted his head.

He knew what it was. It was the fact that he *did* want to be happy. And the thought of allowing himself to care that much again for a woman, even a fraction of that amount, was too frightening. If he allowed himself to love Emma and anything happened to her, he'd be plunged into the depths of despair again, and he didn't want that, couldn't cope with it. He just wanted contentment, a happy, serene life without the possibility of any further grief.

He definitely wasn't doing this.

He took a step backwards and said, 'It's late. We should probably go to bed.'

Emma was just standing there, unmoving, staring at him with a dazed look on her face, as though she couldn't understand what was happening.

He shook his head. 'I...' He should apologise, somehow. 'I'm not... I can't...' He drew a breath and then said, 'I'm sorry. This isn't right for me.'

It was as though his words snapped Emma out of the near-trance she'd been in. 'Of course. Goodnight. Thank you for a lovely evening.'

And then she gathered her skirts and whisked herself through the door into her bedchamber.

Alex stared for a couple of seconds at the closed door before turning to go into his own chamber.

He'd absolutely done the right thing. It was right for both of them. So he should be feeling pleased, positive.

He didn't feel happy at all.

He was sure he would tomorrow, though.

Alex awoke later that morning not feeling remotely refreshed. Despite the late hour, he'd been unable to sleep, and had tossed and turned for what had felt like most of the remainder of the night, replaying the evening in his mind. He'd danced with Emma in order to demonstrate to his friends and neighbours that she was very much his wife, whatever rumours they might have heard to the contrary, for the same reason that he'd kissed her at the inn, and both times it had turned into something unexpected and quite unwelcome.

There was an obvious solution: avoid her as far as was polite when there were no onlookers to be impressed, and avoid actual physical contact when there *were* onlookers. In due course he'd have his physical impulses under control—he hoped really quite soon—and then Emma would be an accepted presence in his life, and they could continue as friends living under the same roof.

So he hauled himself out of bed and down for a quick

breakfast and out for the day before a polite dinner with Emma in the evening.

It worked. It definitely worked.

After their polite and pleasant dinner, they retired upstairs together, entering their bedchambers via their shared sitting room, as was now becoming their custom, and Alex found the strength of mind to go straight into his bedchamber without allowing himself to linger, or dwell on just how much he'd like to...

No, he shouldn't even allow himself to think that behind closed doors. That way lay insanity. It was fortunate that he was so tired after only a couple of hours' sleep last night that he actually nodded off quite quickly, thinking about how he and Emma had joked together over dinner, and her infectious laugh. But it was perfectly normal to go to sleep thinking about your evening...

The next afternoon, having received an invitation from Gideon's sister Letitia, Alex decided to visit the nursery, firstly to spend a little extra time with the boys, and secondly to ask Emma if she'd like to attend an impromptu dinner at Letitia's house the next evening.

Emma was in full flow when he let himself into the room, and the boys were rapt, which was the first time he'd ever seen them like that with a governess.

They were so rapt that they didn't appear even to notice his arrival.

Emma was doing an excellent imitation of a tiger, insofar as it was immediately recognisable, if not accurate, complete with a description of where tigers liked to roam, hunt and sleep.

'Do tigers eat people?' asked John.

'Not very often,' Emma said.

'Do they eat fish?' Harry asked.

Emma's answer morphed into a discussion about the apparently very many rivers in India.

'Papa!' Harry suddenly interrupted Emma, having finally noticed his father.

'Shh.' Alex put his finger to his lips. 'Emma's talking.'

'What's the longest river in India?' Freddie asked, the most animated Alex had seen him about anything other than the stables and horseplay for a long time.

'Have you heard of any of the rivers?' Emma asked. 'What do you think it is?'

'Something beginning with G?' Freddie said.

'That's right,' said Alex.

Simultaneously, Emma said, 'That's what a lot of people think, but in fact it isn't.'

Alex raised an eyebrow and Emma smiled at him and said, 'I believe that the Ganges is the third longest river in India and the longest is the Indus.'

He smiled back at her, impressed.

'Your knowledge of geography is certainly better than I could ever have hoped for in my boys'...' His boys' *what*? He couldn't call her a governess in front of them. She was, after all, legally at least, their stepmother. 'In any instructor of my boys. Or indeed anyone I know, frankly.'

'My grandmother was Indian, and during my childhood she told me a lot of stories about her own childhood. I've been fascinated by the country ever since and have read as much as I can on the subject.'

'Did she live in England?' Freddie asked.

'Yes, in Lancashire with my grandfather.'

'How did she come to live here?' Freddie's questions were almost too much, but Alex decided not to reprimand him.

He was still very young, and also Alex was very interested himself in Emma's answers but didn't want to discuss his own affairs, particularly Diana, and so he couldn't reasonably ask Emma too much about her background.

'My grandfather owned a textile business and travelled to India to find new fabrics. He was asked to dinner by my grandmother's father, who wished to sell him silks from his land. He was a maharajah, and my grandmother was a princess. She met my grandfather and they fell in love, and she embarked on the long journey across the Near East by land and then over the Mediterranean Ocean and all the way to the North of England with him.'

'That's a really long journey,' John said.

'It is.' Emma smiled, and something about her—something wistful in her eyes—told Alex that her interest in India was more than academic.

'Do you perhaps wish to travel there yourself one day? If you don't mind my asking?' he said.

Emma hesitated, and then said, 'Yes.'

Alex nodded, surprised by how unsurprised he was. Women rarely undertook such journeys, but the more he learned of her, the more he realised that Emma was a rare woman. A woman who was very different from him.

'Have you travelled?' she asked.

'I was fortunate enough to do a Grand Tour. Europe. I very much enjoyed it and saw some wonderful sights.'

'But?' She had one eyebrow fractionally raised.

'I like my corner of Somerset,' he told her. 'I enjoy being here, doing my best to be an attentive landlord.'

He counted the schools and the hospital he'd built in recent years as far greater achievements than swanning around the continent as the idle, rich young man he'd been at that stage of his life. And of course his sons were here. His *life* was here.

Emma nodded almost imperceptibly. 'I can see that.'

Their eyes met. She looked as though she was weighing up what she saw before her, much as he was. She nodded again, and he did too. He had the feeling that her urge to travel was as great as his to remain at home.

They were indeed very different.

Emma hesitated for a moment, and then said, 'I would very much like to travel extensively.'

He realised that she'd probably been waiting for the right moment to tell him that. Well, he certainly wouldn't stop her. Indeed, perhaps it would be for the best for both of them that she travel, as long as scandal did not attach to anything she did. When she returned home, any residual attraction between them would hopefully have been erased by time spent apart.

And if the thought of Emma travelling simultaneously scared him and made him realise that he would miss her company, all the better that she go.

'That will be your prerogative,' he told her.

She didn't smile, but just said, 'Thank you.'

Alex felt as though he'd taken a test, but he couldn't tell whether he'd passed or failed. He did know that following their conversation he felt a little miserable.

Emma opted to take her dinner in her chambers that evening, citing a headache, and again, Alex wasn't sure why. He also wasn't sure whether or not he was pleased.

The next morning, the routine into which they seemed already to have fallen since the addition of Emma to the household was disturbed, as they all woke up to a beautiful thick blanket of snow covering everything within sight. The boys were desperate to get outside, and the adults in the household were split between those who agreed with them and those who didn't want to get cold and wet.

The small child in Alex adored the snow, but as Parsons, his man of business, kept telling him, he had a huge amount of bookwork to do.

'Perhaps I might have finished by late morning,' he said, wondering if to Parsons' ears he sounded like a child, pleading to be allowed out to play.

'I hope so, Your Grace,' Parsons said, his creased face impassive.

Alex was still toiling away—how was it possible that these numbers totalled a different amount every time he looked at them—when sounds of shrieking and laughter reached him from the sparkling white lawn outside his study window.

Emma had the boys thoroughly muffled up, and he could see from her gestures and the scarf and twigs she was holding that she was encouraging them to build a snowman. The boys were half engaged in rolling an enormous ball for the snowman's body, half engaged in throwing smaller snowballs at each other.

Alex was struggling even more now to make sense of the figures in front of him.

He'd had enough. He'd done a lot of work this morning; he definitely deserved a break.

If he could get the numbers on the page at which he was currently looking to add up, he'd go outside for a few minutes to show the boys how good snowballs were *really* made.

Five minutes later, he'd come to the conclusion that

the numbers were never going to add up, and that it would be madness not to take advantage of the snow, because who knew when winter playtime conditions would be as good as this again?

Approximately sixty seconds after that he was pulling on a greatcoat and loose walking boots, winding a scarf around his neck and striding outside.

It looked as though he was the first person to emerge that day from the side door by which he'd left the castle. As his feet sank into the pristine snow and he breathed clean, frosty air into his lungs, he took in the beauty of the scene surrounding him. If he were the kind of man who painted, he'd love to attempt a landscape of this. It was…

*Thump.*

Something heavy and wet had hit him squarely in the face.

'Eurmph,' he spluttered, tasting snow.

'Ha-ha-ha,' shouted Freddie from the shelter of a group of trees in a copse to Alex's left, and then another snowball hit Alex on the shoulder.

'War,' Alex shouted, bending down to roll a snowball of his own.

He was bombarded by surprisingly accurate shots until he got himself hidden behind a large oak tree and poked his head round it to see Emma directing the boys in making the snowballs while she held one with her arm back, very much primed to throw, and looked around for her target, presumably *him*.

Well.

Alex bent very carefully and quietly and set about rolling the perfect snowball. Times four. They needed to be big, but not so big that they wouldn't fly perfectly through the air, and also wet, to ensure maximum discomfort when they landed one after the other on Emma and the boys.

Work finished, and his ammunition lined up at his feet, he stood up with a small grunt of satisfaction to check where his prey now were. As he straightened, he realised that they'd gone very silent. He couldn't hear anything at all other than a couple of cracks of twigs and...

*Thump, thump, thump, thump.*

When he'd cleared the snow from his face and could see again, he realised that the four of them, in addition to pelting him with one large snowball each, had jumped on his ones and destroyed them. They'd well and truly trounced him.

For the moment.

He smiled at them all lined up in front of him, laughing. 'Very good. You got me there.'

'You shouted, "War," but we won,' crowed John.

'You certainly did,' Alex said.

And then he leapt forward and swept the boys into his arms and ran with them towards the snowman's body, before dumping all three of them into it.

'Outrageous,' said Emma, standing at a safe distance. 'You've ruined our morning's hard work.' She was definitely smirking. 'And now the boys will be soaked to the skin and will need to go inside to get changed and have warm baths.'

'Have you ever heard the word "hypocrite"?' Alex asked, advancing towards her.

'No!' she said, and then picked up her skirts and ran towards the castle, shouting, 'Boys, inside now.'

Two things surprised Alex: firstly, she was fast, and

secondly, the boys actually obeyed her and sprinted inside after her.

She was an impressive woman, he reflected as he climbed the stairs in order to dry himself off.

She wasn't just an impressive woman, he thought a couple of hours later, as he looked out of the window. She was a determined one.

He wouldn't have noticed if he hadn't happened to glance out at that precise moment, but she and the boys were definitely trying to keep out of sight. They had skirted the edge of the castle, carrying what looked like some of *his* clothes, and now seemed to be occupied in rolling another big snowball. A couple more inches of snow had fallen since they'd gone out this morning, so the conditions were ideal for snowman-building again, and they were clearly planning to build a large one and dress him in Alex's clothes.

Maybe he'd wait until they'd finished and then go outside and land just one perfectly formed snowball on Emma. And then admire the snowman. And then come back inside and finish looking through these blasted books.

Twenty minutes later, he'd achieved strictly nothing further and was feeling as though he was missing out on a lot of fun with the children. He should go outside and find them. And, good Lord, how could he not have had the idea sooner? They had sledges somewhere; he should ask someone to get them out.

He asked Lancing about the sledges, shrugged himself back into his coat and boots, and went outside, following the sounds of laughter and good-natured shouting to a sheltered area.

'My word,' he said, coming to a stop in front of the snowman to which they were putting the finishing touches of what looked like one of his favourite hats, his best gloves and a scarf to which he was—had been—quite partial. They'd already finished its quite hideous-looking face. 'It looks...'

'Surprisingly lifelike?' Emma supplied. 'Like an uncannily good likeness of you, perhaps?'

'Yes, that's right.' He nodded. 'It was on the tip of my tongue to say that looking at it is like looking in a mirror.'

'Why don't you stand next to it so that we can admire our handiwork?' Emma suggested.

'Yes, Papa,' the boys clamoured.

And so he stood next to the gargoyle-like snowman, while the boys told him that it looked *exactly* like him, and Emma congratulated them on how clever they were and laughed at Alex.

He couldn't remember a time when he'd enjoyed himself so much in such a simple way.

He was going to get his revenge on Emma, though.

His opportunity came later, when they'd finished their sledging as dusk fell. The boys' nurse came to take them inside for their second warm bath of the day, leaving Alex and Emma to make their way inside after them.

'The boys have had so much fun today,' Emma said.

'I must thank you,' Alex said. 'I'm not sure how you've done it, but you've worked wonders with them. They actually seem to obey you, and they are learning from you *and* enjoying themselves.'

Emma shook her head. 'You have nothing to thank me for. Without your generosity I could very well be in dire straits now. And the boys are truly lovely. It's a pleasure spending time with them, and I love seeing them happy and enjoying themselves. And who wouldn't enjoy the feeling of victory that for the time being they seem to have called a truce on the introduction of small creatures to my chamber? In fact, I should thank *you* for the opportunity to feel victorious.'

'Very true. Perhaps we should make a mutual agreement to stop thanking each other?' Alex said.

Emma laughed. 'Perhaps.'

'I do have one last little thank-you for you, though.' Moving as fast as he could, for the element of surprise, Alex scooped a large handful of snow from the top of a wall and planted it down the back of Emma's neck.

'You *wretch*!' she shrieked. 'That's so *cold*!'

'I learned all about cold snow earlier today,' Alex said, standing a few feet away from her, ready to dart out of snowballing distance should she decide to retaliate.

She looked at him for a long moment and then smiled. 'I think we're even now.'

She held out her hand and he took it, smiling a gracious smile that said, *I think we all know that I beat you*.

She took his hand in a tighter grip than he'd been expecting, though, and suddenly pulled him very hard. She took a swift sidestep at the same time, and then let go so that he fell into a snowdrift against the wall.

'You look *hilarious*,' she said as he sat up, very much covered in snow.

Alex nodded and smiled, and then very suddenly lunged forward and pulled her down into the snowdrift too, and gave her a little roll for good measure.

'Oh, my goodness,' she gasped. 'Stop! It's so cold.'

'I'm not sure that you should mete out punishments

that you wouldn't be prepared to accept yourself for the same crime,' Alex said with a very serious air.

Emma laughed, and he did too.

And then she stopped laughing. And so did Alex.

Because it suddenly felt as though something had changed; the air between them was practically crackling with tension.

They were lying on their sides next to each other in the soft snow, their faces and bodies only inches apart. Alex still had his upper arm around Emma's waist from when he'd rolled her in the snow.

For fun. It had been for fun.

It didn't feel like fun now. It felt like... It felt like temptation.

It was snowing again, very lightly. He could see snowflakes on Emma's beautiful long, dark eyelashes. Her brown eyes looked deep and mysterious in the twilight, and her lips were slightly parted. He could see the rise and fall of her chest, her full breasts straining against the fabric of her pelisse.

He didn't have the strength to resist the temptation this time.

Very slowly and carefully, he raised himself on his elbow, and then bent his head towards hers.

They didn't sink into a deep kiss immediately. Alex brushed Emma's lips with his own with the lightest of touches, and then drew back slightly. She looked at him for a long moment, a small smile on her lips, before reaching up to him. And then they were almost dancing around the edges of the kiss, nipping at each other's lips, moving away and then back again, like opposing magnets irresistibly drawn together.

Suddenly, it was as though something just snapped

and it happened. His mouth was on hers, or maybe hers was on his, even though he was above her. Their tongues met and he felt his entire body respond to the sensation, as though he'd been waiting just for this for a very long time. He ran his hand down her side, in and out of the dip of her waist, and felt her tremble as he touched her.

'Are you all right?' he whispered.

'Yes,' she said on a sigh.

Alex moved his hand to cup her beautiful face, which he was beginning to know so well, and then slid his hand round to her neck, tugging at her hair, drawing her even closer to him.

As he held her close with one arm, he moved his other hand to cup her breast, and even through several layers of clothing he felt her respond. She arched her back so that she was pressed against him, and pushed her hands into his hair.

This felt like the natural culmination of everything that had come before, the physical temptation, the time they'd spent getting to know each other, talking, laughing together. Now his entire being, from his soul to his body, wanted to get to know more of Emma.

He was dimly aware that this was not wise, but with Emma in his arms like this, he was unable to do anything other than focus on the here and now. And, damn, she was tempting.

He kissed down her neck and undid the hook and top buttons of her pelisse with almost shaking hands, so that he could kiss and lick the hollow at the base of her neck. He undid more buttons and licked and kissed all the way down to the neckline of her dress. When he slid one hand inside and pulled the dress lower, bending his head further to take her nipple in his mouth, she moaned and arched even more. *Damn*, he wanted her, wanted her more than he could have thought possible.

He very vaguely knew that this wasn't the best idea, but he couldn't remember why. All he could think about was the taste of Emma, her seductive scent, the curve of her lips, the way her breast fitted perfectly in his hand, the smoothness of her skin, the eagerness of her kisses, the way his own body was responding to her and the promise of more.

# Chapter Twelve

It was as though every nerve-ending in Emma's body was on fire. Her stomach was dipping, warmth pooling low inside her, as Alex worked magic with his mouth and his fingers on her breasts. Her hands were clutching at his hair and his upper arms—feeling the strength of his muscles there—almost scratching him with her nails in her desire to keep him there next to her.

He continued caressing, licking, sucking, and then he kissed his way back up her chest and neck and took her mouth again, his hands continuing to tease her breasts. When he moved his fingers a little away and traced around them, all she wanted was for him to move them back to her nipples. And when they were there, she could hardly bear the pleasure, and yet she knew that she wanted more, for him to touch her more, in other places.

It was mind-blowing, intoxicating. She couldn't breathe, she couldn't think, all she could do was kiss him back, mould her body to his, loving the weight of him on her and the feel of him pressing against her.

She pulled at his neckcloth and his shirt, wanting to touch his skin as he was touching hers. Wresting his shirt from his breeches, she ran her hands up his muscled torso, shivering as she did so. The hardness and latent strength in his body exactly matched his personality: he was the very embodiment of masculinity.

He pulled slightly away, smiling down at her, and his deep green eyes locked on hers for a long moment before they moved to look at her lips, and then her exposed breasts. The admiration in his eyes was so potent it was making her shiver.

He leaned down again to take her nipple in his mouth again, and then he reached beneath her dress.

'Is this all right?' he asked as he stroked her inner thigh, high up, towards the place where she felt the heaviness between her legs.

'Mmm.' She couldn't speak. All she could focus on were the sensations he was producing and where she was exploring him in her turn with her hands and lips.

And then he began to touch and caress her most intimate parts, and as sensation built she gave a deep, juddering sigh. She knew that she was moist there, and it was as though the rest of her entire body had turned to liquid too. She reached for the front opening in his breeches, fumbling, and he eased himself away to enable her to touch him better, producing a deep, 'Yes,' as she found him.

And then something large and wet landed on her face and she nearly choked.

What was that?

'Snow,' Alex said. 'The tree.'

He brushed snow away from her breasts, the touch of his fingers as they skimmed her skin making her jump.

'The branch couldn't bear the weight.' He smiled at her and leaned down towards her again, and then another large pile of snow fell on them.

He sighed and drew back. 'Maybe we should move.'
Emma nodded, hugely disappointed.
Alex sat up, and pulled her up too.

Immediately, the moment in which they'd been was entirely broken. They were now sitting next to each other in damp clothes, chests exposed, Emma's dress lifted, Alex's breeches open. And now she thought about it she was freezing cold.

Beyond their legal marriage, they weren't truly man and wife, nor in any way romantically involved with each other, so they couldn't just move to somewhere more sheltered in the garden or to a bedchamber, and continue what they'd been doing, because...

Well, they just couldn't. Because clearly neither of them had intended this to happen, and without the impetus of hot-blooded desire, or temptation, or whatever it had been, they obviously weren't going to resume.

They certainly weren't going to, anyway, if Alex didn't suggest it, because Emma was not going to lay herself open to the possibility of his refusing her.

Without looking at him she pulled her dress up and down, so that she was covered, and then drew her pelisse around herself. When she was more properly attired, she glanced at Alex and saw that he'd been busy tucking his shirt in.

The misery and disappointment that struck her in that moment showed her that she'd been hoping that he might somehow find the words—*want* to find the words—to suggest they go somewhere else together, maybe one of their bedchambers, and continue this...whatever it had been.

But of course he'd never been going to do that, and

in the interests of dignity, she certainly wasn't going to demonstrate to him that she was disappointed.

Using the tree trunk as leverage, she began to haul herself to her feet, and immediately slipped on the ground beneath. The snow there had been compressed to near-ice by the weight of their bodies a few minutes ago.

Alex shot an arm out to prevent her falling flat on her face, and had her standing solidly on her own two feet on some fresh snow within seconds, all without making any kind of eye contact.

As soon as it was clear that she wasn't going to fall over again, he let go of her as though she was scalding hot, and said, 'It's getting dark and you should get into some warmer clothes before you catch a cold.'

'You should change too,' Emma told him.

Alex nodded and they set off together in the direction of the house. They walked in complete silence, not a comfortable one, both of them looking straight ahead, and then Emma went directly upstairs while Alex made what she was sure was an excuse about needing to speak to Lancing before he changed.

Jenny was waiting for her when she got to her bedchamber. 'Oh, miss,' she said, 'you're soaked to the skin. You'll catch a chill.'

Emma felt heavy tears behind her eyelids and a very strong desire to be alone for a few minutes.

'Thank you, Jenny. I'm sure I'll be fine. I'm very healthy. And I think I'll dry myself. Thank you so much.' She took the towels from Jenny, who was frowning.

'But, miss, sorry, Your Grace, you're very, very wet.'

'And very, very capable of drying myself,' Emma said, immediately feeling guilty for her impatience. 'I'm sorry, Jenny, I'm just tired. I am so grateful for all that you do for me, but on this occasion I really can dry myself and dress myself for dinner and I will do so. Thank you.'

Jenny left the room, still protesting slightly, half under her breath. Once she'd gone, Emma sank down onto a wooden chair and put her head in her hands. She needed to be very careful. She wasn't completely sure what she was feeling now, but she did know that she had very much enjoyed Alex's company, and the way he'd made her feel just now...

Well, there were no words to describe it. It had been amazing, wonderful, glorious, and she'd wanted so much to continue, to discover how good it might have been if they'd done what she knew people did. Perhaps this was the beginning of love? Yes, she was probably falling in love with her husband. Who had made it very clear that he didn't want to love her, or perhaps just couldn't. He was almost certainly still grieving for his wife, the mother of his children, still in love with her memory.

And they wanted very different things—for example she wanted to travel and he wanted to spend his entire life here in Somerset—and she'd seen first-hand how unhappy her parents' marriage had been, despite their love for each other, because they'd been from different backgrounds and had had different wishes and needs. Indeed, it was almost as though their love had driven them apart, because they'd had such different goals that their relationship, with strong love on one side and different ambitions on the other, had become so unbalanced. She'd seen how their love had turned to near-hatred and it had been awful.

This wasn't good. Sitting alone with her depressing thoughts wasn't going to help her situation in the slightest. And she was unpleasantly damp and cold.

Shivering, she peeled her wet clothes off with difficulty, and then picked up a towel and began to rub herself dry very vigorously.

She didn't know what she ought to do next in regard to Alex, but she did know that she needed to be very conscious of her emotions and keep them under tight control.

Fortunately, it seemed that Alex felt exactly the same way and was going to take things a step further and avoid her, who knew for how long?

He made his excuses about dinner—apparently he had *huge* amounts of work to get through this evening, even though surely a duke had all manner of people to whom he might delegate—and didn't appear at all the next day, even when she sledged with the children and made another snowman with them, and allowed them to scream and shout as much as they liked, just to see if it would inspire him to come outside.

Alex had a note sent to her just as she took the children inside as dusk fell, which definitely indicated that he'd known exactly when they'd finished playing outside.

In it he 'suggested'—his word, which, despite everything she was feeling did make Emma smile, because he'd definitely noticed and responded to the fact that she did not enjoy being told what to do—that they leave at half past six for their evening with Letitia. Apparently, he'd received word that they were continuing with the dinner, as there had been no further snow during the day and the roads were all passable.

'Goodnight,' she bade the children, wondering whether she should tell Alex that she was too tired to go to the dinner this evening.

She'd woken this morning with a headache, due to her lack of sleep during a night the majority of which she'd spent turning over and over in her mind the events of the previous afternoon. Her hours outside in the cold air with the children today had cleared her head, but her headache was returning now, and the last thing she wanted was to spend an evening in Alex's company, knowing what they'd been doing yesterday, but having to behave like relative strangers.

But of course she should go. She'd very much liked Letitia when she met her at the squire's dance, and she had a life to make for herself here in Somerset. If she wasn't going to have Alex's company—which, of course, he had never promised her, so she couldn't complain— she'd be much happier if she had local friends.

She checked the clock above the boys' heads. She would need to hurry to be ready on time.

She was not ready on time.

After spending far too long choosing which dress to wear, and then having Jenny do her hair in three different hairstyles—when you'd been as intimate with a man as you'd ever been, and then he'd spent the next day doing his best to avoid you, for the sake of pride you had to look as good as you could when you next saw him— she hurried downstairs at a quarter to seven.

Alex came out of the library just as she reached the bottom of the stairs, clearly having been listening out for her.

'Good evening,' he said. 'You look lovely.'

'Thank you,' Emma said, suddenly breathless.

Just *seeing* his mouth, which looked so stern and thin in repose, but which when he smiled suddenly seemed so generous, was having a really quite unnerving effect on her. She couldn't help remembering what he'd done with it yesterday.

'Shall we go?'

'Go?' What was he talking about?

'Go outside to the chaise?'

Of course. She was losing her wits.

'Yes, wonderful,' she said.

No, not wonderful. It wasn't wonderful to go out to the carriage. It was just, well, nothing, really.

'Excellent.'

He held his arm out to her and she stared at it for a moment before recollecting where she was and what they were doing and taking it, very gingerly, because right now she felt as though touching him at all might make her feel far too much, and she really didn't want to get flustered again just before dinner. Or at all, in fact, if it wasn't going to lead to anything positive.

They walked out to the chaise, neither of them speaking, and then sat down on opposite benches. The carriage began to move, and still neither of them said anything. Emma concentrated on her gloves, and then on the blackness outside the window.

'I hear from the boys that you made another snowman and that they very much enjoyed more sledging today,' Alex said after some time.

'Yes, it was great fun,' Emma said. 'The boys are lovely. They're a credit to you.'

Alex smiled and inclined his head, and then he looked down at his knees, and then at the wall of the chaise to the right of Emma and above her head. And then in the direction of the window.

Emma, her throat holding a large lump all of a sudden, cast around for something unexceptionable to talk about that might lessen the distance between them.

No, she couldn't think of anything that wouldn't sound like an utterly pathetic and desperate attempt to create conversation out of nothing.

So there was no further conversation between them for the remainder of the journey, which in reality was perhaps half an hour but felt far longer than that.

It was a great relief when they finally arrived and could descend from the chaise.

'I'm so glad that you were able to come.' Letitia had dispensed with formality and was hugging Alex and Emma in turn. 'I hate it when we have snow and the roads are closed and we can't see anyone for ages.'

'And have to suffer only our own company and that of our neighbours to whose houses we can walk in under ten minutes, even in the deepest of snow. It's a hard life.' Arthur accompanied his words with a fond smile at his wife. Emma tried very hard not to think about the fact that Alex was never going to look at *her* like that, in either public or private.

'Honestly.' Letitia pouted at her husband, and he laughed out loud and put his arm around her waist. 'We should go inside before the newlyweds catch their deaths of cold.' She put her free arm through Emma's and said, 'I trust your husband kept you warm in the carriage?'

'Oh, yes,' murmured Emma.

Pretending really wasn't very enjoyable. If you liked the person to whom you were pretending, you felt very guilty. She almost wanted to confide in Letitia this minute the truth of her reality, so that they could begin the friendship she hoped they were going to have with honesty and openness.

'Your house looks so beautiful in the snow. Almost ethereal.'

'Your very abrupt subject-change tells me that your husband kept you *so* warm you really don't want to discuss it in polite company,' Letitia said, laughing. 'Don't worry, I'm not going to torment you any longer. Come and warm yourselves in front of the fire.'

They found four other couples in the drawing room, and were soon absorbed into the group, chatting about inconsequential matters of yet great weight, such as the ribbons newly stocked by the haberdasher in Yarford, the nearest town.

'When the snow has gone we must take a trip there together,' Letitia told Emma.

'I should very much like that.'

It was wonderful that it seemed that Letitia was as desirous as she of forming a mutual friendship. Emma did not need the companionship of Alex who, forbiddingly handsome, was currently standing talking to the other men, having positioned himself about as far from Emma as was physically possible without actually leaving the room. She was already making lovely new friends. There were plenty of women who would be ecstatic to be in her position, and she should make the most of the many positives.

She threw herself with great determination into the conversation and really did enjoy much of it, despite Alex's unnerving presence.

She was still enjoying herself when Letitia said, 'My butler has now caught my eye approximately fifty times, and is starting to look quite put out, so I must ask you all to make your way with me to the dining room, so that the food isn't quite ruined by our chattering for too long.'

She moved unceremoniously towards the door of the room, not waiting for her husband to escort her.

'I'm afraid that I'm being quite fashionable and have seated couples far apart from each other.'

*Perfect.* Emma's eyes flew to Alex's face in reaction to Letitia's words, and his eyes found hers at exactly the same moment. They stared at each other unsmilingly for a second or two, before both shifting their gazes away.

Emma took a deep breath. Things would settle between her and Alex; it wouldn't always be this difficult. She took another breath and fixed a smile to her face before moving into the dining room.

Emma found her name card between those of Arthur and Gideon, both of whom she liked tremendously and with whom she knew she would very much enjoy conversation. The seating plan would have been perfect for her if she hadn't been almost exactly opposite Alex across the wide table; it was going to be difficult to avoid looking at him and getting distracted by his handsome face, sombre this evening in repose, the sound of his deep voice and the way his strong hands held his cutlery.

She noticed with a flash of irritation how very much he seemed to be enjoying his animated conversation with Letitia and their friend Maria. However, both her table neighbours proved themselves to be more than adequate conversationalists, as she had known they would, and Emma found herself thoroughly enjoying herself as long as she didn't look at Alex, and focused very hard on not thinking about him either.

Some time later, they were all exclaiming at Letitia and Arthur's cook's truly wonderful swan-shaped ice cream, and Letitia was recommending that Emma request her housekeeper to purchase or have made any number of ice cream moulds in the shape of perhaps a peacock and a hare at the very least.

Emma nodded. She was definitely going to do so, although she would choose her own designs, perhaps in the shape of one of her kittens, or a pineapple from the castle garden's exotic fruit greenhouse.

Her thoughts were interrupted by Mrs Hardy, the vicar's wife, leaning across Gideon and saying, in a particularly piercing voice, into a lull in the conversation, as the company all enjoyed the creaminess of the ice cream, 'I think we still don't have the full story of how you and the duke first met, Your Grace.'

Emma tilted her head very slightly to the left and regarded Mrs Hardy and her astonishingly smug smile. Clearly, Mrs Hardy believed that she *did* have the full story, and clearly Mrs Hardy was feeling particularly malicious.

'I...' she began, not certain where she was going with her sentence, but very sure that she'd like to make Mrs Hardy feel less smug.

'Her Grace is hesitating—' Alex's voice rang out a little loudly, and every head at the table, including Emma's, shot round to face him '—because we didn't tell anyone initially. Strong, pure emotion feels like a private matter.'

'Oh, but you're amongst friends now,' cooed Mrs Hardy.

Emma found herself gripping her spoon very tightly in lieu of, frankly, *slapping* the woman, who was smiling even more smugly than before, as though she knew that she'd caught Emma and Alex out and was ecstatic to have done so.

'You're right.' Emma turned to Alex and produced a coo of her own. 'Should you tell the story or should I?'

'Why don't you?' If Alex didn't exactly coo back at her, he did manage a fond smile.

'Well. It all began one morning in Hyde Park...'

With a few embellishments on the original—including details about their clothing, their extremely heightened emotions and the weather—Emma reproduced the story they'd concocted in the inn about Alex's horseback rescue and their subsequent secret courtship.

'Even the weather was quite propitious,' she said soulfully as she drew her monologue to a close. 'The sun was warm, but not too warm, and there was exactly the right amount of breeze. It was as though the elements understood that we were at the beginning of something delicate and special and important, and that they needed to nurture it.'

'How very beautiful,' Letitia said, grinning at Emma.

From the way her eyes were dancing, it seemed clear that she'd heard something approaching the real story too, which did make it seem odd that she seemed so certain that Alex and Emma were now a real married couple.

She turned to Alex and said mischievously, 'We'd all love to hear the story from your perspective, Alex.'

Alex coughed. 'I have nothing to add. It was indeed, as Emma says, a...beautiful beginning to what I'm delighted to say is a beautiful...' He tailed off.

'Relationship,' Emma supplied. 'I feel extremely lucky.'

'I'm sure you do.' Mrs Hardy had spoken beneath her breath, but she'd definitely said it.

'The luck,' said Alex, glaring at Mrs Hardy, 'is all mine.'

'I don't know when I've more enjoyed hearing someone's love story,' Letitia said, 'but perhaps we ladies should remove to the drawing room now, to allow the gentlemen their port. Mrs Hardy, I do wonder whether you might be wise to depart quite soon. I hear that there's been a particularly severe snowstorm, very much centred on the road between here and the vicarage, and Mr Hardy would, I'm sure, be distraught not to be able to return to his parishioners. I'll ask Harris to call your carriage. It's been wonderful to see you; thank you so much for coming.'

Once Letitia had completed her skilful dispatch of the Hardys, Emma thoroughly enjoyed herself, drinking tea with Letitia, Maria and the fourth lady still present, Lady Clinthill.

Until Letitia leaned towards her and said, 'I wish to apologise for what Mrs Hardy said. I don't like to see people being rude under my roof. Arthur and I had barely met when we got married—our marriage was arranged very much between our parents—and we're now deeply in love. Obviously that means that I am beholden to my mother forever, about which she reminds me far too often, but aside from that it's wonderful, and it serves as an example of how people can meet in somewhat ridiculous-sounding situations and yet develop very strong feelings for each other. I'm so pleased that the two of you were thrown together in the way in which you were.'

'I... Yes.' Emma just wanted to *squirm*.

'I'm so sorry. I didn't mean to make you uncomfortable. The two of you look perfect together, and are so clearly in love, that I'm sure you'll be able to overcome any obstacles that might arise from two relative strangers marrying. I just wanted to say that others have been in the same position and overcome those issues and become stronger.'

'Thank you.' Emma could feel tears pricking at her eyelids. She wasn't sure whether it was due to the fact that she and Alex were clearly *not* in love, and were never going to be, or to how lovely it was that Letitia was being so kind, if slightly scarily outspoken on fairly regular occasion.

Their conversation was curtailed by the men coming into the room. Emma wasn't sure whether or not she was pleased; she felt that she'd have liked to have had the opportunity to glean some details about the early days of Letitia and Arthur's marriage.

Pleased with her own cunning, she had seated herself on a chair rather than a sofa, so that no comment would be occasioned if—when—Alex chose not to sit next to her. He was the second of the men to come into the room, and after hesitating for a moment, sat himself down on a chair reasonably close to Emma, but not within knee-touching distance, perfectly unexceptionable for a husband.

For no reason at all, things were feeling a lot more complicated now that Alex was here.

Maybe she should confide the truth in Letitia and begin to forge a spinster-within-a-marriage existence for herself sooner rather than later.

'You didn't take long to join us.' Letitia smiled up at her husband. 'Did you miss us?'

'Apparently so.' Arthur plonked a kiss on her cheek and sat down beside her on the loveseat upon which Letitia seemed to have chosen to sit precisely for the purpose of cosying up to her husband. Emma felt another pang that she would never share such an easy familiarity and blatant affection with Alex.

'I think we should play whist,' Letitia said, interrupting Emma's thoughts. 'Eight's the perfect number for it. We can have four sets of two and rotate. How shall we decide on partners? Having been fashionably apart at dinner, should we perhaps unfashionably partner our spouses?'

Everyone except Alex and Emma immediately exclaimed how lovely that would be. The two of them exchanged a quick glance and then both joined in with the exclamations, both perhaps a little too loudly.

Within less than five minutes, Emma was seated at a card table with Alex as her partner. He took the cards to shuffle them and suddenly Emma was fixated on his hands. They were strong, capable and lightly tanned, even though spring had barely begun, so he clearly spent a lot of time outside. And yesterday, in the late afternoon, those hands had been touching her, and just the memory of that was causing her to feel extremely hot again.

'Emma, are you all right?' Letitia asked. 'You look a little flushed. Would you like some ratafia?'

'Yes, please,' Emma said as Alex looked up from the cards.

'Are you sure you're perfectly well?' he asked her in a low voice.

The irony of him asking her if she was all right because everyone thought that she might be ill because she'd just been slightly overcome at the thought of what they'd been doing yesterday. And, oh, for goodness' sake, now she was thinking about his shoulders and his chest and how he'd touched *her* chest.

'Yes, thank you. I'm very well.' Emma buried her face in the glass of ratafia Arthur had just passed to her, took a long draught and nearly choked.

'Are you sure?' Alex asked.

'Yes, thank you, very sure. I hope you're going to prove to be a good player,' she told him, aiming for a playful just-married-and-still-coquettish-with-her-husband tone. 'We've never played cards together before,' she explained to the others.

'I will endeavour to satisfy you,' Alex replied with a little smile, which, had she not known that he was acting just as much as she was, would have caused Emma's heart to leap a little and her insides to flutter again.

He *did* satisfy her. Whist partnership-wise, anyway. He was intuitive, he was able to keep his face entirely expressionless so as not to give away any clues to the contents of his hand, and he adapted his game to hers very well. Emma liked to think that she adapted hers to his as well, and indeed that she had all the same attributes as a player.

Certainly, they beat everyone else quite resoundingly, and one of the most satisfying characteristics in Alex as a partner turned out to be that he was quite as competitive as she was.

'Perhaps just one more round?' he suggested, after the first one for a while that he and Emma hadn't won. *We can't finish on a loss,* he mouthed at her.

Emma was very tired, having slept very badly the night before, but was in complete agreement.

As soon as they'd won the next round, Alex said,

'I'm so sorry to break up the party, and indeed I'd very much like to continue showing the rest of you how it's done, but I think Emma's tired, and I see that it's very late indeed, and we don't wish to outstay our welcome.'

'I hope it hasn't snowed much more,' Emma said.

'You're always welcome here, as I hope you know,' Letitia said, 'and indeed you must also know you will be more than welcome to stay here overnight with us if the snow has made the roads impassable.'

'It has indeed snowed further while you've been here,' Arthur reported from behind the room's heavy curtains. 'I think you might all be forced to stay overnight.'

'That's perfect. I couldn't have planned it better. We will absolutely love to have you,' Letitia said, beaming. 'I will ask Harris to prepare a bedchamber for each couple. An impromptu house party! I already have plans for tomorrow.'

Emma felt that she and Alex had grown adept at reading each other's glances through their card games this evening, but it didn't take a lot of skill to read the horror in Alex's eyes at this moment, mirrored, she was sure, by her own. Well, perhaps not horror in her eyes; perhaps shock. The two of them sharing a bedchamber? Good heavens.

'I feel that we should investigate further,' she said. 'I think Alex and I would both like to return home to the boys tonight if possible.'

'I agree.' He nodded. 'Especially after my recent absence in London.'

'I'm not sure you're going to be able to do so,' Arthur said, still peering out of the window. He let go of the curtains and said, 'Let me go and see.'

'I'll accompany you,' Alex said.

As they left the room, Emma couldn't work out whether she'd rather they could or couldn't get home that night. A traitorous part of her felt that it might be very nice, albeit a little embarrassing, to be forced to share a chamber with Alex.

## Chapter Thirteen

How was it possible that so much snow had fallen in one evening? Ridiculous.

As he and Arthur trod a path around the house, Alex stamped his boots viciously. He was absolutely not going to share a room with Emma tonight. It had been bad enough talking to her at dinner and playing cards with her this evening. He'd enjoyed her company far too much. He hoped he had enough willpower to resist her obvious attractions if they shared a room, but based on yesterday's idiocy he wasn't so sure that he did.

He wasn't going to share a room with her. So at least one of them was going to have to go home and, looking at the depth of the snow in Letitia and Arthur's drive, they weren't going to be able to take the chaise.

Fortunately, there was a full moon, and horses dealt very well with fresh snow; they only had difficulty when there was a frozen crust on top of the snow, which could lacerate their legs. Alex would ride carefully home in the moonlight and Emma could return in the chaise when the snow would allow her. She might have to stay here for several days, which, frankly, would be ideal in terms of allowing them both to cool off after yesterday's insanity.

Back in the house, Alex told the assembled company of his plans and Letitia swept everyone except Emma into the drawing room, saying, 'We must allow the two of you a moment to bid each other adieu for however long it might be.'

'Goodbye, then,' Emma said, her hands gripping each other tightly in front of her. 'Be careful as you ride.'

'Thank you. I will.' It was ridiculous that Alex now felt a wrench at leaving her. In case someone was watching, and because it felt rude not to, he took a step towards her and kissed her cheek, her scent flooding his senses as he did so. 'Goodnight. Sleep well.'

'Goodnight.'

Alex didn't enjoy his journey home. He alternated between walking Star and riding slowly, but that wasn't the problem. The problem was his mood. He felt bereft, as though home would be odd without Emma there. And he felt guilty, as though he'd engineered leaving her behind, and worried in case she was upset.

It was going to be a good thing, though, having time apart.

It was still snowing when he awoke after a short night's sleep. The snow continued until midday, and it was clear that carriages wouldn't be able to travel that day.

By the time Alex took his luncheon with the boys, he still wasn't sure how he felt about Emma's being stranded with Letitia and Arthur.

Extremely heavy snow came with consequences for agriculture, for people living in poverty, for those who needed to travel and for many more, especially this winter after last year's lack of summer. For Alex, it had also had the unexpected consequence of giving him a reprieve from being under the same roof as Emma, having to fight the attraction he felt for her, never sure whether he ought to spend time with her out of courtesy—and enjoyment, if he was honest—or avoid her because he enjoyed her company too much.

Was he pleased to have that reprieve, though?

If he'd been asked a few days ago how he would feel about this situation, he would have stated without hesitation that it would have been very welcome. And it was still welcome, in theory, but in practice he wasn't so sure.

He hoped that she was all right.

'When will Emma be back?' asked John for about the fifth time.

'I want her,' said Harry.

Freddie looked at Alex, and then he looked at his younger brothers. 'We can manage very well without her,' he said.

Alex paused, his fork halfway to his mouth. If he wasn't mistaken, Freddie had calculated that Alex would be pleased that she wasn't there, and had decided to come down on the side of his father rather than his brothers. This was terrible; Alex was setting a very poor example.

'I very much look forward to her returning,' he said. 'And while we can indeed manage without her, I know that we all miss her. I hope that she'll be able to return tomorrow.'

And then he busied himself helping Harry with his food, until he was sure that Freddie wasn't studying his face any more and the conversation had turned to a dead squirrel that the boys had seen being eaten by crows.

The next morning was Sunday and, following no further snow and a rise in temperatures, the roads were passable, albeit somewhat slushy, and Alex attended church with the children. He always chose the village church rather than the chapel on his estate; the chapel was heavy with memories of Diana's funeral, and in addition he wanted the boys' upbringing to be as informal as possible, given that they were the sons of a duke.

'Your Grace,' trilled Mrs Hardy as they left the church. 'Is Her Grace indisposed?'

'She was detained at Letitia and Arthur's by the snow, but we look forward to her return today.' Alex carried on walking.

Mrs Hardy was not a tall woman, but such was her determination to continue the conversation that she managed to lengthen her stride to keep pace with him.

'Perhaps a welcome break from the cosh of wedlock for you?' She accompanied her words with a little titter, while Alex tightened his lips. 'But travelling on a Sunday... I don't believe I can condone Her Grace's intention.'

'My wife's regard for her husband and sons must transcend any small feeling of guilt over undertaking a short journey, which, after all, is not that much further than some people must make between home and church,' Alex said, stony faced.

Mrs Hardy made a sound a little like 'Pfft,' and flounced away, which made Alex smile. He wished Emma had been there to see the flouncing.

Emma was alighting from the chaise as they arrived back at the house.

'Emma!' Harry hurtled towards her, followed by John.

Freddie looked at Alex, who had to struggle not to shake his head at the situation. He actually *was* pleased to see Emma. He did not wish to be pleased to see her, and he did not wish to act on that feeling, but he did need to set a good example of a respectful, if not passionate, union to his boys, particularly Freddie, it seemed.

Living a lie was hard.

He smiled at the boys and then walked forward to greet Emma. He placed his hands on her upper arms and a decorous kiss on each of her cheeks.

'As you see, we're all delighted to see you returned,' he told her.

'Oh,' she squeaked, her cheeks looking a little warm, before she recovered herself and said, 'I'm delighted to see you all.'

As they all went inside the house together, Alex couldn't help thinking that from the outside they must look like the perfect family picture.

He didn't know how he felt about Emma, so it was fortunate that they had the boys to distract them over the luncheon they ate together. Afterwards, in the absence of the excuse of work on the Sabbath, he took Freddie out for a long walk during the afternoon, arriving back only at dusk.

He joined Emma for dinner that evening in the grand dining room. She was dressed in a light green dress, against which her almost black hair looked stunning. The dress was low cut, and Alex caught himself gazing at the neckline for just a little too long, and remembering their interlude in the snow the other day.

He forced his gaze upwards, but that was no better. Emma's lips were slightly parted and she was looking at him as intently as he was looking at her. It was as though there was some kind of indefinable tension between them. Indefinable, but very thick, so thick that he could almost have cut it with the knife in front of him.

'It started snowing again just as we returned to the house after our walk,' he said.

There was a good reason that English people talked about the weather so often: it was the safest of subjects and there was so much of it.

'Quite heavily, in fact,' he continued as they took their seats at the table. 'I wouldn't be surprised if we were snowed in again. Freddie had a lot to tell me about snowflakes and their different constructions, and the fact that geographers believe that no two are the same.'

Good grief, he'd resorted to reciting snowflake facts.

Emma frowned, ignoring his inanities. 'That can't be good for the crops and livestock. The drifts had only barely begun to melt.'

'Indeed.' A week ago, Alex would have been surprised that her mind had gone straight to agriculture, but now he knew her better. 'I will visit my farming tenants tomorrow to discuss what can be done to help, on foot if necessary.'

'And your other tenants? Are they able to cope in this weather?'

'I trust so. They are well-housed, and I ensure that their rent is set at very reasonable levels.'

'I would like to visit the more vulnerable amongst them, if I may. Perhaps the elderly, or any families with numerous offspring who might be struggling.'

'Of course. When the weather is improved.'

'I am also able to visit on foot.'

'It's a long way.' Alex speared some peppered broccoli.

Emma nodded and didn't say anything else, instead focusing on cutting her veal escalope into dainty pieces. Clearly, she was going to ignore him.

'If you *do* go,' he said, 'I would prefer you to take your maid, or a footman, or perhaps both.'

Emma inclined her head and placed a piece of veal in her mouth. Watching her delicate chewing, Alex completely lost his train of thought. She raised her eyebrows at him slightly as she took her next mouthful, and indeed he knew he was staring. Or gazing. Both were a little embarrassing for a grown man at his own supper table. Surely he could find some non-contentious conversation about something beyond snowflakes?

'How did you spend your second evening at Letitia and Arthur's?' he asked. He'd asked whether she'd enjoyed her stay when they sat down for luncheon, but the boys had taken over the conversation from that point on, and they hadn't had the opportunity to go back to it. 'I hope you enjoyed your stay.'

'Thank you; I did enjoy it. We played whist again yesterday evening. I was partnered with Gideon.'

'Oh, dear.' Alex had lost count of the number of times he'd trounced Gideon at the card table. Gideon was not a gifted player, and cheerfully acknowledged that fact.

Emma laughed. 'Indeed. I missed your partnership sorely.'

And then she stopped laughing, and so did he, and he realised that they were gazing at each other's mouths and eyes again. There was something about the word 'partnership'.

'I understand that it often snows very heavily in Lancashire?' Alex said, swallowing.

Snow was apparently the safest topic of conversation this evening, and they stuck to weather-related topics for the entirety of the rest of their dinner, which did less to take Alex's mind off Emma's smile and beautiful eyes than he would have liked.

\* \* \*

They awoke in the morning to the deepest March snow in living memory, according to Lancing, who had a longer memory than most. It had already stopped snowing, though, and while travel by carriage or horse would be difficult, as any flattened snow was icing over, it was possible to walk as men had been out clearing the roads.

Alex spent an hour after breakfast discussing his farmers' needs with Parsons, and then directed footmen and grooms to divert their energies from their usual work to helping on the land where needed, and then set out on foot to check on the inhabitants of a cluster of cottages east of the castle, which were occupied by some elderly people and one couple who had three young children and were expecting a fourth imminently.

He took one of the grooms named Mikey with him. Once they'd checked on those tenants Mikey could send for any necessary assistance, and Alex would walk on to the nearest farm.

The first cottage at which he arrived was that belonging to the young couple. He knocked on the door and it was opened by...*Emma*. Holding a toddler on her hip.

'Emma?'

'Alex?' She opened the door wider to allow him entry. 'I didn't expect to see you here.'

'I thought you knew that I was planning to come?'

'I...' He looked at her. 'Your skirts, though. In the snow.'

'My pelisse is thick, and I'm wearing stout boots and where my skirts got a little wet they're now dry from the fire. The roads are entirely passable as you know.'

'Where's Jenny? Where's *everyone*?' It seemed to be

'Maybe. Maybe not. Just something to think about.'

'Going by your threats, I see that your defeat still rankles.'

'Defeat is a strong word.'

Defeat was completely the wrong word for what had happened. They'd made each other soaking wet, and then they'd...

Why? Why had he brought that up now? Now all he could think about was what they'd done in the snow.

Emma was capable of thinking of other things, apparently. She'd stopped walking and put her hands on her hips.

'I see what you're doing. You're attempting to plant seeds of worry in my mind. There could be a snowball around any corner. And just as my morale is low, which might affect my strategic planning, you will attack.' She started walking again, fast, and said over her shoulder, 'Just be aware that you might have longer and better throwing arms than me, but I'm sure I'm significantly more cunning.'

Alex laughed out loud and took the three strides necessary to catch her up.

He didn't practise any snowball warfare during their walk, not keen to be tempted into any further intimacy in the snow. Instead, he showed Emma various points of interest, from a very ancient oak tree, reputed to date back to the sixteenth century and to have witnessed a visit from Good Queen Bess herself, to a copse in which he and his brother played as children.

As they reached the top of a hill, from which it was possible to see for many miles—all the way to the sea on a cloudless day—the snow suddenly changed to a heavy, driving force. Within minutes, from having been almost able to make out the horizon through light snow, they could see barely a few feet in front of them.

'Oh, my goodness,' a white-covered Emma said.

Alex took two steps towards her, reached for her hand and linked his fingers firmly through hers. 'We must hold hands so that we don't lose each other.'

The swirling snow was incredibly disorientating. Alex knew his land like the back of his hand, and still he was in great danger of losing his bearings unless he concentrated hard. The snow was very wet and very cold, and they would do well not to stay in it for too long. He was beginning to feel chilled to the bone, despite his greatcoat and winter boots, and Emma's clothing was less robust than his. She also had a much smaller frame than he, so she would be freezing very quickly.

They began to walk slowly forward, Alex feeling the way slightly ahead of Emma, using his feet. Within only a few steps Emma tripped. He caught her and pulled her to a halt next to him.

'Are you all right? You haven't twisted your ankle or anything?'

'Yes, thank you.' She was gripping his hand and arm as tightly as he was holding hers now.

'I think we need to take shelter nearby until this is over,' he said. 'I think it would be very difficult to get all the way back. I can't believe it will last more than an hour or two, and there's a barn about a hundred feet to our left.'

It was perhaps two miles to the house, and that was a very long way in a blizzard, especially for someone in female attire.

Arm in arm now, they inched towards where Alex

thought the barn was, guided only by his memory of how the hill's contours went.

'I think I might have misremembered,' he said eventually, after they'd been trudging into driving snow for what seemed like an extraordinarily long time. 'I'm so sorry. Hopefully we will at least find a wall soon, behind which we can shelter.' The snow was biting, literally painful against one's face, and he sensed Emma wince every so often. If they found a wall, he would do his best to shelter her from the storm. 'We can't walk too far, though.'

There was a river running through his land not far from here, and there were several dips in the terrain that were negligible to people who could see them, but which in this weather could cause one or both of them to break a leg or worse.

'Wall!' said Emma about ten seconds later.

'I beg your pardon?'

'Wall. I just hit a wall with my hand.'

Alex turned carefully, with his own free hand outstretched, and felt around. Yes, they'd found a wall.

'Thank God,' he said. 'I'm sure this is the wall of a building. It must be the barn.'

Emma made to let go of his hand, but he tightened his grip on hers.

'I really don't think we should let go of each other at this point,' he said. 'Let's not fail now, when we're so close to shelter.'

'Yes, you're right.' Emma moved back towards him and said, 'Let's go to our right along the wall, not letting go of it, until we come to a door or opening.'

'Good idea.'

They found the opening on the third side, and walked

through the edge of the blizzard inside, towards the back of the barn, which was fully covered and dry and half full of hay.

'That is *such* a relief.' Emma took her hand out of his. 'I can't remember ever feeling so truly ecstatic to find a pile of dead grass.' She reached up to her head and pulled at her bonnet, which had begun the day a fairly rigid, pointed shape, but which was now entirely sodden and drooping. 'My fingers are barely working from the cold.'

Eventually, she had the bonnet off and shook out her hair. 'May I sit on this hay?'

'Certainly.' Alex climbed over towards the back of the barn and held his arm out for her to take. 'If you come here you'll find that it's much warmer, or at least less freezing.'

Emma took his arm for support and climbed over, and then let go and sat down. Alex joined her, although sitting a cautious few feet away from her.

'We were lucky that we were so close to the barn when that started,' she said. 'And that you know your land so well. Or perhaps you have some kind of supernatural ability to see through incredibly heavy snow.'

Alex laughed. 'Yes, I am possessed of a special winter vision belonging only to Somerset natives. No, I've spent many, many days on this land, and I do know it well, even more so now, from a different angle, since I inherited the running and husbandry of it.'

'Well, thank goodness. I'm sure we would have been all right had we stayed out there, albeit extremely cold and wet, but I have to say I vastly prefer being inside, even in a barn. Indeed, at this moment the barn feels positively like a princess's palace.'

'It does. And I'm sure it's very good for us to be re-

minded not to take our creature comforts for granted.'
Alex paused, hearing a slightly odd sound, and studied
Emma. 'Is that sound your teeth chattering?'

'N-n-no...' It wasn't just her teeth that were chattering; her whole body was beginning to judder.

'You're freezing.'

'Please don't worry; this hay will serve very well
to warm me.' Emma pulled some hay against herself,
turning herself into a ridiculously sorry sight as some
stuck to her damp clothes while other wisps floated away
from her.

Alex stood up and took his coat off to wrap her in it.
But, no, that would be no good; it was very wet on the
outside and the damp had penetrated right through it in
parts. His jacket was also wet, and not thick enough to
provide much warmth.

Emma was shivering more and more now, her whole
body jerking. Alex knew that he needed to do something
fast, and could think of only one solution.

'I think you need to take your wet coat off, and then
I'm going to sit very close to you to warm you.'

'Really?'

'Yes.'

She pulled ineffectually at the buttons of her coat,
her fingers clearly too cold to work properly at all now.
Alex moved over to sit beside her and began to undo
the buttons, working as fast as he could, scared by how
very much she was shivering. He had the coat off very
quickly, and laid it out on the hay behind them in the
hope that it might dry a little, before wrapping both his
arms around her. Her dress was a little damp, unsurprisingly.

'I don't see how we can get entirely dry, short of divesting ourselves entirely of our clothes.' He wondered immediately why he'd said that, struggling to force his mind away from the thought of Emma divested of her clothes. 'But I think that if we huddle together like this our body warmth will heat the wetness, which should hopefully warm you up.'

'Thank you.' She could hardly get the words out round her chattering teeth.

Alex was getting even more scared. He could feel Emma's slender shoulders shivering in huge jerks. There was still too much of her exposed to the cold air.

'Come here.' He lifted her onto his lap and wrapped himself around her as much as he could.

'Thank you,' she said again, her voice now muffled against his chest.

They sat like that for a while—Alex couldn't tell how long—until Emma wriggled a little and said, 'I'm starting to feel a reasonably normal temperature again. Thank you so much.'

'Good,' said Alex, not releasing his grip on her. 'Let's not count our chickens too early, though. We must get you as hot as possible before I let go of you. Even when the snow's subsided enough for us to make our way back we're going to get very wet again, and you're going to have to put your wet coat back on.'

'How's it looking now?' Emma raised her head and peered over his shoulder.

'Still remarkably fierce. If we weren't wet and on foot and stranded in a barn a good couple of miles from the house, I'd be lost in happy awe of the elements.'

'It is beautiful,' agreed Emma, wriggling some more, presumably to get a better view out of the barn entrance.

Now that he was a little less worried about her, Alex

was a lot more aware of the fact that she was sitting on his lap, in his arms, and that she was wiggling her gorgeously rounded bottom against him. He really hoped she couldn't feel the effect she was having on him.

She suddenly stopped moving and... Yes, she probably had realised.

There wasn't a lot that embarrassed Alex, but this, yes, this was embarrassing. And there was nothing he could do to extricate himself from the embarrassment because he had to keep holding Emma the way he was, so that she wouldn't get cold again. So he was just going to chat to her about something mundane, and then he'd stop being so aware of her, his body would get itself under control and all would be well.

'I wonder what we'll have for luncheon when we return to the house,' he said.

Food was certainly a mundane topic.

'Something warm and hearty. Perhaps a beef stew. Followed, perhaps, by something deliciously sweet.' Emma shifted again on his lap and Alex almost groaned out loud.

'What's your favourite dessert?' he persisted.

They just needed to talk about food for longer. That way he could absolutely stop his mind and body from being so focused on what Emma was doing with her body.

'I'm not sure. I think...' Emma paused. Alex couldn't see her face, but he knew what she looked like when she was thinking. She'd have her nose ever so slightly wrinkled, and if she was about to say something sarcastic or cheeky, her eyes would be dancing.

'On a day like this, something very rich. A smooth chocolate mousse, perhaps.'

Now Alex was imagining her putting a spoon into a mousse and then into her mouth, her tongue peeking out. And now of course he was imagining kissing her again. God.

'What would you like?' she asked.

'What?'

'What would you like to eat?'

'To eat? Of course.' Alex could barely remember what food was at this point. It felt as though he had one physical need only, and it wasn't food.

Emma twisted her head to look up at him and smiled. It was the smile that undid him. If she hadn't done it maybe he could have resisted, but the smile was both sweet and slightly mocking, as though she knew what he was thinking.

He found himself adjusting her so that he could reach her face better—and, *damn*, it felt good as she moved in his lap—and then, very slowly, he lowered his head to hers. She moved to meet him and suddenly the slowness was gone and they were kissing, hard, urgently, passionately.

Far in the depths of his brain Alex knew that this was a terrible idea, but apparently he was completely powerless to resist.

## Chapter Fourteen

Emma was almost panting as she kissed Alex back as hard as he was kissing her.

From the moment her teeth had stopped chattering so hard it had felt as though she might bite right through her tongue, and she'd had the ability to think about where she was, she'd loved being enveloped in Alex's arms. And from the moment she'd warmed up and moved on his lap and felt the evidence of his desire for her, she'd wanted this.

She had her hands in his thick hair, his arms were round her waist and her shoulders, and his body was still wrapped right around hers. It was truly wonderful, but she wanted *more*.

It wasn't just the physical sensation that she wanted, although she was quite desperate for that. It was also that she wanted some kind of affirmation of how their relationship had developed, in her eyes anyway. They made each other laugh, they seemed to be able to talk about all manner of topics, and Alex was a very kind, decent person whom she *liked*.

She hoped he liked her too.

She didn't just like him. She loved him.

And at this moment, she was in his arms, and she wanted to give him everything she had and receive everything he could give her.

She wriggled against him again and he groaned, deep in his throat, a sound that made her breath catch. She moved one of her hands from the back of his head and ran it up his hard chest. Then she took her other hand and pulled at the fastenings of his shirt, wanting to feel his skin as she had the other day.

She moved further against him and he groaned again, and then he plunged his hands into her hair and pulled very gently, so that her head went back a little. He kissed down her neck, licking, nibbling, nipping, caressing her shoulders with one hand and still holding her waist with the other. His kisses were moving ever lower, but slowly, and Emma felt as though her entire body was becoming taut in anticipation.

And then suddenly he lifted her, so that she was lying on her back, nestled away from any draughts, on a big bundle of hay, with him above her. With one hand he was caressing her breast and the other fumbled with ribbons and buttons, trying to remove her dress. Emma found herself pulling his shirt out of his breeches as urgently as he was trying to undress her.

Alex paused for a moment and found her eyes with his. He raised his eyebrows slightly, as though seeking her consent to continue.

'Yes, please,' she said. And if she sounded as though she was begging, she didn't care.

She smiled at him, a heartfelt invitation, and he smiled back. Then he lowered his lips to hers again, this time kissing her gently, slowly, deeply, all the while exploring with his hands.

Emma's breasts felt as though they were on fire now, and the sensation was spreading to her most intimate parts, so that she was almost *aching* for him in a way that she couldn't even describe.

He drew back for a moment, and just looked at her. 'You're beautiful,' he said.

Emma looked down at herself and gasped. Somehow she was almost entirely naked. Then she looked at him, and gasped again, because he was almost entirely naked too, and he was...magnificent.

And then she lost the ability to think because Alex began to kiss her everywhere, while his fingers touched her between her thighs gently, then more insistently, until she was arching and turning and her body was almost *singing* with sensation.

Then his body was above hers, so close, and he was looking at her again with that raised eyebrow, as though confirming again that she was happy. She nodded, realising through the haze of sensation that there was nothing with which she wouldn't trust him. Kissing her and murmuring her name the whole time, he pushed slowly inside her.

When, after the first shock, she was comfortable—comfortable to perfection—he began to thrust and thrust, and if she'd thought that her body was singing with sensation before, it was positively crying out now.

She opened her eyes for a moment and looked at his face—the face she knew now that she loved, at which she could never tire of looking—and she smiled at him and whispered, 'Alex.'

And then he began to thrust harder and harder, and she was lost, one hand in his hair, the other almost scratching his back, almost screaming with the desire for more and more of him.

Suddenly, she felt the most glorious sensation, her whole body flooded with it, and this time she really did scream, while Alex grunted, 'Yes, Emma, yes.'

And then he gathered her to him as they both lay panting.

Emma looked up at his strong jaw, his kind eyes, his mouth that could set in a forbidding line when he was angry and yet curve in such a sweet way at other times, and knew that she would never be the same again.

She didn't know how he felt about her, but she knew that she'd fallen in love with him, and that it wasn't going to be the kind of love you recovered from quickly. Or maybe ever.

She gasped again—she'd been doing a lot of gasping today—as he eased himself out of her and said, his voice hoarse, 'That was... That was not what I was expecting to do today.'

'Nor I,' Emma said after a moment, her heart cracking, because it was extremely clear that he hadn't been lying there thinking that he'd fallen in love with her.

If you'd just realised that you'd fallen in love with someone the first words that came out of your mouth would not be that you hadn't expected to do that today.

Maybe he could come to love her in time, though? Or at least enjoy her company and making love to her enough to want to live with her as man and wife, properly?

Would he want to make love to her again? Regularly? And would that be enough for her? Would she be able to hide from him how she felt?

If she couldn't hide it from him things could get very embarrassing on both sides.

She could hide it, should hide it, if it meant they could be together. Or should she? Would she in time begin to resent him? Would her love drive a wedge between them, as her parents' love had driven a wedge between them when it had become apparent that they wanted and needed different things in life?

'So.' Alex released her gently and Emma looked down at their nakedness. Alex did too. He was stirring again as they looked at each other. She felt her breath catch in her throat as she felt her own body responding to his obvious desire, and then he cleared his throat and moved a little further away from her.

'The blizzard has stopped,' he said. 'We should return while it's safe to do so, and before anyone becomes worried about us.'

Emma took a deep breath to cover her disappointment, and when she was sure that her voice would sound close to normal said, 'We should, indeed.'

She rolled to one side, away from him, looking for her clothes to cover herself. It turned out that nakedness during lovemaking was wonderful, and natural, but nakedness when the man who had just made love to you just wanted to go home felt embarrassing. And cold when you were in an open barn on a snowy day.

Alex passed her her dress and she said, 'Thank you.'

They dressed with their backs to each other. Emma couldn't remember feeling this miserable for a long time. Ironic that she'd thought—known—she could trust him with anything. She realised now that she could trust him with absolutely everything except her heart.

The good thing about getting dressed in wet clothes surrounded by hay was that it was quite difficult, and it gave Emma time to think a little more and pull herself together. The bad thing about how difficult it was was that she couldn't entirely manage by herself.

She turned to Alex. 'I'm so sorry, but I wonder if you might help with my fastenings?'

'Of course.'

As he carefully pulled her hair aside, his fingers brushed her neck, and Emma almost leapt a mile. She was really going to have to work hard to get herself under control.

'I think you should wear my coat,' Alex told her. 'It's thicker, and it didn't get so wet on the inside.' He held it up against her and said, 'Oh.'

It was many inches too long.

'It might keep me warmer, but I might fall and break a leg instead,' Emma said.

'Indeed. Each to their own coat it is, then.'

They said very little further as they made their way out of the barn, Alex helping Emma clamber over the bales of hay, and their conversation during the walk back was restricted to the most basic of issues, such as Alex's request that Emma hold his arm and hand again, in case the ground was slippery or there was a further sudden snowstorm.

Emma couldn't quite comprehend how the linking of their arms now felt so entirely functional, when their arms had been wrapped around each other so passionately so very recently.

Well, it was a strong sign of how Alex felt, and since she was going to be seeing him every day still, she would have to hide her emotions for both their sakes.

She was sure he was still grieving for his wife.

She remembered their conversation over dinner a

week or two ago, when he'd described Diana in such a tender way. Of *course* he was still grieving for her.

She felt sorry, deeply sorry, for him. She knew that if something awful happened to him now she'd be devastated, and she'd only known and loved him for a few weeks. If something bad happened to him in a few years' time she would find it horrendous.

So, having loved Diana for several years, as he obviously had, and having three children with her, he must have been utterly grief-stricken when he'd lost her. Awful. She hated to think of Alex in pain.

If she was honest, though—and this probably made her a truly terrible person—she couldn't help feeling a tiny bit (very) sorry for her own loss too, because when she thought about it like this it was quite clear that Alex was still deeply in love with the memory of his wife and that Emma would never be able to compete with that.

There was nothing she could say to him now.

They walked on in silence all the way back to the castle.

Perhaps it was a good thing that Alex was still in love with Diana and that Emma couldn't compete with that love. The two of them clearly wanted very different things, just as her parents had, and she didn't want to follow in their footsteps and have her love turn to near-hatred because they were so incompatible.

As they approached the main entrance to the castle, she took a quick glance up at his profile. He didn't twitch. She felt as though she'd lost him today, somewhere in the moments after they'd made love.

'Your Grace,' cried Jenny, hurrying out to meet them. 'Come inside directly. You'll catch your death with that wet coat on.'

Emma realised that she was indeed very cold.

'Thank you, Jenny.' She turned round to bid Alex farewell and discovered that he'd already gone.

'You need to have a bath immediately.'

Jenny and Mrs Drabble both busied themselves calling for so much hot water that the entire household could have had hot baths if the footmen had obeyed them.

'Thank you so much. But I'm very well able to bathe myself,' Emma told Jenny when the bath was ready.

She didn't want to undress in front of Jenny; what if there had been some physical change in her today that Jenny could discern?

'You're shivering. I don't want to leave you, Your Grace.'

'Thank you, Jenny, but I assure you that I will be warm again as soon as I get into the bath.'

Jenny grumbled for so long that Emma feared the bath water might already be cold. When she eventually gave in and left, Emma locked the door behind her and undressed herself before climbing into the bath. She looked down at herself. There did not, in fact, seem to be any noticeable physical change.

She had certainly changed emotionally, though; she was certain now that she'd fallen deeply and irrevocably in love with Alex.

Now she was shivering again.

She rubbed her arms hard to warm herself up. Her body, anyway. It felt as though her heart might never be warm again.

## Chapter Fifteen

Alex spent only the time it took to get changed into dry clothes and visit the kitchen for a flying luncheon—to his chef's expressed horror, but not very well-hidden delight—before readying himself to set off again on foot to visit other tenants. He needed to check that the more vulnerable amongst them were all right, and he also needed not to be alone with his thoughts.

Those thoughts had intruded as he'd changed and eaten and parried comments from his chef, and they continued to intrude as he shrugged on a dry greatcoat.

This morning was the first time he'd been intimate with a woman since he'd lost Diana. He couldn't… He didn't… He wasn't sure how he felt, other than that the experience had been truly spectacular from a physical perspective and utterly terrifying from an emotional perspective.

Physically, he just wanted to do it again.

Emotionally, well, emotionally, what did he want?

He wanted to know that Emma would always be happy. He wanted—that was to say, he was *tempted*—to look after her, cosset her…

Damn it, he wanted to… He almost wanted to love her.

No. He did *not* want to love her.

The image of her smile as they'd lain together on the straw came into his head. Hell and damnation. What if she decided to go out again this afternoon and some accident befell her?

He called Lancing, and every footman he could see, as well as Mrs Drabble and Jenny, to instruct them that they must not allow Emma to leave the house in the snow by herself again.

At the last minute, just before he left, he realised his own hypocrisy. Even if he didn't have a responsibility to himself, he did to many other people, not least his motherless children. He asked his head groom, Jim, whom he knew was very fit and, crucially, also a man of few words, to walk with him.

They set off on a long and silent march into biting wind, enlivened by the occasional sideways flurry of skin-prickling frozen snow, which suited his mood very well.

Visibility this afternoon was dramatically better than it had been this morning, and he could now see the barn from some distance. Thank God they'd found it when they had. And thank God he'd been with Emma. If she'd been alone she might have been killed in that blizzard.

She was so brave. And so stupid. And so adorable. Not to mention beautiful.

He forced his mind away from the memory of her naked beneath him, and then from another, of how, in the aftermath of their lovemaking, her smile had changed from one of physical bliss to uncertainty, when she'd clearly seen that he wasn't going to repeat the experience.

That change in her smile had nearly caused him to gather her up in his arms, rain kisses on her and tell her... Tell her that he felt... Damn. He couldn't. He couldn't love her. He could not allow himself to do so. It would be very easy to do so. But difficult too. Because what if something bad happened to her?

She was extremely competent, but there were things that very few people could survive, like, for example, a fully clothed fall into a near-frozen river in a blizzard. He couldn't bear the thought that she could have died today.

He stepped up his pace and Jim grunted, 'You're in a hurry today, Your Grace.'

Alex found a small smile for him. 'You not up to it, Jim?'

'I'm up to it, Your Grace. Just a little surprised.'

Alex nodded. He was surprised too. This morning had taught him something that he hadn't known. He hadn't believed that he could ever love another woman again after Diana. Now he knew that while he would always carry his grief for Diana with him, he was capable of loving again.

What he was *not* capable of, though, was coping with being in love. Because if Emma *had* died this morning, or even just been injured, it would have devastated him, and he'd only known her for a few weeks. If he allowed himself to make their marriage real it would destroy him if anything happened to her. And the way the boys were going, loving her as they already did, it would destroy them too. He just couldn't do it.

Emma had friends now. She was established socially, he hoped. They should probably move on to the next phase of their marriage. She could move to the dower house and begin to live independently. He would make clear to his friends and acquaintances that she should be respected as a member of their circle. Perhaps he would confide in Letitia as he already had in Gideon.

'Your Grace!'

'Jim?'

'You didn't tell me we'd be running.'

'Not running, Jim, just walking fast.'

Alex increased his pace even more, so that they were working too hard for speech or, importantly, further thought. Thinking was not pleasant today.

Some time later, as they skirted the edge of a small wood at the base of a hill, a bough broke under the weight of the snow it had been holding and fell just in front of them, scattering snow as it went.

The sensation of wet snow on his skin made him think of snowballs with Emma, rolling in the snow with Emma, making love to Emma a few yards away from a blizzard. Which was ridiculous, because he was thirty-three years old and he had encountered a lot of snow with a lot of different people; but it seemed that he couldn't get Emma out of his thoughts this afternoon.

He flexed his shoulders as some of the snow went down his neck and imagined her laughing at him. Damn, he'd miss her if he didn't see her any more. Perhaps he shouldn't make too hasty a decision; perhaps he should think more about their situation first.

They arrived shortly after that at the home of Caleb Wilson, one of Alex's tenant farmers. Caleb was an elderly man who had broken his leg badly a few weeks ago, tumbling from a shire horse that a man of his age really should not have been riding.

As Alex ducked his head to go through the doorway into the cottage's main room, having asked Jim if he would go and check on Caleb's livestock, he saw Caleb huddled in a chair close to a dying fire. There was a large pile of logs on the other side of the fire, but it looked as though Caleb wasn't mobile enough to be able to reach them.

Alex had made sure that all his less well-off tenants had a ready supply of firewood over the winter, so it had to be a mobility issue rather than a financial one. That or Caleb enjoyed freezing in his own home. Other than next to the fire, the room was barely any warmer than the temperature outside.

His heart going out to Caleb, but knowing from experience how proud he was, Alex clapped his hands together, and said, 'It's a cold day out there, Caleb. I'm chilled to the bone. Would you mind if I built your fire up? I'm not sure I'll be able to get through the rest of the day happily otherwise.'

'You're a good lad, Your Grace. Thank you.' Caleb produced a toothless grin for him, and Alex's heart twisted again. Sometimes his responsibility for all these good, decent people weighed on him particularly heavily.

'I hope you don't mind if I join you by the fire?' Alex drew up a stool and sat down next to the old man. 'How's your leg healing?'

Caleb had a lot to say, giving the impression of a man somewhat desperate for company. He would normally be busy all day, and would see his neighbours regularly too, but now with his broken leg he was at the mercy of how much time they could spare to visit him, and in conditions like this they wouldn't have a lot of time.

'Tess, my daughter-in-law, she's been in,' he said. 'She's a good woman, but she's busy with those bairns of hers.' He paused and stretched out a hand to Alex, who took it. 'You'll understand this, Your Grace. I always miss my Jeanie—' his wife had died about five years ago '—but it's at times like this, when I have thinking time, that I miss her even more.'

Alex was not in the habit of talking about his feelings but, looking at Caleb's lined face, into his faded blue eyes, he knew that at this moment he needed to make the effort for Caleb's sake. It didn't come naturally, though. And while he had experienced the terrible loss of his wife, at a horrifyingly early age, he'd never, due to his different station in life, found himself sitting all alone in the near-freezing, near-dark for hours on end.

'Yes. I was reflecting earlier today that too much thinking time is dangerous,' he said, feeling for words that would demonstrate to Caleb that he understood.

'It is. We need to move on with the future. You have your children and I have mine, and I have my grandchildren. We need to think about them, not the past. We're both lucky. Not everyone has children.'

Alex didn't want to think about the fact that he'd effectively prevented Emma from having children of her own. Unless, of course, she'd become with child as a result of their lovemaking this morning. How would he feel if she had? Pleased for her that she'd have a baby but utterly terrified that she'd die in childbirth, as Diana had.

He returned the squeeze of the hand that Caleb gave him and said, 'We might be lucky with our children, but the loss of one's life companion is very hard.'

'It is that.' They sat in silence for a moment, with Alex feeling quite useless, and then Caleb said, 'Thank you, Your Grace. Much appreciated.'

Maybe all Caleb needed from Alex was what he could

give him: his company, and the feeling that they were in the same boat.

He looked up as he heard a muffled sniff from Caleb, and reached over and squeezed his shoulder.

'Thank you again,' Caleb said after a few moments. 'I'm getting emotional in my old age. I just miss her.'

Alex clasped Caleb's hand and looked into the fire. Currently, he was dealing with life better than Caleb was. He'd reached a point where, while still grieving for Diana, he had been able to develop feelings for another woman and enjoy making love to her. He didn't want to regress, be like this again. He didn't want to be a lonely old man, missing his wife so deeply. He wanted to be happy, but not so happy that the loss of that happiness would cause a repeat of his devastation over Diana's death.

'I need to cheer myself up,' Caleb said. 'We have to let go, don't we, when we've lost someone?'

Alex nodded. 'Yes. We do.'

He wasn't talking about Diana, though. It was Emma whom he needed to let go of now. He hoped she wouldn't be hurt, but he had, after all, told her right from the beginning that he couldn't offer her anything more than his name and his protection.

If he and Jim had walked fast on the way there, now, on their way back to the castle, they'd almost give a horse a run for its money.

'May I ask if everything's all right, Your Grace?' Jim panted at one point.

'Certainly.' Alex didn't look at him; he just kept on marching, too fast for further thought.

He and Jim were very hot when they arrived back.

'Thank you for your company,' he said to Jim. 'Apologies if I walked a little fast.'

'I enjoyed it, Your Grace,' Jim said. 'Even if my feet didn't,' he added under his breath, as he headed off towards the stables with a slight limp.

Alex smiled at his departing back. Thank God he had staff who didn't stand on ceremony with him. If he didn't, he could end up as lonely as Caleb. He would make sure that he or someone else from his household visited Caleb regularly until his leg was mended.

Striding into the house, he was stopped by Lancing, who told him that Mrs Hardy had called for tea and had expressed a particular desire to see Alex, should he return before she left. She was currently in the green saloon with the duchess.

'Of course.' Alex could barely imagine a person to whom he'd less like to speak today, and was strongly tempted to turn tail, but he couldn't leave Emma to Mrs Hardy's mercies.

He entered the saloon just in time to hear Mrs Hardy, seated with her back to him, say to a rigid-looking Emma, 'And I must repeat: if you would like any advice on comportment, you know you only have to ask and I shall be very happy to guide you. I am, of course, the granddaughter of an earl. In my capacity as vicar's wife I am here to assist those less fortunate than myself, such as you with your background.'

Emma's eyes had widened as Mrs Hardy spoke. Now she said, one eye on Alex, 'I count myself incredibly fortunate to have you available to assist me should I require such help. Thank you.'

Alex knew that she was being sarcastic, and he knew that she would be able to laugh about Mrs Hardy's ridiculous rudeness, but he was nonetheless filled with real rage at how the woman had spoken to Emma; not least because he was scared that others would hear her express such thoughts and imitate her.

'You are indeed kind to make such an offer, Mrs Hardy,' he said, injecting ice into his voice.

Mrs Hardy turned her head very fast and then rose to her feet, wreathed in smiles, before curtseying. 'Your Grace,' she said, holding her hands out to him.

Alex ignored the hands. 'While you are kind, Emma has no need of your advice. Firstly, she is herself the granddaughter of an earl, through her mother, and also of a princess, through her father. I am certain that she is too well-bred to have discussed her breeding with you, so you were perhaps not aware of that.'

He could see Mrs Hardy's smile fall at his implied criticism and Emma, beyond her, smiling at him, her eyes beginning to dance.

'Secondly, of course, true breeding comes from within, and certainly from my perspective I have nothing but admiration for Emma's character and comportment, and I am sure that the vast majority of her acquaintance feel the same way. Good afternoon.' He moved back to the door and held it wide open and bowed to Mrs Hardy.

'I see that you are in a bad humour this afternoon, Your Grace,' she said, glaring. 'No doubt it is the weather. Much can be excused of a duke, fortunately.'

When she'd huffed herself out of the room, Alex closed the door behind her very firmly and sat down on a sofa opposite Emma.

'Thank you,' she said. 'That was spectacular.'

'I cannot regret my rudeness. The way she spoke to you was completely unacceptable.'

'She was so rude that I just wanted to laugh. But I was very glad that you were there to witness it, to share in my enjoyment.'

Alex laughed. '"Enjoyment" is a charitable word.'

There was a short silence between them.

They needed to talk.

He put his hands on his knees, and then lifted them to adjust his jacket. Perhaps he should have changed before they started this conversation. No, formal clothing would not have helped. He placed his hands back on his knees and crossed his legs, and then uncrossed them.

How to begin?

'How has your afternoon been?' Emma asked into the uncomfortable silence. 'I believe you went to visit other tenants?'

'Yes.'

Describing to Emma his visit to Caleb was a relief: it felt like a partial unburdening, or at least a sharing, of the responsibility Alex felt.

'So he's going to feel his loneliness greatly while he remains incapacitated with his broken leg?' Emma said when Alex had concluded the story of his visit.

He nodded.

'We should arrange for him to have regular visitors. Certainly, I shall visit him, perhaps with one or more of the children, by carriage if you think it appropriate?'

'Yes, I do, and indeed I trust you quite implicitly in your judgement in regard to the children.'

Emma's cheeks flushed. 'Thank you. That's quite the most lovely compliment anyone has paid me for a long time.'

This wasn't really how Alex had envisaged his conversation with Emma going, although he was very grateful to know that she would visit Caleb.

'We need to talk,' he said, more shortly than he'd intended.

'I am at your disposal,' Emma said, her smile gone.

Alex took a deep breath. And then said nothing for a while.

Emma straightened her shoulders and took a deep breath of her own.

'I feel,' Alex began eventually, 'that perhaps now might be a good time for you to move to the dower house.' He looked at her. 'If you would like to.'

No. He couldn't. He could not actually ask her to move out of his—now their—house. How could he have said that? Appalling.

'I'm sorry; that was unconscionable. Please don't move there, unless you'd like to. You might wish to do so. You might not. I'd like to make it very clear that I am, in fact, in no way asking you to move there. I thought that perhaps you would be more comfortable there. But of course you might feel that you would be more comfortable here.'

He stopped talking, aware that he was sounding like the imbecile he apparently was.

For a long moment, Emma just looked at him. Then she leaned forward a little, and said, 'I feel that now is a time for honesty.'

Oh, God.

'And, honestly, you were babbling.'

Alex pressed his lips together and nodded. After Mrs Hardy's departure, he'd sat down, planning to tell Emma that what had happened between them earlier today couldn't be repeated, and that he thought it would be best if she moved to the dower house. Or he thought that was what he'd been planning to say. Now he could barely even recollect what his thoughts had been.

Whatever the case, something had happened in the space of perhaps a minute, and now he didn't know what he wanted. He did know that he'd made an incredible mull of attempting to explain in a dignified fashion that he could offer Emma no further intimacy. All the dignity was on Emma's side.

'My observation,' she continued, 'is that you wanted to tell me that you regret what happened between us today and would prefer not to repeat it. You therefore thought that you wanted me to remove immediately to the dower house, but, on saying the words aloud, you realised that you were telling me that I had to leave your house, and since you are a kind person, you don't feel that you can, in fact, do that.'

'I...' Alex shook his head. And then nodded. Yes. She was probably right. She *was* right. But...

'I have something to say.' Emma was sitting very upright now. She looked very stern and very beautiful, and if he were a different man with a different life he would want nothing more than to take her in his arms and make slow, reverent love to her for the rest of the day. For the rest of time.

But there was no such thing as the rest of time, as both he and Caleb knew.

'Go ahead,' he said.

'It seems to me that you are still grieving the loss of your wife and still in love with her. I cannot compete with that, and I do not wish to compete with that. I agree that what happened this morning was a mistake. I am happy to remove to the dower house if that is what you deem best for both of us, and of course for the boys, but I am also perfectly content to remain in the main house, to live amicable but separate lives. Like you, I would not like to repeat this morning's mistake.'

Alex thought he saw her eyes glistening before she lowered her lids and studied her hands with seeming great interest. He wanted so much to correct her misapprehension that he couldn't love again. But if he told her he loved her he would be doing both himself and her a great disservice.

'Perfect,' he said.

He didn't even know what he was agreeing to.

## Chapter Sixteen

The snow disappeared almost overnight. The temperature rose too, and when Emma and the boys went outside in the late morning to begin a walk, Emma realised immediately that they would need to change their thick coats for lighter ones or be uncomfortably warm in the bright sunshine.

'It feels as though we dreamt the snow,' Freddie observed as they sat down on sun-dried grass, next to the lake at the far end of the lawns directly in front of the castle. 'It's so hot. But there was a blizzard this time yesterday.'

'I agree,' Emma said.

She did agree. At approximately this time yesterday, she and Alex had taken refuge in the barn and made love. Today, only four-and-twenty hours later, it was as though their lovemaking had never occurred. Well, not entirely; it wasn't something she would ever forget. But their relationship had in no way developed as a result of it. Well, it *had* developed, but backwards rather than forwards.

As Freddie had said, it now felt almost as though the whole thing had been a dream.

'Emma!' Harry had his face very close to hers and she jumped as he shouted. 'You weren't listening.'

'I'm so sorry,' she said. 'I was a little distracted thinking about the snow.'

*And your father. And the miracles he was working this time yesterday on my body.*

She shivered. No. She should try hard not to think about that again, and she should try *really* hard not to think about it in front of the boys.

She forced her mind away from Alex and said to Harry, 'Tell me again what you said and I promise you that I will listen very carefully.'

And she did concentrate very well on his surprisingly detailed monologue about dragonflies. She simply needed to apply herself carefully and she would soon be able to stop thinking about Alex in a romantic way. Hopefully.

By the afternoon, the last vestiges of the snow had melted away under a March sun as unseasonably strong as the snow had been, in direct contrast to the frost that seemed to be settling more and more around Emma's heart as the day wore on. An entire day spent with three lively young boys left little time for reflection, and yet, bit by bit, the full reality of what had happened yesterday, and her own and Alex's reactions to it, were permeating her brain.

Later, she couldn't help revisiting in her mind yet again the situation between her and Alex as she finished reading an excerpt from *Gulliver's Travels* to the boys in the nursery.

It had been as though an invisible force had drawn the two of them together. From her side at least it had been based on both a strong physical attraction and a thorough enjoyment—even love—of his company. Their lovemaking had been wonderful and, while Emma had no previous experience to draw on, she was certain that Alex had simulated nothing and had been equally as passionate as she in that moment.

However, where she had then known for certain that she was in love with him—a feeling that was increasingly settling inside her—he had clearly realised that she could never compare to his Diana. He had therefore done his best to inform her that they should henceforth lead separate lives. It was the only time she'd experienced him being inarticulate.

She sniffed.

'Emma, are you crying?' Harry pointed his chubby finger at her face.

Emma shook her head, wiped her fingers under both her eyes and said, 'I think the wind must have blown down the chimney and sent a little smoke from the fire in my direction.'

'Oh.' Harry climbed onto her lap and hugged her. Emma wrapped her arms around him and buried her face in his hair for a moment. Children's affection was so much more straightforward than that between adults.

Alex came in shortly afterwards to see the boys.

'Excuse me,' Emma said, directing a bland smile at them all. 'I must go and change before dinner.'

'And get the smoke out of your eyes where it made you cry,' Harry shouted.

'I think we might all be able to hear you without you shouting so loudly,' Alex admonished gently, avoiding looking directly at Emma.

Did she want to move to the dower house, she wondered as she closed the nursery door behind her.

She didn't want to live by herself. After her father had died, an elderly aunt had come to join her for her mourning period, and the two of them had lived together with her father's servants in splendid and very lonely isolation. Emma had no desire to live like that ever again.

She would also miss the boys, and she hoped she wasn't flattering herself in believing that they would miss her too; and they certainly should not be made to suffer. But she was sure they could be very happy with a new governess, and Alex clearly wanted her to go. And of course she didn't want to make him miserable by inflicting her presence on him.

Dinner was a miserable affair, involving many plates of delectable food for which Emma had absolutely no appetite, and stilted conversation with Alex. The highlight of their interaction was when a conversation about the next day's weather involved a small, unintentional pun involving crows on Alex's part, which they both realised at the same time and which caused them both to smile a little.

Other than that, Alex was very much living up to his Ice Duke sobriquet. Emma didn't feel as though she had the energy to coax him out of it, and she had far too much pride to try. If making love to her once had caused him to be like this, then that was the way it was. She could only be grateful that she'd had the strength to tell him that their lovemaking had been a mistake from her perspective too. If she was going to have to carry on seeing him regularly—and while that would be difficult, it wouldn't be as bad as not seeing him at all—she needed to keep her pride and dignity intact.

\* \* \*

After a miserable night, Emma was delighted at breakfast the next morning to receive a note from Letitia, asking her if she would like to visit the shops in Yarford with her that afternoon. She had her response written and dispatched within minutes of receiving the note.

A few hours later, she and Letitia met outside the draper's on Yarford's high street.

'I hear that they've just taken delivery of the most divine silks, medium-weight, from India, perfect for spring robes.'

Letitia pulled her into the shop.

'Where precisely in India do these come from?' asked Emma as the shopkeeper showed them different fabrics.

'I believe them to be from the Bengal and Gujarat regions,' he said.

After some detailed discussion on the different fabrics, Emma directed Letitia to some plain silks from Bengal and some more elaborate ones with flower designs from Gujarat, which she thought would be ideal for the dresses Letitia had in mind.

'I'm impressed. You're very knowledgeable about both silks and India,' Letitia told her.

'My grandmother was an Indian princess, and my grandfather met her travelling in India to buy silks and calicos for his textiles business, which my father inherited from him.'

'I see, and that's where your famous wealth came from? That's fascinating. Would you care to walk through the town with me for a while? I have so many questions to ask you.'

Emma hadn't realised until now quite how restricted she'd felt in polite company, having had it drummed into her by her aunt that she must not under any circumstances discuss *trade*. She'd spoken to Alex about her background, but very quickly after their marriage he had ceased to feel like *company* and had felt more like, well, family, she supposed.

'I do declare that I'd like to set up a factory myself,' Letitia enthused. 'Think how much pin money we could claim for ourselves. And, on a serious note, it's wonderful that you ensure such good working conditions and pay for the factory workers. It's so interesting to learn all these facts. There's so much wonderful history involved.'

Emma smiled at Letitia. Their conversation reminded her of ones she'd had with Alex, which just showed that she could be perfectly happy spending time with her friends rather than with him. Really, she could be perfectly happy maintaining only a distant relationship with him. She did not need him.

'The weather is so beautifully clement that I wonder whether we should continue our promenade for longer?' Letitia suggested.

'Certainly. I would like that.'

As they strolled, Emma asked Letitia to tell her more about the plans for her husband's land. She'd already learned that the fashionable, frivolous exterior Letitia presented to the world hid a shrewd brain and a strong interest in agricultural advances.

Letitia's shrewdness wasn't confined to agriculture.

'I do enjoy discussing all these things with Arthur,' she said as she concluded her thoughts on field enclosures and the introduction of different crops such as clover to increase soil productivity. 'Of course, whenever we disagree, we discover subsequently that he was wrong and I right. How are you and Alex settling down into married life?'

Emma blinked. Letitia was clever. Emma had not expected her to manoeuvre the conversation so easily in this direction.

'We...' She really wasn't sure what she wanted to say.

'It must be difficult, being married to a widower?' Letitia asked, considerably more tentatively than usual. Emma nodded. Suddenly, she wanted to hear anything that Letitia might know that she didn't. 'I know that he loved Diana very much. Still loves her very much. It must have been incredibly hard for him when she died.'

'Yes, he did and yes, it was.' Letitia paused, and Emma waited. 'Rumour did reach us, even here in the depths of Somerset, that you and Alex didn't have an entirely conventional beginning to your marriage. Although, what is convention in the ridiculous circles in which we move?'

'Indeed,' said Emma. She wanted to say, *Tell me everything you know about Alex and Diana, now.*

'We, Alex's friends here, all care very much about him. Well, not everyone cares about him. Mrs Hardy, for example, before her marriage cared a great deal about his title and wealth and nothing for his happiness, and is quite green with envy that you have succeeded where she did not. However, those of us who are his true friends do wish him every happiness, so we were, of course, a little concerned for him at first, on hearing about his very sudden wedding. But when we met you we were just delighted. I am selfishly delighted, because I like you so much as a friend for myself, and I'm also delighted for Alex, because the two of you seem so, well, so in love. Which is, of course, deeply unfashionable amongst the *ton*, but I'm unfashionable like that and so is Arthur, and so were Alex and Diana. And you and Alex seem so particularly well-suited.'

'Thank you,' said Emma faintly.

'The way he looks at you when you aren't looking at him is too adorable. And you do it to him too. The clearest sign that two people love each other.'

'Oh.' Emma would love to think that Letitia was right. And perhaps Alex *would* have loved her if he hadn't met Diana first. But he *had* met Diana first and that was that, and of course Emma couldn't begrudge him his marriage to her. He had the boys as a result of it, and they were wonderful.

'It is difficult, though—' Letitia flicked an imaginary something off her shoulder, as though she was trying to appear nonchalant, which gave Emma the very strong impression that she'd been planning whatever she was about to say for a while '—in the early days of a marriage, when you are not particularly well acquainted with each other, however easily you have tumbled into love. There must of necessity be a period of adjustment on both sides, which might feel quite difficult at times.'

'You're a wonderful friend to Alex,' Emma said, suddenly wanting to confide in Letitia. 'I do love him, and I do think that he might have loved me if he hadn't met Diana first. But he did. I'd like to tell you something in confidence.'

'Of course.' Letitia took Emma's hand.

'Alex and I do not have a real marriage.'

An image of Alex kissing her on the hay pushed its way to the front of Emma's mind, and she pushed it away again, hard.

'We made a bargain. He is wonderful, and kind, and

did not wish to see me ruined, so he offered me his name when someone else tried to compromise me, as perhaps you heard, but he made it very clear that he was unable to offer more than that. He suggested that if I would like to I could act as informal governess to his boys, and that is working very well. But we do not have a real marriage.'

'And yet,' murmured Letitia, 'when he looks at you he really does look like a man in love.'

Emma shook her head. 'He is a very good actor. As indeed am I. I am feeling a little despondent about our situation, but I think I've hidden my despondency very well from him. From everyone except you now.'

'Oh, Emma. It has been very little time. Love can grow. Perhaps he does not yet realise that he loves you.'

Emma shook her head. 'We have...explored our situation very thoroughly, and we have established together that we will not have an intimate marriage.'

'I'm so sorry.' Letitia squeezed her hand hard.

'Thank you, but I must not be an object of compassion. But for an accident of fate, Alex might not have been there that evening, and then we would never have met, and I would instead be either married to someone quite dreadful or working as a governess or indeed much worse. I count myself fortunate indeed and must never complain.'

'Emma, you have every right to complain, at least to yourself and to your closest friends, if the man you love does not love you. Although I believe that he does.'

Emma shook her head. 'All I need is some time to recover myself.'

An idea was dawning. She couldn't pretend to herself any more that it was going to be easy to see Alex every day in the near future.

'I think that I should perhaps make the journey to Lancashire to visit my family's factories and my cousins. And then perhaps I will journey to France.'

It would be practice for the much longer journey to India that she hoped to undertake in due course. She could visit Paris and the half-siblings she had never met, her mother's younger children. But even Letitia might not be open-minded enough not to be shocked if she described *that* scandal to her, so she wouldn't elaborate on that for now.

'Not alone, I trust?'

'Not alone, no. I will be accompanied by my maid, and perhaps two or three male servants for safety. And I will visit relatives, so that no scandal can possibly attach to my travels.'

'Or you could stay here a little longer first, so that you and Alex can get to know each other better?' Letitia suggested.

Emma shook her head. 'I don't think so.'

She and Alex had already got to know each other quite a lot better than she was going to admit to anyone. She needed some time away from him, to come to terms with her love for him coupled with his inability to love her. Travel would be the ideal distraction, and until then she would make herself very busy in preparing for her journey, together with visiting Alex's more vulnerable tenants and caring for the children.

The next few days passed in a blur for Emma.

During the daytimes she was very busy with the children, and with setting in train preparations for her journey. She also visited tenants, including Caleb Wilson and Eliza and her new baby.

Holding the baby caused Emma's stomach to twist horribly. She would have loved so much to have had the opportunity to bear and hold a baby of her own one day, but unless she was very lucky and last week's lovemaking led to pregnancy, she would never be in that position.

On the first two evenings, she and Alex dined together and made horribly desultory conversation, so on the third evening Emma sent word to him that she had the headache and thought it better to dine alone in her sitting room, and she did the same the next day.

And each night she struggled to sleep, due to the thoughts going round and round in her head, so before long she had extreme tiredness to add to her general misery.

Her misery increased when her monthly courses came and she had to accept that she wouldn't be having a baby.

She knew now, she thought one afternoon, as she walked back from visiting Caleb, that of course a journey to Lancashire wouldn't cure her of her love for Alex.

Somewhere along the way, she'd realised that the fact that her parents' love story had ended badly wasn't relevant to her own love story, or lack thereof. If Alex could love her, she knew that she would abandon her travel plans and stay in Somerset for ever with him rather than lose him.

She couldn't continue like this, and she would find it very difficult to be happy living in loneliness in the dower house, catching sight of him every so often.

What she should do was return to Lancashire and set up home there with Jenny, and make herself busy with local matters and visiting and hosting her friends.

Decision made, she felt her shoulders already less rigid and her step lighter. Perhaps she would allow herself one final dinner with Alex tonight. Not just dinner, if she was honest with herself. It would be one final attempt at trying to tempt him into falling in love with her.

If she didn't succeed tonight, well, she would have lost nothing, and tomorrow evening she would retire very early in preparation for leaving at dawn the morning after. She would tell no one in advance other than Jenny, so that Alex wouldn't make any kind of quixotic attempt at preventing her from going or accompanying her.

She dressed for dinner with care, choosing a new gown of lilac silk overlaid with delicately embroidered net. The dress suited her, she thought, regarding herself critically in the mirror, and, if there was a hint of grey shadow under her eyes from tiredness, Alex would, she hoped, be distracted by the very flattering neckline of the dress.

It was perfect: it looked nice without being too overtly dressy, the ideal dress for a duchess trying for one final time to...yes, seduce her own husband.

At the very least, she decided, as Jenny brushed her hair into an elaborate chignon, she would tell him tonight that she cared greatly about him, so that, even if her seduction of him didn't work, he would have that memory of her. Even if he couldn't love her, she didn't want him to think that she couldn't love him.

Her heart was thudding in her throat as she descended the grand staircase for dinner.

'His Grace is still above stairs,' Lancing informed her as she waited nervously by the great fireplace in the drawing room opposite the dining room.

'I will await him in the dining room,' she said.

It was irregular, but surely she could do as she wished

in what was—for now—her home, and standing there alone was not enjoyable.

Shortly after she sat down, Lancing brought her a note, her name written on the envelope in Alex's distinctive hand.

Emma stared at it for a moment, before opening it slowly, quite sure that she wasn't going to want to read the contents.

Alex had written that he expected she would be eating in her own sitting room again this evening, but just in case, he wanted to let her know that he had supped early, in his study, and was now setting off to visit Gideon for a quiet evening of cards.

'Thank you, Lancing,' Emma managed to say around the enormous lump that had appeared in her throat.

And then, for Alex's sake more than her own, to avoid more gossip amongst the servants than there had to be, she sat in solitary state and ate her dinner. Which she supposed, thinking about it—and there wasn't a lot else to do than think while she ploughed miserably through several dishes—was exactly fitting for her last full evening under the same roof as Alex.

## Chapter Seventeen

The next morning, back from a furiously fast crack-of-dawn gallop across his land, which had afforded him only short-lived respite from thinking about Emma, Alex shoved open a side door to the castle and crashed straight into Emma and Harry.

His superior size and speed knocked them both off balance, and he shot his arms out to hold on to them both, so that for a moment the three of them were effectively locked in a three-way hug, tangled up with his riding crop.

'Papa, you were *running*,' Harry said, throwing his arms round Alex's legs to join in with the hug.

'I imagine that he was in a hurry.' Emma was very much *not* joining in with the hug. Her arms and hands were very firmly clamped to her sides and from where he still had an arm around her shoulders, Alex could feel that her entire upper body had tensed.

'Yes, I was. Very silly of me. I apologise.' Alex let go of Emma fast and swooped Harry up into his arms. 'Where are you off to?'

'Emma has been telling us about Maggan and sailing. We're going to the lake to imagine it's the ocean and think about sailing round it.'

'Maggan?' Alex queried.

'Magellan. I'm killing two birds with one stone—history and geography—and talking about his circumnavigation of the globe.'

'The first ever circumnavigation?' Alex thought he remembered learning about Magellan.

'Yes, we believe so, although of course we don't *know* that the Vikings did not sail all the way around the world.'

'I want to be a Viking,' Harry shouted.

Emma laughed, not catching Alex's eye, and said, 'We should go and find your brothers.' As Alex put Harry down, she glanced at him. 'Their nurse is with the boys. I did not send them to the lake alone.'

Alex shook his head. 'I had not even questioned it in my mind. I have full confidence in your care of them.'

Emma's eyes met his for a long moment and then she said, 'Thank you.'

Alex couldn't take his eyes from hers. One would never tire of looking into their rich brown depths. 'No. Thank *you*. The peace of mind is wonderful.'

It was the only thing that made up for the torture of her still being here in the castle. To be fair, it was a big thing. And the fact that she was so good with the boys did make it very difficult to countenance the idea of her entire removal from their lives. They would still be able to see her every day if she were living in the dower house, but he would not be so conscious of her presence.

'We must go and join the others,' Emma said again, pulling her eyes from his.

'Yes. Of course.' Alex put his son down and Harry immediately put his hand into Emma's.

Alex couldn't help remaining in the doorway for a few moments to watch the two of them as they walked across the lawn. He was indeed lucky that Emma was educating his boys, and with such enthusiasm. He wouldn't mind listening to her lesson on Magellan himself.

After a good hour of dull correspondence at his desk in the library, during which Emma intruded into his thoughts more than he would have liked, he stood up and walked over to where his father—a keen historian— had kept his world history books. Sure enough, after a few minutes of searching, he found an entire book that seemed to be devoted to the life and travels of Magellan.

The book was written in Spanish. Or maybe Portuguese; Alex was not particularly familiar with any of the Iberian languages. It might still be of interest to Emma and the boys, though. It included a number of interesting maps and, knowing Emma, she might well turn out to be proficient in whichever language this was.

It wouldn't be hugely respectful to the memory of his father, or indeed to anyone who might aspire to own such a fine volume, to take it outside on what was now a drizzly morning and possibly ruin it, so he would wait until Emma and the boys came inside before either taking it up to the nursery to show it to them or inviting them into the library to look at it.

Just before luncheon, his correspondence completed for the time being—praise be—he decided to go up to the nursery to show the boys the book.

When he got there the door was slightly ajar and Emma was sitting in an armchair, in full flow, still on the subject of Magellan. The boys were rapt in front of her. Even Freddie's habitual air of nine-year-old cynicism had disappeared.

'Yes, we do remember him today as a very brave man and a hero,' she said, apparently in response to a question from one of the boys. 'While he did die during the voyage—which was very sad—he died doing something he loved, and I'm sure that he would never have regretted his choice to make the journey. It's important to stay as safe as one can, of course, but if one doesn't take any risks at all, one risks never being truly happy.'

Alex stilled. She might have been talking about him. Perhaps she *was* talking about him. No, of course she wasn't; he was being vain. Perhaps she was talking about herself. Or perhaps, and more likely, she was answering a final question about Magellan and attempting to instil some wisdom into the boys.

Her words had resonated strongly with him, though, as she spoke. Would he be better off taking the risk of allowing himself to love again, or just not loving again? With greater risk came the possibility of greater reward, as well as greater misery. How brave was he? Brave enough to allow himself to love Emma and live a rich life full of joy—for now, anyway—or not? Was it better to live a duller, less happy life, but one which would not then be marred by loss?

He was beginning to think that Emma was right, that one should be brave.

He stepped into the room and cleared his throat. 'I found a book in the library that might be of interest to all of you,' he told them, holding it out.

'This is beautiful,' breathed Emma.

'Do you know what language it's written in?' Alex asked.

'Catalan,' she said, not looking up from the book. 'It's surprisingly easy to read if you speak French, much easier than Castilian Spanish, in fact.'

Alex nodded, pleased that he'd been right. Of course she knew.

He continued to be preoccupied with his thoughts as he ate a solitary luncheon. When he had finished, he stood up, knowing what he wanted to do this afternoon.

He sent word to the stables to ask for Star to be saddled for him, and then made his way there. He felt as though he was in too much of a rush to walk.

Twenty minutes later, he dismounted outside Caleb Wilson's cottage.

Caleb was limping around the corner of the building with the aid of a stick. 'Good afternoon, Your Grace. Good of you to come to visit.'

'My pleasure, and I'm delighted to see you on your feet again.'

'It certainly makes life more interesting.' Caleb nodded his head in the direction of his chicken house. 'I'm about to collect some eggs. Just trying to work out how to do it with my stick.'

'Perhaps you'd like some help?' Alex looped Star's reins around a tree.

'I would that.'

'You know,' said Alex a few minutes later, 'I haven't collected eggs since I was very young. There's something very enjoyable about it. I think my boys would very much like to visit you and meet your chickens.'

'They came yesterday, Your Grace. Did Her Grace

not tell you? We had a marvellous time. We agreed to the visit in advance, just to make sure that I wouldn't be out gallivanting when they arrived.'

Caleb roared with laughter at his own joke and Alex smiled, enjoying Caleb's humour and completely unsurprised that Emma had been to visit without trumpeting it, and that she'd brought the boys too.

Eggs—including some beautiful pale blue ones—collected, Alex accompanied Caleb inside his cottage, warm from the now very well-made fire in the corner.

'I have a question for you, Caleb,' he said, accepting a glass of ale. 'I want advice, I suppose.'

'Go on, Your Grace.'

'I wanted to ask...' He stopped and shook his head. 'No, I realise now that it's a stupid question, and one to which I already know the answer.'

Caleb looked at him steadily, but didn't speak.

'I was going to ask whether you had any regrets about marrying Jeanie because you've been so sad since you lost her. But of course you don't.'

'No, I don't. Do you regret loving and marrying Diana, Your Grace?'

'No. I don't.'

'But you're scared of loving again and losing again.' Caleb's words were a statement, not a question.

Alex nodded. 'I think I'm beginning to be less scared, though. Who knows what the future holds?'

'I count myself fortunate, young man, that I've had the happiness I have. I wouldn't have had that happiness without Jeanie, so I could never regret anything. I do miss her, as you know, and I always will, but she lives on in my memories of all our wonderful years together and in the lives of her children and grandchildren.'

'You're very wise, Caleb.'

'Of course I am, Your Grace. I learnt most of what I know about life from Jeanie, and she was a very wise woman. Your new duchess is another wise woman.'

Alex nodded again. 'She is indeed.'

'Seems to me that you might have something to tell her?'

'Yes, I think I do.' He was going to need to be careful with his words, though, not rush straight into conversation and say something stupid. He would spend the evening planning what to say and then he'd ask Emma tomorrow if they could talk.

He'd allowed her to believe that he was unable to love her because he was still grieving for Diana. He needed to explain how wrong he'd been and hope that she felt the same way about him as he felt about her, and that she would believe that he wouldn't be so stupid again.

Alex slept better than he had for a long time that night and woke later than usual. He partook of a leisurely breakfast before going in search of Emma and the boys, none of whom he had seen yet today.

He found the boys in the nursery with their nurse, but there was no sign of Emma.

'I wonder if you know where Emma is?' he said.

'She's going on a journey,' Harry told him very seriously.

'A journey?' Alex replied, not really paying a lot of attention.

He'd spend a few minutes with the boys now, and then ask Lancing if he knew where Emma was. He realised that he didn't know her daily routine; he'd been too busy recently trying to distance himself from her.

'She's gone to see the factories,' John said.

'In Lancashire,' Freddie clarified. 'She said we can visit her there one day when we're old enough, but she needs to discuss it with you first.'

'I'm afraid I don't understand,' Alex said, frowning.

'Emma has gone on a journey to visit the factories in Lancashire,' Freddie repeated slowly, as though to a person with limited comprehension. 'She's gone for a very long time, but we will see her again, because we can visit her there and she can come and visit us here too.'

Damn. *Damn*.

Alex stood up. 'I have to go.'

He went straight to the library for some solitude in which to think. Why had she not told him she was going? She'd told the boys. She'd said they could visit her. But she couldn't have left for good? No, surely not. They must have misunderstood what she'd said. They'd definitely misunderstood; they were only young. She wouldn't have just gone. He was quite certain of that.

A trickle of fear was making its way down his spine, though.

He found himself pacing back and forth beneath the long shelves, his mind going in circles. The library was on two floors, the upper floor accessed by narrow wooden staircases at each end of the room. He walked up one flight of stairs and along the gallery, not pausing to look at any of the books, and then down the flight at the other end.

This was silly, he realised on his second turn past the long windows in the middle of the room. He should ask Lancing now what he knew of Emma's plans. He would word his question so that he didn't sound as though he had absolutely no idea whether or not his own wife had left for Lancashire.

He turned towards his desk to ring for Lancing and saw an envelope propped up against the inkwell, with the word 'Alex' written on it. He recognised the script as Emma's, from letters she had left out to be franked.

The trickle of fear that he'd been feeling turned into a veritable deluge of panic as he pulled a single sheet of paper out of the envelope.

*Dear Alex,*
*I had planned to tell you this in person, but in the end did not find an opportunity to do so.*

*I wanted to let you know that I have decided to travel back to Lancashire and make my home there.*

*I have made arrangements with Nurse to continue the boys' studies according to the notes that I have left, and hope that you will soon find a replacement governess.*

*I have come to love the boys very much and did not wish to leave them. I hope that they will not miss me—but am not sure that growing up with the example of our distant marriage will be good for them.*

*I—like you, I imagine—would hope that they will grow up to marry for companionship and intimacy, or not at all, should that be their choice.*

*I have told them that I am leaving, and that I hope you will allow them to visit me in Lancashire, where the landscapes are quite different from those in Somerset but equally beautiful.*

*I have left the kittens in the stables so that the*

*boys are able to continue to play with them. They have grown quite attached to them, and I did not want to add to any loss they might feel on my departure.*

*I must thank you again for your great kindness in marrying me and saving me from what would, as you rightly said, have certainly been an unpalatable alternative. I will remain forever in your debt.*
*Yours,*
*Emma*

Momentarily stunned, Alex re-read the letter.
She'd left. Left *him*.
Or had she in fact been driven away by his effective rejection of her after they'd made love? Would he ever know now?

What if something bad happened to her on the journey? What if she was set upon by highwaymen? A duchess travelling with only a small entourage must inevitably attract a great deal of attention. She would no doubt have her pistol, which he was sure wouldn't help her in the slightest in such an eventuality.

What if the carriage developed a fault, or one of the horses were injured, or startled, or any one of a number of things, and Emma were injured herself?

What if something truly terrible happened to her and she never knew that he loved her?

He put the letter back in the envelope and then took it out again.

What if, in fact, she didn't love him?

He read the letter for a third time. What would she have written if she *did* love him? If she *didn't*? And what if there was nothing that he would be able to say to convince her to return?

He needed to stop imagining catastrophes and he needed to know.

He stood up, almost knocking his heavy oak chair over in his haste. He was at the library door in a few strides and at the stables only a couple of minutes after that, instructing Jim to prepare Star.

He needed to leave immediately.

The hard ride helped calm the very worst of his fears. By the time he was passing by Bristol he was able to believe it was highly unlikely that any accident would befall Emma. It was also unlikely that he would fail to catch her up or indeed ride straight past her while she stopped for a rest, because, even journeying with just one carriage, a travelling duchess would always occasion comment.

Alex stopped regularly to ask if she had been seen, and ascertained that she was heading directly north. She'd set off very early this morning, and had two or three hours' advantage over him, but the chaise had been built for Alex's mother in her later years and had been designed for luxurious comfort rather than speed.

Perhaps Alex would ask Emma if she would like a new travelling carriage, one designed to her own specification and needs. One built for more regular travel, if that was what she'd like.

When he thought about it, she'd fitted herself into the extremely small space he'd made for her in his life and tried very hard to make the best of it, while he had made little effort to accommodate her.

He spurred Star to go faster, desperate to catch Emma.

As the morning ended, he began to wonder where she would take her luncheon. There was no sign of her at the first two staging inns at which he enquired, and as he left the second one he wondered whether somehow he'd missed her. It was busy and the people at this inn hadn't been able to say either way whether she'd passed by on the road outside.

And then, at the third inn, he found her. Accompanied by Jenny, she was leaving the inn as he arrived in a flurry of dust in the courtyard.

He dismounted, handed Star's reins to an ostler, and strode forward.

'Emma.'

'Oh!' She hadn't been looking in his direction when he arrived and clearly hadn't realised that it was him.

'Alex. Is something wrong? Has something happened to one of the boys? No, you'd be with them if something had.'

'Nothing has happened.' Other than that he'd come to his senses. Hopefully not too late. 'I came to speak to you.' He looked around. 'I wondered if we could talk somewhere, alone.'

## Chapter Eighteen

Emma stared at Alex, standing in front of her, sternly handsome in his riding garb. What was he doing here? Was it a coincidence that he was here? Had he been planning to journey north anyway? Surely not. It seemed a lot more likely that he'd actually ridden all the way here to speak to her. About what, though? Did he think that she ought not to move to Lancashire? Was he worried about the scandal that might ensue?

He was looking at her, bright-eyed, his eyebrows slightly raised, as though he was waiting for the answer to a question.

'Would you be happy for us to talk in private?' he said.

Oh, yes, he *had* been waiting for the answer to a question.

Emma didn't want to speak to him. Even just seeing him here in front of her hurt. But she'd left him with no notice and she owed him a lot.

She drew a deep breath and said, 'Yes.'

'Thank you,' he said, smiling faintly.

He held out his arm to her and after a moment's hesitation she took it, trying not to react to the feel of the corded muscle in his forearm.

'Perhaps inside? In a private room.'

'Of course.'

Her voice sounded a lot steadier than she felt on the inside. She had no idea how she was going to respond to whatever he had to say. If he wanted her to return and live in the dower house, she didn't know whether she could bear to go. He must have something of note to say, though; it was hard to believe that he would have ridden *ventre à terre* such a long way just to say goodbye in person.

The landlord, who'd been very kind to Emma and Jenny, was now bowing deeply in front of the two of them.

'We'd like to be shown to a private parlour, please,' Alex said.

'Of course, Your Grace. Allow me just a few moments to make one ready.'

Shortly afterwards, there was a small commotion. It seemed that several young men dressed in aspiring Corinthian style had been asked to leave the room they were in.

'Alex, we can't—' Emma began.

'We can,' he said. 'Good afternoon, Giles.' He nodded at one of the men. 'Younger brother of a friend of mine,' he told Emma. 'They're young and fit and can very happily go somewhere else. It cannot be possible that what they have to say is as important as what I have to say.'

'Oh.' Emma was beginning to feel so overcome that it was a good job that she had Alex's strong arm for support.

'The room is ready, Your Grace,' the landlord announced a very short time later, having had what must have been almost every member of staff in the entire inn flying around with cloths and brooms, while Alex and Emma stood in uncomfortable silence in the inn's entrance hall.

'Thank you.' Alex pressed several coins into his hand and held the door wide for Emma to enter the room.

She walked in ahead of him and over to the window, which looked out onto an inner courtyard, which was populated by chickens and goats. She clutched the windowsill for support for a moment, feeling momentarily lightheaded.

She heard the door click closed and felt goosebumps from head to toe. This was it. The moment. Alex was about to say whatever it was he wanted to say to her. This could be the last conversation they ever had.

Would she have the strength to tell him now in person that she loved him? Just so that he knew? She'd wanted to tell him before she left, but hadn't found the words to include the sentiment in her letter.

He joined her at the window, standing at her side, perhaps two feet away from her, and then…said nothing.

Emma waited.

Alex cleared his throat twice, but still…nothing.

'This is a very pretty view, isn't it?' Emma said eventually, unable to take any more of the silence, but not wanting to say anything that would precipitate the conversation she knew she didn't want to have. She pointed out of the window. 'I particularly like those black chickens.'

'Delightful,' Alex said. 'Emma…'

She sensed him turn to face her.

'Emma,' he repeated.

'Yes?' She turned her head in his direction, but couldn't bear to look at him properly.

'Emma.'

She looked at his face and her breath caught in her throat. He was gazing at her with a very tender look in his eyes and smiling a crooked little half-smile that caused her...

That caused her to *hope*.

And that hope made her stomach clench uncomfortably and her heart beat faster.

'Thank you for agreeing to speak to me,' he said. 'I followed you here because I want to tell you something.'

'Yes?' Emma found herself clutching the windowsill again.

'What I want to say is...'

What was *wrong* with him? Whatever it was, she just wanted him to get on with it now.

*'Yes?'*

'Um.' And he stopped again.

For goodness' sake.

Emma was on the brink of screaming, *Tell me*, when Alex very suddenly went down on one knee in front of her. She gasped and put her hands to her mouth.

Alex reached up and took her hands while Emma tried to squash the enormous hope now blossoming inside her, just in case, somehow, she was misreading the signs.

Alex cleared his throat. 'This is the way it should have been,' he said, holding her hands tightly. 'What you deserve, and what I would have done if I had already known you and learned not to be scared.'

'Scared?' Emma was so stunned by seeing Alex on his knee before her that she felt as though she'd entirely lost her wits.

'When I met you, I was scared of grieving again the way I grieved after Diana died. I didn't know whether or not I could ever fall in love again, but I did know that I was determined not to, because I didn't want to lay myself open to the pain of loss again, and love does often give rise to grief.'

Emma nodded, unable to speak but still hoping.

'Since we stumbled into each other's lives I've learned two big things.' He drew her towards him. 'Firstly, I learnt that I was able to fall in love again, because I fell in love with you. I know that I allowed you to believe that I was still in love with Diana, and I suppose I am, or at least with her memory, but I'm also deeply in love with you. I was scared to allow myself to become close to you. But I'd already fallen in love with you, and I realised that without you in my life I wouldn't be happy. I overheard you talking to the boys about Magellan and bravery. *I* need to be brave. I want a full, happy life, with you, not an emotionally safe but empty one without you.'

Emma was beginning to smile.

'What I'm trying to say, in a very verbose way, is that I love you. I love you so much, Emma. I love your smile. I love your passion for knowledge. I love the way you tilt your head to one side when you're considering how to reply to me when I've annoyed you. I love your kindness. And in addition to that, I would like to be married to you, properly. If we weren't already married, I would be proposing to you now.'

'Oh,' said Emma.

She could hardly breathe and she could barely process Alex's words. This was everything she could have hoped for and indeed so much more. She sniffed, but a tear still plopped out and landed on their hands. She sniffed again and more tears fell.

Alex folded his lips together and swallowed, and then said, 'Emma?'

'Tears of happiness,' she said.

'Are you sure?'

'Yes.' She sniffed again, in probably a very unalluring way, but Alex just smiled lovingly at her.

Goodness. She hadn't actually replied to him. 'I love you too,' she said, rushing the words out.

'Oh, thank God.' Alex was beginning to beam. 'I was starting to worry that you were crying tears of pity and that you just wanted to get away from me.'

'I *did* want to get away from you, but only because I found it too difficult being near you and yet so far from you.'

'I'm sorry. That was my fault. I was stupid.'

Emma shook her head. 'You weren't stupid. You're a widower. That's difficult.'

'I *was* stupid. But fortunately I came to my senses. I had actually worked out yesterday—before you left—that I wanted to tell you I love you and ask you to live properly with me as my wife. But in a further act of stupidity, to compound all the rest of it, I decided to wait until today to tell you. And then I discovered that you'd gone.' Alex stood up and shook his legs. 'Deeply unromantic, I know, but that floor is both hard and uneven.'

Emma laughed and sniffed again, and then Alex drew her into his arms. He held her against his beautifully solid chest for a long time, with his cheek resting against the top of her head. And then he moved a little, tipped her chin up with his finger and leaned his head down to hers.

Their kiss was different this time. There was the knowledge that it would be good, the knowledge that they both wanted it and that they loved each other. And there was also the knowledge that they could take things to their natural conclusion, and that that would be good too—truly wonderful, in fact.

It was gentle at first, their lips just brushing. Emma almost sighed into the kiss. She wrapped her arms round Alex's neck and he held her very tightly. And then their kiss deepened, their tongues exploring, their hands moving too. There was physical urgency, but it was also as though they both knew that they had time now, and that they should enjoy fully every stage of their lovemaking.

The kiss went on for a long time, the two of them moulded together in front of the window. And then Alex ran a hand up from Emma's waist until it came to rest on the underside of her breast. Even through her dress his touch caused her to shiver, both from what he was doing with his thumb, causing her nipple to tighten, and from the promise of more to come.

And then with both his hands he took her round the waist and lifted her. She found herself with her legs wrapped around his waist, pressed against the wall, with Alex lifting her skirts with one hand to reach between her legs.

'What would you like to do now?' he murmured into her neck.

'I don't have the words,' she gasped as he bit her very gently, while plunging a finger somewhere very moist deep inside her.

'Come home with me.'

'Yes,' she said, beginning to pant.

'But first—' he kissed her mouth again and deepened his touch, and Emma moaned against him '—I think we should take a room here, now, for the night. Just one room.'

'Anything,' Emma managed to say, judders running through her as he touched her deeper and deeper.

'I love you, my duchess.'

'I love you too.'

# *Epilogue*

*Venice, February 1821*

'This is wonderful,' Emma breathed, peeking out of the window of their *palazzo* bedchamber at the carnival in St Mark's Square beneath them.

'You're wonderful,' Alex said, coming to stand behind her and putting his arms round her waist, and looking over her shoulder.

The square was full of puppet theatres and all sorts of performers, including acrobats, tightrope walkers and clowns.

She turned to face him and slid her arms around his neck. 'Thank you so much for arranging this tour.'

They had held a ceremony to repeat their wedding vows on the first anniversary of their London wedding, and Alex had wished to mark their anniversary every year from then on.

On the third anniversary of their wedding, he'd presented Emma with an intricately embroidered mask like those worn at the many masquerades held at the carnival in Venice, knowing that it was an aspect of the Grand Tour that she'd particularly wanted to see, and wanting to give her a clue to the fact that he was planning that they would go on a Grand Tour of their own. And now this year, on their fourth anniversary, here they were in Venice.

He knew that Emma also harboured a strong desire to travel to India, and he did wish to gratify that desire in due course, but it had seemed wise to venture 'only' to Europe for their first foray into travel abroad with, as it turned out, an extremely large entourage.

They were accompanied by their children—they now had twin daughters as well as the boys—and attendant nurses, footmen, grooms, chefs, and others, as well as the stray dog, the abandoned bear cub and the indigent juggler that they—Emma—had collected along the way. For someone who was normally so pragmatic and unfussy, Emma did not travel particularly lightly.

'There's no need to thank me. Thank *you* for being my wife. I'm enjoying our tour.'

Suddenly looking serious, Emma said, 'I really hope you *are* enjoying it. I mean, you seem to be, but I know that you love our corner of Somerset and would happily stay there for evermore without venturing further afield.'

'No.' Alex shook his head. 'I do, of course, love Somerset, and, yes, I am of course a reluctant traveller in anticipation of any journey.'

*Reluctant* was an understatement when it came to his crossing the English Channel. The only person on their boat who was a worse traveller than him in a storm at sea had been Emma. While the rest of their party had been perfectly happy on the boat, the two of them had spent the entire crossing green at best and hideously ill at worst, and had been united in an immediate decision to make the rest of their trip over land only.

'But from the moment the ground stopped rocking beneath us after we disembarked the boat—' it had taken until some time after they'd arrived at Emma's mother's very bohemian but quite delightful villa in Paris for them both to lose the sensation that they were on a rocking boat '—I've loved our journey. My first Grand Tour was good; this is wonderful.'

'What's different about it?' asked Emma, twinkling at him and pressing her body to his, then kissing along his jawline while she ran one hand down his back before bringing it to rest on his backside. 'And, yes, I am indeed fishing for compliments.'

Alex smiled at the promise in her actions and reached down and kissed her full on the mouth, and slid one hand into her hair and cupped her breast with the other. 'I think we could spare a few moments before we go to the masquerade.'

He picked her up and crossed the room with her to land her right in the middle of their canopied bed. He lowered himself over her and began to rain kisses on her eyelids, her nose, her mouth, and down her neck, while she smiled and wriggled and pulled his shirt out of his pantaloons, and he applied four years' worth of expertise to undoing her stays as quickly as he could.

And then, as he traced his fingers around the underside of her breasts, smiling at the way she responded and then groaning as she reached for him inside his open breeches, he remembered that he had a serious point to make.

'What's different about this tour?' he said, still caressing her and smiling as he saw her eyes glaze a little. 'The opportunity to make love very regularly to my beautiful wife is, of course, one difference, but the greatest difference is the chance to share all the different spectacles and experiences with you and witness your enjoyment of them. With you as my companion, every journey that I take will always be better.'

Emma focused her eyes on him and smiled her beautiful smile. 'Thank you,' she said. 'And I, in my turn, know that I couldn't ask for a better companion to share this or any tour with. Nor a better husband to share my life with. I love you, Alex.'

'I love you too.'

He kissed her on the lips again. And then she gasped as, very deliberately, he began a slow but very enthusiastic demonstration of his physical love for her.

\* \* \* \* \*

# HISTORICAL

*Your romantic escape to the past.*

## Available Next Month

**Betrothed In Haste To The Earl** Liz Tyner
**The Wallflower's Last Chance Season** Julia Justiss

---

**Miss Fairfax's Notorious Duke** Eva Shepherd
**Debutante With A Dangerous Past** Samantha Hastings

Available from Big W, Kmart, Target,
selected supermarkets, bookstores & newsagencies.
OR call 1300 659 500 (AU), 0800 265 546 (NZ) to order.

Visit **millsandboon.com.au**

Keep reading for an excerpt of a new title
from the Historical series,
THE LADY BEHIND THE MASQUERADE
by Diane Gaston

## Chapter One

*Paris—November 1818*

The woman tapped the mother-of-pearl counter pieces against the green baize of the gaming table, waiting for the dealer to flip a card on to the three in front of her.

Marcus Wolfdon—Wolf to his friends—leaned against the wall watching her, admiring the concentration in her incredibly dark eyes. She was counting cards, he would wager on it, even though he rarely wagered on anything. She was calculating the probability of her hand coming in under twenty-one. Not cheating, precisely, but giving her a bit of an edge in vingt-et-un.

Wolf frowned. He did not believe any gambling establishment would long tolerate players having an edge, especially this Paris casino, filled with Englishmen like himself, enjoying Paris after Napoleon and enduring the resentment of the Frenchmen running the place.

Wolf knew all about the undercurrent of resentment throughout the city. He was an aide to Sir Charles Stuart, Britain's Ambassador to France, and was aware of every violent incident of French against English. Wolf very much preferred observing this woman, and he was quite at liberty to do so.

His friend Harris had insisted Wolf come with him to this place, then Harris sat down to a high-stakes game of whist and promptly forgot him. Unless Wolf wanted to wager his own funds—which he did not—Wolf had nothing else to amuse him but the mysterious woman playing vingt-et-un.

She was quite intriguing. Her fair skin reminded him of a Sèvres porcelain vase he'd seen in a shop earlier that day. There was a hint of vulnerability to the set of her lush pink lips, but intelligence shone in the depths of those chocolate-brown eyes, an intelligence that bespoke knowledge beyond her years. She looked younger than his twenty-five years, but it was obvious she was no green girl.

Most intriguing was the essence of mystery about her. It attracted him like iron shavings to a magnet.

Wolf fully engrossed himself in speculation about her. She appeared to have come to the casino alone, as had other gaily dressed females. The others, however, attended less to the games of chance than to the Englishmen, batting darkened eyelashes at them in frank invitation.

'*Je n'ai pas d'argent*. I have no money,' he told the few who'd sidled up to him. By no means did he intend to let them know the contents of his purse. It needed to last him until his next pay. Soon enough he was ignored by the *filles de la nuit*.

The vingt-et-un woman took no notice of the men in the room. She rarely moved her eyes from the play of the cards. Wolf, therefore, was at leisure to appreciate the décolletage exposed by a gown scandalous by London standards. Her rich auburn hair was half atop her head, half loose, flowing down to caress creamy shoulders. She was as daringly attired as the women who coveted his purse, but as single-minded in her play as the most dedicated gamester.

Her face betrayed little emotion as she waited for the dealer's hit. He snapped the next card from the deck, placing it in front of her. Wolf watched her eyes lose a bit of their strain. She nodded almost imperceptibly. The dealer glanced from the cards to her face to the cards again. She had sixteen points showing. Slowly the dealer turned up his hidden card. A queen of hearts, giving him twenty-one.

The woman glanced up at the dealer, shocked. Wolf straightened. She snapped her card over, revealing a hand of twenty points. The other players looked disappointed but undisturbed.

The deal began again, two cards to each player. The woman tossed in her two counter pieces. Her hand showed a king. The dealer went round again, but she held with her two cards. The woman's gaze did not leave the dealer's face as he dealt himself twenty points. She revealed her hidden card. A nine. Nineteen points losing to the dealer's twenty.

She stood, her colour high as she glared at the dealer. Wolf thought for certain she would speak, but she abruptly turned away and left the room. He started after her, momentarily impeded by two of the *filles de la nuit* who stumbled against him. He hurried past them, finding her in the supper room seated at a table alone. A servant brought a bottle of wine to the table and only one glass.

Wolf crossed the room.

*'Pardon, madame,'* he said.

## The Lady Behind The Masquerade

She looked up, her face still flushed.

He spoke in French. 'I could not help but notice. The dealer cheated, did he not?'

'Yes.' She gave a Gallic shrug of her shoulder. She looked at him a long time, as if making a decision. She gestured for him to sit. *'Monsieur...?'*

'Wolfdon,' he responded, giving her a smile other women deemed charming. He refrained from offering more detail, such as being aide to the British Ambassador, or son and heir of an English baronetcy. One could never tell who among these French still despised nobility, even as lowly a rank as baronet. 'May I have the honour of knowing your name?'

She hesitated, averting her gaze. 'Fleur,' she finally said, the idea coming, no doubt, from the *fleur de lis* pattern on the papered walls around them.

He conveyed through his voice and by his glance at the wallpaper that he knew the name was false. 'Madame Fleur.'

She lifted her wine glass to her lips.

She had allowed the *'madame'* to go uncorrected, but, since she was inclined to disguise her identity, he could not depend upon this meaning she was married or widowed.

He signalled to the servant to bring another glass. 'You did not confront the dealer, *madame*.'

She gave a soft laugh. 'Naturally, sir. I should be foolish indeed to accuse him of playing a queen that should have been at the bottom of the deck. It would be my word against his. With no one to champion me, I would likely find a dagger in my back for alerting you Englishmen to the true nature of this place.' She fell silent as the servant returned.

Wolf took the glass and waved the man away, pouring for himself. 'What a waste that would be of such a lovely lady. I would be pleased to assist you if you wish it.'

'Be my champion?' She laughed again. 'Then the dagger would be in your back. No, I will not return to this place. That is also my advice to you and to your friend.'

'My friend?' He sipped his wine.

'The fair-haired gentleman who now plays at whist.'

She'd seen that he and Harris had come together.

Wolf raised his eyebrows. 'I noticed you, of course, *madame*. What man could not? I am surprised and flattered you took note of me.'

'One must notice everything.' A distracted look crossed her face. She seemed to force it away. 'You do not gamble, *monsieur*?'

He smiled. 'I dislike losing.' His eyes caught hers, and he felt the jolt of a connection between them.

She held his gaze. 'Why are you here, then? Do you seek a woman for amusement, perhaps?'

Wolf cocked his head, unsure if this was a question or an invitation. 'Are you offering, Madame Fleur?'

She glanced away. 'I assure you, I am a gambler, nothing more.' Her gaze slid back again as she took another sip of her wine. 'I was merely curious, that is all. Men come to the casino to gamble or to find a woman.'

He found himself fascinated by her eyes, as deep a brown as mahogany and at once both expressive and guarded. He almost forgot to speak. 'I am again flattered that you are curious about me. The answer is simple, I fear. I am here for want of other entertainment. One does not wish to spend one's time in Paris idling in one's rooms.'

She tapped on the glass with her fingernail. 'Is that what you have been doing, idling in your rooms?'

## The Lady Behind The Masquerade

'In your beautiful city? Indeed not. I have explored as much of Paris as I have been able.' He reached for his glass of wine and grazed her hand.

She glanced away, and the corners of her mouth turned down into a frown.

He touched her hand again. 'You are unhappy, Fleur?' His voice was soft.

Her fingers flexed, and she slid her hand away. 'I am merely angry at being duped. That is all.' She tapped on her glass again, then gave him a deliberate sort of smile. 'Tell me what places you have seen in the city.'

He told her of visiting the magnificent Notre Dame and the Musée Napoléon, where plundered treasures were displayed. He told of searching the shops for gifts to send home to his family.

'What did you find?' she asked, sounding not so much interested as wishing him to keep talking.

He obliged her. 'A porcelain figurine for my mother. Some lace for my sisters. A penknife for my father.'

'You have sisters?' she asked.

'Three of them,' he replied.

'Ah, three.' She sighed wistfully. 'How lucky you are. Tell me of them.'

Because he would do anything to remain in her company, he'd speak of his sisters, two of whom were barely grown when he'd left in 1811, Harris's father having secured employment with Sir Charles for them both. Sir Charles was Ambassador to Portugal in those days, exciting days during the Peninsular War.

'One is older, the other two younger,' he told her. 'They are all married now.' Aristocrats all, but he'd not mention that in case she was anti-royalist. 'They all have children, but please do not ask me how many or their ages. I cannot keep them all straight.'

'And are they all in England, all your family?' The mysterious Madame Fleur's fingernail continued to tap a tattoo against her glass.

It seemed an odd question. 'Yes. All of them.'

'You are the only tourist, then?' she asked, a hint of scorn in her voice.

'I am not a tourist, *madame*,' he replied. 'I am employed here.'

Her brows rose, but, just as quickly, she took another sip of wine and seemed to lose interest.

'And you, *madame*?' he pressed. 'What is your situation? Do you have family here in Paris?'

She waved her hand dismissively. 'None to be remarked upon.' She stood. 'If you will excuse me, I believe it is time for me to leave.'

One simple question chased her away? Wolf had no wish to let her escape. The company of a beautiful and mysterious woman was a great deal more amusing than watching Harris lose at whist. 'Allow me to escort you to your home, *madame*.'

She responded with another frank stare, and he feared refusal was on her lips.

He quickly added, 'To make certain no dagger ends up in your back.'

She gave a faint smile. 'Very well.'

He stopped by the game room to tell Harris he was leaving. His friend waved him on, barely looking up from his cards. Should he warn Harris about the casino's dishonesty? No. Doing so might endanger Madame Fleur. Besides, Harris never wagered more than he carried in his pockets.

## The Lady Behind The Masquerade

At the door, he helped Madame Fleur into her cloak, fastening it under her chin, enjoying the moment of delicious closeness. She beguiled him. So beautiful and so full of mystery.

They stepped out into the crisp cool night. A rain shower had placed a sheen on the pavement and cleansed the air, leaving only the chill of approaching winter. The streets were nearly deserted. The noise of their footsteps on the stone pavement was the only sound in the quiet night. She held his arm and did not say much as they walked, but he found himself hoping she would issue him an invitation.

She directed him into a narrow alley, to a wooden door. 'We are here,' she said.

The alley was so dark, he sensed rather than saw her looking up at him. She turned to the door, but he caught her arm, not wanting to let her go.

He held her so close he could feel her breath on his face. She finally said, 'Would you like to come in?'

His own breath accelerated as desire surged within him. 'It would be my great pleasure.' He vowed he'd show her great pleasure as well.

The door opened to reveal a narrow wooden stairway. They groped their way up two flights in the darkness and through a narrow hallway, hearing the skittering of mice making way for them. She stopped, and her key scraped against the door, seeking out the lock. Finally, the lock turned, and she opened the door into more darkness. They stepped inside, and he heard her fumbling. Then a spark from a tinder box lit the room for an instant. She was crouched beside a tiny fireplace. After several more sparks, tinder flamed, and from it she lit a taper, then an oil lamp.

It took a moment for Wolf's eyes to adjust before he could see they were in a very small, very spartan room. It held no more than a wooden table and chair, a small trunk and a bed. There were two shelves, mere wooden boards, on one wall. He had not expected a woman dressed as finely as she to have quite such humble lodgings. Why was it? Had she experienced financial reverses? Was she in need of help?

She hung her cloak on a peg by the door. 'May I take your coat, *monsieur*?'

He removed his hat and shrugged out of his greatcoat, which she hung over her cloak. When she turned to face him again, it seemed as if the air crackled between them. He took a step forward and reached out to caress the flawless skin of her cheek, still chilled from the night air.

*New release – out next month!*

# The Rough Rider
by
### NEW YORK TIMES BESTSELLING AUTHOR
# MAISEY YATES

Return to Four Corners Ranch for a marriage of convenience between two unlikely souls — a hopeless romantic and a man who has long given up hope.

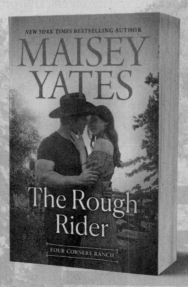

**NEW RELEASE**

**In stores and online August 2023.**

MILLS & BOON

millsandboon.com.au

# MILLS & BOON

## Want to know more about your favourite series or discover a new one?

Experience the variety of romance that Mills & Boon has to offer at our website:

## millsandboon.com.au

Shop all of our categories and discover the one that's right for you.

MODERN

DESIRE

MEDICAL

INTRIGUE

ROMANTIC SUSPENSE

WESTERN

HISTORICAL

FOREVER
EBOOK ONLY

HEART
EBOOK ONLY

f @millsandboonaustralia   @millsandboonaus

# Subscribe and fall in love with a Mills & Boon series today!

You'll be among the first to read stories delivered to your door monthly and enjoy great savings.

## MILLS & BOON SUBSCRIPTIONS

### HOW TO JOIN

**1**

**Visit our website**
millsandboon.com.au/pages/print-subscriptions

**2**

**Select your favourite series**
Choose how many books. We offer monthly as well as pre-paid payment options.

**3**

**Sit back and relax**
Your books will be delivered directly to your door.

# MILLS & BOON

## —— JOIN US ——

### Sign up to our newsletter to stay up to date with...

- Exclusive member discount codes
- Competitions
- New release book information
- All the latest news on your favourite authors

> ### Plus...
> get $10 off your first order.
> *What's not to love?*

Sign up at **millsandboon.com.au/newsletter**

f @millsandboonaustralia  🐦 📷 @millsandboonaus